RAMAGE'S SIGNAL

Historical Fiction Published by McBooks Press

Ramage's Signal

by

DUDLEY POPE

THE LORD RAMAGE NOVELS, NO.11

McBooks Press
ITHACA, NEW YORK

Published by McBooks Press 2001
Copyright © 1980 by Dudley Pope
First published in the United Kingdom in 1980 by
The Alison Press/Martin Secker & Warburg Limited

Cover painting by Paul Wright.

Library of Congress Cataloging-in-Publication Data

Pope, Dudley.
    Ramage's signal / by Dudley Pope.
        p.   cm. — (Lord Ramage novels ; no. 11)
    ISBN 1-59013-008-1 (alk. paper)
        1. Ramage, Nicholas (Fictitious character)—Fiction. 2. Great
    Britain—History, Naval—19th century—Fiction. 3. Great
    Britain. Royal Navy—Officers—Fiction. 4. Napoleonic Wars,
    1800–1815—Fiction.   I. Title
PR6066.O5 R38   2001
823'.914—dc21   2001026696

Distributed to the book trade by
LPC Group, 1436 West Randolph, Chicago, IL 60607
800-626-4330.

Additional copies of this book may be ordered from any
bookstore or directly from McBooks Press, 120 West State
Street, Ithaca, NY 14850. Please include $3.50 postage and
handling with mail orders. New York State residents must add
sales tax. All McBooks Press publications can also be ordered by
calling toll-free 1-888-BOOKS11 (1-888-266-5711).
Please call to request a free catalog.

Visit the McBooks Press website at www.mcbooks.com.

Printed in Canada

9 8 7 6 5 4 3 2 1

For Ian Spencer

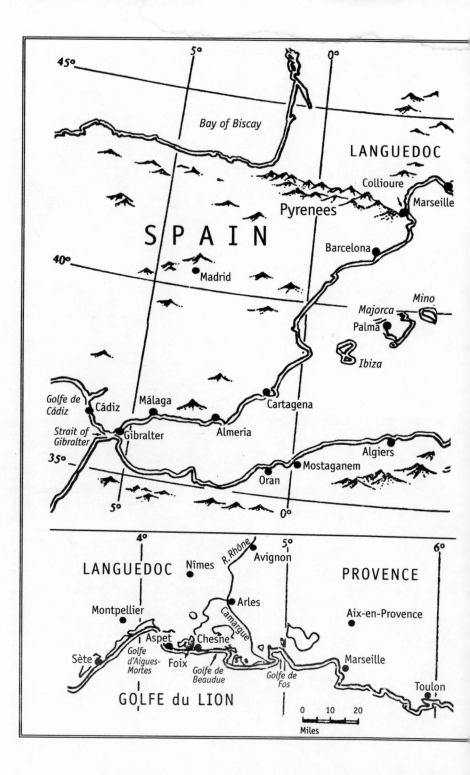

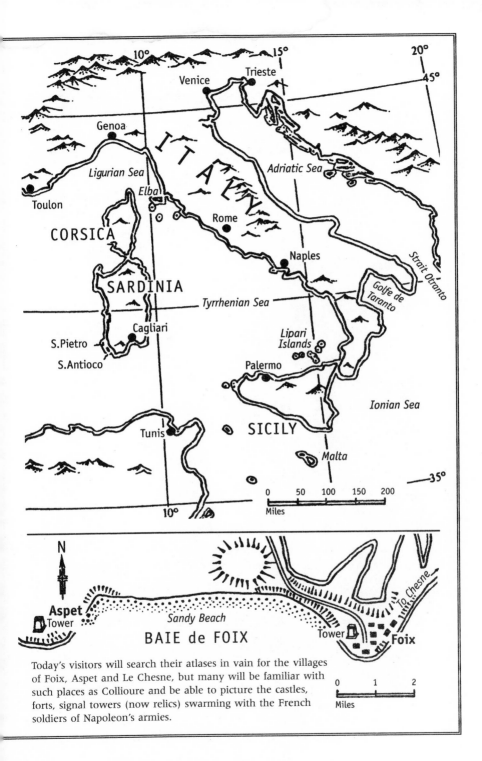

Today's visitors will search their atlases in vain for the villages of Foix, Aspet and Le Chesne, but many will be familiar with such places as Collioure and be able to picture the castles, forts, signal towers (now relics) swarming with the French soldiers of Napoleon's armies.

CHAPTER ONE

ON THE starboard beam the shoreline just three miles away was a gleaming band of sand shimmering in the heat. Beyond it the land, scorched brown by the summer sun, sloped up only a few feet to join the broad, flat ribbon of the plain which seemed to have been carefully placed by nature to prevent Languedoc sliding into the Mediterranean. Farther inland, like haze in the afterglow of sunset, a low line of ridged and dimpled purple hills were slowly turning deep mauve to reveal the beginning of the mass of mountains running north to the Loire Valley, one hundred and fifty miles beyond. Ahead of the ship the same purple, more boldly brushed, showed the lofty Pyrenees finally tumbling into the sea, a jagged line from Collioure on the French side of the frontier to the whitish cliffs of Cabo Lladró on the Spanish.

Ramage was surprised that despite the scorching strength of the noon sun the colours were not harsh; an artist would probably choose watercolours in preference to oils—except, ironically, for the water itself, which was a strong blue. But the heat . . . there was barely enough breeze to give the *Calypso* frigate steerage-way and from time to time the wind collapsed the slight curves of her sails with a flap like a rheumatic washerwoman folding damp sheets.

Although standing under the quarterdeck blue-and-white-striped awning—which stopped him being cooled by an occasional downdraught from the mainsail—Ramage found the sun's glare dazzling because the wavelets reflected it everywhere, like the diamond-shaped pendants of a chandelier, and the muscles controlling his eyebrows ached from squinting. The planking of the deck was scorching, so his feet were swollen from the heat and tight in his shoes. He longed for the West Indies: the Tropics were hotter—but they had the regular cooling Trade winds.

He realized he was dozing although standing up, a trick learned by most midshipmen, when he heard Southwick, the Master, bellowing aloft in reply to a lookout's hail, and roused himself sufficiently to listen to the report—not that it would be anything interesting: this part of the French coast was typically "in between," one of those tedious stretches of uninteresting land on the way to somewhere else.

"The village on the beam, sir: there's a sort of tall framework tower at the western end, an' begging yer pardon, sir, it's movin'."

"The tower or the village?" demanded the practical Master, who was already looking round for his telescope.

"The tower, sir. There! It's—well sir, it looks as though it's *winking!*"

The disbelief in the seaman's voice, as though he was reporting a ghost, made Ramage snatch up his own telescope, pull out the two brass tubes until the eyepiece end lined up with a mark filed on the second, and steady the glass by leaning his elbows on the quarterdeck rail. With so little wind and sea the ship was not rolling and using a glass needed no feat of balancing.

There, encircled by the lens, was the tower. And close to it four or five new wooden buildings which seemed to be more than huts but less than regular barracks. This was what the lookout meant by "the village," and the tower did appear to be winking. He gripped the telescope firmly and stared harder. Or blinking.

He heard Southwick's puzzled grunts and a moment later an exclamation from the Scots First Lieutenant, Aitken. "If there were hills and trees I'd say it was an enormous, great hide for shooting deer," Aitken murmured as though talking to himself, "but here, where it's more like a desert . . ."

As the *Calypso* moved slowly along the coast the tower's angle changed, and Ramage suddenly realized that what at first seemed to be a square, wooden tower was simply a large rectangle of wood perhaps forty feet high, like a door without a frame or wall, its edge at right angles to the sea. As you approached you saw one side as a rectangle and assumed it was a cube. As you came abreast of it, all you saw was something that looked like a pine tree stripped of its branches, and as you passed and looked back you saw the other side of the rectangle.

It was a rectangle which looked like a section of a chess board and in which, even as he watched, one or two squares winked or blinked—or just moved.

Then he realized that it must be one of the new French semaphore towers, and at this very moment it was passing a message along the coast. But which way? The nearest village to this tower was Foix. But where were the other towers? The *Calypso* must have passed several, but unless the angle was right the lookouts would have seen them end-on—and this coast was littered with the bare trunks of pine trees which had died among the sand dunes, killed by harsh winds or goats or rats gnawing the bark.

Southwick and Aitken had both given up looking at the tower and were watching him, puzzled.

"It's one of the new semaphore towers," Ramage explained. "The winking is the shutters opening and closing as they pass a message."

"What are they signalling, I wonder," Aitken mused.

"It shows either that they must have a powerful glass and can see our colours, or they recognize a French ship," Southwick commented.

"More important, no general warning has been passed to them—or any French forces—to watch for a French frigate captured by the British," Ramage said.

"They might be passing the warning now," Southwick said with a chuckle that set his bulging stomach trembling and was a sign that he hoped action was on its way. "Telling someone else along the coast that they've sighted us."

"How far could you distinguish the pattern of those squares if you had a powerful glass on a tripod and good light?" Ramage asked Aitken, who put his telescope back to his eye.

"I reckon it's two miles away now, sir. I can just see the

wavelets on the beach. Ah—there's a man walking, so the shutters are about six feet square. Say a dozen miles, sir."

"Well, I doubt if they're warning anyone about us," Ramage said briskly, "because we must have passed several of these towers already without recognizing them, and each would have seen us and could have reported it."

"Perhaps this one is just reporting that we're passing now?" Aitken ventured.

Ramage shook his head. "What are we making? Perhaps two knots. We've been in sight—close enough for them to identify us as a frigate—for more than an hour. They'd have passed such a message a long time ago."

"They've stopped signalling now," Aitken said. "Two men are walking away from the base of the tower, making for a hut. Ah, now there's a third who seems to have come down a ladder from the top of the tower."

"Where are they going?" Ramage asked sharply. "Note which hut."

"The third man is carrying something rather carefully."

"A telescope?"

"Yes, sir, it could be."

"He was probably watching the next tower acknowledging each word of the signal."

"Ah, I can see a little platform on top," Aitken said. "The ladder goes up to it. Even has an awning. Trust the French. A shelf for a flask of wine, too, I'll be bound."

From the tone of Aitken's voice, with its soft Perthshire accent, it was hard to know whether the sin was in the luxury of the awning, the drinking of wine, or being French. Ramage finally decided it was probably all three.

"Two are going to the first hut on the west side of the headland and which has a flagpole outside; one—the man with the telescope—is going to the next farther inland, probably reporting to the garrison commander. Now another man has just walked round the base of the tower and gone to the third on the east side. The fourth and fifth huts are the same size. There's a sixth, much smaller and with a chimney. Probably the kitchen."

Ramage looked through his telescope. Each hut could accommodate at least a dozen men. What size would the garrison be? Three men were needed to pass a signal, so a signal watch would comprise three men. They would be on duty only during daylight, which in summer lasted about sixteen hours. Four hours on and four off meant two watches a day for six men. Plus a cook. Plus sentries—two on duty at any one time throughout the twenty-four hours. Two hours on and six off. Eight men.

The province's Army commander would hardly have welcomed the setting up of the semaphore stations if each one needed six signalmen, eight infantrymen and a cook. And knowing how expert were soldiers (and sailors, too!) in getting authorization to have the largest complement to do the least work, there'd be a lieutenant as the commanding officer, a quartermaster and probably even a carpenter and his mate to do repairs when an extra strong gust from a *mistral* or Levanter blew out some panels of the semaphore shutters. At least nineteen or twenty men; more counting sergeants and corporals. It seemed absurd but, to be fair, a soldier would never understand why the official complement of the *Calypso*, a 32-gun frigate, was 230 men—not that she was ever lucky enough to have that many, in the same way that any battalion was usually short of men.

Ramage looked up to find Southwick watching him, his chubby, suntanned face wrinkled in an unspoken question. The old man had taken off his hat, and his white hair, in need of a trim and soaked with perspiration, looked like a new mop just dipped in a bucket of water and shaken. Aitken had closed his telescope and was waiting too. Rennick, the Marine Lieutenant, had joined them, anxious not to miss anything.

In the meantime the *Calypso* was stretching along to the westward, a few miles short of the little town of Foix, flying French colours as a legitimate *ruse de guerre*, and Captain the Lord Ramage had, in a lead-weighted canvas pouch in the drawer of his desk, written orders from the Admiralty suitable for one of the few King's ships (if not the only one) left in the Mediterranean, and certainly the sort of orders that one of the most junior on the list of post captains dreamed about.

"What now, sir?" Southwick finally asked. He had served with Ramage for four or five years, was old enough to be his father, and had been in action with him a couple of dozen times, regarding fate as being unfair because while Captain Ramage had been wounded four or five times so far, Southwick had not received a scratch.

"What now, Mr Southwick? Why, we just sail past, dipping our colours politely if the signal station salutes us. I trust you have a lookout watching particularly in case they extend that courtesy, and a man at the halyard?"

Ramage turned away to hide a smile as Southwick's face fell and the old man, utterly dumbfounded, glanced questioningly at Aitken and Rennick. Ramage went below to find his cabin reasonably cool—more than anywhere else it benefited from the quarterdeck awning—and unlocked the bottom drawer.

He took out a canvas pouch, along the bottom of which was sewn a thick strip of lead, heavy enough to sink it if it was thrown over the side in an emergency, and which was held closed like an old woman's purse by a heavy line passing through grommets. He undid the knot and slid out a small book, little more substantial than a pamphlet and printed on cheap, greyish paper.

Boldly printed on the front was a bare oval with an anchor in the middle, and the words *Liberté* on the left and *Egalité* on the right. Inside the oval and surrounding the anchor was *Rep. Fran. Marine*. Beneath, in bolder type and also in French, were the words: *Secret. The Signal Book for Ships of War, third edition.*

Ramage had often used the book since finding it on board a captured French prize a few weeks earlier, and by now knew most of the flag signals by heart. He had been puzzled by a long list of place names in the back, against each of which was a man's name, with no rank hinting that he was, say, a garrison commander. He had recognized several of the places—they were all between Cartagena and Toulon, some six hundred miles of enemy coastline.

Suddenly, when Southwick had named the nearest village a mile or so inland of the tower as Foix, Ramage had finally recognized it as a name on that long list. And here it was, on the next to last page of the book, in very small type, *Foix . . . J-P Louis.* So . . . that was the answer: the list gave the positions of all the French semaphore stations on the Mediterranean coast and, presumably, the commanding officers.

The list began with Toulon and went westward along the coast in steps of ten or twelve miles to Cartagena, more than sixty numbered place names. Some were of ports or anchorages—Sète, Collioure (that was a tiny fishing village near Perpignan), Port Vendres, Rosas and round to Barcelona—then on through names he did not know (probably of headlands) to Tarragona, Valencia, Alicante and finally Cartagena, Spain's greatest base in the Mediterranean.

Damn, the point of looking at the list was to locate the next tower to the west. Foix was followed in the list by Aspet. He reached up to the rack over his head, selected a rolled-up chart, and took it out, holding it flat with unusual-coloured, flat-sided pebbles which some of the crew had found on a beach and polished so that they looked like egg-sized gems. They were his birthday present from them—handed over with much ceremony two weeks ago. They must have consulted someone like Southwick or Aitken, because few people knew that the Captain normally used rough lead castings as weights to hold charts flat.

Aspet . . . He reached for the dividers, opened them so that one arm rested on Foix and the other on Aspet, and then measured the distance against the latitude scale. Eight miles. It seemed a long way, but that was a tall tower, and very visible with the clear Mediterranean light—and probably they did not use it unless the sun was bright. What about urgent messages on rainy, dull

days? In places where the towers were widely spaced, a galloping horse could always bridge a gap, although often the distance
by land between two headlands enclosing a large bay was con-
siderable.

He rolled up the chart and put it back in the rack, gathered
up the pebbles, and then went up on deck, and from the way
Southwick, Aitken and Rennick suddenly stopped talking and
looked embarrassed, they had been discussing their Captain's
extraordinary apparent lack of interest in French semaphore
towers.

"Mr Southwick, using your glass as best as you can, and
helped by Mr Aitken, who no doubt would get a better view
from the mainmasthead, I want as accurate a sketch-map of the
headland, tower, buildings round it and its position in relation
to the beach each side as soon as the two of you can manage."

Both the Master and First Lieutenant gave a grin of relief,
obviously anticipating action.

"As you know," Ramage could not resist adding, "the Admiralty encourages its officers to record unusual sights and views
in their logs and journals: 'Instructions for the Master,' if I remember correctly, says: 'He is duly to observe the appearances of
coasts; and if he discovers any new shoals or rocks under water,
to note them down in his journal . . .'"

"Aye aye, sir," Aitken said gloomily. "I'll use this slate," he
said to Southwick. "You'll have to get another one." With that
he took his telescope and the slate and made for the ratlines to
begin the long hand-over-hand climb to the main-topmasthead.

While Southwick, who was officer of the deck, alternately picked
up his telescope, put it down to mark the slate, then used his
quadrant to measure horizontal angles between the tower and
huts, and the vertical angle made by the tower, Ramage nodded
to Rennick, indicating that he should join him at the taffrail.

The Marine officer, round faced and red complexioned, was
one of the most popular in the ship: his sergeant, two corporals

and 34 men jumped high when he said jump, but they liked him and were proud of him. Rennick exercised them relentlessly but—and Ramage had watched carefully—they did not resent it: they were as keen as Rennick to beat the seamen's times for loading and running out a twelve-pounder gun, and at the moment a Marine crew held the record for loading, running out and firing a carronade on the new slides. The Wednesday competition, as it was called, was one of the *Calypso*'s most popular events—the three carronades on the larboard side manned by Marines competing against the three on the starboard side by seamen, with all of them working to Southwick's whistle and timed by his watch.

Rennick waited for Ramage to speak, but the Marine's eyes were on the distant tower, watching it as a hunter might study a sparsely-covered valley separating him from a fine deer.

"Twenty-five men as garrison, a night attack from boats, no one must escape to raise the alarm, and preferably no muskets or pistols used in case some casual eye spots a flash. Well?"

Rennick paused a few moments before answering. "If we wait until they're all turned in and there's only a sentry awake, sir, I could do it with my men alone. But if the alarm was raised and it's a straight attack at darkness—well, I'd like a second boat with a boarding party. Prisoners?"

"If possible. And I want an attack without the alarm being raised."

Rennick nodded. "There's no moon. The thing most likely to raise the alarm would be the keel of the boat grating on the beach."

"It's sand here, not pebbles," Ramage said, "and the boat party can drop a kedge and ease themselves in."

"A nice run on shore for my lads, sir," Rennick said cheerfully, "and—"

"There are a few conditions," Ramage said warningly. "They might change your views. First every book, log, letter—every sheet of paper in those huts must be seized intact. Once the French realize they're being attacked, they might try to destroy signal books and logs. Secondly, I might decide at the last moment that our party will stay on to occupy the semaphore station for a few days. That means they might have to defend it. Thirdly, I shall be coming along too."

"Aye aye, sir," Rennick said, grinning at Ramage's last few words.

By now seamen were stopping to gossip with one another, pointing at the distant tower and, without knowing what it was, guessing it now held some special significance for the *Calypso*, although obviously puzzled because the frigate was holding her course and already the tower was drawing aft along the starboard quarter.

William Stafford, a Cockney able seaman working abreast the foremast, waved his hand, dismissing the whole thing. "It's very windy 'ere; comes roarin' acrorst that plain from the mountings. They put up the wall to protect the 'uts."

The Italian seaman, Alberto Rossi, laughed derisively. "Is a good idea, Staff, but the *torre* is not between the huts and the plain. Is to one side."

"And it's made of wood; I heard Mr Aitken say so," Jackson added.

"Well, it's tall enough, Jacko," Stafford persisted.

"It has shutters that open and close like windows," Jackson said. "Used for semaphore. I heard them say that, too." As the Captain's coxswain and an American who had served in the Royal Navy for years, even though he had a Protection in his seabag declaring his nationality that would secure his freedom whenever he presented it to an American consul, he was treated as the leader of a small group of seamen who had served with the Captain since he was a junior lieutenant.

"What good are windows?" Rossi demanded.

"How the devil do I know," Jackson said amiably, keeping an eye on the bosun, who would be along in a few minutes to inspect the brasswork which he was polishing with brickdust.

"I've never seen one of those things before."

"Seems funny, just one put up on this bit o' the coast," Stafford said. "What's semifour mean, anyway?"

"Semaphore," Jackson corrected. "I'm not sure. Something to do with signalling, I think."

"Don't see no flags," Stafford persisted.

"That's the reason for the shutters, I expect," Jackson said. "Opening some, closing others—that'd make patterns meaning different things."

"Semaphore: it is from the Greek," a young midshipman said in near perfect English. "It means—well, *sema* is 'a sign,' and *phero* 'to bear.' A sign-bearer."

"Oh," Stafford said, "I thought it was the number four. Like four shutters, or somefing. I say, Mr Orsini, 'ow many languages do you talk?"

"Well, I had to learn Latin and Greek. Italian is my native language and anyway is very like Latin. Spanish—that's like Italian too, and French."

"And English," Stafford added. "That makes six!"

The young midshipman, fourteen years old but tall, with straight black hair, a sallow skin and hooked nose, flushed with embarrassment.

"It is not as you think. My tutor, he made me study Latin, Greek, French, but at home we speak—we used to speak," he corrected himself, "English and Spanish. I have Spanish relatives," he said.

"And the Marchesa?" Jackson asked. "She speaks them too?"

Paolo Orsini nodded matter-of-factly. "Her French is better than mine. She hated the French ambassador."

The three seamen waited expectantly, but Orsini obviously did not consider any further explanation necessary.

"Hated him, sir?" Jackson ventured.

"Oh, not just one but all of them. The last one sent by Louis XVI, and then the two from the Directory. The first of them she declared *persona non grata*—some affair of him stealing Court cutlery at one of her receptions—and his replacement was, how do you say, a boor."

"Yes, they're all boars and should be kept in sties," Stafford said sympathetically, "but why did it make your aunt improve her French?"

"Oh yes," Orsini said, pausing a moment as he worked out Stafford's error, "my aunt occasionally had to talk to the French ambassador, and in the world of diplomacy the language is French. She did not want to give him the satisfaction of hearing her make a mistake."

"Cor, French eh?" exclaimed Stafford. "It oughta be English. Lot of double meanings, that's all French is."

"That's why governments use it," Jackson said. "Now look sharp, 'cos here comes the bosun."

CHAPTER TWO

PAOLO ORSINI had come off watch. He could now be in his berth sleeping, but it was a glorious day and because this was a part of the coast he had never seen before he had come up on deck to look. And he had listened to the talk of the tower with fascination. Semaphore!

He was very familiar with the thick-walled towers built two hundred years ago by the Spaniards along the Tuscan coast and many other places. They were signal towers and watch towers, some round, some square, each within sight of another, so that a fire of brushwood—usually from olive trees which burned readily and with intense flames—lit in a brazier on top would be seen in a moment; within twenty minutes a warning could be passed a hundred miles along a coast. They were admittedly just towers, with walls ten feet thick. These semaphore towers that the Captain had been discussing with the First Lieutenant and Southwick were something quite different.

What exactly *was* "semaphore?" He knew the Greek derivation but had no idea what use the French were making of it. At that moment he heard his name being hailed from the quarterdeck rail and saw that the First Lieutenant was down from aloft. *Accidente*, he had no hat, his shirt was grubby, his breeches stained by that oaf of a boy spilling the apology for stew that had masqueraded as a meal. But it was the First Lieutenant hailing, and he had only slightly more patience than the Captain.

There were times, he thought crossly, as he made for the quarterdeck ladder, when he could not understand why his aunt had fallen in love with Captain Ramage. Then, to be fair, when he recalled seeing her in some of her regal rages in the palace at Volterra, he could not understand why Captain Ramage had fallen in love with her. Anyway, with her now a refugee from her kingdom of Volterra and living in England with the Captain's parents, at least *she* had to be patient.

"Ah, Mr Orsini, how kind of you to come along."

"Aye aye, sir." It was best to humour the Captain when he was in one of these sarcastic moods.

"Cast your eye, Mr Orsini, upon the slate which Mr Southwick is holding, and tell me what you think it represents."

The First Lieutenant, Lieutenant of Marines, Master and Captain: four pairs of eyes were watching him as he tried to make sense out of the small squares and lines marked on the slate. It looked like a maze. A puzzle. A diagram—yes, but of what?

"Come now, Mr Orsini, time flies, and your hesitation hardly flatters the person who drew the diagram."

That was the First Lieutenant, who had been at the maintopmasthead. Ah! That was the clue.

"Il semaforo, commandante!"

Ramage said: "Be more exact."

"That French camp, sir: the huts are here"—he indicated the five rectangles—"and this line is the wall."

"The wall? *Il muro?* Do you know what *un semaforo* is?"

Sheepishly Paolo shook his head. "No, sir, I was guessing."

"Well, it's like patterns on playing cards: each has a separate meaning. With that kind"—he nodded towards the tower, now well past on the starboard quarter—"there are a series of white shutters, like windows. You open some and close others so you make patterns, like rearranging the black and white squares on a chess board, and someone at a distance using a telescope can 'read' it and understand your message. Of course, he has to have the same signal book as you, giving him the key to the meanings."

"Yes, sir." It was so obvious; he should have guessed. But where was the next tower? And the last one? How far could they see from one tower to another? Where did a message come from, and go to? And why was the *Calypso* not attacking this tower? Surely tearing down one tower would have the same effect as cutting a signal halyard?

Paolo realized that in the last few moments all the ship's officers had arrived on the quarterdeck, and it gave him some satisfaction that Kenton, the Second Lieutenant, and Martin, the Third, were even more puzzled than he had been.

"Mr Southwick will take over as officer of the deck; the rest of you come down to my cabin. Bring the slate."

As soon as he was sitting at his desk, with his officers perched on the settee and Aitken occupying the only armchair, Ramage said: "You've been bored since we captured the bomb ketches, and have to stand an extra watch while Wagstaffe takes our frigate prize to Gibraltar. I'm sorry I couldn't keep the bomb ketches as toys for you, but you saw how slow they were, so there was no choice but to scuttle them."

"That seemed to change our luck, sir," Aitken said ruefully.

"Yes. Here we are with orders to attack anything we can find, no British admiral within a thousand miles, and all we see are a few small coasting vessels carrying grain, almonds, rice, casks of wine, olive oil, salt fish and meat. Nothing worth sending in as a prize."

"So that was why you decided to leave the Italian coast and try the coasts of France and Spain, sir?" Aitken asked.

"Yes. What advantage have we, Martin?"

He liked springing questions on his younger officers; it made sure they stayed awake, and, more important, kept them thinking ahead.

"Well, sir, the *Calypso* being French-built and still using French-cut sails, it means we can keep close in with the coast and the Frogs think she's one of theirs."

"And the disadvantage?"

Martin looked puzzled but Orsini asked permission to speak, and said: "It isn't worth sinking these little tartanes and xebecs because that would reveal we are a sheep in wolf's—no, I mean wolf in a sheepskin."

"Exactly," Ramage said, "but as Mr Aitken will probably agree, although we have no choice, it's an appalling waste of the kind of orders we dream about."

"Aye, in a day or so I'll be suggesting we sail into Toulon and attack the French fleet."

Ramage nodded. "In the meantime we might attack this semaphore station."

Aitken, still holding the slate, slowly uncrossed his legs and said warily, knowing by now to be watchful of his Captain when he was in a bantering mood: "I've been thinking about that, sir."

"Go on," Ramage said, sensing the First Lieutenant's unease.

"Well, sir, doesn't the same thing apply? I mean, we're leaving the small coasting vessels alone in the hope of finding better prizes, but knocking down a semaphore tower—well, it . . ."

"It raises the alarm without giving us a decent reward," Ramage finished the sentence for him.

"Yes, sir."

"But, my dear Aitken, we need neither knock down the tower nor raise the alarm. Why, in half an hour we'll be out of sight from the tower, even if anyone is watching us, which I doubt."

"Then how are—"

"Give me your slate," Ramage said, reaching up for a chart, which he unrolled and held flat with his stone weights. "Now, gather round, all of you."

He put his finger on a section of the coast. "You see this large bay, a perfect half moon, sheltered from all winds between south-east and south-west by way of north. It deserves to be better known. Now, here inside the eastern end and a mile or so inland is the village of Foix. Out on the end of the point is the sema-phore tower and the little barracks.

"Now, look at the western side of the bay. No villages until you get to Aspet, twelve miles round the coast but only eight as the crow flies across the water from the semaphore tower at Foix. And what do you notice about Aspet, Mr Martin?"

"It's almost at the end of the headland at the other end of the bay, sir."

"And, Mr Orsini?"

"That's where the next semaphore tower will be, sir."

"I hope so," Ramage said. "We'll soon see. And once we sight the tower at Aspet, we'll alter course for Minorca."

Martin was just about to exclaim "Minorca!" when he noticed that Aitken was using the dividers to measure the distances from Aspet back to Foix. Quite what that had to do with Minorca, Martin could not understand, but he had the wit to realize that one could also phrase the question another way—what had Minorca to do with Aspet and Foix? Then he realized that the distant island was a likely destination for a French frigate; no coastal lookout would be at all surprised to see the *Calypso* bear-ing away in that direction.

Deciding that he would not speak unless in answer to a ques-tion—that was the safest way of not making a fool of himself—Martin watched the Captain, who was now looking at the draw-ing on the slate which Aitken had put down on one side of the desk.

It was curious how his Lordship (Martin still worried about

referring to him as the Captain, which he was, or his Lordship, which he was also, even though everyone said he did not use his title) looked at the slate and then the chart, then at Rennick and then back to the chart, without moving his head. His face was deeply suntanned and lean, his cheekbones high and his nose hooked, but the eyes were what attracted attention: they were brown and deep set, almost hooded, so that as he stood looking down at the chart Martin was put in mind of a hawk he had once watched closely as it sat on a bough: it did not move its head but the eyes missed nothing.

Yet, Martin realized with a shock, the Captain was only six years older than himself: until the birthday a couple of weeks ago he had assumed Mr Ramage was—well, approaching forty, and was startled to discover he was not yet thirty. He did not look forty, or even thirty; it was simply that to have crammed so much action into so few years meant that Captain Ramage was still alive only because of a series of miracles. The hair had just grown back on that tiny bare patch on his head where he had been wounded in the West Indies—taking a Dutch island, Curaçao wasn't it?—although the left arm obviously still gave him trouble: he sometimes held it awkwardly, as though the elbow was stiff with rheumatism.

He saw Ramage point to some soundings marked on the chart, and Aitken wrote them in on the slate. The bay in fact was quite shallow: six and seven fathoms in the centre, but a gradual shoaling up to the beach probably indicated that the sand went well out. The wind was north-east, so it would be calm enough in there.

Martin nodded with the rest of them when Ramage asked casually: "You all have the details in your memories?"

Then Ramage said: "Before I roll this chart up and put it away, can you remember enough to take in a boat tonight, with no moon, and land it fifty yards to the west of the tower, on the bay side of the headland?"

Several sheepish "Well sirs . . ." had Ramage sitting down in his chair again and twisting the chart round for them all, grouped in the front of the desk, to study it more easily.

"Take as long as you need," Ramage said. "If anyone wants to make notes or copy anything, here is pen and paper." He opened a drawer and pulled out a bottle of ink, pen and a pad.

As he looked at the group, Ramage suddenly had an idea which seemed so absurd that for a moment he thought he was just daydreaming. Then he thought about it again with deliberate concentration. It still seemed absurd, but a faint possibility of it working emerged like a drowning man waving a hand. He drove it out of his mind for a full minute, then let it back and considered it for a third time. Even limited success would need a great deal of luck, but there was one important factor in its favour—complete failure neither endangered the *Calypso* nor her disguise, nor killed a lot of men. That was a rare situation; probably sufficient to justify an attempt.

Well, even his first plan, which he was about to describe to these men, had an air of absurdity about it. The second—really only the second part of the first—he would keep to himself for the time being. A few hours spent mulling it over would either improve it or reveal some drawback, when he would quietly forget the whole thing.

Aitken was now back in his chair; Kenton folded a sheet of paper on which he had made notes, carefully wiped the tip of the quill and put the cap back on the inkwell; Rennick read through some notes and Martin crouched down on one knee to look at both chart and diagram for a sea-level view, or rather to see the view he would get from the thwart of a boat. Paolo stared for a few more moments, as though lost in thought, and then sat down.

Ramage looked round at the five of them and said casually: "There's likely to be a garrison of twenty-five to thirty men at Foix. Probably the same at all the signal stations, so there's no advantage in attacking another one in preference to this. In fact this one has several advantages, hasn't it, Rennick?"

"Yes, sir. Sandy beach, so the boats can land without making a lot of noise." He was grateful to the Captain for that casual mention because Aitken looked surprised—obviously, the Marine considered, the First Lieutenant had not thought of it. "It's conveniently placed so we could draw a detailed plan of the position of the buildings and be fairly sure what they're used for. We can see they have no great guns, so there'll be only a normal guard with muskets. It is too far from the village for any general alarm to be raised, and the only road in is likely to be on the landward side of the camp, so the sentry will be there."

Ramage nodded. Rennick had given the soldier's point of view; a sailor would add that a frigate could come into the bay towing her boats and anchor, reducing the distance the landing party would have to be rowed. And since they had no idea of the absurd second half of his plan—in the last few minutes he had decided to attempt it—they could not appreciate the greatest advantage of all.

"Very well, we'll say a garrison of thirty. It hardly matters but I am assuming they have six signalmen working two watches during daylight, so they'll be off watch and asleep when we arrive. Cook, carpenter's mate, various petty officers and a commanding officer—he'll probably be a retired or disabled naval lieutenant—and the rest of the garrison supplying sentries."

He picked up the quill and scribbled on the pad. "Our two cutters carry sixteen men each for cutting out, so your Marines, Rennick, can be split between those two boats. We'll row six men in each, Mr Aitken, so we have a dozen seamen available once the cutters are beached."

"Commanding the cutters, sir?" Aitken asked.

"Kenton can take one, Martin the other." He saw Paolo's face fall. And Aitken, too, was nodding in the businesslike manner which Ramage recognized as his way of hiding disappointment.

"You will command the *Calypso*, Mr Aitken, and you must be ready to deal with thirty or so French prisoners. I will take my gig, rowing eight oars, with a cutting-out party of sixteen seamen, in case Rennick needs a hand. Not with the attack," he added tactfully, "but in getting the prisoners into the boats. Mr Orsini can command the gig."

He added up two columns of figures. "Yes, that gives us nearly fifty Marines and seamen available, without using boats' crews— I hope they're going to be busy rowing back and forth with prisoners."

He glanced across at Martin. "Well, you were the last to pass his examination for lieutenant, so you'll remember what gear a boat needs when sent on 'distant service' . . ."

It was obvious Martin could not remember and thought he was going to be asked. "A compass, sir . . . water . . . yes, and provisions . . ."

"Mr Martin," Ramage said sternly, "you wouldn't reach the horizon. What about your spyglass, quadrant, book of tables, lead-line, grapnel, spare oars and tiller? A lanthorn and candles, tinder box, keg of water, scuttle for bread? An arms chest, flints, watch? You'll stay behind now and write out a complete list.

"However, I wasn't going to ask you about 'distant service,' so I hope you've learned the lesson of never answering a question unless it is asked. You, Kenton, what do we need for tonight's expedition?"

"The Marines and boarding party will have their arms," Kenton said briskly, "so each boat needs a grapnel and line, lead-line, compass, muffling for the oars, at least one axe and a maul, spare tiller, night-glass, handcuffs for prisoners . . . cutlasses and arms chest or skip of pistols for the oarsmen. . . blue lights or whatever you decide for signalling . . ."

"Very good," Ramage said. "We won't use blue lights or rockets, though, because the wrong eyes might see them, and lanterns must be kept shielded." He pulled his chair round so that he was facing the men directly. "Now, listen carefully. This is what we are going to do."

"Sir, excuse me," Aitken interrupted with the sudden anxiety of a man afraid of forgetting something in the forthcoming bustle if he does not mention it at once. "Fever ports. Will we have any quarantine problems in Gibraltar after landing here?"

Ramage thought hard and then took out his letter book from a drawer in the desk. He sorted through several until he found one from the port admiral in Gibraltar, informing Captain Ramage, newly arrived in the *Calypso* from the West Indies, that the following were fever ports, and ships from them were not to be boarded without risk of the *Calypso* having to serve quarantine. Ramage read through the list, which included almost all along the North African coast which had the plague or yellow fever, and several in Spain. "Cadiz, Málaga, Alicante, Cartagena . . . they are the only ones likely to concern us if we take prizes. Toulon is clear, otherwise Wagstaffe would find himself in trouble when he arrives at Gibraltar with our frigate prize, because she sailed from Toulon. Anyway, this stretch of the coast is clear."

He put the letter book back in the drawer and nodded at Aitken. "Thank you for reminding me. We should look silly swinging at the quarantine buoy in Algeciras Bay and just looking at Gibraltar . . . Now, I want the boats prepared like this . . ."

CHAPTER THREE

B Y SUNSET the coastline to the north was a thin, purple band with several gold-tipped peaks to the west, flat land to the north-east—the Camargue and the marshy mouth of the Rhône—and the Alps of Provence to the east, as if balancing the Languedoc peaks at the other end of a seesaw.

Ramage watched Southwick examine the mountains of Languedoc with his telescope and then pick up his quadrant, holding it horizontal to measure the angles between three of them and noting down the figures.

He looked at the chart as the Master put the quadrant away in its baize-lined mahogany box and guessed he must be using Mount Caroux, a second peak just east of Montpellier which was not named, and another anonymous one (as far as the chart was concerned) north-west of Minerve.

"Just where we wanted to be, sir," Southwick reported.

"Not so far from Roquefort sur Soulzon," Ramage commented.

"Is that so, sir?"

"The cheese, you know."

"I'm sure you're right, sir," Southwick said cautiously.

"You don't know what the devil I'm talking about," Ramage said, laughing. "Double Gloucester—now, you'd recognize that!"

"Oh, you mean a cheese for eating? A French one. This— what was it you said, Rockyfour—it comes from near here?"

"Yes, from a place up in those mountains you were looking at. Made from ewe's milk and left in caves to age."

"Ewe's milk, sir?" Southwick repeated suspiciously. He thought about it for a few moments. "I don't think I'd fancy sheep's milk cheese."

"You ought to try the Italian *goat's* milk cheese—so strong that it lifts the top off your head. That's why so many Italian men are bald and have to wear hats."

Southwick instinctively removed his hat and ran his fingers through his mop of white hair. "Is that so, sir? Why do they eat it, then?"

"No, I'm only joking, but it's strong stuff."

At that moment a screeching from forward revealed that the big grindstone had been brought up from below and Marines and seamen were starting to—in their words—"put a sharp" on cutlass, bayonet and tomahawk blades, and the triangular points of boarding-pikes.

A lanky, sandy-haired seaman came up to Ramage and saluted. "Permission to collect your sword from your cabin and sharpen it, sir, and load your pistols."

Ramage felt guilty about both sword and pistols: they had been given to him by Gianna. The sword was a splendid example of the work of one of the best sword cutlers in London, Mr Prater at Charing Cross, and the pistols were a fine, matched pair which she had bought him from Mansfield, in Bond Street, when he was made post. But in fact he preferred to use a seaman's cutlass and have a pair of heavy Sea Service pistols hanging at his waist by their belt-hooks. Sword blades could shatter; a pistol once fired was often flung at the enemy's head as a last resort. He might hesitate for a second if he used Gianna's gifts—and a second could make all the difference between life and death. But the landing? This was a time when he could use them, and he realized that Jackson thought the same. The American seaman had been with him several years and had an uncanny knack of reading his Captain's thoughts—uncanny because sometimes he seemed to anticipate what the Captain would decide before Ramage had even considered the point.

"Ah, you consider this a good occasion to give the Marchesa's presents an airing?"

"Yes, sir," Jackson said firmly. "Knowing her, I reckon the next time she sees you she's going to want to know how many Frogs you've spitted with the sword and shot with the pistols, and, beggin' your pardon, sir, you ain't much of a hand at telling lies. Leastways, not to the Marchesa."

"You flatter me," Ramage said ironically, but Southwick, who had overheard the conversation and knew Gianna almost as well as Jackson, said firmly: "He's right, sir. The Marchesa's bound to want to know, and she'll be hurt if you tell her a tale."

"So you think tonight's attack is going to be a peaceful affair?" Ramage teased Southwick. "That's why you haven't been trying to persuade me to let you go?"

"No, sir," Southwick answered promptly. "At my age I don't fancy traipsing over miles of sand and maquis. It's my feet that aren't willing! Find us a French frigate to board, and I'll be an eager volunteer. But this walking round the countryside . . ."

As soon as the American was out of earshot, Southwick commented: "I wonder how many times he's prepared your sword and pistols? A few dozen, I reckon."

With the shadows lengthening across the deck, Ramage watched as Kenton and Martin stood in the two cutters, checking their contents before they were hoisted out. Earlier he had seen Jackson—who as captain's coxswain was responsible for the gig—going over the various items with Paolo. The boy had taken the task very seriously and Jackson, several inches taller, had bent to listen to him. Jackson had checked the gig, or whatever boat the Captain was going to use, hundreds of times before in previous years and could do it blindfolded, but he had the patience and, Ramage guessed, the affection, to go over it with Paolo as though this was the first time.

The wind was still light and it was time to be heading back for the coast. No one with a spyglass would be able to see that a frigate was steering the opposite course. Nor would they notice her later heave-to and hoist out boats, to be towed astern . . .

William Martin suddenly realized that it was two months to the day since the port admiral at Gibraltar had given him orders to join the *Calypso*, newly arrived from the West Indies. He was, the admiral said, replacing a fourth lieutenant who had quit in Gibraltar after being appointed to her in Jamaica, because the original second lieutenant had been killed in action (and the Captain wounded), so the other lieutenants had moved up a place— Wagstaffe went from third to second, Kenton moved up to third and a new man had been sent over as fourth.

The new man must have had fancy ideas. Martin had since gathered that he was a favourite of the commander-in-chief at Jamaica, and after the spaciousness of a 74-gun ship of the line he probably found a frigate small. Martin also suspected that Wagstaffe, now away taking to Gibraltar the French frigate they had captured, and Kenton, had taken a dislike to the new

Lieutenant. They were an easygoing pair, Wagstaffe lanky and viewing life outside the ship as a humorous affair, while Kenton, small and red-haired, his face always red and peeling from sunburn, took very little interest in anything happening beyond the ship but had Wagstaffe's same amused attitude towards naval life. This occasionally shocked Martin, to whom the volume of Regulations and Instructions, and the slim copy of the Articles of War, were like a Bible.

Anyway, the pair of them had been very good to William Martin, the new Fourth Lieutenant replacing the fellow who quit, and he was lucky they and the Captain (and the First Lieutenant) liked his flute and encouraged him to play it. Certainly the ship's company enjoyed it, and John Smith the Second, who had been the ship's fiddler for years, was thankful not to have to fetch out his fiddle when the men wanted to dance to the tune of some forebitters or old favourites from one of Thomas Gay's operas, which Martin enjoyed playing of an evening.

Martin took a cutlass from the pile now lying on the deck by the grindstone and tested its edge. It had been well sharpened. Occasionally a careless man holding the blade to the stone would burr over the edge but, judging by the way this one was done, the man might well have been an itinerant knife grinder before being swept up by a press-gang. "Knives to grind, scissors to mend!" Martin could remember the tinkers walking the streets of Rochester and Chatham, their grindstone fitted to a wheelbarrow, their jug of water to whet the stone, and their cry, many of them with the addition of "Pots to mend! Put a sharp on y' scissors, ladies!"

For a moment he felt a nostalgia for the Medway, where he had spent his childhood and where even now his father was master shipwright at the Chatham Dockyard. The saltings, the acres of reeking mud exposed at low tide; the sea kale, the footprints of gulls and waders in the mud, the keen east winds of January which they said blew all the way from Russia . . . it was a long distance from here to the Medway. Perhaps two thousand miles, and certainly another lifetime. He found it hard to imagine a young William Martin who rowed on the muddy river in the little skiff that he had built himself. In fact his life seemed to have begun just two months ago, when the Port Admiral had said to him: "I'm sending you over to serve under Captain Ramage. By Christmas you'll be dead or a hero, but if you see the New Year in, you'll have learned enough from him to stand a good chance of being made a post captain by the time you are thirty."

Well, the Port Admiral seemed to be right—Captain Ramage's first foray into the Mediterranean with the *Calypso* had resulted in blowing up one French frigate, sinking a second and capturing a third, which was the one that Wagstaffe was now sailing to Gibraltar. All three frigates had, by chance, been sister ships of the *Calypso*, which in turn Mr Ramage had himself captured in a battle in the West Indies.

But right now Martin had to admit, as he selected two pistols from a couple of dozen in a skip beside the cutlasses and snapped them to make sure the flints were giving strong sparks, the idea of the forthcoming attack on the semaphore station seemed dull stuff. As dull, he thought, as "blackstrap." Ever since he first went to sea as a midshipman there had been a romantic ring to the phrase "being blackstrapped," which was seaman's slang for being sent to the Mediterranean.

No one was very sure how the phrase originated. Blackstrap Bay was on the east side of Europa Point, Gibraltar, and any ship becalmed as she entered the Strait bound for Gibraltar was almost invariably swept past into the Mediterranean by the eastgoing current, and that was called "being blackstrapped" because even with all the boats out towing, the men would be lucky if they managed to work the ship crabwise into Blackstrap Bay and anchor to wait for a fair wind.

To the seamen, however, blackstrap really meant only one thing. It was common for the seaman's daily allowance of one gallon of beer (small beer, admittedly, something just stronger than water but guaranteed not to go bad so quickly) to be replaced by something else when the ship was serving on different stations. In American waters, for instance, he was given a gallon of spruce beer, if it could be obtained. (Martin, to whom it tasted like a vile medicine, was thankful when the purser failed to get any.) In the West Indies it was nearly always half a pint of rum, which was popular as long as it was Jamaican or Barbadian. There was a peculiar rum distilled in Antigua and some other islands which seamen swore would serve better as horse liniment. Even Will Stafford, who would normally happily drink anything, reckoned it "a sovereign cure for a sprain or rheumaticks." Anyway, the regulations said that "In the Streights" one pint of wine was to be issued in place of one gallon of beer.

The wine, usually a rough red that often had much in common with vinegar, was known throughout the Navy as "blackstrap." Still he was thankful that wine-for-beer was the only "exchange of provisions of one species for another," as it was known, practised in the Mediterranean. He had heard the West Indies was the worst station—rice for oatmeal, oil for butter and two pounds of Cheshire cheese for three of Suffolk.

In the meantime, there was the immediate question of the semaphore station and he was commanding the red cutter and carrying half the Marines, while Kenton was taking the other half in the green.

They would be landing on a sandy beach and with no swell out here, it was unlikely there would be any in the bay; just small wind waves. Very well, the cutter drew three feet eight inches forward, so he must make sure that if the Marines had to wade, their powder and flints would be slung on their shoulders to stay dry. Normally they could jump from the stem into shallow water, but there were usually one or two clumsy oafs with three left feet who fell.

Paolo Orsini was standing only a few feet from Martin. The lad brought up in the home of Chatham Dockyard's master shipwright and now the acting Third Lieutenant of the *Calypso* (at least until Wagstaffe returned with his prize crew), and the young Midshipman raised in the *palazzo* at Volterra and, until the Marchesa married and had a son, the heir to the kingdom, were already firm friends.

Martin, knowing Paolo would be in the gig with the Captain, said quietly: "Remember the gig draws three feet eight inches forward. That's when you'll ground on the sand and the boat might start broaching."

"Thanks, Blower," Paolo murmured. "If anyone asked I'd have had to guess, and I'd have said five feet . . ."

With that he snapped the pistol he was holding yet again and cursed the flint, using colourful Italian blasphemy for the weakness of its spark, and tossed the pistol back into the skip and chose another.

"Have you seen the Captain's pair of pistols?" he asked conversationally.

"No, the last time I saw him at general quarters—after he sank that frigate—he was wearing a pair of Sea Service, like the rest of us."

"He prefers them," Paolo said confidingly, "but tonight he's wearing a matched pair given him by my aunt. Hexagonal barrels, and made by Mansfield in Bond Street. Almost like duelling pistols."

"What's he do, then, tuck them in his belt or put them in his pockets?"

"No, they've been specially fitted with belt-hooks."

"I'd be afraid of losing 'em," Martin said. "After all, once you've fired 'em you usually throw them!" He slipped the wide leather cutlass-belt diagonally over his shoulder and slid the cutlass into the frog. He would have to wait to load the pistol; the Captain was very fussy about having powder on deck.

Paolo's thoughts had been running parallel to Martin's, and neither realized that both Kenton and Aitken felt the same—that they were going to a great deal of trouble to capture what Paolo privately regarded as a thin wooden wall and a few hen houses.

The wooden wall looked as though it was supposed to protect the hen houses from the wind, in the same way that many farm houses in Italy were protected by rows of cypress trees which broke the force of the strongest winds.

But the Captain, Paolo mused, had behaved rather curiously when giving his orders for the attack: they must not damage the wall or the hen houses and were to seize all papers and books; particularly they were to ensure that the French did not set fire to anything. They must avoid using pistols as much as possible—unless they saw a man trying to burn anything.

Paolo noted that although Mr Southwick had not been in the cabin when the Captain gave his orders—he had been officer of the deck—he had quite cheerfully helped prepare the ship, refusing to go below to rest when his watch finished, even though he would be up all night. Nor, for that matter, had Mr Rennick shown any reluctance or boredom; in fact he seemed as alert and excited as the night he led the Marines in the attack on that castle at Santa Cruz, on the Spanish Main.

The Midshipman put the cutlass-belt over his head, selected a cutlass and put it in the frog, and then slid the hook of a pistol into his waistbelt. He could feel his dirk slapping against his buttock; a comforting reminder of his favourite weapon.

Jackson came up to him. "Mr Orsini—you're in the gig. Can I leave the grapnel to you?"

Orsini nodded eagerly and Jackson said: "I'll give you the word when to drop it over the stern, but the main thing is not to let the coil of line get twisted up: it's got to run free, otherwise it'll fetch us up short or you'll lose the coil."

"I understand, Jacko."

"And if you'll forgive me reminding you, sir, lower the grapnel slowly until you feel it on the bottom and then keep a steady pull on the line as you pay it out, to make sure the grapnel stays dug in. Otherwise it'll try and skate across the bottom if there's hard sand."

"Yes, Jacko."

"And don't forget to make up the line on the cleat once we're beached."

"No, Jacko," Paolo said patiently, with just enough edge in his voice to remind the American that he had done this sort of thing several times before.

"I know, sir," Jackson said, having earlier detected the resentment in the boy's voice, "but we don't want mistakes tonight."

"What is so special about tonight?" Paolo made little attempt to hide his contempt for the landing.

"Any action is special, sir," Jackson said quietly. "You're more likely to get killed if you're careless, and you're more likely to be careless if you think something's unimportant."

"Quite true," Paolo admitted, "but attacking hen houses!"

"They're barracks, sir," Jackson said sharply, "with thirty or forty French soldiers in them. Each man has a musket and probably a pistol. That's a hundred lead shot, any one of which can drag your anchors for the next world. And thirty or forty swords slicing you up like a leg of salt pork . . . Anyway," he said in a voice which clinched any argument, "the Captain sets a lot of store by us capturing it."

CHAPTER FOUR

I T WANTED a few minutes to midnight with a clear sky when the *Calypso* glided under fore and maintopsails into the bay formed by the headlands of Foix and Aspet. Every minute or so another seaman hurried back from the leadsman at the main chains and gave Ramage the depth of water: it was shoaling very gradually and unless they were unlucky enough to find and hit a high submerged rock they would very soon be anchoring in four fathoms close to the beach.

Aloft, out along the topsail yards, seamen were waiting to furl the sails, but instead of acting at Aitken's bellow through the speaking-trumpet, ship's boys would scamper up the rigging and pass the word, although the topmen would get a preliminary warning as the *Calypso* luffed and came head to wind, backing the topsails so that she would stop and then, gathering sternway, set her anchor.

The splash of the anchor hitting the water should be the only noise that might travel as far as the semaphore station, which was now about a mile away on the *Calypso's* starboard beam.

The stars seemed everywhere, even reflecting in the water now and again as the frigate passed through what Southwick, who was waiting on the fo'c's'le for the word to anchor, would call "a flat spot"; sufficient stars, Ramage noted, to give enough light to distinguish the shape of the land at a mile and recognize a man's face at four feet.

Inspecting the semaphore station yet again with the night-glass, and allowing for the upside-down image, Ramage was surprised to see that the semaphore tower, or screen, or whatever it was called, was in fact built on a small hill, thus raising it another thirty feet or more, although the rest of the headland was flat, reminding him of a miniature Dungeness and making the ends of the barrack buildings stand out like shadowy gravestones.

Even more surprising, neither Southwick nor Aitken had noticed during their close inspection from seaward earlier in the day that there was a low but wide hill two-thirds of the way round the bay, nearer Foix than Aspet, and as far as he could see the hill ran down to the beach and there was no sign of a road. Which meant that any road or lane from the semaphore station to the village of Foix, or joining the two headlands, would have made a long detour inland. So the sentry was likely to be on the north side of the camp, where the lane came in. Yes, a tiny building they had not seen before—was that the guard-house?

He could hear the chatter of the bow wave round the *Calypso's* cutwater, and the frigate's decks looked strangely bare: the red and green cutters and the gig, normally stowed amidships, had been hoisted out and were now towing astern, full of Marines and seamen. Martin and Kenton would be quite happy with the cutters, but Paolo would be excited at the idea of being in command of the gig, at least until Ramage climbed down the rope ladder hanging from the taffrail.

He listened to the last sounding reported by a breathless seaman, looked again at the hill which was now just on the larboard bow, and then at the semaphore tower, now drawing round to the starboard quarter. "My compliments to Mr Southwick," he told the seaman, "and tell him to stand by to anchor as convenient."

Which was a simple way of saying let go the anchor as soon as the way is off the ship.

"Rowlands?"

Rowlands was a sulky but ambitious Welsh boy with no brains who enjoyed nothing more than being allowed to climb aloft, and Ramage had kept him standing by to carry the message to the maintopmen to furl. The moment the foretopmen saw the other sail being furled they would follow suit.

"Here, sir."

"Right, up to the maintop with your message!"

As the boy ran for the ratlines Ramage told the quartermaster to bring the *Calypso* head to wind, and the order was immediately passed to the two men at the wheel while Aitken gave instructions to men standing by at braces, sheets and halyards. All blocks had been greased again during the day—much to the annoyance of the cook, who had to provide the grease, or slush, which floated to the top of the boiler when salt pork or salt beef was cooked. Although it was against regulations, the cook and his mate usually sold the slush to the men, who liked to smear it on their bread—the official name for the biscuits with which they were issued, hard as board when fresh and crumbling when attacked by age or weevils.

The *Calypso* turned to starboard, but so smooth was the water and still the night, that Ramage had the sensation that the ship was stationary and the half-moon of the bay was sliding from right to left, like the swing of a scythe across stalks of wheat.

The chattering of the bow wave quietened to a mutter and then went silent. The coxswain said quietly: "No weight on the rudder, sir; we'll have sternway in a few moments."

The forward movement of the ship, with water flowing past the rudder, meant that the men at the wheel had to use strength to turn the wheel and in turn the rudder, the amount of effort required being proportional to the speed. Once the ship stopped and then began to move astern, the action of the rudder was reversed.

A heavy splash forward, the drumming of heavy rope paying out rapidly and a strong smell of scorching as the friction burned both hemp and wood, showed that Southwick had let go the anchor. The backed topsails gave the *Calypso* enough sternway to make sure the anchor dug well in. The men aloft could see no more cable was being paid out, and a hissing and rustling told Ramage that two big topsails were being clewed up and then furled.

Everything seems to be a compromise, he thought crossly. He had given a lot of thought to the *Calypso*'s arrival in the Baie de Foix. It was essential that the French at Foix—at the semaphore station, anyway—thought she was a French frigate coming in to anchor for her own reasons. They had seen a French frigate pass westward at noon and bear away towards Minorca; now she had come back.

At what point, Ramage tried to decide, did it become a matter of interest to the garrison at Foix? If she came in and anchored in broad daylight the commanding officer of the garrison would expect to be called on board or, more likely, have himself rowed out, in the hope of an invitation to dinner. An evening arrival meant the same thing, with the hope of a half bottle of brandy. But an arrival late at night—not surreptitiously, to raise suspicion, but without a lot of noise to rouse the sleeping garrison commander—might leave the decision to the sentry. If he happened to notice a ship anchoring in the bay he would probably not bother (or dare) rouse the commanding officer, who would curse him for raising the alarm at the arrival of what he knew to be a French ship. And obviously she was French: they had seen her pass flying a French flag, and when had any of them seen, or even heard of, a British ship? Everyone knew the *rosbifs* had been driven out of the Mediterranean . . .

Would that be what was happening over at the semaphore station? He shrugged his shoulders. It seemed likely. Coming in quietly like this would seem natural enough—if the commanding officer of the garrison was by chance awake, he would assume he could hear so little because of the distance. If he was asleep . . . well, he should sleep on.

A seaman appeared out of the darkness to report how much cable Southwick had veered, and pass on the Master's opinion that the anchor was holding well in what the leadsman—who had "armed" the lead, filling the cavity in the bottom with tallow so that a specimen of the sea bottom would stick to it—reported was hard sand and some small shell.

Aitken appeared beside him as the *Calypso* finally swung head to wind, the hill showing clearly as a black lump on the larboard bow and the semaphore tower as a square top to a small anthill on the starboard quarter.

Ramage pulled his sword round, pushed down on the pistols in his belt to make sure the clips were secure, and jammed his hat down hard on his head.

"Well, Mr Aitken, I hand over the ship to you. We should be back within an hour with the prisoners."

Aitken saluted, "Aye aye, sir. I'll have her careened and painted by then!"

Ramage laughed: the young Scot rarely joked, and that he should do so at this moment was an indication that he regarded the operation as about as important as sending a boat away with casks and axes on a wooding and watering expedition.

The cutters had a few yards farther to row than the gig, so he called down for them to be on their way as soon as they were cast off. Seamen at the *Calypso*'s taffrail took the painters from the kevels and dropped them down to the two boats, and Ramage heard both Martin and Kenton give the first of the sequence of orders that would have the oars in the water and rowing briskly, cloth bound round them to deaden the noise where they worked between the thole pins.

Ramage climbed down the rope ladder into the gig and as he sat down in the sternsheets, moving his two pistols slightly so the butts did not dig into his lower ribs, he said to Jackson: "Let's get under way."

As soon as the American had called up to the *Calypso*'s taffrail and Ramage had heard the painter landing in the bow of the gig, where the bowman quickly coiled it, he said to both Jackson and Orsini: "We'll be landing more to the north. Farther inshore."

Martin had been instructed to take the red cutter in a wide sweep round the end of the sand spit to the far side, to land his party of Marines—who were under the command of the sergeant—as close to the second barrack hut from seaward as possible, while Kenton was to land on the bay side by the second barrack hut on that side.

Under the plan, a corporal would attack the seaward hut with a section of Marines while the sergeant attacked the second hut on the far side and the other corporal would attack the third hut, next to it, but farther inland.

Rennick, in Kenton's cutter, would take the nearest hut, the second on the bay side, while a section of men would run to help the corporal attacking the seaward hut (and also cutting off any Frenchmen trying to bolt) and another group of Marines would run inland to secure the fifth hut, the nearest to the semaphore tower.

Ramage's last-minute change was that the seamen in his gig would land well to the north of the semaphore tower, skirt the hill on which it stood and, as soon as they met the track or lane leading to the village, find where the guardhouse was and seize the sentry or the whole guard, if that was how the French had arranged it.

Ramage and his seamen would be the first to catch the rabbits if the Marine ferrets bolted them. But, he hoped, guile would work better than a ferret.

As the men bent to the oars and the gig spurted forward, Ramage could just make out the two cutters to starboard, each diverging slightly, and ahead was the small hill with the strange wooden wall on top of it, high enough to blot out some low stars, as though it was a square sail. It was high; now he could see that the men on Aspet, with a decent spyglass, could read the signals, however they were made. Still, it must be strongly built not to have been blown down by a *mistral* from the north-west, the most frequent strong wind along this coast, or the *labé* from the south-west. Or, for that matter, the *levant* from the east or the *céruse* from the south-east, all of which would hit the tower, or wall rather, more or less at right angles. The *ponant* from the south and *tramontane* from the north should hit it end-on.

In spite of the cloth wrapped round the oars, the thole pins themselves, not a tight fit, still groaned as if protesting. However, thole pins were better than rowlocks for silent work, and he was thankful they were fitted to the cutters. Creak, splash, creak . . . The men were rowing as silently as possible, and as the gig approached the beach Ramage could hear the slap, suck and gurgle of wavelets as they curled over to break on the sand, and a few small wading birds wakened, calling to each other, passing urgent warnings. And now the smell of the maquis: a mixture of pine, dried grass, herbs and, Ramage thought, nostalgia, too, as well as a whiff of soot from the shielded lantern.

He realized the absurdity of wearing a hat and took it off and tucked it under the thwart. The semaphore tower began to look like a poacher's view of the end of a barn. And there was the platform on top described by Aitken. Could he distinguish a system of battens—probably forming slides between which the shutters went up and down to make the signals? They certainly slid up and down: that much was clear when the *Calypso* passed, though he considered hinges on one side, and opening and closing like windows, would have been easier. The shutters must, he thought cynically, go up and down like guillotine blades . . . But how did they form the signals? Did the shapes represent individual letters of the alphabet, words or whole phrases?

About thirty yards to go and he heard Jackson, at the tiller and standing in his little compartment that was cut off from the rest of the boat by the sternsheets, mutter something to Paolo, who stood up, holding the grapnel and lowering it over the stern.

Although Ramage could feel the tension and excitement spreading through the landing party, the men at the oars continued the same steady stroke and he felt detached rather than excited.

"Orsini," he said quietly, "you and I will land first and go round the edge of that hill, looking for the track leading out of the camp. There's bound to be a guardhouse. If there's a sentry, leave him to me; if there's a whole guard we'll have to see." He turned forward and said: "You in the landing party—you will follow Jackson, who'll be fifteen yards astern of Mr Orsini. Any man who makes a noise will have to account to me—after Jackson's finished with him." The men chuckled.

Ramage caught sight of Kenton's cutter two or three hundred yards farther down the coast. It was now near the beach—that was why Ramage had decided to use the gig, which was narrower, shallower and faster than the cutter, and because he would be leaving the *Calypso* after the others he wanted to be first at the beach, knowing at the same time that Rennick would be urging Kenton to make a race of it.

Suddenly there was the coarse sucking and gurgling of the sand and a grunt from Jackson set Paolo taking a strain on the line of the grapnel. And then, as usual, there were a few moments of chaos: Jackson gave a series of swift orders to the men at the oars while he himself lifted the rudder from its pintles so it should not be damaged in the beaching: Paolo was gradually increasing the strain on the grapnel line with half a turn on a cleat and, as Ramage felt the stem of the gig nudge the beach, hurriedly took several turns to secure it.

By now Ramage, jumping from thwart to thwart, was at the bow and he heard Paolo blaspheming quietly in Italian as his cutlass nearly tripped him.

The frothing water was phosphorescent; Ramage had time to notice that as, holding up the scabbard of his sword, he leapt down to the beach and kept moving across the soft sand, knowing Paolo and the rest of the landing party would be close behind. It needed only one man to sprawl on the beach and everyone else would jump on top of him, unable to stop themselves as in turn they reached the stem, poised for a moment and then jumped with cutlass and pistol.

As he moved quickly up the slight slope of the beach and came to the coarse, short grass, the semaphore tower on its hill looming on his right, he knew that behind him Jackson would still be on the beach, mustering his party, while the eight oarsmen left behind as boat-keepers would be digging in another grapnel high up the beach to hold the gig's bow as they pulled her a few feet astern with the grapnel Paolo had laid, making sure she was floating and avoiding any risk that a sudden swell wave would make the stem pound and cause damage. Also, with the gig five or ten yards out, she was safe from a sudden attack.

Paolo was beside him as Ramage slowed down, looking ahead and to his left for some sign of the guardhouse. The hill blocked any view seaward of the five barrack huts but—then suddenly he felt the ground smooth, with no grass. Paolo had stopped abruptly. This was the track, running from left to right. Was the guardhouse towards the huts, or the village? To the right or left?

Paolo nudged him and touched his nose and a moment later Ramage smelled the unmistakable odour of latrines—and they were to the right, towards the barrack buildings. Which probably meant the guardhouse was to the left—even the most inexperienced soldier didn't dig latrines outside the camp's defences . . .

Ramage heard a twig snap several yards behind him and whispered to Paolo: "Go back and tell Jackson we are going left along the track and he is to follow."

Paolo was back in a few moments and Ramage could by now see the track clearly: it was about six paces wide and rutted, showing that an infrequent cart had come on a wet day, its wheels leaving their mark in the mud. Walking along the track had one advantage—they were less likely to step on dried twigs which could sound like pistol shots as they broke.

Paolo had his cutlass in his right hand and his dirk in the left, but Ramage told him to put them away out of sight; for the moment they were two men walking innocently in the night; a sentry would neither see nor, more important, recognize their uniforms in the darkness unless, Ramage suddenly remembered with annoyance, the man noted that they were wearing breeches. In the age of the *sans culotte*, the revolutionaries wore trousers while any escaped aristocrats might still be in breeches—if they still wore heads.

Suddenly he froze, reaching out to stop Paolo. From just ahead of them there was a curious, regular noise. As Ramage concentrated on identifying it and making sure of its direction, he heard several more, muffled and apparently beyond it. Then, almost sheepishly because already he had half drawn his sword he recognized it and whispered to Paolo: "The guardhouse is just ahead. The sentry is asleep somewhere outside: the rest of the guard are sleeping inside. Go back and tell Jackson I want to talk to him."

The semaphore station guard were in for a rude awakening. They were lucky not to get their throats cut with a slash from a cutlass; indeed, Ramage knew that if anything went wrong he would later be blamed for taking needless risks in making them prisoners.

Paolo returned with Jackson and Ramage described what he

had heard and deduced. "We have to work quickly," he added, "because one of the other landing parties might cause someone to raise the alarm. I'll deal with the sentry—knock him out—and I want you and half a dozen men to follow me and go on into the guardhouse and lay out the rest of them. We'll leave them with a couple of seamen as guards while we see if any of the other parties need help. And put two more seamen here outside in the lane by the guardhouse with orders that no one passes— even if they have to shoot."

As Jackson disappeared into the darkness Ramage and Paolo began to creep towards the snoring. "We walk how do you say, 'like a cat on a hot brick,'" Paolo murmured.

"Silent cats," Ramage muttered warningly.

There was maquis on each side of the track; waist-high scrub bushes humming with insects during the day (even now the persistent whine of mosquitoes warned of unseen attacks on his neck, face and hands) and heavy with the smell of wild herbs. He could now hear the waves stirring and gently scouring the sandy beaches on each side of the headland, emphasizing how narrow it was.

He touched Paolo to stop him, and then dropped down on one knee so that anything higher than the maquis would be outlined against the stars. He was immediately startled to see the guardhouse less than five yards away, although the snoring of the one man had lessened considerably,

Paolo had also knelt and, obviously hearing the same thing, said quietly: "He has turned over, away from us!"

Ramage took a pistol from his belt, made sure that it was not cocked, and resumed creeping towards the guardhouse. Suddenly the snoring was interrupted for a moment by a massive grunt—bringing Ramage and Paolo to an abrupt stop—and then once again loudly resumed.

"He's restless," Paolo muttered.

Then they were at the guardhouse. It was a substantial though small rectangular building, built of rough stone with a steeply pitched wooden roof and the entrance at the narrow side facing the track. Ramage guessed the building had originally been a donkey shelter: France and Italy were littered with them, and in times of bad harvests—and probably war—whole families lived inside.

They both spotted the sentry within a few seconds: he was slumped on the ground to the right of the entrance, his back resting against the wall.

Ramage walked over to him and carefully hit him across the right side of the head with the butt of the pistol. The man gave a low grunt and slid slowly sideways, away from the entrance.

There was a low hiss from the track behind and Ramage hissed back. Jackson and his men glided up and Ramage could smell the soot of the shielded lantern.

"All right if we use the light, sir?"

"Yes, it'll prevent accidents. But you'll have to be extra quick in case one of 'em is sleeping lightly."

Jackson turned and whispered to the man behind him—who was, Ramage realized, holding the lantern—and as Jackson glided through the entrance, the man followed, opening the shutter and lighting the inside of the building. Ramage immediately followed the man even though the next seaman in line, not recognizing him, protested. A second later the inside of the guardhouse was like a box full of wild cats.

Jackson knocked out the nearest man but they were sleeping in two-tiered wooden bunks along the walls, and although it was easy to hit the man in the top bunk there was little room to wield a pistol butt to get at the lower one.

The two in the lower bunks farthest from the entrance were awake and trying to roll out by the time the seamen reached them and one was lifting a pistol. Ramage heard him cock it and saw none of the seamen could get to him because of sprawling bodies, before he fired. He hurled his own pistol at the man's head, lost sight of it among the flickering shadows as it spun through the air, and then saw the man's hand drop. By then he had pushed his way through the seamen and found his victim sprawled half out of the bunk, blood dripping from a cut by his ear. He retrieved the pistol and turned to find Jackson methodically checking each of the Frenchmen to make sure he was unconscious.

"Six, sir, and your chap outside. One of 'em must be the sergeant or corporal in charge of the guard."

"Probably. Anyway, hurry up and secure them. Collect up their arms and hide 'em in the bushes. Each will have a cutlass and musket, but that fellow with the pistol may have been the sergeant."

Ramage saw one of the seamen unwinding a line he had coiled round his waist while Stafford stood by ready to cut off lengths with his cutlass, using the end of a bunk as a chopping block.

"'Ere, Jacko," Stafford said hoarsely, "why don't we just lash 'em in their bunks: a bit of line tied round one wrist, under the bunk and securing the wrist the other side? It'll truss 'em up like a Christmas goose."

"Good idea: do that. Start cutting plenty of lengths of line. Here, the rest of you, get these Frogs neatly stowed in their bunks. Two of you fetch Mr Ramage's man from outside the door—that's his bunk there, the empty one."

The American went outside and gave a good imitation of a sea bird—was it a tern?—calling three times. Within a couple of minutes the rest of his party, waiting just down the track, hurried up.

At that moment Ramage, by now standing at the entrance to the guardhouse, was almost deafened by a pistol shot behind him and the grunt of a man hit by a bullet.

He spun round in the lantern light to see that the Frenchman he had earlier knocked out had recovered consciousness, somehow found a pistol and fired it at the nearest seaman. As Ramage cocked his own pistol and lifted it to aim, the Frenchman flung his own empty pistol at the lantern, knocking it off the table and putting out the flame of the candle. As the hut suddenly plunged into darkness, Ramage shouted: "Everyone outside! Jackson, there's a window each side. Cover them in case any of these dam' Frenchmen try to escape."

He waited a few moments hearing his own seamen in the guardhouse—the only ones to understand the order—scrambling out. That Frenchman should have stayed unconscious longer than that, but more important, Ramage knew he should have collected all the pistols: his carelessness had led to one of his men being wounded, perhaps even killed.

"Did anyone see who was hit?" he demanded once they got outside.

"Wilson, sir; we've got 'im 'ere," Stafford said. "Not bad, so he says: just caught 'is right shoulder."

"Is everyone out of the hut?" Ramage called loudly in English. There was no reply, and he asked Jackson: "Windows covered?"

"Yes, sir."

Ramage then said clearly and slowly in French, directing his voice through the doorway: "Surrender! You are surrounded and the camp is taken!"

"*Merde!*" growled a voice from the far end of the hut, and another Frenchman obviously still dazed but able to think, exclaimed excitedly: "The camp taken and not a shot fired? You think we are drunk to believe that?"

Time, Ramage thought; he did not have *time* for a long argument with these idiots. With one shot fired up to now (and, as luck would have it, at the nearest point in the camp to the village) another couple of dozen would not matter.

"You will come out, one at a time," Ramage said conversationally, "with your arms in the air."

"And be shot down like sheep going through a hole in the hedge," a third voice said bitterly. Three out of seven had regained consciousness.

"Paolo," Ramage said, and the boy came to him out of the darkness, cutlass in one hand and a pistol in the other. Ramage said in English: "Curse them in French for fools. I want to confuse them. They'll never credit two French speakers in a landing party."

Succinctly Paolo told them that their hut was not the Bastille; on the contrary it was a pigsty which would in a few minutes become their coffin because they were—

Ramage tapped his shoulder after a suitable torrent of abuse and then continued, in a quiet voice: "If you do not come out, we shall wait for daylight and shoot you down, one at a time, like starlings on a bough."

There was no reply. Ramage heard whispering and crept up to the side of the door, where the sleeping sentry had been sitting. At least four of the guards had recovered consciousness. Two were for surrendering and two, including the man who had fired the shot, reckoned there had been only four or five *rosbifs*, and the seven of them, when the others had recovered, would be able to overpower them. They would all rush the door, he said. Any moment, he added, more of the garrison would arrive, roused by the shot. *"Merde!"* he hissed. "You saw how I shot one of them. Dead, the way he dropped. They're just privateersmen. You'll see."

"What about that frigate that passed this afternoon?" a second man asked.

"We saw she was French—her colours were clear enough."

"Why didn't she capture the privateer, eh sergeant?" the man persisted.

Ramage crouched by the entrance and, knowing the stonework would stop a fusillade of musket shot, waited for a pause in the Frenchmen's discussion and then said, in a conversational tone: "You are outnumbered seven to one, gentlemen.

Your *rosbif* enemies do not care whether they kill you or take you prisoner. They, through me, are leaving the choice to you. If you are thinking of waiting for daylight so you can use your muskets, let me remind you that a grenade thrown in at either window, or through this doorway which has no door, will blow you all to pieces. And if you doubt that . . ."

Ramage lobbed into the room the heavy rock that he had picked up from the edge of the track and waited ten seconds after the ominous thud as it landed on the wooden floor and rolled two or three feet.

"—you can now consider yourselves lucky to be alive because that was a rock, not a grenade. I have just given you your last chance. Do you and your men surrender, sergeant?"

"Yes, *mon colonel!*" the sergeant said hoarsely, obviously deciding such perfidiousness with grenades could be contrived only by someone of such exalted rank. "We lie in our bunks awaiting your orders."

"Very well. Do you have a tinder box?"

"Yes, sir."

"Pick up the lantern and light it."

Ramage heard the man's movement, then the scraping as he found the lantern and set it on the table, the faint click as he opened the door and the scratching as he began striking flint on steel. Then Ramage went back to the track and told Paolo and Jackson what had been agreed.

Paolo, who had heard most of the talk in French with the sergeant, said miserably: "Only one shot fired and it's all over."

"You'd feel differently if you were Wilson," Ramage said unsympathetically. "How is he, by the way?" he asked Jackson.

"Oh, Staff and Rossi bandaged him up and he's around here somewhere—he's left-handed anyway and wants to find a Frenchman to shoot."

By now the glow in the guardhouse was turning into a strong light as the sergeant lit the candle from his tinder box and called: "Colonel—we have the light. Now what are your orders?"

"Wait a moment."

Those bunks were the best places for the prisoners.

"Jackson—we'll tie them to the bunks as Stafford suggested. He and Rossi can do the lashing—the fewer of our men in the guardhouse the better. Have two men leaning in at each window with pistols and tell 'em to shoot to kill at the slightest sign of trouble.

"I'll be inside with Rossi and Stafford; you stay at the door with Mr Orsini—and you'd better hold the lantern," he told the American.

While Jackson passed on the instructions to his men, Ramage gave the French sergeant his orders and stood to one side of the doorway, in shadow but able to see inside, watching as the seven men obediently climbed into their bunks, holding their arms out sideways so that their wrists hung over the edge each side.

Startled by a thudding noise, Ramage discovered that Stafford was cutting lengths of line with his cutlass, using the doorframe as a chopping board, passing each one to Rossi, who was counting in Italian. "Cinque . . . seis . . . siete . . . is enough, Staff."

Jackson called: "My men are ready at the windows, sir. But if there's any trouble, do make for the door, sir!"

"I will," Ramage assured him. "Shooting pistols in a room is fifty times more dangerous than facing a ship of the line's broadside!"

As he walked into the guardhouse, Ramage said to Stafford: "Secure that plump, bald fellow first. He's the one that shot Wilson."

The two seamen had one more man to secure when suddenly there was confused shouting on the track immediately outside the guardhouse. Jackson shut the door of the lantern and in the darkness pushed Orsini away from the doorway, out of the line of fire.

Ramage, nearly blinded by the darkness, made for the dark-grey rectangle of the doorway and as he moved tried to distinguish the voices. Obviously a group of Frenchmen from one of the barrack huts was attacking, or the alarm had been raised in the village and the local militia had been called out.

The moment he was outside the door the first thing he heard—indeed he seemed surrounded by it—was a barrage of cursing in the English of a dozen counties or more. New voices, he realized; not the men of Jackson's party.

"Stand fast, all of you!" he bellowed.

In the sudden silence that followed he said: "This is Captain Ramage's party. Who has just arrived?"

"Sorry, sir, it's Rennick, but we heard a shot and we thought the guards had overpowered you. The lantern was throwing shadows and in the last rush we didn't recognize—"

"Mr Rennick," Ramage interrupted him, "don't apologize for trying to rescue me! I was careless, which is why you heard the shot and Wilson has a bullet in his shoulder. But you? How about your parties?"

"All five barracks are secured, sir; all the French troops embarked in the two cutters and on their way out to the *Calypso*."

"Did you—?"

"And here are all the papers in the camp, sir," Rennick said, handing Ramage a large leather pouch. "Nothing was destroyed. There's just one officer, and I took the liberty of holding on to him in case you wanted to question him immediately. He's under guard and sitting in your gig."

"Very well, Rennick, that's excellent: it's been a good night for your Marines, and give them my thanks. Perhaps you'd take over this French guard—we'll ferry them out to the *Calypso* in the gig, but first I'd like to talk to that Lieutenant."

"The cutters will be back very soon, sir," Rennick said. "They'll be bringing a half platoon of Marines with them—I didn't know whether or not you'd want a garrison here."

Ramage realized that the French prisoners had the uniforms he needed. Suddenly his wild idea seemed possible. "Yes, it's a job for the Marines—but pick small ones: they're going to have to wear French uniforms. We'll strip the prisoners and give them seamen's clothing, and your men will have to get the best fits possible."

Fifteen minutes later Ramage was scrambling over the bow of his gig as it was held by several seamen: in the last hour or so—he could not guess how long they had been because patches of cloud were now hiding the more obvious star constellations— a slight swell had started.

In the darkness he could see a shadowy figure in the stern-sheets, lying awkwardly, sprawled sideways. Rennick reported: "That's the French Lieutenant. They've got him in handcuffs and leg irons."

"You can take off the handcuffs. If he tries to escape by jumping over the side, the leg irons will make sure he drowns. Now, you go back and garrison the place with your Marines and take Orsini with you: he will deal with any stray Frenchmen. I'm taking this Lieutenant to the *Calypso* and I'll be back at daylight, but I'll make sure those French uniforms are sent over for your men."

"Very well, sir; I'll inspect my guards. There'll be no sleeping sentries at the guardhouse!"

"Make sure Orsini is always within hearing of the guard-house: if any Frenchman turns up, the sentries must whistle for him and not talk . . ."

"Yes, sir," Rennick said patiently, having received his orders several minutes earlier and understanding them thoroughly.

The Marine sergeant pulled the French officer's arms up, pushed the rudimentary key into the lock of the handcuffs, and then gave them a bang with the back of his cutlass to overcome the squeaky stiffness of the hinge.

Ramage saw the Lieutenant cringing, obviously assuming that the removal of the handcuffs was a preliminary to removing his head with the same cutlass. Ramage waited while the man sat upright and then said coldly in French: "Sit quietly and nothing will happen to you."

"But—who are you? What happened?"

"You will understand soon," Ramage said, wanting to ensure as much surprise as possible when he came to question the man.

CHAPTER FIVE

RAMAGE turned the lantern over his desk round on its hook so that the dim light fell on the leather pouch which Rennick had handed to him on the beach. Large and made of heavily grained, thick leather, once polished black, it was a relic of the monarchy or, more accurately, a sad representative of the new regime: the royal coat of arms had once been embossed on the flap, but someone had crudely scratched out the gilding of the *fleur-de-lys* without entirely destroying the pattern, merely disfiguring it.

The pouch was stuffed with papers, many crumpled. Clearly Rennick and his men had been in a hurry when they grabbed everything. Ramage shook the papers out and spread them on the desktop.

He reached out for a slim book, and then for something that looked more like a counting-house ledger.

As soon as he opened the slim book he saw it comprised a dozen pages, perhaps more, and was the key to the semaphore code. The ledger was in fact the daily signal log, each entry signed. The first signal was dated more than a year earlier; the latest had been received "from the west" and sent on eastward an hour before sunset the previous evening. Each entry was written clearly and gave the name of "the chief signalman." There were only two names, so presumably his guess about two watches during daylight was correct, and the senior of each was the "chief." The writing was so good that obviously this log was the final copy of a rough log, or they scribbled a signal down on a piece of paper and transferred it to the log after it had been passed on.

He decided to read through the last few days' signals later; for the moment he was more interested in how the semaphore worked. It was an invention of the Ministry of Marine and Colonies, as the first page proudly announced, although the guards at the camp had all been soldiers. Ramage had not seen the Lieutenant's uniform because the poor fellow was still dressed in his nightshirt.

The next page gave instructions for the siting and building of semaphore stations: they should be mounted as high as possible ("always bearing in mind that some desirable peaks or headlands might be too frequently hidden in cloud to be used") and always within clear sight of the other station on each side. This, the Ministry warned, should be checked by direct observation; no reliance should be placed on maps or charts.

Stations were to be manned from first light until dusk and this was to be interpreted as meaning from the time the next tower could first be seen in the morning until it was indistinguishable in the evening. The chief signalman would be responsible for the telescope and keep it locked up at night.

A rough log must be kept "on the platform" and signed by the signalman who took down the message, and this would, as soon as practicable, be copied into the station signal log and signed by the chief signalman of the watch, and once a day by the commanding officer of the station, who was in any case to be told at once if any important signals were received, even if only for passing to the next station.

At all times . . . and so it went on: Ramage reflected that the minds and limited vocabularies of the ministry clerks who drafted such books ran in the same narrow and rutted tracks whatever their nationality.

And then, on page eight, was the key to the code. At first glance the diagrams seemed to be very simple. The big wooden frame had five opening windows or shutters. Four were at the corners of a square with the fifth above in the centre. Each letter of the alphabet was formed by opening shutters to form patterns so that there were twenty letters. J was missing, and single signals represented P and Q, U V W and X Y and Z, so one had to guess which was the correct letter. Numbers were simple—the X Y Z signal, all five shutters open, was repeated twice, and then the numbers 1 to 9 were represented by the same signals as the first nine letters of the alphabet, with the letter 0 also acting as zero. To change back to letters from numbers, the signalmen again sent X Y Z twice.

Ramage saw that it was a laborious, slow but secure way of passing messages. Every letter of every word had to be spelled out, but there would be no mistakes. Nor could there be many situations where there was any urgency, and the garrison of a semaphore station had nothing else to do . . .

Now for the signal log. Yesterday's signals: the last one, addressed simply to Station Eighteen, said: "Powder will be sent." Before that, Station Twenty was told: "Tell ship grain not available here." Where was "here?" Presumably Toulon.

Ramage read back through four pages until he found Station Thirty-four reporting briefly: "First ship of convoy only just arrived." That answered the previous signal, presumably from Toulon, which asked the station when the convoy was due to sail.

In the lower right-hand drawer of his desk Ramage found the signal book he had taken from the captured frigate and looked at the list of names which included Foix and Aspet. He saw that the number thirty-four was printed against Barcelona, while Toulon had number one. Here, Foix, was twelve and Aspet across the bay was thirteen. The last station, at the opposite end to Toulon, was Cartagena, the great Spanish naval base. The advantage of having such swift communication was obvious and the system was ingenious.

He put the signal log book aside. The wind had dropped completely and there was not the slightest cooling draught through the cabin. He glanced up to make sure the skylight was open. Now for the pile of correspondence. Only four or five had the

Ministry of Marine's seal, and they were routine: the Lieutenant commanding the station had been overpaid for several months and the Ministry were involved in an attempt, so far unsuccessful, to get the money back. The letters showed that the Lieutenant was a naval officer, anyway, not a soldier. The remaining letters were from a colonel in Toulon who appeared to head the department responsible for provisioning the semaphore stations.

Ramage collected up the letters and put them in the pouch; he would read them individually when he had some spare time, but it was obvious that if a similar semaphore station could be set up at, say, Newhaven and be responsible to the Admiralty and garrisoned by the Horseguards, its capture by an enemy would produce a similar haul of dreary and routine correspondence.

The Marine brought in the Lieutenant, a mournful-looking man who, unused to appearing in public in a grubby nightshirt, did not know what to do with his bony hands, which stuck out of the sleeves like the crossbar of a scarecrow. His eyes were still bleary; his thin, long face looked furtive because he had not shaved for two or three days and the shadows thrown by the lantern gave him the appearance of a seedy village grocer caught stealing a *gigot de mouton* while the butcher was at mass.

When the sentry, holding the man's arm, jolted him to a stop in front of Ramage's desk, the Lieutenant finally stood to attention, head bent sideways because of the low headroom, his eyes lowered, his mouth so tightly shut that his lips looked like a small wrinkle.

Ramage waved away the sentry and said sharply to the Frenchman: "Jean-Paul Louis?"

The man almost flinched and finally looked at Ramage.

"Yes, sir: how did you know my name?"

Then he saw the signal log and added: "Ah, you've been reading the log."

"I knew your name long before I set foot in Foix," Ramage

said. "Now, sit down in that armchair; your neck will ache if you stand much longer."

The man was tall and with the headroom under the beams only five feet four inches, he could stand only with his head cocked. Cautiously, as though fearing the arms of the chair would clutch him in a deadly grip, the man sat down, showing boots beneath his nightshirt: French Army boots and presumably all he had been able to grab before capture. Or, more likely, Rennick let him get them.

"How long have you commanded at Foix?"

"More than a year, sir, ever since the station was opened."

"And they keep you busy?"

The man shrugged his shoulders and pointed to the log. "Foix is a link in a chain . . ."

"How long does it take to get a message from Toulon to Barcelona?"

Again Louis shrugged his shoulders.

"From Foix to Toulon, then?"

"I don't know, Captain. The messages are occasionally dated but never timed."

"You must have *some* idea, surely?"

But obviously, from the worried look on the man's face as he contemplated the consequences of not knowing the answer to Ramage's question, he neither knew nor, until this moment, cared.

"Provisions," Ramage said. "How are they delivered to your garrison, and from where?"

"Oh, dry provisions come from Sète once a month. Vegetables we grow ourselves—you did not have time to see our garden, but we have a good well and plenty of water, and the men enjoy gardening. We have some cows, so we have fresh milk, butter and cheese. Anything else we need we get from the village."

"You steal it."

"Oh no, sir; we requisition it in the normal way."

"You do not pay cash, I mean."

"We give them tickets which they can cash at the pay offices in Sète."

Ramage then reached the more important question: "Do people from the village visit the garrison frequently?"

"Oh no!" The idea seemed to shock Louis. "No, we have the guardhouse. The whole camp is forbidden to civilians; in fact, only a month ago—"

The man broke off as if realizing he had said too much.

"Only a month ago what?" Ramage asked sharply.

"I cannot say."

"You had better. You can be forced. And I am sure any of your men would be only too pleased to tell us."

"Well, it was a sad business, but a villager was caught in the camp at night, and according to the regulations—you must realize I had no choice; the regulations are there for me to obey—well, I . . ."

"Had him shot," Ramage finished the sentence for him.

The Frenchman looked at Ramage in surprise. "How did you know—have you read the regulations?"

"No," Ramage said quietly, "but I have fought your country for several years."

The Frenchman nodded sympathetically. "I have been lucky. My uncle is mayor of a large town in Normandy, and he was able to arrange for me to have this station. I have no knowledge of the sea, you understand?"

"Yes, I understand," Ramage said dryly. "Now, about your job. Describe what you and the garrison did yesterday."

Ramage opened the signal log as he asked the question.

"Well, about eight o'clock—"

"No," said Ramage, "I want *all* the details. Your sentries . . ."

"Oh yes, there is the guard. One sentry watching the road, to prevent villagers coming in—and, of course, to prevent any of the garrison leaving: they like to go to the village and get drunk and molest the young women. It is dangerous, you understand; the local men try to catch a drunken soldier late at night—then they murder him and steal his musket. Every man must carry a musket if he leaves the camp."

"Tell me, this man you shot," Ramage said conversationally, "why had he come to the camp?"

"Oh, hunting rabbits. He had a ferret, nets and snares. And three dead rabbits."

"So he was not spying or stealing French government property?"

"No—except that rabbits on French government land, which the camp is, are French government rabbits, of course. And anyway, there are the regulations."

Ramage felt a chill creeping over him at this stupid, cruel reasoning. "It is a rule of war, is it not, that any enemy not wearing a uniform is treated as a spy and shot."

"Oh yes, indeed," Louis said eagerly. "There you have it. This man was not wearing uniform, he was caught on French government land, so he had to be shot."

"But he was a Frenchman, so not an enemy," Ramage said.

"Not an enemy like the English, no, but a traitor, which is far worse."

Ramage nodded his head judiciously, and then said quietly: "You are on board a British ship-of-war, you are French, we are at war, and you are not wearing uniform . . ."

"But, Captain!" Louis protested, "I was—"

"Whatever explanation you have to avoid being shot, I am sure the poacher had one too. You know the regulations. No doubt you have a wife and children—"

"Yes, indeed, four children!"

"—and no doubt the poacher had, too."

Louis nodded miserably, understanding only too well the parallel Ramage had drawn. "Yes, two children."

"Very well," Ramage said crisply, "I want honest and quick answers. You have guards on the track to Foix. Who, in the next week or two, do you expect to visit you from Foix—to come along that track?"

"No one," Louis said. "The month's provisions arrived five days ago, no inspection is due. And now the village knows we shot the poacher, no local people."

"Good. Now for signals. How does the system work?"

"Well, at daylight the men go on watch, with the chief signalman taking the telescope to the platform on top, and looking at Station Eleven—that's at Le Chesne, just to the east—and Station Thirteen, Aspet, just to the west. If one or other has the signal flag up he indicates he is ready to receive."

"The signal *flag?*"

"Yes, that is a recent idea. There is a flagpole on the platform now, and when a station has a signal it hoists a yellow flag. The next station hoists a yellow flag in answer and the first station begins sending when the second lowers its flag."

"How is the signal actually sent?"

"By opening the shutters to make the patterns in the book." He pointed to the small volume.

"The whole signal is sent without acknowledging it word by word?"

"Yes. If there is any misunderstanding the receiver hoists the flag and the sender repeats the last word until the receiver lowers the flag."

"And then?"

"Well, the receiver passes on the signal to the next station beyond."

"But surely hoisting a yellow flag can be confusing."

"Oh no!" Louis said, anxious to avoid any misunderstanding. "Each station uses a square yellow flag to communicate with the next one to the east of it, and a triangular red flag for the one to the *west.*"

Ramage nodded, giving the man a reassuring smile. "You pass on a message immediately?"

"Not always," Louis admitted guiltily. "An unimportant one received while the men are having bread and cheese and a glass of wine might be left for perhaps half an hour, or until they've finished a game of cards. Not anything *important*, of course."

"So yesterday there were just these signals: that was all that the signalmen did yesterday?"

"Yes. It was a quiet day."

"You do not report passing ships?" He had deliberately taken his time in leading up to that question in case the man was sharper than he seemed.

"Oh, no, we have no orders to do that. Nor," he said, anticipating Ramage's next question and anxious to help, "do we keep a watch to seaward, in case you wondered why the guardhouse is on the landward side of the camp."

"So when you saw the frigate passing to the westward about noon, you merely noted that she flew French colours and then ignored her?"

"Did she fly French colours? I did not look. Most passing ships fly no colours, you understand; this is an isolated part of the coast."

"Do many ships anchor in this bay?"

"Some—occasionally a ship-of-war stays for a week or two, sometimes a privateer. Of course, we have convoys in here; especially when one is forming up, with ships joining from many ports near here. You know merchant ships—they're always late."

"Yes," Ramage said, and called for the sentry.

CHAPTER SIX

RAMAGE managed to get two hours' sleep before washing and shaving and then going on shore at daybreak with Aitken to inspect the semaphore station. The insects were still whining and the metallic buzz of the *cigales* was loud. An occasional startled bird bolted into the maquis, squawking its alarm. Rennick was waiting on the beach, self-conscious and bulging in a French soldier's uniform made for a slimmer man.

He saluted as Ramage, holding the leather pouch, jumped down from the boat. "Welcome to the Foix semaphore station, sir. Everything is under control—except the semaphore!"

"I'm sure it is," Ramage said. "I've come over to inspect the tower and see how the semaphore works, and give our signalmen their instructions."

"You have the code, sir?" the Marine said eagerly. "It was among those papers we found?"

"It was, and you must have made a clean sweep!"

Ramage and Rennick, who led the way, went up the narrow track to the semaphore tower perched on the hill, followed by Orsini, Jackson, Rossi and Stafford, all dressed in French uniforms.

"Too dark when I was up there a few minutes ago to see how it works, sir," Rennick said. "Looks very complicated."

"It'll give Orsini and Jackson something to do," Ramage said and opened the pouch. He selected a sheet of paper and gave it to Rennick. "That's your copy of the semaphore alphabet. There's no code, as you'll see. Orsini and Jackson must make a copy: that one should be kept up on the platform."

Rennick glanced over the diagram of the twenty squares as he walked. "There's a note here about flags."

Ramage explained how the red and yellow flags were used and by the time he had finished they had arrived at the base of the tower. Apart from big baulks of timber sunk into the ground and the bracing holding it vertical, the only thing that could be said about it was, Ramage realized, that it was not a tower. A section of wooden wall, a huge, wooden door with no doorway or walls . . . As he glanced up he could see the five shutters, closed now like blank sash windows, but each raised and lowered by tackles.

The rope tails of the tackles all led to the ground at the middle of the eastern side and were made up separately on large cleats, each of which had numbers from one to five painted on it corresponding to the shutter it controlled. One series of numbers was in red; the other in yellow. Ramage was puzzled for a moment, and then realized that a signal to Aspet would have to be reversed, as though seen in a mirror, for Le Chesne to read it properly.

The three seamen and Orsini were examining the ropes and the shutters, and Ramage pointed out the reason for the different positions for the red numbers and the yellow. Then Orsini found a ladder fixed to the framework and leading up to the small platform which, as the sun rose, they could now see quite clearly fixed on top. Orsini scrambled up and a minute or two later called down: "There's a small flagpole and a couple of flags bundled up, one red and the other yellow. Just as the book says."

"Stay up there," Ramage said. "You have the telescope. Can you see the tower to the east yet?"

"Yes, sir, but I wouldn't be able to distinguish the flag."

Ramage looked at his watch. "What about the one to the west, Aspet?"

"I can make out the tower clearly, sir, but the flags would be difficult. Both towers have high land behind them in the distance. It won't affect seeing the shutters, but a waving flag . . ."

"Very well. We'd better try out these shutters before the other towers start their watch. You stay up there and keep a lookout," he told Orsini. "You—" he pointed at Stafford and Jackson— "haul on the purchase marked in yellow with '1.'"

The two men gave a prodigious heave, there was a heavy thud and Rennick, who was standing farther back and was looking up, shouted: "That's the top one—you're showing "A," but remember you're only hoisting up a light shutter, not a maintop yard!"

"Lower gently," Ramage added. "We don't want to spend the rest of the morning doing repairs."

"Flag, sir!" Orsini yelled, "from Aspet."

"Hoist your yellow one," Ramage called, "only don't be too quick about it."

After Orsini had it hoisted Ramage said: "Are you ready with

your telescope and the crib for the alphabet? Very well, lower
your flag and call down the signal letter by letter."

"C . . . I . . . N . . . PQ. . ." Orsini called. "Now a space—ah, it
starts again, UVW . . . A . . . I . . . S . . . S . . . E . . . A . . . UVW
. . . XYZ, . . . S . . . O . . . N . . . T, . . . A . . . R . . . R
. . . I . . . UVW . . . E . . . S . . ., space, figures signal, 3 . . . 4. Now
the flag hoisted and dipped twice, so it's the end of the message."

"Hoist your yellow one once," Ramage said, turning to Jackson. "Well, that's an easy signal for you to start with. 'Cinq
vaisseaux sont arrivés,' Barcelona is telling Toulon 'Five ships have
now arrived,' and don't forget the '34,' which identifies the station. You saw how the single signals PQ and UVW were used for
the Q in 'cinq' and the V in 'arrivés?'"

"Yes, sir, and they don't seem to hurry, do they?"

"Just as well," Ramage said, and called up to Paolo: "Hoist
your red flag and watch for Le Chesne to answer."

A full five minutes elapsed before an exasperated Paolo
shouted: "They're answering now; they've just hoisted a yellow."

"Lower yours," Ramage said, and to Jackson he said: "Have
you the correct halyard for 'C?'" Then, before Jackson had time
to answer he shouted to Orsini: "Did Aspet's shutters open simultaneously when there was more than one?"

"It varied, sir. A very slack crowd over there."

Maybe so, Ramage thought, but Foix is not suddenly going
to become the fastest station in the whole chain. He walked back
a few paces and joined Rennick, looking up at the shutters.

"Very well, let's have 'C.'"

The shutter slid up and opened at the bottom right-hand
corner.

"Now 'I.'"

Ramage noticed that the pattern for "I" was the opposite of
"F"—the top one and the upper of the two on the left.

Jackson and his team had just finished "vaisseaux" when Ramage looked at his watch.

"Slow down, you're sending twice as fast as Aspet."

The American laughed at some comment from Stafford. "I was just telling Staff, sir, that this is a good way to teach him how to spell, and he was saying it was too fast."

Ramage took a small book from the leather pouch and handed it to Rennick. "Give that to Orsini when he's finished: that's his signal log. All messages to be signed and the time of receipt and sending noted down. And make sure he records whether the signal is going east or west."

With that he looked round to see Aitken coming up to the mound, having just finished his inspection of the camp. Although Ramage did not know whether the seamen and Marines would be occupying them for a few hours, days or weeks, he wanted to examine the huts and, confident that Paolo and Jackson would be able to transmit the message, walked with Aitken towards the nearest hut, the most westerly, and the nearest to where the gig had landed.

Almost at once he noticed a well-cultivated garden, fifteen yards square and with a big cask at one corner and a watering can beside it. Some vegetable that Ramage did not recognize was growing in neat rows.

"The Lieutenant said they provided everything for themselves except dried goods," Ramage commented. "They must enjoy gardening."

"There are four plots like this, sir," Aitken said. "And the well is thirty or forty yards along the track past the guardhouse. Three cows live in a fenced-in meadow along with the powder magazine."

Ramage was not sure whether Aitken saw any irony in that. It was not that the Scot lacked a sense of humour; rather that it took a lot to surprise him.

By now they had reached the first hut, walking along a roughly paved path, and Aitken held open the door. The building, the lower half stone and the upper wood, but substantial and cool, held six beds. This must be the quarters of the signalmen. There was a locker beside each bed, and Ramage

remembered the French Lieutenant saying that the chief signalman kept the station's telescope under lock and key.

He glanced at the windows and door to determine which was
the coolest bed, looked at the padlock on its locker and then
noted that none of the other lockers could be secured.

He saw Aitken was wearing a cutlass. "Prise off the door,
please," he said, and the startled Scot slid the blade into the gap
on the hinge side of the door while Ramage held the locker
steady between his knees. The door flung open with a crash and
Ramage, without looking down, said: "Take out the telescope. If
it's better than the one Orsini has, let him have it."

Aitken grinned as he examined the glass. "You'd make a good
magician, sir." He noted the tripod fitting, pulled out the tubes,
adjusted the focus by looking out through the door and up at
Orsini perched on his platform, and then slid them shut with a
snap. "It's a very good glass; much better than the one the boy
has."

He tucked it under his arm as Ramage finished inspecting the
room. The beds were strong but crude, the mattresses were stuffed
with straw, and there was a table and two long forms.

"I was thinking about these gardens, sir," Aitken said cautiously.

"You feel like an hour's weeding?" Ramage joked.

"No, sir, but if we're not staying long we might as well collect the fresh vegetables, and milk the cows, and if we're staying
a mite longer, it'd be worth watering the plants."

"I've no idea," Ramage said, but went to the door, followed
by Aitken, and pointed up to wispy clouds which were beginning to come in from the north-east. "I have a feeling the *mistral*
will be blowing in a few hours, and all this low land over there
to the north-west isn't going to give the *Calypso* a scrap of shelter."

"I'd spotted the clouds but that's the first sign of a *mistral* I've
ever seen," Aitken said. "It's a strong wind, isn't it?"

"Too strong for us to stay at anchor in here. Well, let's finish our inspection."

The next hut, the southernmost on the headland, was twice as large and had twelve beds, table, forms and a single chair at the head of the table.

"For the sergeant, no doubt," Aitken said, pointing to the chair. "And you'll notice the wine, sir . . ." he nodded towards a demijohn of red wine in one corner.

"Are the other huts—er, similarly equipped?"

Aitken nodded gravely.

"Well, have them all taken to the signalmen's hut. Orsini can issue the men their ration and be responsible for the rest."

The two men went on to inspect the cookhouse, which was surprisingly clean and, compared with a ship's galley, very well equipped: copper saucepans, well polished, hung on hooks from the wall, several different types of carving knives were in a rack over a heavy, wooden table, the top of which was several inches thick, and along one wall were demijohns of olive oil.

"They have plenty of hens running among the cattle," Aitken said, "and they probably had boiled or roast chicken yesterday." He pointed at a large box half full of feathers. "Looks as though the cook wants to make a feather mattress."

"For the Lieutenant," Ramage said, remembering how thin he was and thinking of bony hips trying to get comfortable on a straw mattress.

At the magazine, a low, stone building little more than a large chest with a door big enough for a man to crawl through and then squat down inside, Aitken produced a heavy key to open the padlock. "Watch out for scorpions if you go in, sir: there's one under every stone, and the floor is made of loose pebbles."

"Much powder?"

"Just enough for the sentries' muskets. Rennick worked out there was enough for each of the Frenchmen to have fired twenty rounds."

"If we're going to stay a while we'll need to bring over more powder," Ramage said, half to himself. Aitken glanced at him, hoping to get some clue to the Captain's intentions.

Ramage sat on top of the magazine for a few minutes, facing eastward with the beach and sea a few yards away, the guard-house thirty yards behind him and the well twenty yards farther along the track. The cows gave discontented moos and Ramage, noticing the swollen udders, said suddenly: "See if we have any men who can milk cows. These poor beasts haven't been milked since yesterday."

"Well, I can, sir," Aitken said.

"No doubt," Ramage answered amiably, "but it's hardly the job for the first lieutenant of one of the King's ships. Ask Jackson; he's bound to know someone."

As Aitken walked away towards the signal tower, Ramage added: "Make sure they scour out the milking pails. Boil up some water if necessary—I see there's stacks of firewood at the back of the kitchen."

The waves were becoming larger and the time between them breaking on the beach longer; the wisps of cloud of a quarter of an hour ago were already collecting like pieces of wool, and by noon the sky would be overcast. Unmilked cows behind him, he thought, semaphore stations to left and right, quite apart from the one here on the Foix peninsula, and the *Calypso* swinging quietly at anchor. And in the drawer of his desk Admiralty orders to capture, sink or destroy as many enemy ships as he could.

He had been lucky off the Italian coast, meeting three French frigates, but this swing westward along the French coast towards Spain had, so far, been disastrous. His strongest card, of course, gave him a weak hand for most of the game: the fact that the *Calypso* was a former French frigate with a distinctive sheer, and still using the original French sails with their very recognizable cut, meant she could cruise along the coast flying French colours, a perfectly legitimate *ruse de guerre*, which she would drop and hoist British colours before opening fire. So—and he was quite

sure of this, particularly after questioning the French Lieutenant—
the French had no idea that a British frigate was patrolling the
coast.

They had sighted several small coasting vessels which he could
have sunk: xebecs with their gull-wing rig, tartanes with the
lateen sail, heavily-laden galliots carrying wine or olive oil, even
caiques that came round with cargoes from the Adriatic and
Aegean to ports like Marseilles. Small—fifty or a hundred tons
of cargo at the most and five men in the crew. Far too small to
waste his men by putting prize crews on board, and far too
insignificant to sink and reveal his disguised presence to the
French authorities. A couple of good plump merchantmen
(though preferably a convoy) would be worth it; he could strike
and then make off to some other part of the Mediterranean. But
one could not lure fat merchantmen over the horizon with the
same tricks that caught hens pecking and scratching in dried
grass, or brought the cows to the post where the French soldiers
moored them for milking.

The second part of his idea, which had fluttered across his
mind like a scorched moth when he decided to seize the semaphore tower, now seemed much less absurd. Admittedly it could
be wrecked by sharp-eyed and suspicious signalmen at the Le
Chesne station, but would men who had already spent a year
on this job be sharp-eyed or suspicious? It took Paolo long enough
to rouse them this morning.

Yes, the idea might well work. Paolo's French was quite good
enough. With bad weather coming up, the *Calypso* was going to
have to sail for a while, but who could he leave in command at
Foix? Aitken was competent enough, but it was taking an unnecessary risk to leave there the man who would command the
Calypso should anything happen to her Captain.

Kenton? The acting Second Lieutenant was reliable enough,
but did he have that—well, the sudden capacity to spot an unexpected opportunity and exploit it? He was brave and loyal but,
Ramage finally decided, not the man to deal with something that

was just as likely to gallop up the track from the village, as appear on the Aspet or Le Chesne semaphore towers.

Martin—the Fourth, now acting Third Lieutenant. He had made good use of Paolo in the affair of the bomb ketches. Whomever Ramage chose had to work well with Paolo because, in an emergency, it might well be Paolo's fluent French and ill-fitting French uniform that kept up a deception that would pull them through. Well, that settled it; young "Blower" Martin would have the job.

Aitken was walking back towards him with three seamen, one of whom was coming from the direction of the kitchen holding a pail in each hand. Although Ramage had never noticed it on board, all three had the walk of men used to uneven ground; they walked looking ahead while Aitken, for instance, kept his eyes down, knowing an anthill could twist his ankle.

"What should they do with the milk, sir?"

"Share it out among the men—use it for cooking if any of them has the skill. They could make a fine omelette if they found out where the hens are laying."

The three men grinned and one went over to the milking post, where there was a halter. "We'll manage somehow, sir," he said with a broad grin. "This is like home to me."

CHAPTER SEVEN

SOUTHWICK was apologetic when he met Ramage at the entry port. "I had the two cutters hoisted in, sir, because they'd finished taking over provisions and those bundles of French uniforms, and I don't like the look of this sky."

"Neither do I," Ramage said briskly. "Send Martin down to my cabin. I want ten minutes with him, and then the gig can run him on shore and come straight back. Then hoist it in and prepare to weigh."

"Aye aye, sir," Southwick said. And, Ramage thought, that brief conversation told a bystander more about Southwick than a full-length portrait in oils by Lemuel Abbott and two columns of biographical notes in the *Naval Chronicle*—or even three pages, which they had recently devoted to an utterly undeserving, time-serving but very senior admiral just returned home with a pocket full of prize-money after a couple of years as the commander-in-chief of a very lucrative station abroad. Southwick was a fine seaman, ready to act as he thought fit if his commanding officer was not on board and, for that matter, far from nervous about disagreeing (as discreetly as a shire horse attempting a quadrille) if he thought his captain wrong.

Martin came into Ramage's cabin like a guilty schoolboy expecting a birching from his headmaster.

"What have you been up to?" Ramage asked.

"Why, nothing, sir," a flustered Martin answered.

"Don't look so guilty, then. Now, yes or no, and be honest: with this *mistral* coming up, the *Calypso* has to sail and may be away three or four days. Can you go on shore and take command of the seamen manning the semaphore station and run it?"

"And Marines, sir?"

"Rennick will carry out your orders, but he will handle his Marines in the normal way. Otherwise," Ramage added coldly, not wanting to influence the youth's judgement, "you'll be responsible for every man, seaman or Marine."

"Can I have Orsini, sir?"

"Yes, of course, you'll need his French. And Jackson, Stafford and Rossi, because they're the only ones who know how to work the semaphore, though I suggest you train a spare crew."

"What happens if French troops arrive, sir?"

"If Orsini can't tell them a good tale and they are not impressed by your French uniforms, I should think you'll all be shot as spies."

"Yes," Martin said reflectively. "Well, thank you, sir."

"For what?" Ramage asked cautiously.

"Giving me the command, sir."

"Very well. Now listen carefully."

For the next five minutes, William Martin, 23 years old, who had been serving as a lieutenant in one of the King's ships for a matter of weeks, could hardly believe his ears.

By the time the gig had been hoisted on board and secured, clouds looking like strips of sheep's wool caught on a thorny bramble were beginning to race across the sky from the northwest and the wind was fluking round the big hill towards the end of the Baie de Foix. First a gust would come round the east side and hit the *Calypso's* starboard side, making her heel with its violence; then as she began to right herself another circled the western slope to hit the frigate's larboard side.

Ramage nodded to Aitken. "When you have the awning stowed below, you'd better get down the awning ridge ropes."

"Aye aye, sir," Aitken said patiently, knowing that the Captain would notice in a few moments that two seamen were already undoing them.

The wind was beginning to sweep across the bay itself, whipping up lines of white caps as though it was a giant flail. Ramage, knowing it could be blowing half a gale in half an hour, again nodded to the First Lieutenant: "Get under way, please, Mr Aitken."

The First Lieutenant reached out for the speaking-trumpet. The men were already alert and waiting for the first in the long sequence of orders that would have the *Calypso* sailing.

"Man the capstan!" he shouted.

The bars were already shipped, sticking out chest-high from slots in the barrel of the capstan like the spokes of a wheel, and within moments two men were standing at each of the nine spokes while another hurriedly secured the outer end of each bar to the next one with a line, a routine known as "passing a swifter" and ensuring that the strain of the eighteen men pushing was equal on all the bars and none could slip out.

"Bring to . . . heave taut . . . unbit . . . heave round . . ."

Aitken's orders had the capstan turning and the thick anchor cable began to come home, water streaming out as the strain squeezed the strands of the rope, and ready to be "nipped" to the messenger. This endless rope went round the capstan, through a block forward and back to the capstan and brought the cable farther aft, where it was dropped down into the smelly depths of the cable tier and stowed by the day's delinquents.

It was a busy time for the ship's boys: seamen used short lines to take a quick turn at intervals seizing, or nipping, the anchor cable to the moving messenger, and then each boy took a line and ran along keeping a strain so that it did not come undone. When they reached the hatchway to the cable tier they quickly undid the nipper, the line which gave them their nickname, letting the anchor cable down into the tier, and ran forward again to repeat the process, each boy handing his nipper to a waiting seaman to be used again as the capstan rumbled and the cable came in.

Ramage's manoeuvre for sailing the *Calypso* out of the Baie de Foix was simple but, like so many examples of seamanship, the simplicity was the result of having a well-trained crew. The frigate was lying head to wind, pointing by coincidence directly at the land at the centre of the crescent made by the bay.

He intended, when the anchor was off the bottom, to let the wind blow the *Calypso* stern first out to sea. Once he had plenty of room the helm would be put over. Going astern—having sternway in other words—meant that the effect on the rudder was the opposite of going ahead; the blade of the rudder had to point in the direction the stern was to go.

The *Calypso*, sails still furled on the yards, moving only because of the windage on her hull, masts and spars, would come round in a luff circle until her bow was heading out to sea. Then sails would be let fall in the regular sequence and reefed at once, and the helm put over again. Ramage wanted to stay as close to Foix and Aspet as possible, although if the *mistral* blew for any length of time and became a full Gulf of Lions gale—which was likely—

he might have to worry about raising French curiosity as to why one of their ships should want to stay close to land in that weather.

John Smith the Second was standing on top of the capstan barrel, turning as the head turned—*girasole*, Ramage suddenly thought, remembering the big Italian sunflower—scratching away at his fiddle, the wind just carrying back to the quarterdeck the sound of a favourite "forebitter," a tune which kept the men at the capstan heaving on the bars in unison and had those with spare breath joining in.

Soon Southwick was signalling the cable was "At long stay," meaning that its angle was the same as the mainstay, and then "At short stay," the same as the forestay. That was followed by "Up and down," so the anchor was now off the bottom and the cable hanging perpendicular. At once the *Calypso's* bow began to pay off and the men at the capstan, spurred on by Smith's fiddle and with the weight lessened because they were no longer hauling the *Calypso* through the water towards the anchor, soon had the anchor up to the hawse.

Ramage gave brief helm orders as Southwick dealt with catting and fishing the anchor—getting the hook from a tackle on to the anchor and hauling it up horizontally to deck level, where it could be lashed securely in its chocks, safe against seas which might well, within the next few hours, be breaking green over the fo'c's'le.

With Aitken standing beside him, Ramage passed on his orders and the Scotsman now had to bellow loudly through the speaking-trumpet as the wind piped up to make his voice heard forward.

"Away aloft . . . trice up . . . layout . . ."

Ramage saw the topmen first go up the ratlines hand over hand as if they were weightless, then, after a pause for the next order, swarm out along the topsail yards as the stunsail booms, lying along the top of the yards, were cocked up out of the men's way.

"Man the topsail sheets!" That was an order for the men

down on the deck. Then the speaking-trumpet pointed aloft for "Let fall!" and down again for "Sheet home!" as the topmen let go the gaskets and the canvas tumbled down, and the men at the long ropes sweeping down from the lower corners of the sail to the deck heaved swiftly to get the sails under control, the wind quick to belly the cloth.

"Lower booms!" The topmen dropped the stunsail booms back in position.

"Down from aloft!"

With that order the *Calypso*'s finest seamen swarmed down the ratlines again while others on deck took the strain on the braces to swing the yards round. More men were standing by at the topsail halyards and, at Aitken's order, hauled the yards up several feet.

Ramage always found it satisfying when sails on different masts were set as though they were one, but the fore and main-topsails hardly had time to get the creases out of the material because of the press of wind before Ramage, looking astern over the taffrail, saw that the frigate was already well out of the bay, the semaphore tower of Foix sitting on its hill like a playing card stuck into a tiny pile of sand, while the big hill between Foix and Aspet now seemed little more than a hummock. Behind it, stretching it seemed right over Languedoc, were fast-moving grey clouds, racing towards them like lancers across a plain. The temperature was dropping now the sun had vanished, and the *Calypso* began pitching as she came clear of the headlands.

"Comes up as fast as it does in the Tropics, sir," Aitken commented.

Ramage nodded but warned: "In the Mediterranean it lasts longer. Off Martinique we'd forget a squall like this in an hour. Here it can last three days."

He waited five minutes and then said: "Close reef the top-sails, Mr Aitken, and make sure there are plenty of chafing mats in position. Have Kenton make sure that all the guns are properly secured."

For as long as the *mistral* lasted, the *Calypso*'s greatest enemy would probably be not wind and sea as such but chafe, caused by the continual movement of everything in the ship. Sails furled on yards were long sausages with lines, or gaskets, round them at intervals, and the bulges—the bunts—were easily chafed if they touched rigging, so chafing mats had to be positioned to protect them. Everything that could move unnecessarily had extra lashings put on it; the hawseholes on each side of the bow, through which the anchor cables ran, were sealed by bucklers, large wooden shields blocking the holes like tight blinkers over a horse's eyes.

"I'm going below for an hour or so," Ramage said to Aitken. "Call me if there's any wind shift."

Before he went down the companion-way he looked aft again. Across the expanse of sea that an hour ago had been blue but was now a dirty grey and closely speckled with tumbling white caps, he looked at the headland of Foix. There were Martin and Orsini, and Rennick. And all but half a dozen of the *Calypso's* Marines. And Jackson and his crew. They would now be watching the frigate leaving. For a moment he wondered if his luck would turn against him and he would never see them again.

After the wind slowly increased to gale force by evening, Ramage knew for certain as darkness fell that they were in for a storm. For several hours the *Calypso's* men had been preparing for it: relieving tackles were put on the great tiller to ease the strain on the wheel ropes and the spare tiller was ready to be fitted in case the regular one broke under the strain; four hefty men were needed at the wheel, each with a rope round his waist secured to a deadeye on the deck to prevent him being washed overboard.

All the small sails had long ago been lowered from the tops and stowed below; the royal and topgallant yards had been sent down and securely lashed on deck, followed by the royal and topgallant masts, reducing both weight and windage aloft. Preventer braces were rove on the topsail yards; extra gripes had been passed over and round the boats, Southwick himself checking that their plugs had been removed so that flying spray and driving rain did not collect in them like water cisterns.

Once an hour the carpenter went below with his sounding rod to sound the well: to check, in fact, how much water was getting into the *Calypso* as her hull worked in the big seas. He had been told to report to Ramage the moment he found the ship was making a fifth more water than usual, and he had yet to make any report.

Ramage was thankful that Jackson had taken his long, tarpaulin coat and sou'wester hat and tarred them afresh as soon as they came through the Gut into the Mediterranean: the name of the sea always sounded so beautiful and inviting in Homer but it was far more treacherous than the Caribbean and North Sea put together. Storms could and often did spring up in an hour or so and last for days; the seas were short, high and more vicious than anywhere else—except perhaps off the north-west Dutch coast, the Texel, in the late autumn.

By the early afternoon of the second full day of the storm, the *Calypso* had been unable to do anything except wear every few hours so that she kept as close in with the coast as possible but not so close that a sudden wind shift would put her on a lee shore.

Ramage, bored with sitting in his cot—the only reasonably comfortable place in a cabin that otherwise seemed to have a lot in common with a runaway carriage careering down a rough track into a stone quarry—stood up and holding on to rails made his way outside to where the seaman sentry, under orders not to try and stand up, was squatting with his sword beside him, a curious-looking replacement for the usual Marine.

Ramage took the tarpaulin coat off its hook and struggled into it, helped by the sentry, both men grinning as sudden pitches and rolls sent them reeling helplessly, often holding on to each other instinctively for support. Finally, enveloped in the tarpaulin coat and with the sou'wester pulled down to shelter his eyes,

Ramage struggled up the companion-way, at times having to stop and hold on as the frigate rolled so that he was hanging away from the steps.

He slid back the hatch and stepped out on deck. Kenton was officer of the deck but Southwick, a shiny black tent in his tarpaulin coat and trousers, was standing with him. Both men looked tired, and from their deliberately limited movements Ramage guessed their tarpaulins had leaked so that their clothing beneath was sodden, cold and probably chafing, with the reek of wet wool, which Ramage hated, overpowering the smell of tar from the tarpaulins.

"Sky's a bit lighter, sir," Southwick said cheerily, "and the wind has definitely eased."

"The glass?"

"Steady now, sir. Last drop was a couple of hours ago. I doubt it'll go down any more."

"What's the course and distance back to the bay?"

"About nor'-nor'-east, fifteen miles, sir," Southwick replied. "Two tacks and four hours."

Ramage nodded, a movement completely obscured by the sou'wester, "We'll be able to shake out a reef in a couple of hours: we could just get in by daylight."

"Once we get in the lee of the coast the sea won't be so wild," Kenton commented, to be reproved by Southwick: "That'd be true anywhere but the Mediterranean. But as soon as it shallows up . . ."

"You're sure about the course?" Ramage asked Southwick who, as Master, was responsible for the navigation of the *Calypso*.

"Not to within a quarter point," Southwick said, "but by the time we've worn round I'll have checked it."

Ramage turned to Kenton. "See how she'll take nor'-nor'-east. Don't rouse out everyone: just use the watch on deck. And try and get the sails trimmed while the rain has stopped: there's no need to soak the men again."

Half an hour later, with a reef shaken out of both fore and

maintopsails and staysails cautiously set, the *Calypso* was plunging up to the Baie de Foix, the wind slowly backing so that sheets could be eased and now, not hard on the wind, the frigate was slipping easily across the wave tops instead of pounding or, as Southwick grumbled, "digging the same hole twice like a forgetful sexton."

Ramage reckoned there was an hour of daylight remaining as the *Calypso* stretched up to the coast with the Baie de Foix on her starboard bow. He held on until she was close to the western side, giving himself a look at the other semaphore tower at Aspet. Then he gave the order for the *Calypso* to tack into the bay itself. Her sails started flapping and, for anyone not used to a ship going about, there was sudden confusion for a few minutes and then almost complete silence after sheets and braces were hauled home and tacks settled.

Through the glass the semaphore tower at Foix seemed undamaged by the wind, which was dropping quickly, and Ramage was startled to see the yellow flag run up on the platform at the top and stream out like a board. They had a signal to pass to Aspet—and yes, Aspet hoisted the red flag: they were ready to receive it.

Southwick offered to get the semaphore signal book so that they could read the signal as Orsini, Jackson, Stafford and Rossi worked the shutters, but Ramage, at last free of his tarpaulin coat and sou'wester, shook his head. Very soon he would be reading the Foix tower's signal log, and seeing the latest news of the convoy assembling at Barcelona . . .

There seemed to be a deputation to meet him on the beach when Ramage jumped down from the bow of his gig in the late evening to find Martin, Rennick and Orsini standing to attention on the sand a few feet back from the line of breaking waves.

"Welcome back, sir," Martin said. "That was quite a gale."

"Yes, I half expected to hear your flute," Ramage said teasingly.

"It wouldn't have been my flute, sir," Martin said, almost crossly, "it'd have been that damned tower: the wind goes through it like an abandoned windmill: all creaks and groans and whistles. Hard to sleep."

By now Ramage was leading them towards the signalmen's hut.

"Much signal traffic?"

"Our hands are raw, sir: needed three men at each halyard to raise a shutter in that wind, and Toulon and Barcelona have been signalling like neighbours chatting over the fence."

"They probably have fine weather: ours was just a local Gulf of Lions gale."

Ramage turned to Rennick. "Well, what have the Marines to report?"

"All well, sir—except for the sand: this dam' wind drives it in under doors and gets it into the men's muskets—until the rain came and settled it down. At least we haven't had to water the gardens."

"Had any trouble with discipline?" Ramage asked Martin casually.

"None, sir: even though the weather was bad the men seem to enjoy their run on shore. They scrubbed the floors and tables in their barracks before I could stop them; now they're having the devil of a job drying them out."

By now they had reached the signalmen's hut and Martin led the way in. A lantern on the table showed the signal log and beside it, under a brick used as a paperweight, were the original signals copied down by the men on the platform.

Ramage motioned the three men to sit and said to Paolo: "Did you have any trouble understanding the signals?"

"No, sir. I've written translations under each signal for the benefit of Mr Martin."

"And very useful it's been, sir," Martin said emphatically, obviously anxious that Paolo should not miss any credit.

Ramage nodded and opened the signal book. The signals were

written in neat copperplate, giving the time that Aspet or Le Chesne began sending, the time the last word of the signal was received in Foix, and the similar times when it was passed on. Beneath each signal was the translation, each one signed with a flourish, "P.O."

It took Ramage a few moments to remember the day and date the *Calypso* sailed, and then he read slowly through the signals, first in French, then Paolo's translation to make sure neither of them missed some nuance. There had been a signal to the east or west roughly every half an hour in the two days of daylight. That meant the men had been hauling on the shutter halyards almost continually, able to rest only when a signal was being received.

So eleven merchant ships were now assembled in Barcelona, bound for Marseilles, Genoa and Leghorn. And the final two signals, passed in the last of the light that very day, complained that the two frigates had not arrived to escort the convoy, which was now being delayed.

Ramage read for the third time all the signals concerning the assembling of the convoy. Martin, Rennick and Orsini watched him, each man perfectly still. Each was watching Ramage's face which, in the light of the lantern, with its flame flickering in the draught from the wind and throwing dancing shadows, seemed as if it had been carved from a block of mahogany, the sun-and-wind tan emphasized by the candlelight.

Paolo did not know whether to be disappointed or elated. Certainly the Captain was pleased with the way they had received and passed the messages, and Blower had been good enough to praise him. The translations of the signals—well, they were simple and he knew he had made no mistakes. Yet the Captain was now reading the signals—which seemed routine enough—for the third time. Fourth, in fact, because he had just turned to the first page again, and was reading even more slowly, running his finger from word to word, like a schoolboy.

Martin's original confidence too was ebbing fast: the Captain had not spoken for ten minutes: he just continued reading the signals, turning back to the first page as soon as he finished the last.

He was reading both the original French and Orsini's translations, but Orsini's translations could not be faulty because the Midshipman would by now have received an angry blast.

Ramage's head was still; just his eyes moved from word to word along one line and flicked back to the beginning of the next. The eyes were bloodshot, as one would expect in a man who had spent the last couple of days at sea in a gale: indeed, there were still grains of dried salt on his cheeks. The eyes seemed more sunken than usual, but that could be tiredness or, more likely, the shadows thrown by the lantern.

What was fascinating the Captain about the signals? To Martin they seemed routine; the same as the dozens and dozens of signals passed in the previous year and which Orsini had skimmed through to make sure he understood the French system.

Rennick was soon intrigued enough to begin watching Martin and Orsini. He had very quickly recognized what was going on in the Captain's mind because he had seen the expression many times before, that fixed position and just the eyes moving, but he was interested to see that neither of the two lads understood: from Blower's expression, clearly he thought he had done something wrong; Orsini, on the other hand, was fairly certain he had made no mistakes but the Captain's continued silence was raising doubts in his mind.

All three jumped as Ramage suddenly flipped the signal book shut, smiled pleasantly, and said: "Very well, lads, carry on; I'm going back to the ship now, but I'll be over again at dawn."

He was just walking to the door when he turned and said to Martin: "Those halyards for the shutters: you're watching them for wear, I hope."

"Yes, sir," Martin said thankfully. "Jackson is the last man off the platform and he climbs down the framework, checking it all—blocks, tackles, the frames in which the shutters slide . . ."

Ramage knew he should have guessed Jackson would leave nothing to chance. He looked across at Rennick, remembering the Marine officer might be feeling left out of it. "I'll be inspecting your men at daylight," he said. "A glance with a lantern now will satisfy no one."

The grin on Rennick's face showed that just being remembered was reward enough, and such was human nature that the Marines would enjoy polishing their equipment before dawn in anticipation of the Captain's inspection.

The row back to the *Calypso* in the gig lasted long enough for him to realize how tired he was. He made his way down to his cabin, stripping off his wet boat-cloak as he went.

Waving away his steward, who wanted to serve him a bowl of hot soup, he sent for Aitken and when the First Lieutenant arrived he said: "A convoy is waiting to sail from Barcelona. Eleven ships. The French escort of two frigates has not yet arrived."

"That's too bad," Aitken said in his soft Perthshire accent. "Delayed by this same bad weather, perhaps; or just late . . . they'd be sailing from Toulon, and we've seen nothing of them— I wonder if they'd go direct or keep in with the coast?"

"Keep close in with a *mistral*," Ramage said. "That is, if they've sailed at all."

"Aye, that's the puzzle," Aitken mused. "If they've sailed at all . . ."

Quickly Ramage described the gist of the signals that had passed between Barcelona and Toulon. Then he told Aitken of the wild idea he had had and was slightly disappointed that the Scotsman's only reaction was a brief nod and the comment: "We can start that going first thing in the morning. We'll look daft if those French frigates get to Barcelona first."

CHAPTER EIGHT

THE distant outline of the Alpes de Provence was just appearing to the eastward, shaped by the first hint of dawn beyond, when Ramage jumped on to the beach from his gig and answered the respectful greetings of Martin and Rennick with a cheerfulness that startled them and made Paolo glance quickly at Jackson.

The acting signalmen, with nothing to do until daylight showed the towers at Aspet and Le Chesne, had come down to the beach to help hold the gig, anticipating heavy swells from the previous days' storm, but the sea had calmed.

"Somefing's up!" Stafford whispered to Jackson. "Whenever 'e's so cheerful this time o' the morning it means trouble."

"Action, not trouble," Rossi corrected.

"'S what I mean. I'm getting fed up wiv pulling them bloody 'alyards, I don't mind telling you. Black an' white squares," he exclaimed scornfully. "Beats me 'ow people can stay awake playin' chess!"

"They're usually yellow, not white," Jackson said.

"Even worse. Wearin' a yellow dress can make you miscarry, so my sister says."

"Yes," Jackson said briskly, "that's why I never wear one. Now the Captain's on shore we might as well get ready to go up the tower."

"We got *hours* yet," Stafford protested.

"All right, you stay here and let the mosquitoes eat you. But that tower is just high enough that the lazy ones don't bother to fly that high, and they'll be swarming in another ten minutes."

"Is right, I come with you," Rossi said, slapping at early-risers who were already biting his bare arm. "The higher you go the not so many *zanzari*."

Inside the signalmen's hut, appropriated by Martin as the officers' quarters and serving as his combined headquarters and gunroom, the lantern light seemed very yellow, an even stronger hint that dawn was breaking. Again Ramage indicated the trio should sit down, and from his jacket he took a slip of paper. "This signal must be sent westwards at first light. I don't want the Le Chesne station to see it, so we must try to send it off before they man their tower."

He unfolded it and gave it to Paolo. "Read it aloud in French," he said, and when the midshipman had done so, he said: "Now translate it for Mr Martin and Mr Rennick."

Paolo paused a few moments, obviously changing the French construction into English, but equally obvious to Martin and Rennick was that reading the French version had brought first puzzlement and then excitement to the Midshipman's eyes.

Paolo began reading aloud: "*'Figures 34, Convoy to sail immediately for Baie de Foix where escort will join. Figures 1.'* That's the signal and," he added for Rennick's benefit, "it's to the station at Barcelona, which is 34, from Toulon, which is number 1."

Martin gestured impatiently for the paper but Ramage realized that the movement was a delaying action as much as anything: young "Blower" Martin, confronted with an entirely unexpected situation, was giving himself time to think. And then, as he realized the consequences, he gave a cheerful grin.

"Shall we have enough men to make up prize crews, sir?"

"Don't count your prize-money before the prizes are caught," Ramage said. "There are just two or three possible snags, aren't there, Rennick?"

He knew the Marine had spotted them—more perhaps by instinct than logical thought, because Martin was twice as clever as the burly Marine.

"Yes, sir: if the French authorities somewhere between here and Barcelona get suspicious and send two or three frigates to see what's going on in the Baie de Foix, or the real escort arrive in time or meet the convoy on the way and sail with it to here. Or, a third alternative, they meet the convoy, hear of the signal from Toulon about going to Foix, reckon it no longer applies because the convoy now has an escort, and sails direct to its original destinations."

Ramage nodded. "The first two are risks; the third will be the disappointment."

Martin said: "But, sir, supposing the merchantmen refuse to risk sailing without an escort? If they're anything like our own shipmasters, they can be a damned independent crowd."

"It could happen, but Barcelona would report to Toulon. We would intercept the signal and after a suitable interval send back a reply threatening the shipmasters. I doubt if they dare play the games the British ones do: they have no Committee of West India merchants or Lloyd's Coffee House to back them up . . ."

He glanced up as there was a knock at the door, and at a word from Martin, a Marine came in with two jugs, which he put on the table, went to a cupboard and came back with four mugs.

"Tea, sir?" he asked Ramage politely, and when Ramage nodded and watched a mug being neatly filled from one jug was surprised to hear the Marine ask: "And milk, sir?"

Then he remembered the three cows in the meadow behind the guardhouse. "A little, please," he said.

Ramage had stood on the tower platform with Paolo and Jackson while Rossi and Stafford hauled on the halyards, watched by an anxious Martin. Before daylight they had hoisted the yellow flag, warning Aspet there was a signal for them, so that the first signalman at Aspet to look at Foix would see it. Ramage had watched the tower at Le Chesne for signs of movement, particularly when Paolo exclaimed that Aspet had answered and the signal could be sent. A shout down to Stafford and Rossi started the shutters rising and falling, Jackson watching Aspet for any request for a repetition while Ramage kept an eye on Le Chesne for any indication that they had noticed that Foix's shutters were working.

Finally, after Paolo had shouted down the last letter of the signal and the shutters had risen and then crashed down again, so the tower was once more without window-like openings, Jackson took the halyard, raised and lowered the yellow flag twice, and said to Ramage: "Now the signal's on its way, sir. As the post-chaise coachman says: 'Next stop Barcelona.'"

And, Ramage thought to himself, it will probably take all day to reach Barcelona, allowing for a noon delay for the meal and siesta at about station twenty . . . so the convoy could sail about noon tomorrow. The distance from Barcelona to Foix was almost exactly one hundred and fifty miles, and the course followed the coast because the ships had to round the cape just north of Palamós. They needed plenty of south in the wind to bring them north without too much delay.

Without an escort to crack a whip behind them, they would make perhaps four knots with a fair wind, so at the earliest there would be no sign of them until 36 hours after they sailed. Thirty-six hours from noon tomorrow. It was a long time. And he had to spend the rest of the day on shore, just in case a signal came back unexpectedly before sunset. In the meantime he looked across at the *Calypso* swinging at anchor in the bay, a glorious sight washed by the pinkish-orange of a good sunrise following the gale.

Ramage climbed down the ladder, telling Paolo to hail the moment a signal started to come through from either Aspet or Le Chesne—he was more curious about the method than what the message might say. His first task for the morning was to inspect the Marines.

This was set for eight o'clock, and Ramage knew Rennick would be happy for the rest of the day—even if, by some miracle, the Captain spotted a dulled button or a speck of sand on a musket barrel. Flints—ah yes, just to tease Rennick (without the men realizing it) he would insist on all muskets being "snapped"—

cocked and fired, without being loaded—to check the strength of the spark in the flintlock. And he would play merry hell if even one failed to spark, because in action a misfire could cost the man's life.

At eight o'clock, on the only flat area between the huts not dug for a garden—but certainly not used as a parade ground by the French—Rennick had his men drawn up, and when Ramage strode out with all the nonchalance expected of the captain of one of the King's ships, Rennick gave a smart salute and bellowed: "One sergeant, one corporal and twenty-eight men, all present and correct, sir! One corporal and six men on detached guard duty!"

"Very well, Lieutenant; I will inspect the men."

Escorted by Rennick and followed by the sergeant, Ramage began to walk along the first of the four ranks of men. The corporal was the first he reached.

"Have him make sure his musket isn't loaded; then I want to see him snap the lock."

Rennick barked out the order with his usual confidence; the corporal flipped up the pan cover and blew into the vent while the sergeant blocked the barrel with his thumb over the muzzle and then took it away suddenly so that a "whoosh" of the corporal's breath showed the gun was unloaded.

"Cock the piece and squeeze the trigger," Rennick ordered. Ramage watched the flint strike the steel. There was no spark.

"Cock the piece and squeeze the trigger," Rennick repeated.

Again there was no spark.

"Take this man's name, sergeant," Rennick said as Ramage walked on to the first Marine in the front rank. The locks of 28 muskets sparked satisfactorily and Ramage, already feeling sorry for the wretched corporal, decided not to check the sergeant's musket.

After Rennick dismissed the men, he led the way to the guard-house where the second corporal and six men were drawn up outside the hut. Knowing their muskets would be loaded,

Ramage confined himself to inspecting the French uniforms the men were wearing.

"They were never as smart with Frenchmen inside 'em," he commented to Rennick. "Even if the Frenchmen were shorter."

"Yes. I've been trying to persuade the sergeant that although a couple of inches of ankle showing at the trouser leg would cause a sensation at Portsmouth, it doesn't matter here. He now agrees. He issued the uniforms," he added, "so it's hardly surprising his own is the only perfect fit."

Suddenly Ramage heard Jackson hailing from the top of the tower. "Captain, sir! Captain, sir!"

Ramage, knowing the limitations of his own voice, nodded to Rennick, who bellowed: "The Captain is here, at the guardhouse."

"Signal coming from Aspet, sir."

"Very well."

Ramage looked towards the corporal. "Your men are a credit. Don't forget though, if anyone arrives, no talking, and blow the whistle for Mr Orsini."

With that Ramage hurried over to the tower, noting that Rennick and the sergeant were heading for one of the huts, presumably to deal with the unfortunate corporal whose flint refused to spark.

By now the sun was well above the horizon, bringing warmth with it and putting new vigour into the insects which were beginning to buzz about the yellow flecks of flower among the gorse bushes. Feeling he needed the exercise, Ramage climbed the ladder, although he did it at a speed which made it clear to any onlooker that the Captain was simply climbing the ladder to get to the top of the platform, not to demonstrate how topmen should go up the ratlines wearing breeches.

Paolo, eye glued to the telescope on its stand, and aimed at Aspet, was calling out letters of the alphabet which Jackson was writing down on a slate. Ramage looked over the American's shoulder and saw it was a signal from Barcelona to Toulon.

"That's all," Paolo said briskly, "now dip the flag twice and then they can go to sleep again over there, happy in the knowledge we have the signal."

"I wonder where that signal spent the night," Ramage reflected. "It started off from Barcelona in broad daylight yesterday, for certain, but it was benighted before it travelled very far. It can't have travelled through only two or three stations today."

"Probably delayed by rain, sir," Jackson offered, "especially when you remember how the thunderstorms roll down the side of the Pyrenees. Cuts visibility to a few yards."

Paolo took the slate from Jackson and held it out for Ramage to finish reading. Then he asked: "Do we pass it on, sir?"

Ramage shook his head. "No, put it in the log and add a translation."

"The fools may have trumped your ace, sir," he said sympathetically. "One can never trust the Spanish."

The signal when translated said quite simply: "Convoy now fifteen ships refuses await escort and sails tomorrow." Obviously "tomorrow" meant today, because it was now only half past eight in the morning.

Ramage knew that only one question needed an answer now: would the Spanish (and probably French) merchantmen have left Barcelona before his faked order arrived telling them to make for Foix?

Most British convoys Ramage had ever seen—admittedly large West Indian ones, often comprising more than one hundred ships—took all day to get out of the harbour and sometimes all the next day to form up properly.

With Aitken, Southwick and Kenton on board the *Calypso* Ramage could spend the day at the semaphore station, although apart from giving an immediate answer to any questions concerning signals there seemed little else for him to do, and he enjoyed the atmosphere of the maquis.

Thirty-six hours from noon: that was about the earliest he could hope to sight the convoy, providing his signal arrived in time—and providing the real escort had not reached Barcelona. It was a sequence of events, he reflected gloomily, in which the word "providing" appeared too frequently.

Idly he watched the *Calypso* and saw the red and green cutters being hoisted out. As soon as they were in the water they would be filled with water casks—Aitken's men were to spend the rest of the day "wooding and watering": parties would be collecting firewood for the *Calypso's* coppers within the limits of the camp while others were filling casks with fresh water from the well. With luck the *Calypso* by the end of the day would again have thirty tons on board, the amount with which she had left Gibraltar to begin the present cruise. The cook was not going to be pleased with the wood, though; most of the trees were stunted and would yield logs more suitable for brightening the hearth of a cottage than heating a frigate's big coppers.

"Le Chesne, sir," Jackson reported to Orsini. "They've got their flag up."

"Answer and stand by," Orsini said, swinging the telescope round to the eastward and focusing it on the Le Chesne tower. Jackson hoisted and lowered the red flag and then picked up the slate. The signal was from Toulon and directed to station sixteen, which Ramage guessed was Séte. As Orsini called out the letters and Jackson wrote them down, Ramage realized the signal was a routine one about a discrepancy between stores reported used and the amount actually found in a recent inventory, and the commanding officer was required . . .

As he climbed down the ladder and recalled the contents of the original French signal log, he decided that pilfering, selling government stores and taking inventories were the main occupations of the commanding officers of the various semaphore stations.

Two days later Ramage sat on the *Calypso's* quarterdeck in a canvas-backed chair in the shade of the awning, which was rigged again to provide shelter from the blazing sun returning after the *mistral.* The sea was calm with a gentle breeze from the west so that the frigate was lying parallel with the beach. Over at the semaphore tower, which he could see on the larboard quarter, the tiny awning was rigged on the platform and he could just make out two figures, Paolo and Jackson, swinging the telescope round from time to time, keeping a watch on Aspet and Le Chesne.

Aloft in the *Calypso* seamen kept watch seaward, but by now he was sure that the convoy had sailed from Barcelona direct for their destinations before his signal had arrived ordering them to Foix, and no doubt the French escort had joined them.

Tonight, he decided, the *Calypso* would sail to look for the convoy—though he was uncertain whether to head eastward, close along the coast, on the assumption that it had passed in the darkness, or south-east because perhaps it had found a different wind once it left Barcelona and could comfortably lay Marseilles, its first destination.

He was not sure whether his semaphore signal had been a wild idea and a waste of time, or whether it had been a good idea unluckily ruined by the impatience of the French masters of merchantmen. Anyway tonight, as soon as it was dark, the tower would topple under the Marines' axes, the barrack huts would be wrecked, the powder casks rolled into the sea, and the cattle turned loose—the villagers would soon find and appropriate them. Burning down the whole place would attract far too much attention to the *Calypso*—the flames would be seen for miles—and to the French the important part of the camp as a link in the signal chain was not the accommodation (which could be replaced by tents) but the tower, which was as easily destroyed by axes as flames.

A fruitless chase after the convoy, he thought miserably, then a few weeks' cruising along the French and Spanish coasts sinking xebecs, tartanes and suchlike small coasting vessels, and then back to Gibraltar because the time limit for his orders would have run out. He could destroy a few of the semaphore towers, every fourth one, say, but he could not see their Lordships (or even the port admiral at Gibraltar) realizing what a blow that would be to the French naval communication system. The Board and admirals could understand ships captured or sunk; signals were dull affairs.

A few seamen in the waist were exercising French prisoners, allowing them up a dozen at a time. They were made to run round the fore and mainmasts a few times (they showed a great reluctance to exercise themselves voluntarily) and before they were sent below had to be inspected by Southwick.

Although the old Master spoke not a word of French, he always made himself clear: a tug at a shirt collar and a growl told the man it needed washing; an accusing finger pointing at uncombed hair or a badly tied queue was enough of a warning.

The French Lieutenant was proving a worry to Ramage: the man had sunk into a deep gloom, convinced that if the British did not shoot him they would hand him back to his own people, who would lop off his head, although for what crime Ramage could not discover, because being taken prisoner was no offence on either side.

He decided to have another talk with the wretched fellow: he was still irritated at having more than thirty French prisoners on board and was thinking of releasing them as the *Calypso* sailed. However, doing that meant the *Calypso*'s French disguise would be revealed.

Ramage called to a seaman to fetch another canvas deckchair and signalled to Aitken, whom he told to send a reliable seaman to bring the French Lieutenant who, once he was seated in the chair, was to be guarded only from a distance.

"He's a sad puir fellow," Aitken said after the seaman had departed. "Lost a *louis* and found a *centime*. I canna believe it's just because he's a prisoner."

The "sad puir fellow" came up the ladder from below, squinting with his eyes almost closed from the glare, and shuffling his feet as if on his way to the scaffold. The seaman guided him to the chair and when the man stood as though puzzled what to do next, gave him an unceremonious shove to make him sit.

Ramage nodded to him and said in French: "The sun is strong."

The French Lieutenant said sadly: "Yes, and my eyes are weak." He looked incuriously round the *Calypso*'s deck, appeared to notice the big hill in the centre of the bay, and equally incuriously looked farther round to the semaphore tower and the camp which for a year, until a few days ago, he had commanded. Now, Ramage was certain, he had no interest in it at all; he looked at it just as a sleepy dog looks up when roused in front of a fire.

"You are satisfied with the way your men are being treated?"

"My men?" He paused, obviously puzzled, and then said: "Oh yes, they are all right, or so the sergeant tells me."

"And yourself?"

The Lieutenant shrugged. "It is all a farce, *m'sieur*, and the sooner it is over the better."

"What is a farce?" Ramage asked casually.

"Treating me as a prisoner."

"What do I intend to do, then?"

"Shoot me."

"I do not shoot my prisoners."

"Then hand me back to the French authorities, which will be the same thing."

"Why should setting you free—for that's what it would be—amount to the same as shooting you?"

"I shall be punished."

"For what?" The man seemed to be almost in tears and Ramage was reminded of stories of penitents submitting to the Inquisition.

"There . . . a . . . deficiency . . . they had an inventory . . . when they return to Sète and compare what we have in our stores with what the inventory shows . . ."

"There will be a difference?"

"A big difference."

"In what materials?" Ramage was curious now; the scope for speculation seemed limited.

"Rice, flour, olive oil, wine . . ."

"How did it happen? Where did it go?"

"The villagers paid a good price: their crops failed this year and they were hungry."

"So you sold them Army stores?"

"It was not quite like that," the Lieutenant said lamely. "They were starving, you understand."

"You could have *given* them food."

"It came from them in the first place, all except the rice," the Lieutenant explained.

"From *them?*" Ramage was puzzled but a suspicion was forming in his mind.

"Yes—you see, we requisition what we need for the troops."

"But what did you sell to the starving villagers?"

"Well, the surplus."

"How could there be a *surplus* if you requisitioned only what you needed?"

The Lieutenant shrugged his shoulders. "It was hard to estimate."

"So—having deliberately stolen—not requisitioned, but stolen—more than you needed, you then made a cash profit by selling it back to the villagers?"

Ramage's voice was so cold and his eyes seemed but slits, like sword blades viewed from the point, that the Lieutenant said nothing.

"How did the Army authorities find a deficit?"

"We kept two sets of books and the wrong ones were given to the quartermaster's department at the time of the survey."

Ramage stood up and stared down at the Lieutenant, trying to control his anger. "You rob your own people of their food and sell it back to them, and when your quartermaster's department find out, you feel sorry for yourself and fear the guillotine, eh? Well, I'd hang you—slowly. Get out of my sight"—he pointed to

the ladder leading below and the seaman escort hurried back—
"in case I decide to do the job for your authorities."

As soon as the man had gone below—bolting like a rabbit, in
comparison with the way he had shambled up—Aitken came
over to find his Captain sitting down again and shaking with
rage.

The Scot, who had never seen Ramage like this before, asked
bluntly: "What happened, sir?"

Ramage told him, and Aitken commented: "It's a temptation
to hand him over, isn't it, sir. But it'd give ourselves away. Of
course," he added slowly, "we could keep the French seamen and
hand him over to the villagers. They'd probably string him up
from a tree."

Ramage shook his head. "There's always a government
informer in every village. It'd end up with the people of Foix
being massacred."

"We'll just make his life a bluidy misery then," Aitken said.
"We'll have him wakened every half an hour at night for a start,
with someone asking him if he's hungry."

Ramage told him the phrase to use, and the Scot repeated it
to himself a few times. "That's not too difficult; I'll have some
men from each watch practise it. His water ration can be a bit
smelly. And his wine issue vinegary. And if he finds more weevils in his bread than usual, well . . ."

Ramage nodded. "But this sort of requisitioning is going on
all over France where there's a garrison: the French Army lives
off the land—even in France."

The sun was dropping so low now its rays were coming under
the awning. Down on his desk were fifteen sheets of paper, each
intended for the master of one of the ships in the convoy, and
each neatly written in French by Paolo last night. Paolo's handwriting was typically that of a Latin: he wrote French easily, his
pen flowing without the hesitation of someone pausing to check
the spelling of a difficult word.

Had the convoy arrived, Paolo would have been rowed to

each of the ships in his French Army uniform and delivered a letter to the captain—in fact a brief paragraph of new orders—and the convoy's departure and subsequent capture would have been assured without a shot being fired. But Paolo's time—and the candle consumed in the lantern at the signalmen's hut—had been wasted.

Aitken said tactfully: "Should I take over the saws and axes to the camp and arrange what the men have to do tonight, sir?"

"Yes. Make sure they destroy completely the mechanism of the tower, once they've brought it down."

"Aye aye, sir."

"And don't forget to make sure the cattle are freed."

"Aye aye, sir."

"And make sure Orsini brings back the signal log and the copies of the semaphore code."

"Aye aye, sir," Aitken said patiently, sensing how his Captain's disappointment over the convoy was now mixed with anger over the despicable French Lieutenant. It would be unfortunate if any of the *Calypso's* officers or seamen made a bad mistake today—at least, within sight of the Captain.

Aitken was just climbing down into the red cutter when there was a bellow from aloft, and out of habit he paused to listen.

"Quarterdeck there—foremast here!"

"Deck here!" Ramage shouted back, not bothering to use the speaking-trumpet.

"Sail ho, being sou'-sou'-west, sir."

"How distant?"

"Just sighted her topsails. And there's another—there's two of 'em, sir."

"Very well, keep a sharp lookout."

Two ships. He could sail out, seize them and be back in Foix to take off the Marines at nightfall. Olive oil, grain and that sickly, sweet, red wine from Banyuls that's as bad as Marsala, Ramage thought crossly. Perhaps some hides, just to add their hideous stench to everything. Well, xebecs, tartanes, droghers, caiques, fishing boats—he did not give a damn; from now on they would be captured and sent in as prizes, or scuttled. He might keep a fast little xebec to act as a tender; young Martin could command it and he and Orsini would learn fast about the xebec's extraordinary rig. It could act as a scout and get into shallow places where the *Calypso* dare not venture.

"Deck there, foremast here. Three ships, sir, and maybe more: I need a bring-'em-near up here."

Ramage realized he was becoming lethargic; a few days ago a lookout's hail of a single ship would have meant someone immediately going aloft with a telescope. And now Aitken was coming back on board again.

"Deck there!" the lookout bawled. "There's dozens of the buggers, sir! Stretching from sou'-sou'-west to west by south."

"It must be the convoy, sir," Aitken murmured, and as Ramage nodded doubtfully he said: "I'll get aloft with the glass. Fifteen ships, wasn't it?"

"Fifteen. Any extra might mean the escorts found them."

Aitken grabbed a telescope from the binnacle box drawer and ran to the ratlines while Ramage turned his own glass to the south-west. He could see nothing; from where he stood the ships were still hidden below the curvature of the earth.

He had been so sure he had missed the convoy that even now he suspected the sails belonged to a flock of coasters which, after sheltering in the same port from the recent *mistral,* were now sailing together out of habit; the old routine of "Let us proceed together for mutual protection."

Aitken was perched comfortably aloft and Ramage had to walk out from under the awning to watch him. Now he was pulling out the tubes of the telescope, checking that they were lined up with the marks giving the right focus for his eye, and then looking out to the south-west. He seemed to be taking an age and it was as much as Ramage could do to avoid calling up to him. Finally the telescope was lowered.

"Deck there, sir."

"Deck here."

"Fifteen ships, sir, and all apparently steering for this bay."

"No escorts?"

"None in sight, sir; just merchantmen jogging along under easy sail. They've a soldier's wind out there; south from the look of it. We might be lying to a local breeze in here."

"Very well, Mr Aitken, come down when you're satisfied. Lookout! Report any change of course or increase or reduction of sail."

"Aye aye, sir."

By now Southwick, roused from below by the shouting, was standing beside him, a happy grin on his face.

"So our signal did get through, sir!"

"Seems so," Ramage said, mildly irritated that Southwick had said from the start that it would, an example of the Master's usual optimism swamping logic. "We'd better change into trousers and shirts and join the ranks of the *sans culottes* because this is supposed to be a French frigate and we may get a visit from the senior master of the merchantmen."

"Do you think we could fool him, sir?"

"No, which is why I want to spot him early and, if necessary, pay *him* a visit."

"He'll probably be flying some sort of pendant and throwing his weight about," Southwick said.

Aitken walked up, rubbing his hands on a piece of cloth, trying to remove tar stains picked up from the rigging and balancing his telescope under his arm.

"Half a dozen of them are fair-sized ships, sir," he reported. "The rest range from large coasting brigs to tartanes and a small xebec. They're in no sort of formation, although they're following what seems the largest ship. She probably wants to get into the bay first to find a good depth. There'll be a few foul berths and fouled anchors in here before the night's out!"

Aitken's words reminded Ramage that he had many decisions

to make before the merchantmen arrived, and he went aft to the taffrail and began striding athwartships, still protected from the glare of the setting sun by the awning, and able—for what it was worth—to look at the semaphore tower.

Twenty short paces from the larboard side to the starboard let him form in his mind the question of the semaphore tower. Leave it or cut it down? In favour of leaving it was—well, nothing: the French Army would find out soon enough that its garrison at Foix had vanished, and perhaps Aspet would mention the French frigate that had been at anchor near by. Would the Army put the two together? It was unlikely; there were no signs of a struggle; the French would just find the barracks empty and the tower unmanned. And the cows missing, providing they knew about the cows. The villagers would be no help—they would be hiding (and regularly milking) the cows, and from what that despicable Lieutenant had said, would be delighted that all those robbers had vanished. No doubt the older folk who did not agree with the Revolution would regard it as intervention of Divine Providence and say a few prayers of thanks—until the replacement garrison arrived.

So cutting down the tower would raise the alarm with the French Army authorities; leaving the tower and the rest of the camp intact would puzzle them as well. And, Ramage realized, he knew enough now about semaphore camps to attack a dozen of them once he had disposed of the convoy.

Five turns back and forth across the quarterdeck was a hundred paces, and had been enough to make up his mind about the tower. The cutters could go over at sunset—which would be before the merchantmen were close enough to see what was going on, but the time when sending semaphore signals stopped for the day—and bring back the Marines, leaving them enough time to tidy up the camp and remove any sign of their visit. The idea of the French Army (through the men at Aspet and Le Chesne) slowly discovering that their Foix camp was deserted appealed to him; he knew it would have a ghostly effect on many French soldiers who, though atheism was the official creed, had been born and bred as Catholics, and no matter what Revolutionary talk had subsequently been dinned into them, still retained enough of their childhood training to cross themselves in moments of extreme danger and have a healthy fear when nearly forty men suddenly vanished without trace.

He turned once again—the sun was lower now and peeping under the forward side of the awning—and considered the convoy now approaching under orders (his orders!) to anchor in the Baie de Foix to await an escort.

One 36-gun frigate should be enough of an escort, though a few cautious masters would no doubt complain. The longer the ships stayed at anchor the more chance there was that people from the merchantmen could discover that the *Calypso* was British: men might row to the camp at Foix, planning a night's carousing with the garrison, and raise the alarm.

It would take a day or two for Aspet or Le Chesne to react to having no answer to their flags—Ramage realized that Foix had no horse, so it was reasonable to suppose the other two were without horses too, so they would have either to march to Foix or commandeer a horse from a village (more likely a donkey or mule) to find out why the answering flag was not hoisted. He could just imagine a soldier sitting astride a donkey, feet nearly touching the ground, and jolting his way to Foix. The poor fellow would probably prefer to walk; in fact from Ramage's own experience walking was always preferable to riding bareback on a donkey.

That made eleven more double crossings of the quarterdeck; 220 paces to decide about the merchantmen. He realized he had examined the problem in detail and from every angle, but had made no decision. His feet ached, his eyes ached, his head ached. And the *Calypso* had swung close enough to the shore to have mosquitoes arriving any moment, each demanding their pint (it seemed) of blood. Very well, the merchantmen would have to come into the Baie and anchor while Orsini was rowed to each of them to hand over the written orders.

So that was decided, and it had taken another forty paces, a total of 260.

What was he to do with the convoy once he had control of it? He could not expect them to sail to Gibraltar and deliver themselves up to the prize marshal, but he could not spare fifteen prize crews and guards for all the prisoners.

Would they sail to the place he really wanted to have them anchored, where he could deal with them at his leisure? For three turns across the quarterdeck he repeated the place's name, as an infatuated lover might say the name of his mistress. It might work, and he had nothing to lose (except for fifteen merchant ships) if it did not. He went down to his cabin for one more look at the chart before the light went.

CHAPTER NINE

PAOLO climbed back on board the *Calypso* in the darkness, and while the cutter was being hoisted in under Jackson's directions he decided that the last hour and a half had been the strangest in his life—so far, anyway. Serving with the man he hoped would one day become his uncle by marriage produced more surprises than did a Three Kings' party every January when he was a little boy in Volterra.

He petted his coat pocket to make sure his notes were dry— there was always a slop thrown up when a boat went alongside a ship, and the cutter had just done that fifteen times: sixteen counting her return.

"The Captain is waiting for you in his cabin," Aitken said, his figure shadowy in the lantern light.

"Aye aye, sir." First lieutenants do not waste time, Paolo grumbled to himself: three hours ago, he and Martin were shifting their gear out of the signalmen's hut and making sure they had left nothing behind that could reveal the British had been there. Since then he had boarded fifteen enemy ships . . .

Paolo could not get used to trousers and a white shirt, open at the throat, even if it did have lace at the cuffs. The Frenchman for whom it had been made—that miserable Lieutenant—was too thin; Paolo was afraid that any exertion expanding his chest would rip it in half.

"Orsini! The Captain!"

"Aye aye, sir." Mr Aitken was such an impatient man. One could not report to the Captain wearing sodden boots.

A bellow from the Captain coming up the skylights from the cabin proved him wrong, and he scuttled and squelched down the companion-way, ignoring the sentry's salute in his agitation, and burst into the cabin without knocking.

Ramage looked up from his desk, his face seeming daemonic in the shadows of the flickering lantern.

"Go outside again and knock."

An embarrassed midshipman went outside, shut the door, said "Evening" to the sentry—the nearest he could get to an apology—and knocked on the door just as the sentry, not to be outdone, announced loudly: "Mr Orsini, sir!"

"Send him in."

Once again Paolo ducked his head and entered the cabin. Seeing the Captain in an open-necked seaman's shirt was a shock; the hairiness of his chest was also a surprise. Because the Captain's stock was usually tied high under his chin, Paolo realized, one did not think of there being a body—not in the hairy sense, anyway—'twixt stock and sole. Ah, there was a fine phrase; he had recently come across "'twixt" but had spent the last few days in the company of "Blower" Martin and Jackson, both splendid men but unappreciative of such a word.

"Why is that dam' silly grin on your face?"

"I was—er, well sir . . ." Paolo fumbled for a reason, unwilling to take a chance with "'twixt sock and sole,'" and finally dragged his notes from his pocket. They were wetter than he had realized. His hands had been wet when he added paragraphs to them and even wetter when, a few minutes ago, he had checked to see if they were dry.

"What on earth have you got there—a wet rag?"

"The list of ships and their cargoes, sir," Paolo said miserably. "I think I can still read it."

Ramage took out his pen, ink and sheet of paper. "Start reading, then."

"I went to the largest ship first, sir, as you told me. She's the *Sarazine* of Toulon, 560 tons, pierced for eight guns but carrying only four, all nine-pounders from the look of it. Seven men and the master—he complains of several desertions before sailing.

"He says he has been the commodore of the convoy from Barcelona to here and is very angry about the lack of escort. He complains of the responsibility. I told him I was only an *aspirant* and knew nothing about it all and my orders were to deliver the orders. He calmed down after a while and accepted the new destination but says he has no charts for that coast."

Ramage nodded. "You reassured him?"

The question relieved Paolo who, faced with the same complaint by all fifteen shipmasters, had promised each of them that copies would be sent on board long before the coast came in sight. "Yes, sir; I said we'd send one over."

"And the other ships?"

"The same, sir."

"Very good," Ramage said, adding dryly: "You're going to be busy making all those copies."

"Er—yes, sir. Well, she has a mixed cargo and is under charter to the Ministry of Marine. She's carrying fifty tons of powder for the garrison at Leghorn, stowed in half hogsheads, as well as flints for flintlocks. Five thousand for great guns, five thousand musket size, two thousand carbine and three thousand pistol."

Ramage wondered if there was a good source of flints and enough skilled flint knappers in Spain, then realized they might have come overland, across France and the Pyrenees: it would still be an easier journey to Leghorn than across the Alps.

"The second largest ship is the *Golondrina*, Spanish obviously. Also under charter to the Ministry of Marine. I thought it best not to understand Spanish, sir, and they had an officer who spoke French. Six guns, pierced for ten, mixed cargo. Everything from lumber—for the shipyard, they said—to bolts of canvas. Oh yes, they must be short of casks in Leghorn: she has twenty tons of iron hoops, and thousands of staves for butts, puncheons, hogsheads and barrels, and head pieces of course. Olive oil, Madeira—they must like it in Leghorn, or else they tranship it— and several tons of currants and raisins.

"The master was complaining to his officers in Spanish, not realizing I could understand, that one frigate was not much of an escort, and with the *Golondrina*'s bottom so foul, she was going to have the frigate alongside of her most of the time firing guns and screaming at him to set more canvas, but as they were so short of sails the French—he used a very strong word, sir—would have to put up with it."

Ramage looked up. "How many men apart from officers?"

"Only five that I could see, sir, and the master, mate and someone who would be a master's mate in the Royal Navy. Very undermanned, except in light weather."

"The next?"

"A very nice brig, the *Bergère*, captured from us by the French in mid-Atlantic, brought into Toulon, refitted and commissioned as a transport. Three hundred tons, and carrying great guns for ships, carriages for land artillery, harnesses for horses, and bales of hides which have been cut out and now need stitching to make them into harnesses. Very short of men, she was: the master and the mate are doing watch and watch about, and they have only eight men."

Ramage had heard, as a dismal descant sung by all captured French officers, that they were always short of men, and this was proof enough: undermanned ships in the West Indies could be explained by the loss through sickness and the distance from France. Yet, here, along the Mediterranean coast, they were sending ships to sea with so few men that any master carrying topsails at night—let alone topgallants—in unsettled weather would be asking for trouble: four men trying to furl or reef a topsail in a sudden Gulf of Lions squall might just as well stay in their hammocks and let the sail blow out; they would be unlikely to beat the wind.

"Any of the rest of those ships worth mentioning?" Ramage asked.

"Five of them are carrying quantities of powder. Some for Genoa, most for Leghorn and a certain amount for Civita Vecchia." He read out the names of the ships and the amounts.

"The quantities look like the normal replacement one would expect," Ramage commented, half to himself.

"Yes, sir. I wonder what sort of quality it is."

"Hmm . . . why not have one ship carrying all the powder?" Ramage mused, and then provided his own answer. "Probably put on board whichever ship happened to be loading as the convoys of carts arrived in Barcelona."

Ramage looked up at Paolo, who was obviously trying to pluck up enough courage to say something.

"Well, what ship has taken your fancy?"

Paolo's jaw dropped at the way the Captain seemed to have read his thoughts. "She's a tartane, sir, the *Passe Partout*. Laden with olive oil in hogsheads. Master, mate and four men. Pierced for four guns, but at the moment mounts only six swivels, three-pounders, I think."

"*Passe Partout*, 'the master key,'" Ramage mused. "What lock do you hope she'll open for you?"

"If we took her, sir, she'd make a fine tender for the *Calypso*: tartanes go to windward so well that she'd double the area we could search. Or . . . well, sir, I could sail her to Gibraltar as the *Calypso's* prize."

"Paolo," Ramage said affectionately, the first time he had used the boy's name on board, "would your navigation stand up to a seven hundred-mile voyage?"

"Yes, sir," Paolo said stoutly and, before a startled Ramage could contradict, he added: "To Gibraltar, anyway. From wherever we took her—I suppose it'd be near the destination—even though it's seven hundred miles to Gibraltar, I have only to sail west. If I see land to starboard, I keep it there; if to larboard, I keep it there. That way I'm bound to sight Europa Point and sail into Gibraltar Harbour."

"Like water poured into a funnel, eh? It has to go down and come out of the spout."

"Yes, sir," Paolo said lamely, wishing the Captain had chosen a less mundane comparison.

"I'll bear it in mind. Why a tartane, as a matter of interest?"

"This one was built in Italy, sir, and her master reckons she's the most weatherly afloat."

"Never believe a master or owner's description of his vessel," Ramage warned mockingly. "Criticize his wife, his mistress, or his house, but never his ship . . . Now," he said, pulling out his watch. "Ah, nearly time for our convoy to get under way. Go and tell Mr Southwick that you have orders from me to check the trim of the poop lanterns and make sure the glasses are clean."

Ramage knew that either Southwick or Aitken would have done that already—the novelty of carrying three lanterns on the stern, one on each side of the poop and one higher in the centre to make a triangle, would have been enough for them to check that the lamptrimmer had done his job properly. He could not remember when they had last used a poop lantern. He could only hope that the quality of the stone-ground French glass was good enough that it did not crack in the windows so that the flames blew out.

He picked up his hat and went on deck. It was dark but cloudless, the stars reflecting just enough light for him to be able to see that the *Calypso* was almost surrounded by merchant ships. He noticed that they had let go just enough cable from the anchor to hold and not a fathom more; not one of them would have a single man to spare while weighing anchor. Even the cook in some of them would be heaving down on the windlass or straining at the capstan.

He found an angry Southwick on the quarterdeck, peering anxiously from one side to the other with the night-glass.

"Some of these beggars haven't anchored, sir," he exclaimed. "Too damned lazy to weigh an anchor. They've been drifting across the bay and then tacking back up again . . . it's only a matter of time before one gets caught in stays and hits us."

"All of them short of men, it seems. The sooner we get under way the better."

"Aye, sir, otherwise we'll find ourselves with a brace of tartanes on the end of our jib-boom; it'll be like spitting pickled onions with a skewer."

"We'll weigh and get out of the bay before we light the poop lanterns; that'll give us a lead of half a mile," Ramage said.

Aitken, who had joined them in time to hear the last few words, laughed and said: "I was going to suggest that m'self, sir: it's like being surrounded by fifteen drunken bullocks."

"Or nervous old ladies clutching smoking grenades," Ramage said. "They're so scared of collision that at first most will be out of control because they daren't set enough canvas to have proper steerage-way."

"We'll play the highwayman, then, and make a quick escape. Starting now, sir?"

It was a good half an hour before the sailing time Ramage had put in the orders, a copy of which Paolo had delivered to each ship, but by that time the *Calypso* must be well clear of the bay, steering the correct course and the triangle of poop lanterns acting as a guiding star for the merchant ships.

Ramage, knowing that a collision tearing away shrouds and bringing down a mast would not only wreck this operation but bring the whole cruise to a stop and result in them being made prisoners, gave the order. Southwick went forward while Aitken passed the word for the bosun's mates to rouse out both watches without using their shrill calls and without hearty bellows in English. Their voices would carry a long way on a night like this.

The topmen had already been instructed that all they would hear from the deck would be a sequence of numbers hailed in French. In fact—although Ramage had not made the point—it did not matter if they forgot the actual words for the numbers as long as they remembered the sequence. The third order, or hail, for instance, could only mean "Trice up booms."

Ramage silently ran through the list of things to be done or checked before going to sea. He had done it hundreds of times in the past when, as a midshipman or lieutenant, some of the tasks had been his responsibility. Now he had three lieutenants and a master to make sure they were done; but if even one was accidentally omitted and the ship damaged or endangered, the court martial would find the captain guilty of negligence. That was what captains were there for . . .

All but the bower anchor stowed; boats hoisted in and secured; ensign staff down—the Tricolour had already been taken in—and the dog-vanes put in the bulwarks, their feathers checked in the corks, the lines securing the corks inspected for wear and twists; sails ready for loosing—he had looked them over with the glass before darkness fell; tiller and relieving tackle inspected—he had done that immediately once they had anchored after the *mistral.* If they were leaving from one of His Majesty's dockyards, he or Southwick would check that they had all the charts needed for the voyage, which reminded him that young Orsini must make a start on the copies of the charts for the French ships, and Ramage decided his clerk could lose a night's sleep too, helping him. The clerk was an idler, the official word for a day worker. There were not many of them in a frigate and they included people like the cook and his mate, the carpenter's crew, men whose regular routine was interrupted only by general quarters or, as in the case of the clerk, an unusual situation . . .

He could hear the steady clunk, clunk, clank as the pawls dropped into place with the turning of the capstan barrel. There was none of John Smith the Second's fiddle tonight; although he played it as another man might strangle a cat, the men liked to have him standing on the capstan head, sawing away. A seaman glided up to Aitken in the darkness with a message from Southwick—the anchor was at long stay, Ramage guessed. He looked around for any French merchantmen anchored in the way—this was just the sort of situation when you found a badly commanded ship lying between you and your anchor so that as you hove in your cable you came up to her. The result was usually unpleasant, the other ship complaining that they mistook your anchor buoy for a fishpot marker. How few people realized that it often took more skill to anchor a ship properly than sail her. It was an old adage in the Royal Navy that "A ship is known by her boats," because badly painted and badly handled boats always came from slackly commanded ships. Ramage had his own addition to that—a badly anchored ship was always incompetently commanded.

By now the *Calypso*'s anchor was up and Aitken was calling aloft the unaccustomed: "*Un . . . deux . . . trois . . .*"

Southwick had been correct in his claim that some of the ships had not anchored, because as soon as they saw the *Calypso*'s topsails let fall, they began setting sail.

Once the frigate was clear of the Baie de Foix, Ramage told Aitken: "Have the poop lanterns lit," and a few minutes later was cursing the sooty smell that the gentle north-westerly breeze would keep drifting forward across the quarterdeck.

Southwick came bustling up, his work on the fo'c's'le completed. "It's the same as being the first out of church, sir; you avoid meeting all the people you don't like."

"I can't picture you in or out of a church."

"True, but my sister always makes me go to both matins and evensong when I am on leave."

"I should think so," Ramage said. "She has a well-developed sense of duty."

"She's more concerned with showing her brother off to the neighbours," Southwick grumbled. "I don't get the impression she worries too much about my immortal soul."

"Well, someone ought to, because I have the feeling"—Ramage waved astern towards the merchant ships now setting sail—"that it's going to be strained for the next few days."

"Escorting a convoy with one ship is like leading a flock of sheep without a dog," Southwick said crossly. "No one to chase up the laggards."

"Cheer up," Ramage teased him. "It could be worse."

"I doubt it. I've never escorted a convoy of British ships where at least half the masters weren't mules. But a mixture of French and Spanish—can you imagine it, sir?"

"I can, only too vividly," Ramage admitted. "And the Dons don't trust the French anyway, and the French are already angry that the escorts—they were expecting more than a frigate—did not arrive."

"I know what I'd like to do," Southwick muttered.

"What's that?"

"Board the biggest two, send 'em to Gibraltar as prizes, and sink the rest."

"So would I," Ramage said quietly, "but the prizes would never get there. They'd be recaptured by the French or Spanish in a few hours, and we'd end up losing a couple of good prize crews."

"I suppose so, sir," Southwick said grudgingly, puzzled because he knew the order sent to each of the ships was to make for a place in the opposite direction to Gibraltar, and that the *Calypso* was going to lead them there. And a discreet inquiry of Aitken showed that the Captain had not given a hint to the First Lieutenant either about what he intended to do with these mules.

Look at them, he told himself, they've only just left the bay, and have the *Calypso's* three lights to make for, as clear as a light-house, and they're already spreading out across ten points of the horizon.

CHAPTER TEN

WILL Stafford had worked it all out without any difficulty, he told Jackson and Rossi. The Captain had very cunningly ordered the convoy to come to the bay; now he was going to lead it to Gibraltar, lowering the French colours as the *Calypso* hauled her wind to make up for Europa Point.

The three men, off watch, were sitting on the fo'c's'le gossiping and enjoying the mellow Mediterranean night, finding it too hot with the light following wind to go below.

Jackson, pointing at the Pole Star, said mildly: "We're steering about south-east. That means Sardinia, Sicily, Egypt or the Morea. It doesn't mean Gibraltar, which happens to be in the opposite direction."

"We're just getting a good offing before we turn into the Gut," Stafford said airily. "We don't want to get caught in a Levanter with Spain to leeward. These mules couldn't claw off a carpet, let alone a dead lee shore."

"They've been clawing off lee shores for years," Jackson commented. "You don't live long in the Mediterranean otherwise."

"Italy," Rossi said, as though announcing its discovery. "The Captain is sailing back to Italy."

"On this course it could be—the southern part, anyway," Jackson agreed. "But why Italy?"

"He has friends there—I *know,*" Rossi said darkly.

"The Marchesa's living in England, Volterra's occupied, we've just finished making the *Calypso* very unpopular round Elba, so

I can tell you the Captain has no friends there—I *know!*" Jackson said.

"Why did Mr Orsini go to all the ships when they arrived then?"

"Because he speaks fluent French," Jackson said.

"And Italian," Rossi said triumphantly.

"And Spanish!" said Stafford, not to be outdone.

"So he could talk with the Spanish captains as well as the French," Jackson said. "If he spoke a word of Italian tonight, it was to swear when he banged his shin on a thwart."

"How do you know he banged his shin on a thwart?" demanded Rossi. "You weren't in the boat."

"My oath," Stafford grumbled, "you really are 'ard work, Rossi my old sparrer."

"Sparrer? Who is he?"

"Sparrow," Jackson said. "Stafford's English is not very good. The bird. Little brown things, you see thousands of them everywhere."

"Why does he call me a sparrer, then? *Rossignol,* perhaps. I sing not so good as the nightcap—"

"Nightingale," Jackson corrected him.

"—as the nightingale, then, but as for this sparrer—"

"Look, t'aint nothing ter do with singing," Stafford said. "It's— well, where I come from to call someone 'My old cock sparrer' is like, well, 'mate,' or 'chum.'"

"Perhaps, but this cock sparrer I do not like," Rossi said firmly. "They shit all over you. I know. Even in Milan Cathedral during the Blessing."

"All right, all right, I'm sorry," Stafford said. "But why are we going to Italy?"

"I didn't say we were definitely going," Rossi said impatiently. "I just hope we are."

"Why?"

"This bloody Spanish blackstrap, that's why," Rossi said crossly.

"The only true red wine is from Toscana—Tuscany, you call it. This Spanish vinegar the purser was given in Gibraltar—even Napolitani wouldn't drink it, and they're not particular if it is free."

"Mention it to the Captain," Jackson teased.

"*Mama mia*, you know how much *he* drinks."

Jackson looked astern. "Well, the convoy is forming up astern of us, so the course is south-east for the night anyway."

"Very strange," Stafford said. "You must admit that, Jacko; it's very strange."

"I admit that," Jackson said readily enough, "but it's 'very strange' things on Mr Ramage's part that's put a pile of prize-money in your pocket. How much are you worth now?"

"A few 'undred guineas," Stafford admitted. "Enough to buy a nice quiet inn whenever I feel the urge to 'run' or the war ends."

"Don't 'run,'" Jackson advised. "They'd pick you up in a couple of days, and the soldiers would relieve you of your guineas, too."

"I was only jokin', but I got enough put away for a nice wife and a nice old age. In fac' I was thinking only the other day, the press-gang did me a good turn."

"Yes, you certainly wouldn't have made a tenth of that burgling."

"Burgling?" Stafford was horrified. "I was a locksmith."

"Yes, we know," Rossi said ironically. "Always working by night."

"Shut up!" hissed Jackson. "What's that noise?"

It was not a single noise but a continuous one, starting off with an eerie creaking and groaning aloft which quickly merged into a crackling like the snapping of dried sticks and reached a climax with a bang like a gunshot. The three men looking aloft and aft, up at the foremast, saw the foreyard break into halves and come crashing down to the deck, leaving the topsail on the yard above ripped to pieces and beginning to flog in the wind.

Both Rossi and Stafford began to run aft but Jackson shouted to them to stop. In the few seconds it had taken to happen he had realized that as the two halves of the great yard—the second largest in the ship, seventy feet long and a foot and a half in diameter—hit the deck there had been no screams of pain, so it was unlikely that any injured men were trapped. And there was still more wreckage to fall—blocks the size of small church bells, perhaps the stunsail booms were still up there, caught in the rigging and yet to fall . . . As he waited his fears were confirmed; heavy objects thudded down on to the deck like falling round shot, blocks slid off the ropes or ripped tackles, great sections of the torn foresail, which had been furled on the yard, fell like bales of straw, still bound by gaskets and tangled in clewlines and buntlines.

Then he saw men coming from aft with lanterns, advancing cautiously. "Right lads, now we can go, but watch for anything else coming down."

Aitken and Southwick had been standing with Ramage on the quarterdeck when the yard broke; both had begun to run forward, both had been halted by Ramage for the same reason Jackson had stopped the two seamen.

Once lanterns had been hurriedly lit, Ramage stayed at the quarterdeck rail as the First Lieutenant and Master went forward to begin with a search for injured men. Ramage knew only too well what had happened; all that mattered was first that no men had been hurt and second that the yard could be repaired. The carpenter was a good man and no doubt he and his mates could fish the two halves together again, because although the *Calypso* had spare topsail yards and topgallant yards stowed along the booms beside the boats, she did not have spare fore and main yards. He picked up the speaking-trumpet and called for the bosun.

The man came running up the quarterdeck ladder as though answering a routine hail.

"Get the spare topsail sent up on deck from the sailroom, and a pair of slings. Leave the new foresail for the time being. I want that topsail hoisted up and bent on first. From the look of it there won't be much to save from the old one."

"No, sir. Pity the sheets didn't part . . ."

The topsail sheets passed through shoulder blocks at each end of the lower yardarm so that when the yard broke and fell its weight wrenched down on the sheets, which were secured one at each lower corner of the topsail, and tore it in half as one might rip a sheet of paper by pulling on the two lower corners.

Now was the time that Ramage detested being the Captain: he would prefer to be forward there, going through the wreckage, making sure none of the men were trapped, seeing exactly what the damage was (apart from the broken yard, he would be lucky if two guns each side had not been dismounted and the carriages smashed), and assessing the best way of repairing it. Carpenters were skilled men but he found that sometimes they were narrow in their ideas.

He turned away deliberately and walked slowly aft, making sure he did not have his night vision affected by the reflection of one of the poop lanterns on a shiny section of the taffrail. With his night-glass he looked at the ships astern. No formation, not a set of masts in line to show they were on the same course. To work out which tack they were on he had to reverse in his mind what he saw with his eye, as well as visualize the ships the right way up. He shut the telescope with an impatient gesture: all the ships lacked was a drover and his dog, then they would look like ewes on their way to the market. However, he had to be fair; the three largest ships were reasonably close to the *Calypso's* wake and no doubt the rest would soon follow like children scared of the dark.

He called to the quartermaster and was told the ship was handling well under the maintopsail alone, despite the flogging remnants of the fore-topsail, and even as the man replied, Ramage heard the noise lessen and, glancing up, saw that topmen were already out on the topsail yard, cutting the lacings securing the remains of the sail, which floated down like ghostly nightshirts.

Kenton came out of the darkness and saluted.

"The First Lieutenant ordered me to report, sir. The foreyard broke in a split twelve feet long and Mr Aitken says it will be easy to fish. The foresail, as far as we can see because the gaskets still secure most of it to the pieces of the yard, can be repaired. Five guns—three to larboard and two to starboard dismounted, but only one carriage smashed."

"The injured," Ramage interrupted. "How many?"

"Oh, none, sir," Kenton said, the surprise showing in his voice. "The deck is badly scored, a section of the starboard bulwark is stove in, but not a man hurt."

"Very well, what else?"

"That's all for now, sir: the carpenter is inspecting it. He will be reporting to you in five or ten minutes, but I heard Southwick say he reckoned the heat of the Tropics had made the wood brittle, and that bad weather a few days ago . . ."

"Twelve feet, you say?"

"At least, sir. A nice clean split. Glue, fish and woolding . . ."

The carpenter was the next to report. He was a small, wizened man but because he refused to wear a hat his face and forehead always had a deep tan—a colour, Southwick always maintained, halfway between oiled teak and varnished mahogany, teasing the carpenter that he was carved from a wood unknown to man.

Lewis was a Man of Kent, not a Kentish Man. He was always careful to explain that it was a matter of which side of the Medway a man was born. He had been born, in fact, within a few miles of one of Ramage's uncles: while repairing a drawer of the Captain's desk one day he had casually mentioned that as a boy he poached regularly over the uncle's estate, and even as a grown man before the war, whenever he had leave he enjoyed taking out a ferret of a night and netting a few burrows.

"Yer uncle never missed them rahbbets, sir," he said. "Bein' as 'ow 'e'd have given me permission ter snare, net or shoot any rahbbets I wanted, though 'e'd have drawn a line at pheasints or partridge. But poachin' 'em was wot gave 'em the aroma, sir; catchin' 'em legal like would have taken the taste away, like bilin' 'em too long."

Now Lewis was reporting to the landowner's nephew and, Ramage reflected wryly, everyone in the *Calypso* was taking part in a kind of poaching . . .

"Larboard side, sir, startin' abowt ten feet outboard of the jeers; the yard just split like an 'ead o' fresh celery. The split be fourteen feet three inches long, clean as a whistle, none o' the wood lorst. Glue up a treat, it will; bolt every foot, then six or eight fishes 'bout eighteen feet long, and wooldin' over the 'ole thing and the yard'll be stronger than afore it broke."

"You deserve a brace of pheasants, Lewis, and I'll tell my uncle!"

"Ah, 'ave 'em 'anging in the barn a week an' they'll roast up a treat."

"When can I expect to have that yard across again?"

Lewis scratched his head and then, holding his fists out in front of him, began sticking out one finger after another. Finally he had all the fingers and thumb of his right hand and the thumb and two fingers of his left.

"What be the time now, sir, then?"

Ramage looked at his watch by the light of the binnacle lamp. "Just before midnight."

"If I can have some men to help haul the two sections of the yard so I can true 'em up before gluing and bolting, and then help me and my mates turn it while we's driving the bolts and then fitting the fishes—well, ten or twelve hours, sir."

"No signs of rot?"

"None, sir; clean as a whistle."

"Why did she go?"

"Reckon the wood just got brittle from the tropical 'eat, sir. Sun's always beatin' on the top of the yard. And French wood, sir. Must have been an old yard from another ship, 'cos it's in one piece. A new one at the time this ship was built would be two trees scarphed together; they'd do a vertical scarph in the middle. Short o' long timber, they are."

"Anyway," Ramage said thankfully, "you can glue, bolt, fish and woold without having to cut scarphs?"

"Easy, sir, just so long as the sea don't get up and set those two pieces rollin' about the deck!"

Ramage nodded and Lewis went back down the ladder. How long had it all taken? Perhaps twenty minutes. In twenty minutes, on a calm Mediterranean night, the *Calypso* had been changed suddenly from an efficient fighting machine—capable, for example, of sinking every ship in the convoy with the ease of Lewis and his ferret chasing rabbits out of the burrow and into nets, to despatch them with a sharp blow across the back of the neck—to a wretched hulk that could not work her way to windward or manoeuvre against much more than a laden merchant ship.

Well, Aitken and Southwick had been complaining that patrolling off the coast of Languedoc was a dull business but now, although they might be short on fighting, they could hardly complain there was little to do: summoning up a convoy of fifteen French ships by juggling with a giant chess board, a bout with a Gulf of Lions gale, and now the foreyard crashing down around their ears should keep them occupied for a while.

Ramage was mistaken. Southwick was back on the quarterdeck five minutes later, bustling because he tended to bustle after any unusual physical exertion, as though it wound him up like a grandfather clock.

"Shall I sway up the spare maintopsail yard in the meantime, sir, and set the spare fore-topsail on it? Just in case we meet something."

Having thirty or forty extra seamen working round the fore-mast sending up the spare yard while Lewis and his men started on the broken yard would slow up everything.

"No, we'll replace that fore-topsail just as soon as they get the spare up from the sailroom, but after that we concentrate on Lewis and his mates. It's a case where jury-rigging is likely to delay proper repairs by twelve hours."

"How long does Lewis want, then?"

"He says ten or twelve hours."

"By noon, eh? Well, he's a reliable man, sir, and if that's his estimate we can rely on it."

"I hope so. Will you keep an eye on the bosun while they bend on the new fore-topsail?"

"Set her flying, sir, once we're ready?"

Ramage looked astern at the merchant ships, found he could not make out more than one or two, and once again searched the horizon with the night-glass.

"No, leave it furled until we have the foreyard repaired and swayed up: these damned mules astern are so slow we'll proba-bly have to put a reef or two in the maintopsail just to avoid leaving them too far astern."

Southwick gave one of his typical sniffs. He had a dozen or more, each of which had a different tone and meaning. This one, Ramage knew, was reserved for situations of which Southwick disapproved but was powerless to change.

A fast frigate in a stiff wind would be hard put to keep these fifteen merchantmen in any sort of formation; closing and firing shots across their bows would not hurry them up; shouted threats of putting a round shot into them would result in a shower of Gascon, Breton and Norman abuse. So, since the *Calypso* was for the moment a disabled frigate, and far from there being a stiff wind there was only a mild breeze, the only thing was to be thankful that of all times the foreyard decided to split, now was the most convenient, because the *Calypso* was hardly rolling at all, and repairs should be comparatively easy.

C H A P T E R   E L E V E N

AT DAWN, when the *Calypso*'s ship's company were at quarters, guns loaded and run out, ready for any enemy that might emerge as the darkness vanished, Ramage slowly walked forward, stopping to talk with the guns' crews.

He found these "dawn promenades," as Southwick called them, a useful way of communicating with the men. Sometimes a seaman had a genuine grievance which only the Captain could settle, but because he was a shy man or feared upsetting the First Lieutenant to whom he was supposed to go first, he would say nothing, and that sometimes meant he would become morose, surly or a troublemaker with a chip on his shoulder.

Ramage's habit of walking casually from one gun to another, often with some comment on the weather or the shape of a headland if they were near land, put him physically close to most of the men. He knew them well by name; he knew the family history of many of them; he had been in action with all of them.

Sometimes a hint would come from Jackson, or perhaps from Bowen, the observant Surgeon. It meant that often Ramage, pausing at a gun to ask one man if the rheumatism was now gone, would be able to talk to the actual man who had a real or imagined grievance or problem.

These usually multiplied after a sack of mail arrived on board: letters from home seemed to bring as much misery as joy: interfering neighbours relating gossip, money problems, pregnant wives, sick children, aged parents—a seaman could rarely do anything to help any of them because he was a quarter of the hemisphere away, or about to sail from Britain.

It was a chilly morning but a clear sky warned of a scorching day. Dawn was coming fast—soon they would be able "to see a grey goose at a mile," so the lookouts would then go aloft and the rest would stand down from quarters. Ramage had not passed the mainmast before he discovered one thing: the men who had been on shore at the semaphore station for several days were still bubbling over about it: to them walking on grass once again, being able to compete with each other to see who could hurl a stone the farthest, even swimming from the beaches (though few of them could actually swim, most of them enjoyed ducking their heads under) had been like special leave.

He cursed the *mistral:* but for the need to sail for those three days he would have been able to rotate the men so that all had a chance to stay on shore.

The two guns on one side and the three on the other dismounted by the falling yard were all back on their carriages again, although two on each side were hauled up to the centreline clear of the space where Lewis and his mates were working.

Already Ramage could smell the hot glue and the yard, now lying fore and aft, was once again a continuous piece. Every foot or so there were a dozen turns of rope, each with a handspike stuck in it. Lewis had used handspikes for the Spanish windlasses of rope clamping the two pieces of yard tightly together while the glue set. There was not a man within several feet of the yard: the carpenter's mates were busy preparing long planks—Lewis would call them battens—to fish the yard. They would be laid along where it had been glued, overlapping the length of the split, and eventually completely encircling it, like many splints supporting a broken leg. The fishes or battens would sit on "flats" specially planed along the curved surface of the yard and be held in position by bolts and nails.

Lewis saw Ramage coming and, running his fingers through his hair after rubbing his hands down the sides of his trousers to remove some of the glue, stood ready to report.

Ramage eyed the repair so far. There was enough daylight now to see the runs of glue from where the two split pieces had been fitted together. Plenty of glue had dripped on to the deck planking, too, which would later need holystoning, but he could see very little damage from the spar's fall. The lifts must have held each side just long enough to make the two halves swing down like pendulums, rather than crash down as though rolled off a cliff.

The black objects, several feet long and narrow, like giant corkscrews, were augers, and after Lewis saluted he pointed to them.

"All going well, sir; so far I think we're even a bit ahead o' ourselves. Got her glued up and held by them Spanish wind-lushes and as soon as we got enough light to sight 'em, we go in with the augers and drill for the bolts. The armourer's mate's goin' to cut a few more bolts down to size (I got almost all I need that fit; just short of six) as soon as we can get the galley fire going to give him 'eat."

Ramage watched as Lewis showed where he had marked the positions for the bolts. "They'll be set into the wood so they won't chafe nothing, and anyway the woolding will cover 'em."

"You can't hoop it, I suppose?"

Lewis shook his head. "We just don't have the iron 'oops, sir. Nothing I'd like better than drive an 'ot iron 'oop every three feet; that'd set it up like a new spar. No, sir, it'll 'ave to be woolding. Not that there's anything wrong with that, sir," he added hastily. "These 'ere blacksmiths swear by 'ot 'oops but I b'aint so sure. 'Ere, sir," he said confidentially, taking a pace nearer and dropping his voice, "it's on account of rust."

"Is that so?" a startled Ramage replied.

"Yus, sir. They 'oop masts and spars now as a matter o' course when they make 'em, but once there's a few coats of paint on the 'oops, yer can't see what's goin' on underneath. But I seen it, sir; I seen masts and yards where, when they've got the 'oops off, underneath it's been rusting away for years and the 'oops is thin as paper. As paper," he repeated disgustedly. "I ask yer, sir, what's the good o' 'oops like that? Might just as well put on a few pages of the *Morning Post* like a winding sheet and paint it over.

"No, sir," Lewis said firmly, "woolding's the answer, and it

stand to reason. With 'oops you can't see what's going on under-
beneath—and that rust makes the 'oops swell, too. I've seen
some that the rust has swelled so much they've split orf by their-
selves. But with wooldin', you can *see*.

"First you use good stretched rope. It's bin used so you know
it's strong an' sound. You nail one end to the yard and then start
passin' it round, 'eaving a good strain on it, and nailing. That
way a nail every couple o' feet 'olds the strain you've 'eaved,
and by the time you got six or eight turns on and nailed, you've
got that spar gripped better than with an 'oop and now, sir, you
tell me the two big advantages you've got over the 'oop."

Ramage could see more than two, but it seemed unfair to
spoil the climax of Lewis's exposition. "You tell me," he said cautiously.

"Well, sir, stands to reason. 'Ow many turns have you got on,
eh?"

"Let's say eight."

"Right, sir. Diameter of the rope used—say one inch. Eight
turns of rope lying side by side and well nailed down means that
bit of wooldin' is at least eight inches wide and is 'olding eight
times the breakin' strain of the rope. And 'ow wide is an 'oop?"

Ramage was saved having to guess by Lewis's exultant, "You
see, sir, stands to reason. But"—he held up an admonitory finger—"that's only one of the advantages. The other one—and by
my reckonin' it's the greatest one—is that you can go along every
few months and check it over. You give the wooldin' a good bang
with a mallet and you'll soon see if the rope's still sound and the
nails 'oldin' in the wood. Not like an 'oop 'iding its weakness
under coats of paint."

"So woolding it is," Ramage said, knowing that he would be
there for half an hour if he let Lewis carry on. The man talked
sense and Ramage would have happily listened to his wisdom
for the rest of the day—if the foreyard was not lying on the deck
beside them.

"Ah," Lewis said, "that be light enough to start drilling for them bolts. If you'll excuse me, sir—now, Butcher, let's start turning them augers."

By nine o'clock, with the sun just beginning to get some warmth in it, Ramage heard a clattering of metal and looked forward from the quarterdeck to see the armourer's mate emptying a sack of bolts at Lewis's feet beside the foreyard. The carpenter bent down, picked up one of the bolts and examined it critically. He looked round for a heavy hammer, went over to the first of the holes drilled right through the yard and the fish on each side, and pressed in the first two or three inches of the bolt, motioning to the armourer's mate to hold it steady while he swung the hammer, which had a handle five feet long.

The rest of the carpenter's mates stopped to watch and, at an order from the carpenter, leaned against the yard to steady it, standing alternately. The armourer's mate held the bolt at arm's length, obviously afraid one of the carpenter's blows would miss, glance off and hit him.

The carpenter struck one blow, and then called to one of his men, who had a jar of Stockholm tar and a brush. He dabbed the bolt with tar and after each blow with the hammer wetted the bolt and wood again.

As the bolt drove into the wood one of the mates crouched down to watch for the other end to emerge. He had to make sure that the wood did not split and that the lower fish was held securely by the turns of the Spanish windlasses, even though the glue had not yet set hard.

"Here she comes!" he called, and at once the carpenter began delivering lighter strokes. "An inch to go . . . end's level . . . out half an inch and no splitting . . ."

The carpenter dropped the hammer with the proud gesture of a skilled craftsman: other and lesser men could drive the remaining bolts now he had shown them how it should be done, and then clench the lower ends over the big washers, or roves, so that each bolt became a great rivet.

Already the bosun was cutting lengths of rope, each one long enough to go round the yard eight times, and his mates were busy putting whippings on each end to prevent the strands unlaying. Several men with chisels and gouges were cutting grooves round the yard just deep enough for the rope to lie in for a third of its diameter, but because of the fishes the grooves need be only along the edges of the planks. Lying ready were piles of copper nails, awls to drill the holes in the wood and fids to make holes through the whole rope, rather than let the copper nails drive down between the strands.

Southwick came up the quarterdeck ladder after a tour of inspection and reported to Ramage: "He'll have finished it by noon, sir: a good man, Lewis; he's got a sense of order. Prepares things so that as he finishes one part the next one is ready."

"One of those bolts could make a bad split if it's a fraction too big or the hole bored too small," Ramage said. "I'd like to see Lewis drive them all."

Southwick nodded. "Aye, sir, that's the one thing that really could set us back a day. I'll go down and tell him."

As the Master left, Ramage looked astern gloomily. It did not seem possible that fifteen ships could occupy so much space: they were spread from a mile astern of the *Calypso*—that was the *Sarazine*—in a vast semicircle to the horizon. As soon as Lewis has driven those bolts, Ramage vowed, the *Calypso* would be forcing them into the formation described in the orders that Orsini had delivered to each master.

Martin was the officer of the deck and it was Orsini's watch. Martin was proving a very competent watchkeeper and Ramage was thankful that his next letter to Gianna would still be able to give Paolo honest praise because he was (apart from mathematics) improving almost daily.

Ramage guessed that both youngsters were giving impatient glances astern, waiting for the Captain to turn the *Calypso* back to crack the whip round the merchant ships. Neither of them appreciated that for the time being it did not matter; what mattered was that an unexpected roll did not upset the foreyard, which could not be chocked up, shored up, roped down, wedged or lashed too tightly at this stage because it was important that when drilled and bolted it was in its natural shape. In an emergency, yes, it would be worth risking bolting in a slight bend, but at this stage with the convoy at least following, albeit like sheep ambling across a field in search of fresh grass, and no risk of an enemy, good formation did not really matter. Not, Ramage realized, that he could say such a thing out loud in front of his officers.

"We could do with the *Passe Partout* now, sir," Orsini said cautiously. As a rule midshipmen did not initiate conversations with captains, and Paolo was more than anxious that he should not appear to take advantage of the fact that the Marchesa was his aunt. The result was, of course, that he spoke to the Captain less than if he had been a complete stranger.

"We could also do with another frigate," Ramage said sourly.

"But in these light airs, sir, a tartane . . ."

Ramage gave a sniff that he was sure Southwick would envy; a perfect blend of understanding Paolo's motives in making the remark, a superior knowledge of the sailing ability of tartanes in general and the *Passe Partout* in particular, and some information that Paolo did not possess.

"If I was the master of the *Sarazine*," Ramage said, "I don't think I'd be bothered by any tartane in my wake."

"But she has swivels, sir. Three-pounder shot whistling round your ears . . ."

"And the *Sarazine* has nine-pounders, and a stem that could cut the *Passe Partout* in half without scraping any paint . . ."

"Yes, sir," Paolo agreed regretfully. "Still, the *Passe Partout* is keeping well up; she's only one ship astern of the *Sarazine*."

"I've noticed that," Ramage said heavily. "Fetch me the French signal book: it is in the binnacle drawer."

Ramage glanced at it to check a signal, and said: "Mr Martin—hoist the French signal for *'The convoy is to take up close formation at once,'* and fire a gun to draw attention to it. Leave it hoisted until I give the word." He handed the signal book to the Lieutenant, pointing out the flags.

Three minutes later, with the flags hoisted, one of the *Calypso's* sternchase guns was fired. The smoke drifted forward over the quarterdeck and as it cleared Ramage looked at the French ships with his glass, shut it with a snap, and said to Martin: "I'm going to my cabin. Pass the word if those mules pay any attention to the signal."

As he sat down on the settee, remembering he had not filled in his journal for the previous day's events, Ramage knew that although Paolo wanted to get on board the *Passe Partout* simply because he was a young lad who dreamed of his own command, the fact was that Lewis would have the yard repaired by noon; it would be hoisted and the foresail bent on and the lead of the fore-topsail sheets corrected by two o'clock at the latest, and it would be better if the convoy was in some sort of formation by then, rather than having the *Calypso* chasing round in light airs . . .

The *Passe Partout,* according to Paolo, had a master, mate and four men on board. That, the boy admitted, was all he saw. So there would also be a cook, and perhaps another couple of men who were sleeping when Paolo was on board. Nine men, say a dozen at the most. The problem was not how to overpower a dozen men and seize the ship, but how to do it without fourteen other ships seeing it, getting alarmed and bolting.

He told the sentry to pass the word for Aitken, who arrived breathless, assuming something had gone wrong.

"No," Ramage assured him, "quite to the contrary. It is just that we'll very soon need a sheepdog to yap at the convoy's heels."

"Ah—that tartane, sir, the *Passe Partout.*"

"You've been listening to young Orsini!"

"Yes, sir, but I must admit I think she's the one I'd choose."

"You're more concerned with sparing the fewest men for a prize crew," Ramage said teasingly.

"Aye, that's true, sir, but I can find a dozen without much strain."

"And who would you put in command?" Ramage asked out of curiosity.

"Orsini, if we just want yapping at their heels; Martin if there are likely to be any serious decisions to be taken which he can't refer to you."

"You have a good opinion of Martin."

"Yes, sir, he'll go far. And he's having an excellent influence on Orsini. They work well together. That sort of thing is, in my experience, unusual: normally a midshipman wants to show off and a lieutenant won't listen to him. But they both like and trust each other, like a younger and older brother. Orsini has, well, I suppose it's a cosmopolitan view because of his background, and Martin is a fine seaman. Each wants to learn what the other has to offer—at least, that's my impression, sir."

Ramage nodded because Aitken's opinion coincided with his own, though the Scot had phrased it more succinctly.

"So we want the tartane, then, and Martin can command it with Orsini as mate."

"Night attack, sir?"

"No. We don't want them firing off those swivels and alarming the rest of the convoy. No, we must take her without a shot being fired, and the only way I can think of is this." For the next five minutes Ramage gave Aitken his orders.

Within an hour of the men finishing their midday meal the great foreyard was hoisted, using the capstan to raise its fifteen hundredweight up the foremast. Running rigging was fitted and by the time the fore-topsail sheets were properly rove, the foresail, the second largest sail in the ship, was lying at the foot of the mast ready to be hoisted and bent on.

The sail was made up of more than one thousand five hundred square feet of canvas; along the head of the sail, where it would be laced to the yard, it measured within inches of fifty feet; along the curved foot it was a couple of feet less, while the luffs—the vertical sides—were 31 feet.

The sailmaker, bosun and his mates had already checked over the sail and made repairs, and Ramage was surprised how little damage it had suffered. Most of the tears had been vertical along the seams; the cloth had held while the stitching gave way. Reef points had been checked over and many replaced—not through damage but because of wear. Two reef cringles had also been replaced, along with all the bowline cringles on the starboard side of the sail.

Now fifty men were busy round the sail. Yard ropes were rove to the reef cringles; buntlines, running vertically along the sail and normally used for hauling it up to the yard for furling, were rove through their respective blocks which were once again secured to the yard.

Topmen went aloft and out along the yard; slowly the sail was hoisted up as Aitken shouted his orders through the speaking-trumpet. Once the head of the sail reached the yard, like a great sheet being pegged out on a washing line, the topmen secured it, hauling the canvas taut. With that done, Aitken gave the orders to furl the sail, which was then hauled up to the yard, gathered like an enormous sausage, and secured with gaskets.

"The yard seems to sit well enough," Southwick commented to Ramage. "As straight as before. Not so much spring in her, but she's bound to be stiffer where she's bolted and fished."

"The yard is stronger than before, anyway," Ramage said dryly. "She won't break there again!"

"You won't be setting stunsails for a while, sir?"

"No—why?"

"Lewis mentioned to me that—well, in the rush to get the yard repaired he hadn't noticed that the larboard stunsail boom is in two pieces, and he has to make a new one. Matter of an hour or so."

"If that's all he's forgotten, he did a good job," Ramage said. "Send for him and his mates: they deserve some praise—and some sleep, too."

As soon as the men were lined up on the quarterdeck, Lewis

standing a pace in front of them, Ramage thanked them briefly. More than a dozen words of praise had them shuffling with embarrassment, and Ramage could see that three or four of them were almost asleep on their feet, having been working on the yard for nearly twelve hours.

Once the carpenter had led his mates below, Ramage explained to Southwick his plan for the *Passe Partout* and the Master chuckled. "Ah, I wish I was a youngster again; they get all the fun."

"You've had your share," Ramage said unsympathetically, "and there'll be more to come before you go over the standing part of the foresheet."

"Aye, I hope so," Southwick said.

"There'd better be," Ramage said, "otherwise I'll go back to Cornwall and breed horses."

Knowing how much Ramage disliked horses and riding, Southwick gave a broad grin, and nodded when Ramage said: "Send Martin, Orsini, Jackson, Stafford and Rossi down to my cabin, and look up the *Passe Partout's* number in our version of the convoy orders. Eight, I think it was. Then,"—he took out the French signal book and looked up a signal—"be ready to hoist '*Pass within hail.*'"

The *Passe Partout's* big triangular lateen sail bulging from the curving yard hoisted on her single mast reminded Ramage of a shark's fin slicing through the water as she came up astern of the *Calypso*.

Most of the ships in the convoy had made some attempt to get into formation, or rather they bunched up closer to the *Sarazine*, which in turn was obviously trying to stay in the *Calypso's* wake. Most were three miles or more astern now that the frigate, unknown to the convoy, was deliberately outpacing it.

Aitken admired the way that the Captain had first hoisted the signal for the convoy to take up closer formation, one he knew they were incapable of obeying with any sort of efficiency, and given them a couple of hours to do their best. As the Captain had predicted, they had simply closed up on the *Sarazine* like chicks following the mother hen.

Aitken then had noticed that the Captain's telescope was more often pointing out to the sides than directly astern and he later commented that he was more concerned that the convoy formation became narrower than wider; that the ships bulged out astern rather than strung out across the width of the horizon.

Then, simultaneously with hoisting the *Passe Partout*'s number and the signal for her to pass within hail, Mr Ramage had almost imperceptibly edged the *Calypso* over to one edge of the convoy: all the merchant ships were now over on the *Calypso*'s larboard quarter. And, he guessed, the *Passe Partout* was going to be ordered up on the starboard side, out of sight of the rest of them . . .

The tartane, her hull blue and mast white, was now a mile astern, gliding up and over the slight swell waves like a gull, her foresail flapping idly as the big lateen sail took all the wind in a great bellying curve swelled out by the following breeze. There were two men in the waist of the ship, almost hidden by the bow because of the tartane's deep sheer, and Aitken could see two more men at the tiller. In this wind it could be handled by one, so the other was probably the master just standing there giving orders.

There were three lumps down each side on top of the bulwarks looking rather like horses' heads, and which Aitken recognized as swivel guns, covered in protective canvas covers that distorted their shape.

"How many men can you distinguish?" Ramage asked.

"Only four, sir. Perhaps more will come up when she gets closer."

Ramage looked across at Martin. "It's going to be quite a jump down. Are you sure you won't break your necks?"

"Quite sure, sir."

Ramage looked at Paolo, who had changed his usual weapons of a cutlass with his midshipman's dirk to use as a *main gauche,* to two pistols clipped in his belt and the dirk, which was shorter than the cutlass.

Jackson favoured a half-pike and two pistols. Four feet and a half long including its sharp iron head, the half-pike was a good jabbing weapon with an ash staff stout enough to ward off a slashing cutlass. Both Stafford and Rossi remained loyal to pistols and to cutlasses, with the belts pulled round so that the blades hung down their backs, out of the way and less likely to trip them up.

The remaining two seamen were made by a wilful Nature as the exact opposite of each other, although they were close friends. Baxter and Johnson came from the same village in Lincolnshire, attended the same tiny school together for two years before going to work with their fathers as labourers on adjoining farms—and were picked up by the same press-gang sent out on a swing through the countryside from Lincoln.

Baxter, at six feet two inches, was the tallest man in the *Calypso* and had wide shoulders and a chest that looked as though they could break a capstan bar by leaning on it. He also had one of the quietest voices and gentlest natures of anyone aboard. He had only one weakness, drink. When, as Johnson would say fearfully, "the drink was in him," Baxter became an enraged ox who could interpret a shipmate's accidental glance as a mortal insult.

By contrast, Johnson was so small that the top of his head barely reached Baxter's shoulder. His voice was shrill and when provoked—which was rarely—he sounded like a nagging shrew, but his was the only voice that Baxter really listened to, apart from petty officers and officers giving orders.

Both men were superb pistol shots. No one knew how it happened because, as Johnson once admitted, the only guns they used as boys were shotguns, and then only for poaching. As if to partner the ability with pistols, both men were excellent with cutlasses. Baxter could use his height and strength to chop his way through a crowd: Johnson was as nimble as a Morris dancer and could swerve, duck and parry to the utter confusion of enemy seamen trained to use a cutlass as a slashing weapon with the same finesse as the ship's cook using a cleaver to cut twenty-pound blocks of salt beef.

Ramage spoke once more to Martin: "The canvas bag—ah, I see you have it. You've checked it holds all you need?"

"Aye aye, sir. Chart, tables, signal books—French and English—and a list of the convoy. Orsini has my sextant, and Jackson the set of French flags we've just sewn up."

Ramage glanced astern and was startled to see how fast the *Passe Partout* was approaching. Martin and his men looked a fine party of French seamen: white trousers (grubby) and blue shirts (torn) were not the French naval uniform because at this time there was not one for seamen, but it was just the rig that a smart captain would insist his men wore, because sewing their own clothes (or paying a shipmate to do it) made it as easy to use white and blue cloth as any other.

"Deck there—foremast here!"

Damn! The last thing Ramage wanted with that tartane so close was a lot of bellowing in English, and Aitken snatched up the speaking-trumpet, which would at least funnel his voice upwards.

"Deck here!"

"There's another ship coming up well astern of the convoy, sir. Enemy, I reckon, because they're all keeping away from her!"

"Very well, I'll send a man up with a glass."

Southwick lumbered over to Ramage, sniffing as he walked, like a disgruntled bloodhound. "Can only be one of two things, sir," he said.

Ramage nodded. "I know."

"Either," Southwick said, drawing out the word and carrying on as if he had not heard his Captain's reply, "Algerine pirates up from the coast, or a British privateer."

"Yes. Which are you putting your money on?"

"Algerine. We can sink an Algerine and all the Frogs will cheer us, but a British privateer . . ."

"Yes," Ramage answered shortly, his mind working fast. Fifteen French merchant ships would be waiting—were at this moment waiting for him to beat back to them and drive off or sink whatever it was, Algerine or British. He looked aloft impatiently and saw that the man sent up with the telescope was just settling himself and opening the lens tubes.

But the *Passe Partout* was now very close—and, damn and blast it, was obviously intending to come close alongside to larboard in plain view of the convoy.

"Deck there—French ship's—"

"Shut up!" Aitken's brief shout was deliberately slurred.

Ramage swung his glass across the convoy and saw that several of the ships were now hoisting flag signals with a speed that contrasted with their earlier leisurely response to his. As he watched he saw a string run up on the *Sarazine,* to be followed by a flash, a spurt of smoke and a muffled bang as she fired a gun to draw attention to it.

Aitken looked with his glass and then opened the French signal book. "On the first hoist is *'Enemy vessel,'* the second signifies *'bearing'* and the third is *'north-west.'*"

"Ignore them. I didn't know you spoke French," Ramage said.

"A little. I read it better."

"The book gives only 'Enemy,' doesn't it? Not more explicit—ah, here comes the man with the glass. What did you see, Kelso?"

The man was almost breathless from his climb up and down the mast, and he gave the glass back to Aitken, handling it carefully as though it would explode.

Do not rush him, Ramage told himself, just be calm and nonchalant; do not scream at the poor fellow a question like: "Well, what did you see, you damned fool?" After all Kelso did have the sense not to shout down what he had seen, a shout which would almost certainly be heard by the *Passe Partout,* which was

being waved—thank goodness for that!—to the starboard side by
Orsini, who was standing on the taffrail, holding on to one of
the poop lanterns and using the speaking-trumpet to shout his
shrill French.

"I had a good look at 'im, sor," Kelso said, unsure whether
he should report to Southwick, Aitken or Ramage, who were
now gathered round him in a group.

"You did, eh?" Ramage said to get the man's attention before
the poor fellow's head swivelled off. "And what did you make
of her?"

"Scunner-rigged, goes to windward like a round shot, an' got
every stitch o' canvas set, even ringtails on the main, I reckon."

"A schooner, eh?" Ramage said unhurriedly. "You didn't get
a sight of her flag, of course."

"Oh noo, sir, she's too far away for thaat!"

No more Devonians, Ramage swore to himself; I'll never ship
another Devonian, however fast he says he can talk.

Southwick jabbed the man in the ribs with his forefinger.
"British or Algerine?"

"Oh, British, sir," Kelso said at once. "I reckon I recognize
her, too, unless someone's copying her style o' paintwork."

"Well?" Southwick demanded.

"She's the old *Magpie*, used to sail out o' Brixham. I was a
privateersman afore the press took me up, an' she was m' first
ship after the war begun. Her hull, y' carn't mistake it: alternate
strakes o' black and white, carried well up under the run."

"*M'sieu! M'sieu!*"

It was Orsini, shouting to draw his attention and gesticulat-
ing over the starboard side. And there Ramage could see over
the bulwarks the upper part of the *Passe Partout*'s lateen sail only
a few feet away, a great bird's wing of canvas.

He had only a moment to make up his mind as he absorbed
the situation. The *Magpie* might already be attacking the convoy,
but whatever she was doing she must be sent off—preferably

happy at saying goodbye to the pick of fifteen enemy ships. But in this wind a frigate so obviously French as the *Calypso* could not get within five miles of a fore-and-aft rigged vessel like a schooner, and what would the convoy think of a French frigate talking to a British privateer instead of trying to sink her? The *Passe Partout* was close alongside, racing along as only a tartane or a xebec could in this breeze.

Ramage snapped at Aitken: "Take command of the *Calypso!*"

With that he grabbed the Scot's arm and pulled him to the ship's starboard side, where they could look down on the tartane, whose captain was obviously showing off to the Navy how close he could sail his ship to the frigate.

Ramage pointed down at her. "Lay us alongside her for two minutes," he told Aitken, "but don't do her any damage. Watch for that lateen yard!"

Ramage looked round for Martin. "Are your crowd ready? Come on then, lads, let's go!"

CHAPTER TWELVE

RAMAGE jumped down on to the *Passe Partout*'s deck, realizing as he dropped that it was farther than he'd thought, and landing with a thud that brought him to his knees. As he stood up he caught a foot in a ringbolt and sprawled across the deck. A moment later a French seaman helped him up in a cloud of garlic and he saw, eight or nine feet farther forward, another seaman helping Baxter.

Hurriedly thanking the seaman in French and noting he was not armed, and dodging more men dropping from the *Calypso*'s deck, Ramage hurried aft to the big ornate tiller where the man who was obviously the master stood looking up at the *Calypso*'s quarterdeck towering over him.

"Bear away gently, we're all on board!" Ramage called, anxious that the upper end of the lateen yard should not catch in the *Calypso's* rigging.

"As you say!" the master replied cheerfully, patting his enormous stomach and leaning against the tiller. "Fed up with the Navy's food, are you?"

"Urgent work," Ramage said, noticing there were still only four men on deck—the portly master, the helmsman who until a few minutes ago had been at the tiller, the man amidships who had lifted him to his feet, and the one who helped Baxter.

And now, as the *Passe Partout* curved away from the *Calypso,* Ramage saw his heavily-armed boarding-party was standing along the tartane's side deck looking very sheepish. Martin was beside Orsini, who by now was having an amiable conversation with the two French seamen amidships. They obviously believed that the eight men who had just jumped down from the frigate were, like themselves, true upholders of the Republic, "One and Indivisible."

As the turn showed the frigate's transom and her name painted on the scroll, Ramage realized for the first time exactly what he had done on the spur of the moment: he had quit the King's ship that he commanded and on a whim was now a supernumerary on board a French tartane. A French tartane which was about to become a British prize under the command of Lt William Martin, Royal Navy, known to his intimates as "Blower" and who had, without a doubt, hidden his flute somewhere among the prize crew's gear.

Well, neither Martin nor Orsini seemed to want to strain the good relations they were establishing with the two enemy seamen, but the *Passe Partout* had an urgent appointment with the *Magpie* on the far side of the convoy, so Ramage turned aft again, walked up the rising deck to the plump master and said, unable to keep the apologetic note out of his voice, as though he was a well-dressed bandit forced to reveal his true identity and rob the host who had just given him a fine dinner: "*M'sieu*—consider yourself and your men my prisoners; this ship is now a prize to His Britannic Majesty's frigate the *Calypso*."

The fat man looked startled, then began roaring with laughter. Keeping one eye on the *Calypso* as the tartane caught a good puff of wind and heeled as she increased speed, he slapped the helmsman on the back and said: "Well, that's one way of asking for a bottle of wine! Take the tiller and keep her on that course, Alfonse, while I get some up. And then *m'sieu* can tell me what he wants of us."

Ramage, realizing he was unarmed and dressed like a Frenchman, knew that only a flourished pistol would convince this jolly fellow that his ship was now captured. He turned and shouted forward in English: "Martin! Come aft with Jackson and send Orsini below to secure the other prisoners!"

Looking back at the master again Ramage saw he had gone white; his face was sagging and his brow speckling with perspiration. The welcoming grin had vanished; in its place was raw fear.

Ramage held up a reassuring hand. "There need be no bloodshed; we are British. I am a British officer."

The French master gestured helplessly at the convoy and then at the *Calypso*. "She has the French flag," he protested weakly. "This is a French convoy."

The flag: that was a mistake. A genuine one, but if the Admiralty heard about it they would not like it. It was a legitimate *ruse de guerre* to fly the enemy's flag providing that before opening fire you dropped it and hoisted your own. Well, on the other hand the *Calypso* had not opened fire and had not threatened to and, Ramage thought angrily, becoming furious with himself for bothering, this fellow General Bonaparte had not been fussy about protocol when he suddenly attacked half the countries in Europe, the Kingdom of Volterra included, without reason, pretext or warning.

"I am sorry," Ramage said. "We will take over your ship peacefully and providing you do not try to resist, no one will be hurt."

By now several men were walking aft from the fo'c's'le, all obviously just awakened, and followed by Martin's men.

"Tell them," Ramage told the master, "tell them no harm will come to them unless they try to retake the ship. Where is your arms chest?"

The master pointed down the companion-way near his feet. "In my cabin. Six muskets and six pistols."

"And powder and shot for those swivels?"

"There is a small locker at the forward side of my cabin. A half-cask of powder and a net of shot, and powder and shot for the small arms. Wads, too."

Ramage nodded as he counted up the Frenchmen. Paolo had been right: only six, and that included the cook. And the lateen rig was so simple that they needed no more. But for the moment only Paolo, Rossi and Jackson understood the working of the lateen rig.

The sun was scorching. For a few minutes the big lateen sail gave some shade on one side; then the *Passe Partout* had to tack again, zigzagging through the convoy as Ramage watched for the slightest shift in wind direction that might give the *Passe Partout* an advantage in the struggle to beat up to the *Magpie*.

The privateer was a puzzle. Ramage had expected her to swoop on the rear ships, the ones right at the stern of the convoy and therefore dead to windward of the *Calypso,* but the schooner was simply tacking back and forth across the wake of the convoy, as if biding her time.

Had her master a better plan? Ramage thought for a few moments, putting himself in the position of the master of the British privateer suddenly coming across a French convoy escorted by one frigate. He would go for the biggest ship, but she was the *Sarazine* and the nearest to the frigate.

Very well, he would wait for darkness. Work his way round the convoy—not difficult with a following wind—and sneak in quietly to board in the darkness, having the *Sarazine* captured and sailing out of the convoy before the *Calypso* could do anything. If the frigate tried to recapture the *Sarazine*, then the *Magpie* would board another merchantman, put a prize crew on board and sail her out of the convoy. Ramage knew that if he commanded the *Magpie* he would try for three prizes and hope to get away with two, expecting the third to be recaptured by the frigate.

In the meantime the *Passe Partout* had to work her way up to windward and get close enough to the *Magpie* to establish communication. But how? At the moment the schooner was staying far enough astern of the convoy for the *Passe Partout*, if she could only get close enough to the *Magpie*, to hoist a white flag without any of the French ships seeing it. Would the *Magpie* think it a trap? Hardly, because there was no way a little tartane in open water in bright sunshine could trap a heavily-armed privateer schooner. A pity merchant ships and privateers did not have the Navy's numerary code, because then Ramage could hoist a series of numbers which the *Magpie* could read out of the signal book as a message.

Again he nodded to Rossi, who had spent the last quarter of an hour at the helm; again the Italian leaned against the tiller; again the *Passe Partout*'s bow swung across the horizon, to put the wind on the other side and bring the lateen yard slamming across as she tacked.

Martin, Orsini and Jackson were busy with the swivels. They had found ten round shot for each of them and a copper-lined half-cask of powder in the locker forward of the master's cabin filled with cartridges. The wads were damp, so Martin had spread them out in the sun to dry before loading the guns. Several pieces of slowmatch were also hanging up to dry like lengths of stiff line—the guns were fired by slowmatch wound round linstocks; not for them the complication (and expense!) of flintlocks. Nor, from what Martin reported, the luxury of clean barrels: the bores of all of them were rusted, and they had trouble unblocking the touch-hole of the forward one on the starboard side.

By now there were only two merchant ships in the convoy remaining between the *Passe Partout* and the *Magpie* schooner. Scared of the killer in their wake, they had set every stitch of canvas; and Ramage used the tartane's master's telescope to satisfy his curiosity. The topgallants of both merchant ships had lines of mildew on them, especially in bands where the wide canvas gaskets had held them furled against the yard, with every shower or downpour keeping that strip of canvas wetter for longer.

The next tack took the tartane close to the last ship, and Ramage could see two or three men aft watching, one holding a telescope and no doubt curious why a tartane should be making for the schooner. The fact that their escorting frigate was staying to leeward at the head of the convoy might be something of a surprise but more likely it was providing an incentive for the ship to catch up with the *Sarazine*. Anyway, they would have seen the tartane go up to the frigate.

Ramage carefully watched the *Magpie*, estimated her speed, assumed she would hold the course that was now taking her diagonally across the stern of the convoy to the south-west, and tacked the *Passe Partout* again.

Rossi was quite at home with the tartane; he had commented about them twice to Ramage, indicating he had served in them during his youth, nominally spent in Genoa. He had searched the fo'c's'le and found half a *parmigiano* of an age, size and hardness, so Stafford claimed, making it suitable for repairing the stonework of St Paul's Cathedral. Certainly it withstood some violent cutlass blows from Rossi, who quickly found an axe and, later, a rasp in what was obviously the ship's tool chest. *Parmigiano*, he swore, was proof that there must be pasta somewhere in the ship and the ingredients for making some kind of sauce, and Ramage had given him fifteen minutes—until it was obvious that his skill was needed at the tiller—to find it. He had then discovered some spaghetti in a cask in the galley which, he declared, had not been completely eaten by weevils and from which he could make them a good supper. Several suppers, he had added, obviously hoping that would draw from the Captain an indication of how long they would be in the *Passe Partout*.

Martin came aft to report that all six swivels could be fired and, thanks to a liberal application from the greasy slush found in the cook's slush bucket, the swivels now turned easily in the fittings in the bulwarks, and the trunnions of the guns moved freely in the swivels. There was no shot gauge to ensure that no shot was oversize or swollen by rust but it had been easy enough to try every shot in a gun: matter of rolling in the shot and then—with the muzzle inboard—tilting the barrel down so that the shot rolled out again into waiting hands. All the socket fittings for the swivels in the bulwarks looked sound enough. "The guns have just been neglected for the past year: they were originally fitted well enough," Martin reported.

A year, Ramage thought: just a little less than the length of time the Royal Navy left the Mediterranean because of the demands for ships of war in other seas and other oceans. Clearly no Algerine pirates came far enough north to persuade this tartane's master that his swivels needed anything more than canvas covers by way of maintenance. Or, more likely, the tartane usually hugged the coast.

The schooner was still holding her course: obviously the Britons on board were either curious or uninterested in the tartane—staying on a course which would very soon have them crossing tracks could mean either.

Martin examined her with the glass, wiped the objective lens with a piece of cloth to remove specks of spray, and looked again.

"That hull hasn't seen a paintbrush for a year or two," he commented. "And her jibs have an odd cut to them. Like flour bags, they belly so much."

"I noticed that," Ramage said, taking another bearing of her across the top of the *Passe Partout*'s steering compass.

"And those quarter-boats—they weren't built in a British yard: look more like bananas."

"Probably lost her own months ago and took those from an Algerine prize."

"Still, she has British colours, so we shouldn't have any problems, sir."

Ramage looked astern and saw that the last of the ships of the convoy were now two or three miles away, and Jackson, Orsini and Stafford were standing by the line reeved through a block at the after end of the lateen yard and used as a flag halyard.

He then looked across at the *Magpie* and called to Orsini, who promptly gestured to the two seamen and the French colours came down at the run. Another glance forward reassured him that on this tack the curve of the *Passe Partout*'s sail made a big enough belly of canvas to hide any flags from the convoy.

As soon as the Tricolour was down and removed from the halyard, it was replaced with a flag twice as large, one which Jackson, Stafford and Rossi had hurriedly cobbled up from a bolt of canvas found in the bosun's tiny store in the fo'c's'le.

"Hoist it slowly," Ramage said, and a large white flag—as white as sail canvas could ever be—rose to the end of the yard.

Ramage took the glass and watched the afterdeck of the *Magpie*. A white flag was accepted universally as a flag of truce, and on the matter of colours, Ramage noted, the *Magpie*'s were faded. There was just enough for it to be recognizable as a Red Ensign, but—there were a lot of swarthy faces on her fo'c's'le. She must have shipped a crew from—where? And there were many more men with swarthy faces on the quarterdeck, too. Swarthy! They were Arabs! They even had the Red Ensign upside-down, something he had only just noticed because it was flapping spasmodically in the *Magpie*'s soldier's wind.

"Go about," he snapped at Rossi and with seconds counting leaned against the tiller.

"Man the swivels, she's an Algerine!"

The *Passe Partout* spun round to the north-west, away from her rendezvous with the schooner, and almost at once Ramage heard the faint pop-pop-pop of muskets and then the deeper boom of six-pounder guns.

There was a heavy crash of spars and flapping of canvas as the *Magpie* wore round to try to intercept the tartane on her new tack and, with Rossi now holding the tiller over, Ramage was able to use the glass once again.

Yes, the larboard side of the *Magpie*, hidden until she wore round, was damaged and had been temporarily repaired but not painted—and now the Red Ensign was coming down and the green-and-white crescent flag used by the Algerines was going up in its place, an enormous flag that seemed more suitable for a fortress than a ship.

"Jackson—signal flags—British: hoist number sixteen where the *Calypso* can see it. Martin, Orsini, get those swivels firing—don't worry about hitting the *Magpie*, make plenty of smoke so that the *Calypso* sees it!"

"Number sixteen, *'Engage the enemy more closely'* going up, sir," Jackson yelled, overhauling the halyard.

"Yer gotta laugh," Stafford said gloomily as he slid a flannel cartridge into the muzzle of a swivel. "Here we are, British mustering under Frog colours, and there they are, a crowd of h'Arabs musterin' under British colours to attack the Frogs."

"Yes," said Paolo indignantly, pushing in a wad and rolling a shot after it, "but you heard what the Captain said—they had the British flag *upside-down:* they're just damned *Saraceni.* Barbarossa's brood."

"Barbey Rossi—I'd forgotten 'im," Stafford said. "You'd think he was an Italian with a name like that, just like our Rossi."

"No," Paolo corrected him. "'Barba' means 'beard' and 'rossa' is 'red.' Redbeard was his nickname, not his true name."

Ramage watched the *Magpie* as the Algerines trimmed the sheets of the big mainsail and foresail. Obviously they were much more used to the lateen than the gaff rig, but reaching as she now was, with the wind on the beam, they would not need the sail-trimming skill necessary to get her moving fast to windward.

She came round into the *Passe Partout*'s wake and about half a mile astern. Her masts were now in line.

"Martin! Your quadrant. Give me the elevation of the *Magpie*'s foremast!"

The young Lieutenant opened the mahogany box as the first of the tartane's swivels fired. By the time the third had fired he was balancing, sighting the *Magpie* in the quadrant's mirror. A few delicate movements with the quadrant's arm and Martin was reading off the minutes and degrees.

Ramage looked at his watch and said to Rossi: "Keep her masts in line; I want to see how quickly she can overhaul us on a reach."

"Very quickly," Rossi muttered. "Only to windward can we escape!"

And that, Ramage knew, was the irony of the situation. The only ship with the guns to deal with the *Magpie* was the *Calypso*, at the far end of the convoy and who could only get to the Algerine vessel by beating to windward—a long, slow task in this light wind.

The *Passe Partout* could not escape from the *Magpie* by running away before the wind to join the *Calypso*; the schooner would overtake her long before that. If she raced away on a broad reach, north or south, taking the *Magpie* in pursuit, she was making it a little easier for the *Calypso*, whose speed would increase with every point she could sail free. But the *Magpie* would catch the tartane long before the *Calypso* could get near.

Only by beating to windward, away from the *Calypso*, could the *Passe Partout* escape. Would the *Magpie* continue chasing her? If so, it would keep her out of the *Calypso*'s hands but—ironically enough—save the French convoy.

The fifth swivel fired. It was absurd to waste the shot when the whole point of firing was to make smoke to attract the *Calypso*'s attention because at this range a three-pounder shot would not harm a privateer schooner any more than a soggy dumpling.

"Fire blank charges," Ramage shouted. "Don't waste shot. Just make smoke!"

He looked astern across the convoy at the *Calypso* and just managed to steady the glass in time to see the frigate wearing round, sails shivering as she steadied on a course hard on the wind. Aitken and Southwick were going to be busy as they tacked back and forth through the convoy. There were bound to be at least three merchant ships whose masters lost their nerve at the sight of a great frigate, guns run out, racing in their direction and, instead of holding their course, they would do something silly and risk a collision . . .

"Martin," Ramage snapped after another glance at his watch, "have another look at the *Magpie*'s foremasthead."

The degrees and minutes he reported confirmed what Ramage had already seen with his naked eye: he hardly needed the quadrant to tell him that the angle subtended by the *Magpie*'s foremasthead was increasing so fast that the schooner would be ranging alongside within minutes.

He glanced at Rossi, who was loosing a powerful stream of blasphemy in Italian at the *Magpie* such as can be achieved only by an imaginative Italian Catholic.

"Very hard on Catholics, these Arabs," Ramage said teasingly. "They flay them, I believe."

Rossi grinned as he said: "Yes, sir, even lapsed Catholics."

The Genoese seaman was handling the *Passe Partout*'s tiller as an artist might his brush; he was responsive to every variation in the wind's strength, reacting to puffs and lulls, like a gull hovering over the edge of a cliff.

Martin turned to Ramage and said cheerfully: "I am sorry, sir, someone wrote *andante ma non troppo* on this ship's keel!"

Ramage gave a great gust of laughter which stopped every man in his tracks, and knowing they had very little time left for anything, Ramage called: "Mr Martin says the *Passe Partout* has a musical direction—an order by the composer to the soloist or orchestra—which means in Italian, 'Fast, but not too much!'"

"Ho, I was wondering what was delayin' 'er," Stafford said.

There were seven French prisoners locked in the fo'c's'le and who had been guarded, until the swivels were needed, by Baxter and Johnson. He must not forget to free them at the last moment and give them, too, a chance to kill an Arab or so before that screaming horde swamped the *Passe Partout's* deck.

He turned to Rossi, waving to Martin to attend to the sheets and braces: "Bring her hard on the wind. It's not much of a chance, but we'll give 'em a run for their money!"

Within two or three minutes the tartane was heeling as she sliced through the waves, lively as a young pony let loose in a meadow. With the glass Ramage saw the men in the *Magpie* hauling on headsails, foresail and mainsail sheets so that the schooner could sail closer to the wind and stay in the tartane's wake until she overhauled her.

Martin, standing by him, commented: "They seem to be a lubberly crowd over there, sir!"

Ramage nodded, an impression in his mind giving way to an idea. "Tell Orsini to fetch the French master here, but leave the rest of the Frenchmen locked up. Send Baxter and Johnson with him."

The fat Frenchman walked most of the way staring at the *Magpie* almost in the *Passe Partout's* wake, but when he reached Ramage he held his arms out in front of him, palms facing forward.

"What is happening?" he asked. "I hear the guns firing—but she is British, like you!"

"She is an Algerine pirate. She was British, but the Algerines captured her."

"You won't get away from her," the Frenchman said philosophically. "We have more barnacles on the bottom than the Republic has debts. We are all making mistakes today—I mistook you for French, you mistook those villains for English. Your mistake is going to be the most expensive for all of us: if we are lucky, they'll cut our throats. If not—well, they have many cruel games to play with 'infidels'. . ."

The Frenchman, fat as he was, and slightly ridiculous to look at, was no coward; his attitude was droll and he was genuinely amused that both he and Ramage had made mistakes over identity.

Ramage looked astern at the *Magpie*, glanced at Rossi, who shook his head to indicate the *Passe Partout* was not gaining a yard, and said to the Frenchman: "*M'sieu*, I've no doubt you and your men share our reluctance to become prisoners of the Dey of Algiers or any of his men. If I release you all, will you give me your word that you'll remain our prisoners at large, help us, and surrender yourselves again when we have escaped?"

"Escaped? *Quelle blague!*" he exclaimed at such crazy talk. "But certainly we will help make those camel-lovers pay dearly for our skins. Yes, you have our parole; we'll help you sail and fight the ship—whatever you propose to do. Fight against all *that* mob!" The notion made him chuckle as he made his way forward to explain to his men, and Ramage called Baxter and Johnson aft as he told Martin what he was doing.

"I'm glad they'll be helping with the sheets and downhauls, sir," Martin admitted. "This rig is effective, I'll admit that, but it's as tricky as a Thames barge. A man and a boy can work a barge up a narrow gut against a foul tide—as long as they know how!"

"Orsini," Ramage said, "I'm putting you in charge of the Frenchmen because you'll hear me giving orders in English and can translate."

"Aye aye, sir. And sir," he reminded Ramage, as if to excuse his future behaviour, "the *Saraceni* have been the natural enemies of Italians for centuries."

Ramage remembered how the various Arab rulers of Algiers and Tunis along the north coast of Africa had always made passing ships pay enormous "tributes," quite apart from capturing hundreds of seamen to work the oars of their galleys. "Yes, they've lacked friends for a long time," he said dryly. "They have some curious habits."

"The *Magpie,* sir," Martin said as he put his quadrant away in its box, having carefully wiped spray from the brass fittings. "She's catching up very fast!"

"Ah, there are your Frenchmen," Ramage told Orsini. "Tell the master to show you where their muskets and pistols are kept, and then make sure his men have them."

The wind was piping up; it was now a fresh breeze, cooling the decks a little, and increasing the belly of the sail. The *Magpie,* he had to admit, looked a fine sight, although he would be quite satisfied if he could admire her a mile away, instead of a few hundred yards.

The Algerines were obviously going to pass to leeward and give the *Passe Partout* a broadside; then they would probably drop astern and come up again on the weather side and board. There must be a couple of hundred of them, judging from the crowd lining the weather rail, and, he suspected, by habit they were acting as human ballast, as they would in a xebec or tartane.

The French master came waddling aft, and suddenly held out his hand. "Chesneau," he said. "Albert Chesneau."

Ramage shook it and introduced himself, giving his name the English pronunciation. Chesneau did not hear it clearly because at that moment the tiller creaked louder than usual, so Ramage repeated it with the French pronunciation.

"Ramage—*the* Ramage?" Chesneau was obviously impressed. "Ha, I've heard of you and I've said a few prayers that I'd never meet you at sea. I imagined different circumstances!"

By now Orsini was leading the French seamen from the cabin and they were busy checking over muskets and pistols. Ramage looked round for Martin.

"Listen, this ship should have been your command and I'm sorry to be interfering, but the next half an hour is likely to be busy, so I'll give you a hand. Orsini can use those Frenchmen like Marines, and their muskets will help. I want you to look after the sail-handling. I suggest you put Jackson in charge of the swivels. Leave Rossi at the tiller, and I'll give him a hand if he needs it."

"Aye aye, sir," Martin said and then looked almost shy. "Will you pardon me for saying it, sir, we all know the *Magpie*'s going to do us in, but it's an honour to be beside you, sir, and none of us would be anywhere else."

Suddenly all the men round gave a cheer which was swamped by a bellow from Baxter: "Three cheers an' a tiger for 'is Lordship—'ip 'ip, 'urray!"

An embarrassed Ramage stood still until they had finished, then gave the men a salute in reply and a grin of encouragement.

"Right lads, I've a deal of paperwork to finish in the *Calypso*, so let's hurry up and finish off this bird astern!"

The men roared with laughter, Orsini hastily translating for the Frenchmen.

"Remember this," Ramage shouted to make himself heard above the increasing wind and the laughter, "that schooner is expecting to give us a broadside or two and then board.

"Now you know that, forget it. Forget everything except the job you now have. Men at the sheets, braces and downhauls: that's your entire life for the next half an hour—if you want to live. You men at the swivels—fire as fast as you can but as accurately as possible. Your target will always be the *Magpie*'s quarterdeck if your gun will bear, otherwise her topmasts."

He lapsed into French. "You new allies are the sharpshooters. Try and pick off the magpies and jackdaws on the quarterdeck, particularly anyone that looks like an officer."

He looked at the *Magpie* and realized that the new sound of popping was musket fire from the Arabs swarming out along the *Magpie*'s bowsprit and, he noted, getting in each other's way. She was less than a hundred yards astern and spray was slicing up from her bow as she raced up to the *Passe Partout*.

"One last thing," Ramage shouted, "and make sure you translate this, Orsini: don't waste a single shot. Aim and fire. If you can't aim properly, wait for a target to present itself."

The *Calypso* had tacked again, weaving in and out of the ships of the convoy. Neither Aitken nor Southwick would ever guess what he was originally going to try to do with that damned convoy, and if they had any sense they would grab the *Sarazine* and *Golondrina* and make for Gibraltar.

Southwick would eventually visit Gianna, of course, and he would tell her what little he had seen of the last few minutes of her sweetheart and her heir, and Jackson, Rossi and Stafford. She would mourn but she would be proud, even if the Admiralty made a fuss about him leaving the ship.

He mopped his face with his handkerchief, not because he was dripping with perspiration but because he wanted to wipe away the black thoughts. And, being human, he could be permitted some black thoughts when nine Britons and six Frenchmen in a tiny tartane found themselves about to be boarded by a schooner crowded with a couple of hundred Algerine pirates, whose shrill shouts and screams he could now hear, a noise of wild animals—how he imagined wolves chased their quarry.

He looked around the *Passe Partout*. The six swivels were loaded; men stood at them with linstocks round which were wound smoking slowmatch. The Frenchmen were settling themselves down in comfortable corners with their muskets, arranging powder, shot and rammers to hand.

Chesneau, having talked to each of his men, was now waddling aft to join Ramage and Rossi right aft. He jerked his thumb over his shoulder at the *Magpie*. "The owners of that schooner allow the captain even less paint than mine do for the *Passe Partout!*"

"I don't think they've had her long," Ramage said. "You see she has damage down the larboard side? I think that was done when they captured her from the British."

Chesneau shivered. "I hope your countrymen had quick deaths; otherwise they are still chained in the galleys."

"You do not have the build for rowing," Ramage said, "so perhaps we had better not be captured."

"I would kiss the Pope's ring and never dodge another tax to avoid that," Chesneau said, "but our fate is only a couple of ship's lengths astern now."

"Yes," Ramage said, looking round at Rossi, who was watching the leech of the *Passe Partout*'s sail, a cheerful grin on his face as Stafford shouted some teasing obscenity at him.

"You are very calm, M'sieu Ramage; you even smile."

"I'm smiling because I am about to do something of which I do not entirely approve, M'sieu Chesneau."

"Indeed? You've left it late in life to acquire a new bad habit!"

The *Magpie* was perhaps forty yards astern now and the black marks appearing in the *Passe Partout*'s sail were being made by musket balls.

"It may not be a bad habit; it's just one I avoid as much as possible."

"You intrigue me. What are you going to do, M'sieu Ramage?"

"Gamble, M'sieu Chesneau: *Les jeux sont faits!*"

C H A P T E R T H I R T E E N

ADMITTEDLY it was a bet for which he would be hard put to find a taker, whether among the bookies on Newmarket Heath or the pallid gamblers at White's or Brooks's or Boodle's. He was betting the life of the fifteen motley crew of the *Passe Partout* on a single chance: that the couple of hundred or so Algerines who had captured the *Magpie* only a few weeks ago were still bewildered; that the towering masts and running and standing rigging of a gaff-rigged topsail schooner was such a complex mass of spars and rope, to men used to simple lateen sails hoisted on stubby masts, that they were certainly unused to it and probably still nervous.

He stood close to Rossi and gave his instructions. The tip of the *Magpie*'s flying jib-boom was less than forty yards astern; the musket balls were beginning to rattle and Jackson, having been warned by Ramage, was waiting the signal to fire his swivels into the screaming and gibbering mass of Arabs on the *Magpie*'s bow while Orsini held back his Frenchmen.

"This ship," Ramage said to Chesneau in a conversational tone, "she handles easily?"

"Like a dancer," the fat man said. He was pale now and perspiring but Ramage sensed it was due to more of a feeling of helplessness than fear.

Thirty yards to the tip of the *Magpie*'s jib-boom, and it would be only a matter of moments before some of the Passe Partouts were hit by musket balls.

Ramage pointed at Jackson. "Fire, when you're ready!"

He pointed at Orsini and repeated the order.

The guns thundered out at twenty yards: by the time the smoke cleared it was ten yards, the great jib-boom high above them.

Then he turned to Rossi. "Round we go!" and with that helped the Italian push the big tiller over to larboard so that the *Passe Partout* suddenly turned to starboard, jinking right across the *Magpie*'s bow and missing the jib-boom by only a yard or so. Chesneau, the moment he saw what they were doing, jumped over to add his weight to the leverage on the rudder and as Ramage tried to look over his shoulder at the *Magpie*, he saw the great schooner with its towering masts and topmasts already passing astern, at right angles to the *Passe Partout*'s course. As her quarterdeck raced by, the tartane's swivels were grunting again and spurting smoke, slamming three-pounder round shot across her decks while the unhurried firing of muskets showed that the Frenchmen were picking their targets.

The *Passe Partout's* sheets were eased as Martin hurried his men to trim the sail on the new course, with the wind now broad on the larboard quarter.

Ramage stood back from the tiller, saw the lateen sail bellying nicely, noticed that Jackson's swivel gunners were already sponging and ramming, and saw the Frenchmen hurriedly reloading their muskets as they scrambled into positions from which they could fire at the *Magpie* when she turned after them.

The schooner herself, Ramage then realized, had been taken completely by surprise: not one of her broadside guns had fired as she raced across the *Passe Partout's* stern—yet she should have given the tartane a devastating raking broadside: that had seemed to Ramage his greatest danger when he weighed up the idea several minutes ago.

But now the schooner was beginning to turn; already her masts were separating as she turned to starboard to wear round after the *Passe Partout,* but even as she turned Ramage felt something clutch at his heart, because she was a beautiful vessel.

The wheel had obviously been put over and the great ship was turning on her heel, the big booms slamming over from the starboard side to the larboard as she began to come round after the tartane and her stern passed through the eye of the wind.

But in their excitement the Algerines had not cast off the running backstays; the booms had swung across only a short distance before jamming hard up against them, and the ship continued turning so the wind filling the sails exerted enormous pressure on the booms and through the booms on to the running backstays.

Ramage looked aloft. From the running backstays the pressure was, of course, spreading to the masts, to which the stays were secured, and he could now see that her rigging was slack—or, rather, the result of months of scorching sun drying and stretching it and rain shrinking it. The Algerines, he was sure, had not set up the rigging from the day they captured her.

The fools had gybed her all standing, the fear of all seamen in fore-and-aft rigged vessels, and suddenly the ship seemed to vanish. One moment the sails were there, great billowing masses of canvas distorted by the hard lines of the ropes into which they were being pressed, and the next moment they had disappeared. Instead there was a long, low hulk wallowing in the water, covered with canvas like a shroud, which was rapidly darkening as water soaked into it.

Ramage was puzzled as to why he had been so surprised, because the *Magpie* had done just what he had hoped: that was why he had taken the *Passe Partout* across her bow. He hoped that the Algerines, unused to the *Magpie's* complex rig, would have become so excited in their chase of the tartane that when the *Passe Partout* suddenly jinked across her bow like a hare being chased by hounds they would spin the wheel over and forget to let go the running backstays on one side and take them up on the other.

"*Accidente!*" Rossi said, "the Algerine could do with you as their admiral, sir, just to teach them how to sail our ships!"

Chesneau simply shook him by the hand. "We are your prisoners again, *m'sieu*. Our freedom was brief—thanks to you."

Ramage grinned, and then noticed that they were rapidly drawing away from the dismasted *Magpie*.

"Perhaps your men would be kind enough to lower the sail: it will take my men another five miles' sailing to find out how it is done!"

Chesneau barked out orders and the Frenchmen, putting down their muskets and pistols and grinning cheerfully, hurried to the halyard and vangs.

Ramage caught Jackson's eye and pointed to the muskets, and within a minute Baxter and Johnson were collecting up the small arms and taking them aft to the little cabin.

Lying stopped half a mile to leeward of the *Magpie*, the *Passe Partout* looked as innocent as a vessel waiting in a calm and giving her men an hour or two to try their luck with fishhooks.

Ramage and Martin watched the hulk of the *Magpie*. It was, Martin commented, hard to see the wreck for the Algerines: the ship looked more like a floating log covered with busy ants. Already they had cut away the sails to clear the after part of the ship, and now they were chopping at the shrouds holding the broken masts alongside the ship.

"They're in a panic," Ramage said, "and either they do not have an effective captain or he was killed."

"Certainly Jackson's swivels were quite effective—he found a few bags of musket balls and used them instead of round shot."

Ramage turned to Martin in surprise. "That was smart of him. Where were they?"

"Actually the French master mentioned them to Orsini: he thought they'd be more useful than round shot. Jackson managed to get 25 into each swivel."

"One hundred and fifty musket balls in every broadside! Did he . . ."

"Yes, sir: as the *Magpie* went across our stern, they managed to fire each swivel at her quarterdeck."

That was typically Jackson: he did not bother his Captain with the question of whether or not to substitute musket balls for round shot because he knew the answer and just went ahead and did it. And as a result it was unlikely that a man had been left alive abaft the *Magpie*'s mainmast.

"There go the remains of her mainmast and the topmast," Martin commented.

"And the main boom and gaff," Ramage said as he watched the spars float away.

"Now they're chopping like madmen to get the foremast clear."

"Yes," Ramage said cheerfully, "and very soon someone over there is going to realize they have nothing left with which to jury-rig her."

Martin gave a boyish chuckle. The main boom could have been hoisted on shears and used as a jury mainmast, and the gaff could have made an emergency foremast. "They must have spare sails stowed below, but I can see the deck's swept clean—yes, look over there, sir," he said pointing to the east. "All that floating wreckage must be her smashed boats and the spare booms stowed alongside them."

"Well, they've a long row ahead of them," Ramage said sourly, and Martin stared at him.

"We don't . . . ?"

Ramage shook his head. "Here, take the glass and give me an estimate of how many men you think there are still alive on board."

Martin balanced himself, adjusted the focus of the glass and began counting in fives and had reached a hundred in less than half a minute. The next hundred took longer, and after two hundred and fifty he was counting in pairs.

Finally he gave the glass back to Ramage. "Three hundred and seventy at least. Round the wheel the bodies are almost piled up."

"And the actual complement of the *Calypso?*" Ramage asked, to ram the point home.

"Two hundred and twenty."

"And we have forty French prisoners from the semaphore station."

"I see what you mean, sir."

"No, you are just doing sums, two hundred and twenty of us against three hundred and seventy Algerines and 48 French. You don't realize that every one of those Algerines regards you and me—in other words people who don't worship their god—as infidels. When they capture an infidel they kill him or make him a slave. They do not surrender to infidels; they'd sooner die, which is why you can never capture an Algerine. If they're outnumbered, they'll blow the ship up or fight to the last man."

"So we leave them?"

"We leave them," Ramage said. "If they'd caught us, by now they would be flaying us, or using us as live targets for their muskets, or chopping off limbs with those damned scimitars of theirs."

He did not tell Martin that when the *Calypso* arrived, the *Magpie* would be battered until she sank. There were too many galleys rowed by hundreds of captured Dutch, Danes, French, British, Italians, Spaniards—anyone who did not come from Algeria or Tunisia and fell into their hands—for any Algerine to be shown mercy.

The *Calypso* was a mile away now, tacking yet again in the long zigzag against the wind. He could imagine Aitken and Southwick running from one side of the quarterdeck to the other with their telescopes, trying to see exactly what had happened, and no doubt the lookouts aloft were receiving their share of abuse for not supplying more detailed answers.

Rossi was proud of the way he had steered the *Passe Partout* and was just telling Jackson and Stafford for the third time how he and the Captain had turned the tartane under the *Magpie*'s flying jib-boom when the Cockney said impatiently: "While you was leaning comfortable against the tiller, Jacko and me and Baxter and Johnnie was usin' the swivels to knock these h'Arabs down like starlings on a bough. 'Ow many you reckon we got, Jacko?"

"Twenty with each gun," the American said soberly.

"*Madonna!* These *Saraceni* die of fright, eh?"

Jackson explained how, at the last moment, the French master had produced the bag of musket balls. "Nice and rusty, too," Stafford said. "Teach them h'Arabs to chain up our chaps in galleys."

"And the Frenchies were cool enough, too," Jackson said. "Each of 'em was firing aimed shots with muskets and pistols, just like Mr Ramage told 'em."

"Well, I thought we was all done for," Stafford admitted. "I could feel me anchors draggin' fer the next world. Surprisin' how quick yer can fire a swivel when you 'ave to."

"Now what is we doing?" Rossi asked Jackson.

"Waiting for the *Calypso* to sink that schooner, I reckon."

"Is best," Rossi said. "We rescue them and they kill us. More than three hundred and seventy of them; I heard Mr Martin counting."

Stafford shivered. "Ooh, I can feel 'em nailing out my skin to dry in the sun. I'd make a lovely cushion cover in a harem."

"Here comes the *Calypso*," Jackson said. "This tack'll bring her practically alongside us."

"Jackson," Ramage called. "Hoist number sixteen again."

"Aye aye, sir, number sixteen, *'Engage the enemy more closely.'*" As he extracted the flag from the bag he murmured: "If those heathens have any sense they'll stop what they're doing and start asking Allah, or whoever it is, to lend 'em a hand."

As soon as the signal was hoisted the *Calypso* acknowledged it and bore away slightly. She looked a fine sight, spray slicing up from the stem, her port-lids open, the muzzles of her guns protruding like a row of stubby black fingers. Jackson noticed she was flying no colours—Mr Aitken must have decided he would not fight under French colours. Not that this was going to be a fight.

First the *Calypso*'s fore and main courses were furled with all the speed and smartness as though she was coming into harbour with the admiral watching; then her topgallants followed until she was sailing under topsails and headsails, the fighting rig for a frigate.

Paolo, standing amidships in the *Passe Partout*, felt cold, even though the sun was still scorching: his skin was covered in goose pimples and he wished he was on board the *Calypso*, commanding a division of her guns.

For centuries the *Saraceni* had raided the coasts of Italy; even now there was barely ten miles of coast not covered by a watch tower built—on the Tyrrhenian coast anyway—by Philip II of Spain as a warning system and defence against the *Saraceni*, who regularly landed from the sea by day or night and raided towns and villages. There was not a town in Tuscany that did not have a long history of attacks. La Bella Marsiglia—wasn't that the name of the woman in one of the legends? She was beautiful beyond description and lived on the coast not far from Volterra. She was kidnapped by *Saraceni* raiders and taken away to their headquarters but, in the only *Saraceni* story he knew of that had a happy ending, the bey or dey of the city saw her before she was sold off as a slave, fell in love and married her.

Thank goodness they never reached as far inland as Volterra, though the high walls with the nine gates should keep them out. Do the French continue the rule that the gates were shut an hour after sunset until an hour after dawn? Nine gates—and he was startled to find he could hardly remember their names now, except that the road from Rome came in at the Porta all' Arco; from Siena and Florence by the Porta a Selci. He found it equally difficult to picture the *Palazzo;* all he could see in his mind was the great carved griffin over each main doorway, the arms and crest of the Kingdom of Volterra. He never did discover what dragon the griffin in the coat of arms was killing, but the griffin was certainly rampant and the victor.

And there was the *Calypso*—he found himself cheering with the rest of them at the First Lieutenant's seamanship: he backed the fore-topsail just to leeward of the *Magpie* so that as the frigate turned and stopped, the gun captains of the whole larboard broadside could aim almost at their leisure.

There was a rumble, like the first hint of thunder in the mountains, and smoke spurted along on the *Calypso*'s larboard side and then began coming out of the open ports on the starboard side as the wind blew the rest of the smoke through the ship.

Now the maintopsail was backed and the *Calypso* began making a sternboard so that her bow swung through 180 degrees and as she went slowly astern, passing the *Magpie,* she fired her starboard broadside.

Paolo could picture the men hurriedly reloading the larboard guns now as the frigate's yards were braced sharp up and she went ahead to pass under the *Magpie*'s stern and luff up on the schooner's other side, once again backing her fore-topsail while her starboard broadside fired again. For the second time Aitken backed the maintopsail for another sternboard so that the frigate's bow paid off and the larboard broadside would bear. Again the guns fired and Paolo could see the rippling flash from the muzzles, but the ship was becoming so full of smoke from four quick broadsides that the flashes were becoming glows. Despite the breeze the smoke was remaining, a low cloud hanging heavy, oily and opaque, blurring the *Calypso*'s outline.

Paolo walked aft and asked Martin if he could use the glass: neither he nor Mr Ramage were using it. Before he turned the glass on the *Magpie,* Paolo saw that the Captain's face was taut, as though the skin had shrunk; his high cheekbones seemed to have no flesh over them and his eyes were sunken, as if he had not slept for a week. Martin, too, was obviously upset; his face was white, and he was gripping the bulwark capping.

The glass showed Paolo that the *Magpie* had been so battered by the *Calypso*'s broadsides that her planking and decking looked more like the sides of a cage. Men, *Saraceni,* were leaping over the side to avoid the round and grapeshot but they could not swim. And some of them, in moments before they jumped to their death, shook their fists first at the *Passe Partout* and then at the *Calypso.*

Obviously Aitken was waiting for the smoke to clear, and Paolo saw Martin glance up at flag number sixteen, still hoisted at the peak of the *Passe Partout*'s lateen yard. Ramage saw the glance and knew what thoughts must be passing through Martin's mind.

"You must understand," he said harshly, "that killing, robbing and raping are a religion to these men. You can't train a fox not to kill hens; you can't stop Algerines killing everyone who won't bow before Allah. If you lowered a boat and rescued one of them now, the moment you dragged him on board he would pull out a dagger and kill you."

"Aye aye, sir," Martin said. "So Orsini told me."

At that moment the *Magpie* disappeared, sinking evenly as though lowered below the waves by some mechanical contrivance.

Ramage said: "Mr Martin, would you be kind enough to signal for a boat so that I can return to my ship. You will remain in command of the *Passe Partout* until Mr Orsini feels confident enough to take over. In the meantime I presume you do not intend to keep number sixteen hoisted any longer."

CHAPTER FOURTEEN

THE *Calypso* and the *Passe Parout* sailed back through the convoy and received a hero's welcome: all the merchant ships cheered as they passed, three or four of them even firing salutes. Ramage thought of Chesneau, now a prisoner below in the *Calypso* along with the garrison of the semaphore station. Chesneau would hear the salutes and appreciate the joke; in fact Ramage decided to have him to dinner one day with Southwick, Aitken and young Martin. Orsini could come as well to help with the translation and enjoy a few hours' rest from the *Passe Partout*.

It was good to be back in the *Calypso*. Neither Aitken nor Southwick discussed his precipitate departure; in fact both took it as a matter of course, Southwick commenting that whether the *Magpie* had proved to be British or Algerine, he would have had to be there to make decisions.

One fortunate effect was that the merchant ships now kept better station, and Martin, after the *Passe Partout*'s welcome by the convoy, was sent to the rear with orders to chase up any laggards.

"When can we expect Martin back, sir?" Southwick asked that evening.

Ramage told him what he had said to Martin and Orsini, and Southwick gave a rumbling laugh. "That'll be the first time young Orsini ever badgered someone to teach him more mathematics!"

"It should have an effect on both of them: Martin will have to keep on his toes and dredge his memory in order to run the ship, and Orsini will be prodding him—I hope."

Ramage went down to his cabin, telling Southwick to send down the master's log. Sitting at his desk he saw the noon position noted down and the usual routine entries about winds, courses, distances and sail carried. Today's entries recorded how much fresh water remained, that the ship's company were employed "A.S.R."—the abbreviation for "As the Service Required"—and that a cask of salt beef just opened and marked as containing 137 pieces in fact contained only 128. The contractor's number stencilled on the cask was given and it was now up to the purser to try to get a refund from him. Like every other purser in one of the King's ships, the *Calypso*'s would no doubt try, but government contractors thousands of miles away— indeed, even just down the road—had little to learn from the Algerines about robbery, and the Navy Board took no notice: commissioners of dockyards, notably ones like Sir Isaac Coffin, once a brave officer, were now rich men because of the bribes the contractors regularly paid them to look the other way. The contractor was paid by the Government for the amount of meat stencilled on the cask and the commissioner was paid off by the contractor, and the only ones who went short were the seamen . . .

The noon position. The convoy was moving slowly. He took down a chart and unrolled it, put a finger on the position and looked across at their destination. Well, they would probably make better time after today's scare, and with the *Passe Partout* cutting in and out, none of these mulish merchant ships would be reducing sail tonight. It was a habit of all shipmasters and no doubt forced on them by penny-pinching owners who did not want to give them big enough crews to reef and furl in the darkness if a squall came up. For the escorts, however, it was a wretched business because over most of the world's oceans the wind usually dropped at night, not increased, and some of the big West Indian convoys would, no matter what the escorts did, make hardly any progress between dusk and dawn; indeed if there was a foul current, they would often lose ground.

Most frigate captains—*all* frigate captains, he corrected himself—did everything they could to avoid convoy duty. In the West Indies, being ordered to escort a homeward-bound convoy was a sure sign that the captain was out of favour with the admiral. Favoured captains were sent off cruising, searching among the islands and along the Main for enemy ships, capturing prizes, making plenty of prize-money—in which the admiral shared, of course.

Now consider the case of Captain Ramage who by now, thanks no doubt to a few deaths among the hundreds of captains senior to him, and the fact that a few deserving lieutenants had recently been made post and thus joined the list below him to push him up a few places, had achieved a little seniority. At least, he was no longer the most junior.

Captain Ramage had received orders from the Admiralty which many of his rivals would claim he did not deserve; to water and provision the *Calypso* for four months and then enter the Mediterranean and sink, burn or capture any enemy ships that he could and generally irritate and inconvenience the French.

Wonderful orders, he had to admit. So what did Captain Ramage do? He deliberately arranged a convoy for himself! Not a British convoy, mind you, but a French one. And where was it sailing? Not in the West Indies or westward across the Atlantic, where one could usually rely on brisk Trade winds during the day, but the Mediterranean, where in 24 hours the wind, at this time of the year, could blow from nineteen different directions and vanish completely for the other five hours, leaving ships rolling and pitching, booms slamming, yards creaking, masts straining first the shrouds on one side and then the other, stretching so that the lanyards would have to be set up again at the first opportunity, and reducing men's movements along the deck to a series of hurried lurches.

Blackstrapped with a French convoy! Well, it would make an amusing story when told in the Green Room at Plymouth or by the naval members of Boodle's or White's, but for the moment he could only hope that Orsini knew the finer shades of French obscenities and Martin would not hesitate to let drive across a laggard's bow or stern with one of those swivels.

He opened a drawer and looked for the list of French and Spanish ships drawn up by Orsini. Fifteen ships in all, and the *Passe Partout* by far the smallest, so crossing out her original crew made little difference. Fourteen ships, then. Slowly he added up the masters, officers and seamen, sometimes pausing to make sure of one of Orsini's hurriedly written figures. Yes, the fourteen ships had at least two hundred men by the time you added in the extras, because Orsini had noted down only the men he had actually seen (and one could be sure there were always several more below), plus the forty or so from the garrison of the semaphore station and the *Passe Partout* already on board the *Calypso*.

He would need fifty men to guard two hundred and fifty or so prisoners, and none of these could be topmen or idlers. That also meant fifty fewer available as prize crews. No, he had been right the first time; right when he had sent the signal from Foix. He could understand why Aitken, Kenton and Southwick were puzzled.

He put the parallel rulers down on the chart with the top edge passing through Southwick's noon position and then moved them crabwise across to the destination. If only this wind direction would hold. It was increasing nicely—not enough to scare the timid masters into premature reefing and furling, but giving signs of settling in for the night.

Ramage was vaguely conscious of boots clattering down the

companion-way, and a few moments later the sentry knocked on the door and called: "Mr Southwick, sir."

"Send him in," Ramage answered, removing the weights and letting the chart roll up. He put the parallel rulers away, and while Southwick acknowledged his gesture and sat down on the settee, Ramage closed the log.

"Well, Mr Southwick?" Ramage knew the old Master had come down just for a chat, but he always had an excuse and Ramage waited to see what it was.

Southwick fished a piece of paper from his pocket. "The log, sir, I'm afraid it's not up to date: the expenditure of powder and shot was not entered. I have the figures here."

Ramage took the paper. "Nor was the departure in a French tartane of the Captain, acting Third Lieutenant, Midshipman and five seamen, and the Captain's subsequent return."

Southwick grinned and admitted: "I wasn't sure how you wanted to deal with that, sir. It so happens, if you'll look just below the reference to the shortage of salt beef in that cask, there is space enough to enter the departure, and the Captain's return would be the last entry, after this one about expenditure of powder and shot."

"You'd better enter it all," Ramage said. "Their Lordships may raise their eyebrows at my brief absence, but it was in a good cause!"

Southwick scratched his head in a gesture Ramage knew so well that he could guess what the old man was going to say.

"Beats me how you knew that privateer schooner, the *Magpie*, was going to turn out to be sailed by Algerines."

"I didn't," Ramage said, surprised.

"Then why did you go in the *Passe Partout*, sir?"

"I didn't have time to tell Martin how to negotiate with a British privateer—it meant persuading them to let several prizes sail away."

"Martin could have gone on board and torn up the letter of marque," Southwick said grimly.

"That wouldn't have helped. There are not many British ships of war to inspect it, and if the French catch a British privateer I doubt that they care much about letters of marque."

"But you could have let Aitken go off in the *Passe Partout*," the Master persisted.

"I could, but he learned more by being left in command of the *Calypso*. He handled her very well."

Southwick nodded. "Especially the way he sank the *Magpie*. But he worries too much."

"How do you mean?"

"Well, when you hoisted number sixteen, he was afraid he wouldn't be able to tack up to you in time."

"So was I," Ramage said grimly. "In fact, if the *Magpie* hadn't had her masts go by the board . . ."

"But she did: I was telling Aitken that you'd do something, and you did."

Ramage sighed at the thought of the thin line by which his life was at times suspended: a thin line of faith that he could perform miracles. "Don't depend on it. We were lucky this time, but if those Algerines had been sailing the ship for another couple of months it would have been a different story."

"Yes, sir," Southwick said comfortably, "and we are all thankful they weren't. How long before you'll give young Orsini command of the *Passe Partout*?"

"I was going to leave Martin with him tonight, to hold his hand if necessary in the dark, and launch him off on his own tomorrow."

"I'll pack up his quadrant, tables and glass: he didn't have time to take them with him."

"It seems unfair to Martin," Ramage said, having second thoughts.

Southwick's eyes twinkled as he said casually, "I don't expect she'll be the only prize we'll take. I'd have thought that a tartane rated a midshipman's command, not a lieutenant's!"

"It sounds to me as though you are trying to exercise patronage on behalf of the Marchesa."

Southwick gave a bellow of laughter. "That's about it! Anyway, I'd like to be. She'd have enjoyed watching the *Magpie* business."

"From the *Calypso*."

"No, sir, from the *Passe Partout*," Southwick corrected him with mock severity. "You haven't seen her for so long you've forgotten what she's like when there's a whiff of action in the air."

Ramage hadn't forgotten, but it had been so long since he had seen her that now memories brought pain rather than pleasure.

Southwick pointed at the chart which was still lying curled up on Ramage's desk. "If this wind holds, we should sight land before noon the day after tomorrow, sir."

"That's some 'if.' When does the wind stay in the same direction for more than a few hours in this part of the world?"

"When it's blowing a *mistral* or Levanter," Southwick reminded him.

Next day the *Passe Partout* came close to the *Calypso* and one of the frigate's boats took off Martin and brought Paolo on board the *Calypso* to receive his orders and collect his navigational equipment. Before he was taken back to the tartane Ramage sent for him and gave him his official orders. They were brief and written in the stylized form laid down by the Admiralty.

By Nicholas Ramage, Captain and commanding officer of His Majesty's frigate *Calypso*

To Paolo Orsini, Midshipman, hereby appointed to the *Passe Partout*, prize to the *Calypso* frigate.

By virtue of the power and authority to me given, I do hereby constitute and appoint you midshipman in command of the tartane *Passe Partout*, prize to His Majesty's frigate *Calypso,* willing and requiring you forthwith to go on board, and take upon you the charge and command of her accordingly; strictly charging and commanding all the petty officers and company . . . to behave themselves jointly and severally . . . And you likewise to observe and execute as well the General Printed Instructions, and such orders and directions you shall from time to time receive from your captain . . . hereof nor you nor any of you may fail, as you will answer the contrary at your Peril; and for so doing this shall be your warrant.

The document was then dated, Ramage's seal impressed on it, and his signature added, and for the first time in his life Paolo commanded a ship and was responsible for the behaviour of every man on board.

When the Captain gave it to him, Paolo read it and found no difficulty in understanding the neat handwriting of the Captain's clerk, but was intimidated by the wording. He read the last paragraph yet again, this time aloud—"hereof nor you nor any of you may fail, as you will answer to the contrary at your Peril . . ."

He looked at Ramage, not realizing that this was standard wording. "But, sir, this last part . . ." It seemed very unreasonable of the Captain to be so hard on him—presumably because . . . Well, he was not sure quite why.

"'At your Peril,' eh? That frightens you, I expect."

"Yes, sir; after all . . ."

"Well, you are in good company, my lad; every naval officer given command of *anything* has that in his orders. Commanders-in-chief, commodores, captains, lieutenants—even midshipmen in command of captured tartanes."

"You mean, sir, *your* orders say the same?"

"The same and a lot more."

At that moment Paolo understood why the commanding

officer was always such a remote figure; why the attitude of the seamen, for instance, had been different where Martin was concerned on board the *Passe Partout:* they were more reserved, keeping a distance between them. Now, Paolo realized, he had—however temporarily—crossed the line separating carefree midshipmen skylarking on board without any papers or passing any examinations from officers who must not fail without "answering to the contrary."

He saw Ramage was watching him.

"Nothing has changed," Ramage said quietly. "Always do what you think is right, be just, don't give an order you would not carry out yourself and you won't fail. And once you've made up your mind, *do* it. Hesitation and indecision loses battles—and reputations."

"Like you did not hesitate when you jumped on board the *Passe Partout,*" Paolo said eagerly.

Ramage winced at such a recent memory. "That's not a very good example, but just do your best. And remember, your men have to do their best as well."

He motioned Paolo to put the order in his pocket. "Now, we should be arriving at our destination tomorrow afternoon if the wind holds. For various reasons I don't want the whole convoy arriving at the same time, so from sunset tonight don't chase up the laggards. Let them lag. Ideally, I'd like half a dozen ships to arrive in the first hour or so, three or four an hour later, and the last of them at dusk . . ."

"Aye aye, sir."

"And there's one more thing. You can keep Stafford and Rossi, but I need Jackson back. You can pick a good man to replace him. Now, listen carefully; this is what you will do when the convoy arrives."

Paolo listened for four minutes, nodded, was reprimanded for not saying "Aye aye, sir" to acknowledge the orders, and then left the cabin and climbed down to the waiting boat in a haze of excitement: he commanded a ship-of-war and had a document to prove it. Suddenly he found the prospect and responsibility did not frighten him. At least, not very much.

The *Calypso*'s lookouts first sighted land lying low on the horizon to the east two hours before noon, but apart from there being cliffs along the coast no one, apart from Southwick, was sure that they were on course for their destination.

The advantage of the destination lying on a coast that ran north-west and south-east was that a noon sight gave the latitude, which ran almost at right angles through the coastline. If the latitude from the sight was greater than the latitude of the destination, they had to turn south, if less then north.

With fifteen ships following the *Calypso*, Southwick knew that his navigation was important, but as the sun climbed higher towards its zenith in a cloudless sky the Master only grinned when Ramage and Aitken teased him.

The effect of the *Passe Partout* lying out on one wing of the convoy and not swooping down to make a laggard set more sail to catch up was very apparent. The *Sarazine* was still the closest to the *Calypso*, but she was now a good two miles astern, with the Spanish *Golondrina* abeam. After those two ships, the other thirteen were spread out to the westward so that four of them had almost dropped below the horizon, all but their topgallants hidden below the curvature of the earth.

The *Passe Partout*, recognizable because of her lateen sail and in the far distance looking even more like a shark's fin, now seemed as much of a straggler as any other merchant ship in the convoy, although Ramage guessed that Orsini was keeping his men busy with the hundred and one jobs that needed doing—checking over, cutting into proper lengths and drying slowmatch, cutting more wads for the swivels; filling more cartridges—and Ramage knew that meant sewing more flannel cartridges, because one of the items Orsini had taken with him was flannel. Orsini, Rossi, and Stafford would carefully check for wear on the vangs holding the big lateen yard and the sheets and the downhauls at the lower end of the yard. The sail had been lowered for an hour yesterday, so all the holes from the *Magpie*'s musket balls would have been repaired.

Baxter and Johnson, Ramage was prepared to bet, were scrubbing out the after cabin, the master's, which Orsini was proposing to use as his own as he had to be close to the man at the tiller in case of an emergency. The fo'c's'le, too, was suffering from several months of too many seamen being careless with scraps of food. Orsini would be hoping for a captain's inspection of the *Passe Partout* when they arrived but, Ramage thought ironically, he had never yet tried to give one of those big lateen sails a harbour furl—and it was unlikely the French would have any of the neat canvas gaskets, in effect straps, to which Orsini was accustomed; more likely one of the vangs would be wound round and round the yard in a spiral to furl the sail in a long bundle.

It would be interesting to see if Martin's Medway and Thames background had rubbed off on Orsini. Among the Thames barges, whose long sprits were Britain's nearest to the lateen yards of tartanes or xebecs, the vangs—the heavy ropes which controlled the upper end of the sprits and stopped them slamming about in heavy weather—were almost invariably referred to by bargemen as "wangs," just as seamen pronounced "tackle" as "taickle." Martin would almost certainly have called them "wangs" and it would be interesting to see if Orsini had assumed that was the proper English pronunciation. *Palan de retenue* in French, *oste della mezzana* in Italian, *burdas de mezana* in Spanish. They made "vang" seem a very bald and ugly word; still, in a gale of wind, he would sooner shout "vang" through a speaking-trumpet.

Ramage glanced at his watch and looked round for Southwick. The Master was waiting with his quadrant in his hand. There was no need for a midshipman standing by with a watch or minute glass; the sun would "hang" for many seconds as it reached the highest point in its meridian passage and Southwick adjusted his quadrant to measure the altitude. They were in

roughly the same latitude as Ibiza and between Valencia and Alicante, he thought inconsequentially; thirty degrees north of the
area in which he preferred to serve, the Caribbean.

The Tricolour streamed out in the wind: at least the breeze
had stayed steady since dawn after easing down for the night.
Easing down just enough, Ramage admitted, to let the convoy
straggle to its heart's content. Now Southwick was, for once,
becoming impatient waiting for local noon, for the moment when
the sun reached its zenith and its bearing was due south.

Southwick walked over to the starboard side of the quarterdeck and held the telescope of the quadrant to his eye, making
sure that no shrouds, rigging, lanyards or blocks obscured his
view. He flipped down a shade, looked at the sun through it, and
flipped down a second. Then he set the arm against a figure on
the ivory scale.

Ramage winked as Southwick glanced across to see if this act
of supreme confidence had been noticed. Southwick was in fact
doing it backwards: he was in effect saying he knew already the
precise latitude in which the *Calypso* and the convoy were sailing, and in that latitude at noon on this day in the year the
altitude of the sun should be a certain number of degrees and
minutes measured by his quadrant. By putting the altitude on
the quadrant he should (if he was correct) put the telescope of
the quadrant to his eye and, as the sun hovered at the zenith in
the course of its meridian passage at noon, he should see it
reflected in the mirror and apparently sitting on the horizon like
a bright red plate balanced vertically on a shelf.

Ramage watched to see if the Master's left hand reached up
to make a slight (and probably surreptitious) adjustment—an
indication that the *Calypso* was north or south of Southwick's
reckoning. He counted three minutes and saw Southwick smile
to himself as he lowered the quadrant and walked to the slate
which was on top of the binnacle box.

"San Pietro and Sant' Antioco islands are dead ahead on this course, distant about ten miles, sir," Southwick reported. "Thirty-nine degrees and two minutes of latitude."

"Very well, Mr Southwick." He looked round for Kenton who was the officer of the deck. "I'll trouble you, Mr Kenton, to let fall the t'gallants, and once they're drawing we'll have a cast of the log. Keep an eye on the convoy and pass the word for Mr Aitken and Mr Rennick to come to my cabin." He gestured to Southwick to follow and went down the companion-way.

He had a large-scale chart open on his desk, and Southwick was placing the stone paperweights, by the time the sentry's call announced the arrival of Aitken and Rennick.

Aitken immediately looked at the chart as if hoping to see pencilled lines that would reveal the Captain's plans. Instead he saw a fifty-mile stretch of coast running north-west and south-east down to form Capo Teulada and Capo Spartivento at the south-western corner of the island of Sardinia.

Forming, Aitken realized, one of the great corners of the Mediterranean. Once a ship sailed into the Mediterranean past Europa Point and left Gibraltar astern, Capo Teulada and then Capo Spartivento, forming the southern tip of Sardinia, and Capo Passero at the south end of Sicily, had to be rounded before turning up into the Adriatic or the Aegean, or passing on south of Crete—he could not remember the name of that cape—for those places with magical names: Sidon, Tyre, Acre and the Biblical villages and towns, none of which seemed to be on the coast, as though the early Christians were wary of the sea, despite St Peter being a fisherman.

The four men stood round the desk looking at the chart, and Ramage put his finger down at a point about halfway along the coast.

"There's the Golfo di Palmas," he said to Aitken and Rennick, "and Southwick assures me it lies just ahead. That island protecting it to the north is Sant' Antioco and the smaller one north of that is San Pietro. The Golfo di Palmas is reckoned one of the best anchorages in this part of the Mediterranean: ships can find shelter because even a south wind doesn't kick up too much of a sea."

"And for our purposes not too many villages or towers overlooking the anchorage," Southwick said.

"None that need bother us," Ramage agreed. "I haven't been in here for ten years or more, but last time there were a few fishermen living in huts, a tower or two and churches, and a Roman acropolis. They fish for tunny. Anyway, they need not concern us. Now, with our topgallants drawing we should be pulling ahead of the convoy, and because each master knows we are making for the Golfo di Palmas, that'll seem natural enough: they can see land ahead and those who could be bothered to take the sun's meridian passage will know that it is the right spot."

"I wonder where they think the convoy is going to after that," Rennick said in an elaborately casual voice, obviously hoping to draw a hint from Ramage.

"Once they've rounded Capo Spartivento the whole of the eastern Mediterranean is open to them," Ramage said blandly. "Venice, Ragusa, the Morea, Constantinople, Egypt . . ."

Rennick grinned and said: "Which would you choose, sir?"

"For a visit in time of peace? Venice, Constantinople . . . scores of places."

"That wasn't quite what I meant, sir."

"I know," Ramage said, "but I'm making you add patience to your long list of virtues."

He picked up Orsini's list of ships and the sheet of paper on which he had made an estimate of the number of their crews.

Now is the moment, he told himself. You can give one of two sets of orders to these men. One will result in a small but *certain* victory; the other gives a *chance* of a very much larger one. But only a chance; a chance in which he could take no precautions against things like a random sighting at sea, a night of gale . . . And the question the Admiral at Gibraltar—or the

Admiralty, since he was sailing under Admiralty orders—would ask was why he did not take the smaller assured victory.

"Under Admiralty orders"—it meant, in a case like this, so much more than just receiving orders direct from their Lordships. When a captain acting on orders from an admiral captured a prize, the admiral received an eighth of the prize-money, which had to come out of the total shared by the captain, officers and ship's company.

However, if a captain and his ships were sailing "under Admiralty orders," when they captured a prize they shared nothing with any admiral—with no one, in fact, except the prize agent. Not unnaturally the Admiralty were always on the watch for a captain abusing this situation. It was an obvious temptation for some captains. However, his father, one of the most intelligent admirals serving the Navy, although eventually his career was ruined when he became a political scapegoat, had once said to him: "Always aim at a complete victory. Remember that a battle half won is a battle half lost. A man losing a leg doesn't say he's half lame."

Rennick was examining the chart for forts and fields of fire, and seeing what landing beaches there were in the gulf, while Aitken was noting the soundings in the gulf itself, and between Sant' Antioco and San Pietro and the mainland, which formed a much smaller but obviously good anchorage.

Southwick, who had already spent a long time examining the chart and had inspected each copy made by Orsini for the French masters and delivered to them the first day out of Foix, waited patiently for the Captain to begin.

Finally Rennick looked up at Ramage, and then Aitken said: "It certainly is a fine anchorage, sir. Room enough for a fleet and you can get in or out in almost any wind: a little like Falmouth but without that narrow entrance. Well, sir . . . ?"

In his imagination Ramage saw the letter written by the Secretary to the Board, with its stylized beginning, "I am commanded by their Lordships . . ." and he could hear a man walking with a wooden leg.

He sat down at the desk and motioned the others to make themselves comfortable on the settee and the one armchair. Then he thought for a moment. Whatever he did, Kenton and Martin were involved, but Southwick, whether he liked it or not, was going to have to stay with the *Calypso*.

"You'd better relieve Kenton," Ramage said to Southwick, "and tell Martin to come down, too."

An hour later he was standing at the quarterdeck rail with Southwick, examining with his telescope the hilly land ahead of them.

"That's Sant' Antioco island," Ramage said. "It's difficult to distinguish from the hills behind, but check the peaks against the chart as I call them out.

"The highest is in the middle of the island. That'll be Perdas de Foga. Nearly nine hundred feet, isn't it?"

"According to this chart, sir."

"At the south end of the island there are three more peaks, the middle one being the highest. That'll be Monte Arbus, I take it."

Southwick grunted agreement.

"Now, there's a pointed peak at the north end of the island. Scrocca Manu, eh?"

"If that's how you pronounce it," Southwick grumbled. "About five hundred feet. It all fits."

Ten minutes later, Ramage again put the glass to his eye.

"Ah, Southwick. The north end of Sant' Antioco—are you ready with the chart? Good. There's a small town there with a tall, white, circular tower. A hundred feet high, I should think. And—yes, a church with a white cupola."

"That's right, sir," Southwick said matter-of-factly. "It's Calasetta, but you're wrong about the tower, it's only 95 feet. By the way, off the south end of the island, a couple of miles or so—"

"Yes, the land of Sant' Antioco comes down low there, and then there's a very small island, steep-to but high."

"That's it: Isolotto la Vacca."

"Now, the island to the north of Sant' Antioco, Isola San Pietro. Not much to see—seems fairly low, plenty of trees. Olives and figs, and I can pick out some vine terraces. The south end looks like salt pans. Wait—yes, on the mainland beyond, I can see another big tower. Octagonal—at least, not round. Very prominent."

"That's at Portoscuso, sir. How about looking down to the south, at the southern end of the Golfo di Palmas?"

"Well, on the mainland in line with the south end of Sant' Antioco there are various hills inland, but it begins with a white sand beach, then what looks like marshes. That must be the north side of Porto Pino?"

"Seems so from this chart, sir."

"Then as you trend south there's a headland with—yes, a tower on top. Too far off to see shape and colour; in fact it looks like a tree stump!"

"That'll be the tower on the north side of Cala Piombo, sir, 633 feet high. If we get strong nor'easters or sou'easters, that's the anchorage for us. Good holding in six to ten fathoms, the chart says; I've a special note on it."

"Well," Ramage said, shutting the telescope, "let's hope we get fine weather so we can stay out of the Cala Piombo."

"It's an odd sort of name," Southwick said. He paused and then gave a sniff. "Still, I can't think why we'd ever want to be down that end of the gulf."

"*Piombo* is Italian for lead," Ramage said. "I wonder who built the tower . . ."

CHAPTER FIFTEEN

THE moment the *Calypso* was anchored in the lee of Sant' Antioco, Rennick had his men drawn up in the waist with the sergeant checking their pistols and cutlasses while Aitken attended to hoisting out the boats. Fortunately the frigate was lying with her head to the north-west, so that her starboard side was for the time being hidden from any ships entering the bay. Which, the First Lieutenant thought to himself, was just as well.

A frigate carried six boats, two (usually the cutters) secured in quarter davits and the other four stowed on deck amidships with the spare yards and booms. When she anchored, normally the two quarter-boats were lowered—the first one away traditionally carrying the master or bosun in a circle round the ship making sure all the yards were square.

So a frigate might have her two cutters in the water and no onlooker would be surprised; but for a frigate, or any ship-of-war, to have six boats in the water—that could mean one of two things: that they were all being sent off wooding and watering, and would be stowed with casks, or they were going to attack something, in which case they would be full of men.

First Aitken had the larboard cutter, the red one, lowered and brought round to the starboard side, when the other cutter was lowered. Each one was designed to carry sixteen men for cutting-out expeditions and was rowed by six oars. The launch was then hoisted out on the stay tackle, the biggest and heaviest of the *Calypso*'s boats, carrying 24 armed men and rowed by eight oars. The pinnace was the next to go over the side, and like the cutters carried sixteen armed men but rowed eight oars. With the launch, the pinnace was intended for more distant expeditions. The gig, long and narrow-beamed and the fastest of them all, was hoisted out next. She could carry sixteen armed men and rowed eight oars. Finally the little jolly-boat was hoisted out—rowing four oars, she carried eight armed men.

All the boats had been secured by painters and stern-fasts by the time Ramage came up to the entry port and said to Aitken: "The first of the merchant ships is just passing the end of Sant' Antioco and Isolotto la Vacca, that rock south of it. She'll be anchoring in half an hour. She's the *Sarazine*, with a dozen men. You'd better take the launch, your party and a section of Marines under the sergeant."

"Aye aye, sir."

"Damn—there's another ship just nosing round the headland. Ah, the *Golondrina*. I think I'll go in the gig with Kenton to deal with her; it's a long time since I heard Spanish spoken."

Aitken shouted: "Launch crew and boarders fall in beside number five gun, starboard side; green cutter's crew and boarders to number nine gun."

Ramage watched Aitken and his men leave, looked round for Martin, saw him eyeing the two approaching merchant ships and called over: "You'll recognize your ship and go off to her at the right moment. Don't forget the signal to Southwick, otherwise you might find some round shot whistling round your ears."

Martin was excited and nodded his head. "Aye aye, sir. Will Orsini bring in the *Passe Partout* and anchor her?"

"Yes, all being well. Don't forget, he's already several jumps ahead of us!"

Martin nodded again, clearly preoccupied. Not frightened, Ramage realized, but on the verge of being overwhelmed with the apparent importance of his orders and what he thought would be the consequences of failure.

"You and Orsini are a lucky pair," Ramage said conversationally. "You went off comfortably to your first commands. Mine was different. I was knocked out by a splinter and woke up to find that I, the Fifth Lieutenant, was the sole surviving officer and therefore in command—of a sinking frigate being battered to pieces by a French ship of the line."

"I heard about that from Jackson, sir: he was with you. He said you treated it as—well, as a great joke, sir."

"I assure you I didn't," Ramage said laughing. "My head was ringing like a church bell from being knocked out."

"That's one of those scars . . . ?"

"The upper one," Ramage said, automatically rubbing the scar above his right eyebrow. "Now, I think that's your bird coming into sight, isn't it?"

"Yes, sir: if you'll excuse me!" He gave a shout: "Red cutter party fall in here! Red cutter party to me!"

By the time Martin had cast off with the red cutter, Kenton was calling for the gig's crew and boarding-party and Rennick, who would be commanding the pinnace and sixteen boarders, apart from the eight oarsmen, was still inspecting his men.

Aitken's launch was already half a mile from the *Calypso*, the men rowing leisurely and not heading directly for any particular ship. Then, if anyone was watching the frigate, they would have seen the red cutter leave and row round the ship a couple of times before heading seaward. A few minutes later the pinnace came from under the *Calypso*'s stern and suddenly she picked up speed, Rennick calling for a fast pace, and then after a mile she slowed down to a more normal speed. Again, there was nothing very odd about that; the gig would soon be doing the same. She was a long, narrow and fast boat, and was often the private property of the captain of a ship. The gig usually had gold leaf picking out the ship's name, and the sternsheets were either scrubbed teak, or varnished so that they and the thwarts shone like a dining-room table, and when not in use were protected from the sun's rays by canvas covers.

Now more merchant ships were coming into the gulf, the more careful of them with leadsmen in the chains calling out depths, though the majority of the masters obviously looked at ships like the *Sarazine* and *Golondrina*, which they knew drew much more water than they did, and steered straight for them, assuming they had kept on a straight course after rounding Sant' Antioco.

The *Calypso*'s pinnace was now rowing between the merchant

ships. The Marine Lieutenant had been on enough cutting-out expeditions to be perfectly at home in the eight-oared boat, and the only thing that seemed at all strange was that all the men in her were dressed either in French uniform or ragged clothes.

Jackson, usually Captain Ramage's coxswain in the gig, was commanding the green cutter for the time being, and threatening the sixteen boarders and six oarsmen with dire punishment if they did not stop talking: he did not mind the teasing but he was afraid they might be overheard by someone on board one of the French ships.

Clearly the captain of the frigate had decided to exercise all his boats' crews—that was the opinion of the *Sarazine*'s master, who had just noticed three or four of them, and he was wondering how he could use the French Navy to help him with watering— there was bound to be water available somewhere in the gulf. His casks had leaked, thanks to the pounding the ship had received in the seas left over from the *mistral,* and he could never force his men to make do with only their daily ration of water: abetted by the mate, they simply drew more at night, when he was asleep.

Now, however, he was faced with having to launch his own boat, which was too small to carry more than one cask, and he had plenty of work on the rigging to occupy his seven seamen without sending them off watering. So perhaps, if he could speak to one of those Navy officers, they would take a couple of casks, and . . . He remembered he had some bottles of manzanilla, bought cheaply in Alicante, which might help. At that moment he saw that the frigate's launch would pass close astern, and he walked to the taffrail to give a hail.

Ramage, sitting in the sternsheets of the gig with Kenton, said quietly: "I think the ships are used to the idea of us rowing round, so we'll board the *Golondrina* now. If you go alongside to starboard, none of the others will see us."

The gig turned and appeared to be going close along the edge of the beach until she was almost abreast the Spanish ship, and then she turned four points to larboard, which brought the master of the ship to the bulwark to give a friendly wave.

Ramage waved back and when the master saw the gig was coming to his ship he called for seamen to take her painter and stern-fast. As soon as the gig was alongside, Ramage scrambled on board and greeted the master cheerfully, making a joke about the privateer schooner as he went aft, so that when the master turned naturally to walk with him, his back was towards the entry port.

"The tartane was fast," the master said. "I could not believe my eyes when I saw those masts falling. The British must have been sleeping!"

"She was not British," Ramage said, touching the side of his nose mysteriously. "You did not see the affair of her flag?"

"No, only that she had the English flag, the red one."

"Ah, but at the last moment she changed it! She hauled down the British flag and hoisted another . . ." Ramage let his voice die away mysteriously.

"Hoisted *another?* What other? With whom else are we at war, *señor?*"

"The crescent and star . . ."

"An Algerine? *Caramba!* They must have captured her from the English and kept her colours!"

"It has been done before and will be done again, I've no doubt," Ramage said gloomily, a note of sorrow in his voice as he gave a signal to Kenton. "As you said of the privateer when she lost her mast, it is hard to believe one's own eyes."

The Master found himself staring at the muzzle of a pistol with a hexagonal barrel, one of the two that he had admired when he saw the French officer wearing them with belt-hooks.

Now the French officer had his thumb on—that click: now it was cocked! "Be careful!" the master said hastily, "do not point that pistol at me, anyone would think—"

He broke off as he looked round and saw his ship's company

all lying flat on the deck, a man from the gig standing over each of them.

"What is this? Have you gone mad? This is not an Algerine—nor an English ship!"

Ramage pointed across to the *Calypso*. "No," he could not resist saying, "but she is."

"But . . . but . . . she is French. Why, I recognize the class. And the young officer from her who brought over my orders at Foix—you are not going to tell me he was English!"

"No, Italian, but he is an officer of the Royal Navy, as I am. I must introduce myself," Ramage said, "and may I take it that this"—he gestured with the pistol—"is not necessary?"

The master nodded vigorously. Ramage lowered the hammer gently and slipped the hook over his belt.

He gave a slight bow. "Ramage—Captain Ramage, at your service."

"*Nombre de Dios,*" the master said, and sat down on the deck with a thud, his face white, his upper lip and brow beading with perspiration. "Excuse me, *señor,* I suddenly feel faint. I know that name."

"It might be someone else," Ramage said politely, helping the man to his feet again. "Breathe deeply. It helps usually."

The Spaniard took a few deep breaths, exhaling, it seemed to Ramage, pure garlic.

"There may be others called Ramage, but only one would—*Caramba!* How did you know that at the last moment the convoy would go to Foix?"

"I sent the signal," Ramage said blandly. "The French semaphore system is most useful."

The Spaniard shrugged his shoulders, as a priest might admit the Devil's existence. "Now you capture the whole convoy, eh? And I thought you were simply exercising your boats."

"Oh, but I am," Ramage assured him. "Now, if you'll join your men—I suggest you sit there by the mainmast. I have a few words to say to them."

By now the men of the gig's boarding-party were bent down below the level of the bulwarks. Two of them returning from searching the fo'c's'le were pushing along a man they had found sleeping.

Ramage raised his voice. "You may sit up," he said in Spanish, and noted there were ten men in addition to the master, and one of them was, from his dress, the mate.

"This ship is now a British prize. You will all go down to the gig, and I warn you that if you shout or try to signal any of the ships, you'll be run through with a cutlass. Do as you are told and you will not be hurt."

He walked over to Kenton and said: "I leave you to your new command. And don't forget to hoist the signal for Southwick; he worries about you."

The Spanish crew of the *Golondrina* climbed down into the gig, in which there were only the six oarsmen, but close by Jackson steered the green cutter so that his boarding-party covered the prisoners. Ramage followed the Spanish master and took the tiller, and with a farewell wave to Kenton, the painter and sternfast were cast off and the gig headed back for the *Calypso* and then, without any of the other ships noticing them, turned away for the beach.

Ramage said to the Spanish master: "I am going to be generous. If I was an Algerine, I would cut all your throats, eh?"

The master nodded miserably and rubbed his unshaven chin in a reflex gesture.

"I am going to land you on the beach. You will all immediately go inland out of sight. Cagliari is to the south-east, and I suggest you follow the coast road. Do not try to raise the alarm because there are fourteen other ships in the convoy, and you could cause a great deal of bloodshed."

Ramage saw that the man understood. He would be marooned on an alien island, but there were many towns and ports in Sardinia, and he would eventually get back to Spain. The gig's keel scraped on the sand, and the men of the *Golondrina* scrambled on shore while Jackson's men kept them covered from the cutter.

Southwick wrote carefully in his log, using the slate to help his memory: "Two PM wind W by S. Anchored with best bower in five fms, Vacca I. bearing SW by W, white house on S. Antioco NW by ½ W, ruin on P. Botte E by S. 2.30 PM all boats hoisted out, manned and three PM, left under general command of the Captain. Pumped ship at ten ins. Fresh water remaining twenty-one tons. 3:15 PM first ships of French convoy entering gulf and anchoring as convenient."

Southwick sniffed as he wiped his pen dry. "As convenient" be damned; they were just sailing in, clewing up or brailing sails, turning head to wind and tipping anchors over the side as though disposing of rubbish. The *Sarazine* would foul the *Calypso* the moment the wind had any east in it; the *Golondrina* needed only a north wind to bring her crashing into the *Calypso*, and two other ships only a little smaller than the *Sarazine* obviously had not let out enough scope on their cables and would drag on to the frigate if the wind picked up. And the damnable thing was that he could do nothing about it: no one left on board the *Calypso* spoke a word of French: Mr Ramage was away with the boats and Mr Orsini was only just now coming into sight with the *Passe Partout*.

He had not heard a shot fired so far: not a pistol, not a musket, not a great gun: it was waiting for the sound of a shot that was making him so bad-tempered. If anything went wrong, what could he do, with no boats and fifty men left on board, all of them old wrecks like himself, short of wind—a quarter of them wearing trusses, half of them bleary of eye, and most shaky of gait? All of them had spirit enough, but a warlike yell and threat of a broadside would not be enough to get even one of them up to the main-yard in under five minutes.

He, Edward Southwick, had to admit that at the moment he was a Falstaff at the head of a rag-tag and bobtail party of seamen who, when mixed with the rest of the ship's company, did their jobs well enough: there was no need for the cook to have two legs and no reason why his mate should not be cross-eyed—except in a situation like this.

"Signal from the *Golondrina*, sir," a seaman called down.

Cursing, Southwick grabbed his hat and sword and hurried up the ladder.

"French flags, sir, I've worked it out as being this one." He pointed to it in the signal book. "I don't understand the lingo, sir, but the book mentions '*charpentier.*' Perhaps it means send over the carpenter and his mates?"

Southwick nodded, and said: "Just acknowledge it." He did not need to know French to understand the message: it was a code arranged by Mr Ramage so that he and the other boarding parties could use the French system to send signals to the *Calypso* which, read by any other of the French ships, would seem innocent enough.

So Mr Ramage had secured the *Golondrina* and would be leaving young Kenton in command with his party while he took the Spanish crew on shore in the gig. He opened his telescope and a few moments later saw the gig appear round the stern of the Spanish ship, followed by the green cutter. He had to admit that Mr Ramage was right; with so many of the *Calypso*'s boats rowing round apparently at random it all seemed quite natural and no one would notice. The mixture of French uniforms and old clothes, for example, was typically the way the French would do it, so that the gig making for the beach with ten or more Spaniards from the *Golondrina* looked no different from when she first went alongside with a boarding-party from the *Calypso*. The substitution of Spaniards for boarding-party was not noticeable.

The *Golondrina* would have been no problem because, of course, Mr Ramage spoke Spanish, but what about Aitken with the *Sarazine?* Still, the muzzle of a pistol pointing at you had a language all of its own.

He saw a movement of colour just as the seaman spoke: the

same signal was being hoisted from the *Sarazine* and the launch was leaving her and rowing steadily along the coast: obviously Aitken had ordered his prisoners to be landed a long way from the *Golondrina* people.

Martin steered the red cutter another point to starboard. The brig *Bergère* had now anchored and he could distinguish the master, a fat man wearing a beret and looking as though he would be more at home sitting under an old plane tree in the *place* of a small town in the south of France, and the mate, a lanky man in a red shirt. He had counted nine seamen and petty officers, only one more than Orsini had noted, so the boy had done a good job.

He saw that both the *Golondrina* and *Sarazine* were flying the signal, so Mr Aitken and Kenton had taken their prizes.

It was easy enough to see that the *Bergère* brig had been built in England and, remembering what he had learned all the time he had been growing up as the son of the master shipwright at Chatham Dockyard, he guessed from her sheer and the shape of her stern that she had been built on the south coast not too far from Portsmouth. At Bursledon perhaps, or even East Cowes. Getting on for three hundred tons and down on her marks—he could see that she was pierced for six guns and carried them, nine-pounders from the look of it. According to Orsini her holds were full of carriages for land guns, harnesses, hides and a ground tier of guns to mount on the carriages.

There were fewer Frenchmen on deck now: with the anchor down and sails furled (bundled up, to his way of thinking) they probably thought their day's work was over.

"Stand by, men, I'm going alongside now."

He pushed the tiller over with his shoulder as he crouched for a moment to check that his pistols were held tightly by the belt-hooks.

One of his seamen was standing up in the bow, holding a boat-hook horizontally across his chest. No one in the *Bergère* showed the slightest interest; in fact the red cutter was now so close that a man in the brig would have to stand on the bulwark and peer down to see her.

He could scramble up the side—none of the other ships would see—or go on board in a dignified fashion, followed by his men and pretending until the last moment to be French. Mr Ramage had said they should get as far as possible with bluff, and from the indifference of the men in the *Bergère*, Martin was sure he and half a dozen men could get to the wheel without being challenged.

Then the cutter was alongside, the men using the oars without orders and then boating them, while the seamen forward hooked on to an eyebolt with the boat-hook. A second seaman climbed up the ship's side in a leisurely fashion with the painter while a third went up with the stern-fast. Martin, mouth dry, his heart seeming to skid over cobblestones rather than beat regularly, jammed his hat (according to the label inside it belonged to someone called Pierre Duhamel, now prisoner in the *Calypso*) firmly on his head and climbed up the side battens.

For the last few seconds, as his head appeared over the level of the deck at the entry port, he looked round the *Bergère* and saw the fat man in the beret standing right aft and unaware that there was a boat alongside. Catching sight of Martin he gave a cheerful wave and bellowed for the mate, whose red shirt Martin could see on the foredeck.

Martin waved back and walked to the centreline to leave room for his boarding-party, who were following him. As soon as the bosun's mate who was his second-in-command arrived beside him, Martin said casually: "Everyone except the captain is forward. Secure them—watch the man in a red shirt, he's the mate."

With that Martin strolled aft in what he felt was a casual manner, hoping the captain would watch him and not the boarding-party going forward.

The Frenchman looked puzzled and called something to

Martin, who grinned and waved reassuringly, increasing his pace. A few moments later there was a yell from forward and Martin guessed it was the red-shirted mate.

Three quick strides brought him up to the master with a pistol in his right hand. He stopped and pulled the hammer back with his thumb, the click seeming to sound like a small hammer on an anvil.

He then repeated, parrot-fashion, the French phrase that Mr Ramage had made him learn, which told the master that his ship was now a British prize and any attempt to raise an alarm would mean death. To emphasize *"mort"* Martin jammed the pistol in the man's stomach, and as he bent forward in an instinctive reaction, Martin could not resist the schoolboy gesture of pulling the floppy beret down so that it covered the man's eyes, the band jamming across his nose.

With the captain momentarily blinded, Martin spun round to look forward in time to see the French mate collapsing into the arms of one of his own men, having just been punched in the stomach by the *Calypso's* burliest boarder. The rest of the French promptly raised their arms in surrender and were told by the bosun's mate, using sign language, to go down into the cutter.

Martin, wanting to keep him occupied until all the men were in the cutter, pushed the French captain so that he lost his balance and fell over. At that moment one of the Calypsos, who had climbed up on to the bulwarks, called out. "The gig's coming, sir, with the Captain!"

Martin waved an acknowledgement: it was part of the plan that the gig or red cutter would help convoy the boats taking crews to the beach. As soon as Martin saw the red-shirted man helped down into the cutter, he jerked the captain's beret upwards —and saw why the man wore it: he was completely bald. The Frenchman blinked in the sudden light, looked round for his men and saw Martin pointing to the entry port. He walked over to it, watched by the wary bosun's mate with a cocked pistol, and Martin jumped up on to the bulwarks.

Ramage saw him almost immediately, waved as if congratulating him, and then pointed aloft. For a moment Martin was puzzled. Then he remembered.

"Bosun's mate, hoist the signal."

He now had his command. Yes, he had commanded the *Passe Partout* for a few hours but, much as he enjoyed having Orsini with him, it was not quite the same. Now he commanded a brig of three hundred tons, worth hundreds of pounds in prize-money.

Rennick was still circling with the pinnace, waiting for the *Matilda* to anchor while the bosun with the jolly-boat edged over towards the *Rosette* schooner, which had anchored and whose crew would, in a few minutes, be busy furling the sails and unlikely to take much notice of a frigate's boat coming alongside.

CHAPTER SIXTEEN

BY SIX o'clock in the evening fifteen ships and the *Calypso* frigate were at anchor in the Golfo di Palmas, and unknown to eight of them, the masters, mates and ships' companies of the other seven, with the Foix garrison, were tramping over the Sardinian hills in the dry, dusty heat, looking in vain for a town or village which could understand their French and Spanish, give them drink, food and shelter, and help them raise the alarm. Instead, the people assumed they were bandits and opened fire with fowling pieces, unleashed their dogs and bawled threats in Italian.

The *Sarazine*, the largest of the merchant ships, was providing comfortable quarters for Aitken: her master's cabin was bigger than the coach on board the *Calypso*—the captain's day cabin, bed place and dining cabin—and the Scotsman, whose own quarters in the frigate comprised a box eight feet long and seven wide, felt almost guilty at the luxuriousness of it.

Kenton was counting himself equally lucky in the *Golondrina*, except for the smell of garlic. He refused to believe that the heavy smell was simply the residue over the years of masters eating garlic-treated food and breathing out garlic-laden breath: he was convinced that somewhere, having rolled under something, must be a clove which had been trodden on and squashed. He had a seaman search the cabin but without success, although the man at the end of an hour's crouching, peering and sniffing, did comment to an exasperated Kenton that: "I'm partial to a bit of garlic meself, sir, an' Watkins, what's going to be the cook, has found a great string of 'em. If you like, sir, I can get you a fresh clove."

In the *Bergère*, Martin was inspecting sails and rigging with the bosun's mate, making his topmen let fall one sail and check it for tears or chafe, before furling it and letting fall the next. As soon as that was finished he went to the wheel and had the bosun's mate turn it slowly while he made sure there was no wear where the ropes to the tiller went round the drum. Then together they inspected the rudder-head, tiller, wheel ropes and the relieving tackle. When they climbed back on deck the bosun's mate, Maxwell, gave a contented sigh. "Everything seems to be all right, sir, an that's just as well, because whatever Mr Ramage has got in mind, this old brig is going to have to sail faster than she's done for years!"

Martin looked at his watch. An hour to go. He could now tell the men exactly what Mr Ramage intended.

"Muster the men aft, Maxwell," he said, "then you'll all know what Mr Ramage has in mind."

While he waited, he saw the gig go alongside the *Passe Partout*, take off three or four men, and then row towards the other brig in the gulf, the *Caroline*, smaller than the *Bergère* but French-built.

Jackson took the gig alongside the *Passe Partout* and, while the bowman held on, scrambled up the side of the tartane to hand over sealed, written orders to Orsini.

For a few moments the midshipman thought they must mean

he had lost command of the tartane, and rather than let Jackson, Rossi and Stafford and the rest of the men see his disappointment—he knew he was not far from tears—he went aft to his cabin with the unopened orders stuck carelessly in a pocket.

The moment he was in the cabin he shut the door, pulled out the folded paper, broke the seal and began reading. The orders comprised only a few lines—were similar in fact to those for the *Passe Partout*—but he read them again carefully, and then a third time. Then he sat down, angry that his hands were trembling. There was no disguising the trembling, and he knew two things were causing it. Three rather. First, the shock because he thought he was losing the tartane because the Captain was dissatisfied with him; second, excitement at his new command; and third, fear, or to call it by a less harsh name, apprehension.

Who, he wondered, would not feel apprehension in his position when ordered to take possession and then command of the *Caroline* brig? She must be all of three hundred tons. She bore the same relationship to the tartane as a ship of the line to a frigate . . .

He folded the orders and put them in his pocket, slipped the cutlass-belt over his shoulder and hooked two pistols into his belt. Then he held out his right hand, palm downwards, and examined it. It was no longer trembling, and he went out on deck to find Jackson talking to Rossi and Stafford.

Jackson stepped forward and handed him another letter. "The Captain said to give you this, sir, after you'd read the other one."

Paolo grinned because there was no hiding anything from Jackson: like the Captain he seemed to be able to see through a thick plank.

He broke the seal and read the letter. He was to take Rossi with him as second-in-command. To capture the *Caroline* he would use Stafford and Jackson's boarding-party in the gig. All the ships captured so far had been taken by just boarding as though paying a friendly visit . . .

"You've been busy," he said to Jackson. "We missed the fun."

The American shook his head. "No fun, really, sir; it's been like picking ripe apples. But they tell me you ran out of wind."

"Three hours and not a breath," Paolo said angrily. "We've been slamming and banging a couple of miles beyond this island. Very well, now," he pushed down on his pistols to make sure the hooks were holding, "we'll go over and take possession of our next ship."

It was, he thought, a splendidly offhand remark; it was the kind of thing that Mr Ramage said so well.

"Aye aye, sir," Jackson said, but hesitated a moment as Rossi and Stafford led the way down to the gig.

What was Jackson waiting for? Oh yes, the *Passe Partout* could not be left without someone in command of her, and the Captain had left the choice of a man to him.

He turned forward. "Reynolds!" As soon as the red-haired seaman was standing to attention in front of him, he said: "I am leaving you in command of the *Passe Partout* until you receive further orders from Captain Ramage. Keep a good anchor watch, and pump the bilge every hour."

"Aye aye, sir," Reynolds said, almost numbly, and Orsini knew just how he felt. "You goin' somewhere, then, sir?"

Orsini pointed to the brig. "Yes, I've been given command of the *Caroline*."

The news braced Reynolds, who grinned cheerfully. "Well, sir, if you've got to command 'er, I s'pose it's up to me to do me best with this old girl!"

Impulsively Orsini shook him by the hand. "Thanks—and the best of luck."

As the gig approached the *Caroline*, Orsini could see a man on deck. Finally, when the gig was forty or fifty yards away, an unshaven man, shirtless and covered in rolls of fat, came to the entry port and emptied a bucket of rubbish over the side, spat and disappeared.

"I could just see that happening in the *Calypso*, sir," Jackson murmured. "Mr Southwick would shoot him with a blunt bullet."

"A blunt—oh, I see what you mean!"

Then the gig was alongside and Orsini led the way up the side. He pictured the signature "Ramage" on his orders and knew that his hands were not trembling, nor would they. There was no one on deck, not even the grubby man with the bucket.

"Come with me," he said to Stafford and Rossi, and to Jackson he said: "Take your men and secure the ship's company: we'll make do with the master!"

As he went down the companion-way, Orsini pulled a pistol from his belt, then changed his mind, thrust it back and drew the cutlass, because close by he could hear heavy snoring.

They found the master of the *Caroline* deep asleep in an armchair; it took more than a minute to waken him. As soon as it looked as though he could haul in the fact that he had just lost his ship, Paolo said conversationally in French:

"*M'sieu*, forgive me for waking you, but your ship is now a prize to His Britannic Majesty's frigate the *Calypso* . . ."

He could have said it more briefly but he liked the way the words flowed. Now the poor fellow was wide awake. Dressed only in a long pair of underpants—he was obviously from the south of France where, as in Italy, they believed it was medically perilous not to wear wool next to the skin at all times—he had the trapped look of a calf in a slaughterhouse.

"Can I move?" the man asked cautiously.

"Certainly, stand up and dress, because in a few minutes you must leave the ship."

"To go where?" The man was used to people being taken away in tumbrils to guillotines set up in town squares.

"To a firing squad, eh? Or to a noose dangling from a yardarm? Or a push over the side with a heavy piece of ballast tied on your back?" It was a macabre sort of teasing, but in escaping from Volterra and making his way to Naples, Paolo had seen thirty or forty guillotines set up in small towns, and beside most of them the rusty iron replica of a tree of liberty.

"Do I choose?" the man whispered, as though invisible hands were trying to strangle him.

"You had better dress first," Orsini said, and while the man pulled on his clothes he told Jackson of the conversation so far.

"I wondered why he suddenly went white and started perspiring, sir. Has he said which he prefers?"

"Not yet; he's probably making up his mind now."

Finally the *Caroline*'s master was dressed and Paolo said: "The ship's papers—where are they?"

The man went to a cupboard and took out several documents. "They are here—ship's certificate of registry, charter party, bills of lading, manifest . . ."

"Muster book, log . . . ?"

The man put his hand back in the cupboard. "All in here, with my quadrant, tables, almanac."

"Put them back," Paolo ordered and, as the man shut the cupboard door again, asked casually: "Have you made up your mind?"

The man took a deep breath which ended in a sob. "Firing squad. Not the noose nor drowning, I beg of you . . . And *m'sieu*, is there any way I can send a message to my wife? You see, I hid some money in the garden: buried it—for security, you understand."

"Oh yes, it will be secure enough—unless your wife's new husband begins to plant potatoes . . ."

The thought of it brought tears to the man's eyes and Paolo, glancing at his watch, decided the joke had gone far enough. "You may yet be lucky enough to dig it up yourself; go down into the boat alongside. You and your men are going to be put on shore. You will at once start making your way inland: if any of you stay near the beach you will be hunted down and shot."

The man hurried out of the cabin as though afraid this crazy youth would change his mind.

Ramage walked from one side of the *Calypso*'s quarterdeck to the other, listening to the "thunk . . . thunk" of the capstan pawls on board the five ships and the clacking of the schooner's windlass. All six were weighing on time, and Southwick was cursing the *Sarazine*. In hauling up to her anchor she was coming very close to the *Calypso*, just as he had feared when her original French captain anchored her.

Ramage looked across at the *Golondrina*, which was on the other side: she was creeping ahead and in three or four minutes would be clear of the *Calypso*. He picked up the speaking-trumpet and hailed the *Sarazine*.

"Mr Aitken . . ."

As soon as the Scot answered, Ramage called, keeping his voice low: "'Vast heaving for a few minutes, until the *Golondrina* is clear of us. Then I'll let fall our mizen topsail so we can give our stern a sheer to starboard out of your way. But have them step out lively at the capstan!"

"Aye aye, sir. The way these Frenchmen anchored, you'd think they were leaving haycarts in a farmyard for the night."

Southwick looked at the Spanish brig with his glass and saw Kenton watching the *Calypso* warily. Suddenly her topsails were let fall while the headsails soared up the stays.

"Kenton had lashings in place of gaskets on those topsails," Southwick commented to Ramage. "Good idea when you're shorthanded and there's not much room."

"As long as the topmen have sharp knives." Ramage looked round again. "I think we can let fall our mizen topsail and back it, Mr Southwick."

The Master gave the orders for the topmen, had the quartermaster put the wheel over, and watched as the yard was braced round until the sail was backed, the wind pressing on its forward side and pushing the *Calypso*'s stern away from the *Sarazine*, whose capstan once again continued its rhythmic clanking.

Then Ramage saw one of the other ships already under way: a brig, the *Caroline*. She was making the first tack to leave the gulf under topsails. He guessed Aitken would be cross; but for the pause to avoid the *Calypso* he would have led out his convoy.

"Orsini's lads were determined they'd be first," Southwick commented. "It'll do him good: build up his confidence for when it gets dark."

How right the Master was. For a moment Ramage was surprised that Southwick, who must be sixty or more, could remember, although Ramage himself recalled as though it was yesterday the first prize he commanded as a midshipman, and how his courage had gone down with the setting sun—or, to be more honest, his cowardice arrived with the dusk.

The *Golondrina* was under way, and Martin had the *Bergère* tacking under topsails—Ramage could imagine him being pleasantly annoyed at being beaten by Orsini. Now Rennick was tacking across the gulf with the *Matilda*, and he saw that the main and foresails of the *Rosette* schooner had been hoisted, with the headsails following. There was a pause as the peaks of both gaffs were hoisted another foot or two to give a tighter leech and take out some creases; then the schooner bore away as the bosun confidently hardened in sheets and set off after the *Caroline*.

Now the *Sarazine's* anchor was being catted as her topsails were sheeted home and she headed for the southern end of Sant' Antioco island, where the other five ships would join her.

"I wonder what the rest of these Frenchmen are thinking now," Southwick said, half to himself, and gesturing at the remaining anchored ships. "Just imagine, eight left—nine, rather; I keep forgetting we have the *Passe Partout*—and not one of the masters suspicious or coming across to ask us questions."

"Not one of them bothering to watch, as far as I can see," Ramage said, closing his telescope, "and that's just as well."

Southwick nodded happily. "Yes, we've a busy night ahead."

"Have you that anchorage diagram?"

"Yes, here it is," Southwick said, opening the binnacle box drawer and taking out a sheet of paper. He put it down on the top of the binnacle, holding two sides of it against the wind as Ramage put an arm across the other.

Eight ships were drawn at the precise positions in which they were anchored. They were all linked to the *Calypso* by lines radiating from her like spokes from an axle, and along each line was written the particular ship's bearing, so that at night a boat with a compass could be sent from the *Calypso* to find her.

"According to Orsini's list," Southwick said, "there are about one hundred men on board them."

Ramage shook his head crossly. "You know, it's my own fault. There's Aitken setting off for Gibraltar with his convoy of ships, and I've had to use my First, acting Second and acting Third Lieutenants, midshipman, bosun and Lieutenant of Marines to command them, just because we carry only one midshipman, instead of half a dozen."

Southwick gave one of his particularly disapproving sniffs. "Orsini's an exception, but midshipmen can be a mixed blessing, sir. What's more trouble in a ship than a thirty-year-old midshipman who's spent ten years trying and failing his lieutenant's examination? He's bitter and usually a troublemaker and drinker, and if you send him off in command of a prize, then you'd best use it as an opportunity of getting rid of all your bad men and search 'em all for liquor."

"Well, we're lucky in *that* respect."

"Aye, sir, not a man I'd want to get rid of—except that damned gunner."

The gunner, a warrant officer, should have been in command of one of the prizes; instead he was the only person in the *Calypso* to whom Ramage found it hard to be civil, because he was incompetent and sly. The man dodged any responsibility, did not know his job—Ramage often wondered how he obtained his warrant from the Board of Ordnance in the first place—and was more than content to leave everything to his mate. Fortunately for the *Calypso* the young gunner's mate was both enthusiastic and competent. Ramage usually managed to get rid of incompetent men or anyone who had an abrasive character, but the gunner was appointed by the Ordnance Board and, as Southwick had once bitterly complained: "It takes an Act of Parliament to get rid of any of *their* people."

The gunner treated powder as though it was his own personal property and he had paid for it, and when he first joined the *Calypso* he had tried to avoid allowing powder or shot for the men to exercise muskets and the upper-deck guns. Finally Ramage had the man brought down to his cabin and, with Aitken and Southwick present, had read him number eleven in the Admiralty's Printed Instructions for the Gunner:

> By direction of the captain, he is to allow a proper quantity of powder and shot for exercise, viz. once a week for the first two months, and once a month afterwards, six charges of powder to each man for exercise of small arms, and once a fortnight four pounds of musket shot for them all, and once a month five charges of powder and five of shot for the exercise of the upper-deck guns.

Faced with the Admiralty instructions, the wretched fellow had, within a fortnight, then claimed that "each man" did not include idlers, such as the cook and his mate, the captain's clerk, sailmaker and others whose name came from the fact that they did not stand a watch.

Once again Ramage had taken him down to his cabin and pointed out there was nothing in anyone's instructions that said the cook had to cook food for him, that the purser had to provide him with water, or the clerk with quills, ink or paper. In the meantime there were precisely forty individual instructions covering the gunner's duty, and it was up to the captain to make sure, with suitable strictness, that they were obeyed. Number twenty, for example, which in its entirety said of the gunner: "He is to observe upon the guns, the notches or sights on the base, or muzzle rings, for the better guiding the aim."

Ramage had asked the gunner what he thought that meant and, getting an evasive answer, had asked Aitken to give his opinion as the ship's First Lieutenant. The Scotsman, who detested the gunner, said flatly: "It means he is to stand and observe the notches. 'Observe' means 'to keep a watch on,' the dictionary tells us that, so obviously the gunner must stand and watch the notches on all the guns every day during the hours of daylight."

By now the gunner was becoming very nervous, his fear of authority overcoming his meanness with the Board of Ordnance's powder and shot, and before dismissing him Ramage said: "You will report to the First Lieutenant every Monday, in the forenoon, with a copy of your Instructions, and he will check with you that you have done your duty the preceding week. In the meantime every man in this ship, watchkeeper, idler or waister, must be proficient with a musket. That is one of your responsibilities."

Ramage cursed to himself for wasting his time now thinking black thoughts about the gunner, and concentrated on South-wick's chart. The *Calypso* still had her six boats, a dozen Marines under a corporal, and plenty of seamen. All she lacked, Ramage thought crossly, were commission and petty officers.

Eight merchant ships left, and about a hundred men in them who had to be captured and dumped on shore to follow their fellow countrymen along the dusty road to Cagliari. Should he wait for nightfall, in case one of the ships became suspicious? He almost laughed aloud at the idea: the *Calypso* could sail through the anchorage sinking a ship with each broadside; likewise any two of her boats with boarding parties could seize a ship. The whole need for secrecy was now gone because, as he looked westward, the *Sarazine* was leading her convoy out to sea: six fine and undamaged prizes taken without the expenditure of a single musket shot or a human life—unless one counted the Algerines.

No, two boats could go to each ship and remove the crew. If they went to a ship at one side of the anchorage first, and after the French seamen were landed went to a vessel at the opposite side of the gulf, the chances were that no one would notice anything and the task could be accomplished quickly.

Ramage wrote a number against each of the ships on South-wick's chart.

"Jackson, six Marines and six seamen as boarders and eight men to row the gig; Stafford, the corporal and the other six Marines, six seamen and eight to row the launch . . ."

He thought a moment, and then added: "We'll have eighty men standing by, armed: they can go off in the cutters, pinnace and jolly-boat, if there's an emergency."

"Don't forget our men in the *Passe Partout*, sir."

"No, we're keeping her as our tender. She's one of the few in the convoy that could keep up with us going to windward!"

"Pity we couldn't have kept young Orsini in command of her."

"I thought about that, but he'll learn a great deal more by going to Gibraltar."

Southwick stumped from one side of the quarterdeck to the other, after putting his telescope on the chart to hold it down, and then said bitterly: "It's enough to make a saintly man swear."

He was talking to himself but a curious Ramage asked, "Has your rheumatism started again?"

"No, sir, it's just painful to look at eight prizes without being able to do anything about them."

"Well, our lads will only be losing the value of the hulls; most of them are laden with powder and shot. If they weren't bound for so many different ports, I'd think the French are planning a new campaign somewhere, but they're obviously just re-equip-ping garrisons."

"Aye, but it's a pity the Admiralty pay so poorly for French powder."

"Be fair! It's such poor quality you remember we changed it when we captured the *Calypso*."

"Oh, I know all that, sir," Southwick said. "And it's not the money either—thanks to you most of us have plenty of prize-money in the Funds now. It just seems a waste of ships."

"You would have sunk them all if you'd found the convoy at sea," Ramage pointed out, "and been very pleased with yourself."

"I suppose so, but we didn't find them at sea," Southwick said morosely, "we *sent* for them, using the Frogs' own semaphore!"

By nightfall Ramage was bored. Perhaps bored was the wrong word, because he was rarely bored. Unsettled would be more accurate, the jumpy feeling which always came when he had to stay on board while some of his men went off to meet the enemy. This time it really was "meeting," almost a social occasion, because with the Frenchmen from seven of the ships already taken on shore, there had been no shooting.

The moon would be rising in the next ten minutes; already the sky to the eastward had a golden tinge. Ah, there were the boats leaving the fifth ship and heading for the shore.

"We've been lucky with the weather," Southwick said as the two men stood at the quarterdeck rail. "With anything of a wind or sea, it'd take all night to get those men ashore. I wonder if the first of them have reached Cagliari yet."

"Not unless they ran all the way: it must be sixty miles or more, whether they go south round the coast or north to Iglésias and then across to Cagliari. They'll keep to the tracks; I can't see any of them climbing rows and rows of hills."

The boats were leaving the beach and at this distance, now the moon was over the hills and lighting the gulf, they looked like water beetles as they headed for the sixth ship, anchored close to Sant' Antioco. Ramage glanced over towards her and as he did so his eye caught sight of a dark patch to seaward.

Was it Isolotto la Vacca, the little rock just south of Sant' Antioco? No, he could see that, and this patch was small and much farther out to sea. A ship—perhaps one of Aitken's convoy returning?

"There's something out there, just south of Vacca," Ramage said to Southwick as he hurried aft to the binnacle box drawer to get the night-glass. He was back in a moment and resting his elbows on the capping of the rail to steady the glass.

"It's a ship . . ."

"What's her course, sir?"

"I think she's heading for the gulf . . . Blast this glass; it's hard to work out everything upside-down . . . Yes, she's on the starboard tack, the moon is lighting up her sails well. Not much wind out there . . . Yes, I have the line of her masts now . . . she's probably heading for Cala Piombo. That's about twelve miles from here at the south end of the gulf, isn't it?"

"Yes," Southwick said. "An easy anchorage to make for on a moonlit night 'cos you can pick up that tower."

Ramage concentrated for another minute or two, knowing it was very easy to make mistakes with the night-glass because, apart from showing ships upside-down, it also made them appear to be on the opposite tack.

"Our lads will have a long row down there with boats," Southwick said. "Still, if she sights us all anchored this end of the gulf, perhaps she'll change her mind and join us."

"That might be a mixed blessing," Ramage said grimly. "She's a French ship of the line."

CHAPTER SEVENTEEN

WHILE Southwick sent away the two cutters and pinnace to take off the French from the three remaining merchant ships and the jolly-boat rowed over to recall the gig and launch when they left the beach, the bosun's mates hurried through the *Calypso* sending the men to quarters.

Quickly and quietly they wetted and sanded the decks, put match tubs between the guns, half filling them with water, and set out larger tubs in which the sponges could be soaked when sponging out the guns. The gunner took the large, bronze magazine key from Ramage and went below to begin issuing flintlocks, lanyards, prickers and powder horns to each of the gun captains and be ready to issue cartridges to the powder boys.

Southwick was looking at his watch and cursing.

"We're lucky the dam' French 74 isn't steering for us; I've never known the men to take so long!"

"You must be patient," Ramage murmured, knowing his own reputation as the most impatient man in the ship. "Don't forget we hardly have a gun captain left on board: nearly all the men are doing someone else's job, and they're not used to it."

"Aye," Southwick admitted, "but they've been exercised enough at exchanging jobs."

"It's not the same. Telling every fourth man he's a casualty and making the rest move round is no good because each replacement sees what the previous man was doing."

"I hadn't thought of that," Southwick said, and Ramage admitted the thought had only just come to him. In future—if there was a future, with a ship of the line coming into the gulf like the door of a trap closing—he would start all exercise at the great guns by jumbling the men's numbers. Or perhaps just subtracting three, so everyone had to change.

He swung the glass back to the French ship. She was still well outside the gulf and clewing up her main and forecourse, so she would enter the gulf in a leisurely fashion under topsails alone. In this light breeze! If her bottom had the usual crop of barnacles and she was in fact making for Cala Piombo, or even the one to the north of it, she had at least fifteen miles to sail, and she must be making only three or four knots.

All that made sense. If the French captain had never been into the gulf before, he was coming in under the worst possible conditions (barring a gale, of course): running in at night before a west wind meant he was coming up to a lee shore and sailing straight towards a full moon still low on the horizon, so that all the hills and cliffs were shadowy, making it very difficult to judge distances. The land at six miles would look as though it was only three miles away.

In fact, Ramage realized, almost giving an audible sigh of relief, the *Calypso* herself would be indistinguishable against the shadow of the cliffs and hills behind her, which from the Frenchman's position were higher than her masts. The French 74 would spot some of the merchant ships anchored much farther out, but they would be easily identifiable; just the coasting vessels she would expect to find anchored for the night in a place like the Golfo di Palmas.

With the night-glass Ramage could see the jolly-boat, gig and launch returning to the *Calypso* from the beach and, a moment later, spotted one of the cutters leaving a merchantman. Only one? Then he detected movement beside another merchantman and saw the second cutter leave her and head for the shore. Either the men commanding the cutters were confident or disobedient, because both cutters were supposed to tackle a ship together . . . Well, as long as there were no flares or flashes of musketry to attract the attention of the 74, it did not matter. It was, he thought, the sort of thing young Orsini would do—or Martin. Or, he admitted, himself when he was a midshipman or lieutenant.

Southwick now went through what Ramage knew only too well as his disapproving ritual. First he took off his hat and scratched his head; then he ran his fingers through his flowing white hair to straighten it out; then he jammed his hat back on again, rubbed his stomach with a circular motion, as though trying to assist his digestion, and then gave a sharp sniff.

"We cut and run, eh, sir, as soon as she's anchored?"

It was, of course, the only sensible thing to do: they would be able to see the 74 anchoring down at the other end of the gulf and the moment she had an anchor down and was busy furling sails the *Calypso* would cut her cable—indeed, they could start weighing now if they wanted to avoid losing both anchor and cable—let fall her topsails and courses, and beat out of the gulf, staying as far to the north as possible: shaving between the south end of Sant' Antioco and Isolotto la Vacca. The Frenchman, eight or ten miles to the south, would never catch them . . .

"Seems a pity, doesn't it?" Ramage said casually, trying to remember the details in Orsini's list of the main cargoes carried by the remaining merchant ships. Aitken had gone off with the six ships carrying the most valuable cargoes; those left here at anchor, and which he had been intending to burn tomorrow, were stowed with mundane things like the poor-quality powder, whose prize value Southwick had just been bemoaning.

Half an hour later Ramage and Southwick finally reached a compromise in the quiet of the cabin, and Ramage admitted that it improved the chances of success. Ramage had first intended using one ship, which he would command, leaving Southwick on board the *Calypso*.

This had brought an immediate and explosive protest from the Master.

"Sir, I'm beginning to think you reckon me too old, or getting too stupid; this job is one for a lieutenant or master, not a post captain. I'm the only officer you have, but . . ."

"Nonsense," Ramage said, and to smooth Southwick's pride, freely admitted: "It's not lack of faith in you; I'm just being greedy."

Southwick had guessed that from the start, but he also knew that a display of injured pride represented his only chance of seeing any action tonight.

"Let me look at the list of cargoes again," Ramage said.

Orsini's writing, never very clear, had been little more than a scribble, done standing up as he talked to each master at Foix.

Most of the eight ships were carrying powder, but only two, the brigs *Muscade* and the *Merle*, carried any substantial quantity. The first had more than seventy-five tons on board, the second more than one hundred and fifty.

Ramage tried to picture one of them exploding. Unlike powder in a gun, where the only way the explosive force could go was up the barrel, powder stored in a ship's hold would explode in every direction; there was no way of aiming or channelling it.

It was like prize-fighting: if your opponent swayed back when you punched him on his jaw, much of the force of your blow was lost. But if you managed to hold his head with your left hand and then hit him with your right, you might not kill him but would certainly knock him out, because the full force of the blow would be concentrated on a small area. The crowd betting on him might well set about you with stools, bricks and walking canes, but you would have the satisfaction of winning the fight.

He needed exactly that for the attack on the French 74—a hand holding one side to avoid losing most of the effect of a merchantman exploding on the other.

The answer was, of course, to have a merchant ship exploding on each side at the same moment. And that was how the compromise came about.

"Who will you leave in command of the *Calypso*, sir?" Southwick asked.

"I've no choice: under the regulations it must be the next senior officer after you, which means the gunner."

Southwick gave a rumbling laugh that lasted a full minute. "The gunner!" he finally gasped unbelievingly. "He wouldn't even take responsibility for eight men and a jolly-boat, let alone command of one of the prizes in Aitken's convoy. Now he's going to be stuck with the *Calypso*. Sir," he asked pleadingly, "may I be the one to tell him?"

"Yes—and you'd better warn him that if neither of us comes back, he'll have to take the *Calypso* to Gibraltar."

"I think Bowen had better be standing by with some medicinal brandy!"

"You know, Bowen wouldn't even blink if I told him that he had to get the *Calypso* to Gibraltar."

"He certainly wouldn't," Southwick agreed, "but he's an unusual surgeon."

"Yes, and he can play chess."

Southwick grinned ruefully. "I'm getting the average down, sir; I doubt if I lose two games out of five to him these days."

"I'm glad of that, but we'd better start preparing those two ships. The Frenchman won't be inside the gulf for another half an hour, but it's going to take time for us to get the *Muscade* and the *Merle* down to Cala Piombo, if that's where she anchors."

"These blasted French names," Southwick grumbled, "what do they mean?"

"*Muscade* is nutmeg—I expect she was sailing to the spice islands of the West Indies before the war. *Merle* is simply 'blackbird.'"

Southwick nodded and picked up his hat. "I'll go up on deck and see where our French friend has got to. I expect you'll want to pick our men."

After the Master had gone, Ramage took a pencil. He did not need the muster book to choose the men. From what he could remember of the *Muscade* and the *Merle*, both were brigs of similar size, about two hundred and fifty tons. He had not considered them for Gibraltar because he guessed the Admiral would refuse to buy in French powder.

He and Southwick needed the minimum number of men for the operation to keep the boats light. Escaping afterwards would mean rowing like madmen for several minutes. The fastest boat was the gig, so Southwick should have it for the *Muscade*. He would take one of the cutters with the *Merle*.

There would be no seconds-in-command; it would be a brief voyage for both brigs. A man at the wheel, eight topmen, three men to handle grapnels, three more for sheets and braces, and then light fuses, and a boat-keeper, and that would be all. That made sixteen, seventeen adding in himself or Southwick. The gig carried sixteen, with eight at the oars, so each boat would be only two-thirds full. The same for the cutter. The totals did not allow for casualties, but that could not be helped.

Small arms? A few pistols and cutlasses, but there should be no fighting. They would need several axes, plenty of slowmatch, flint and steel, and some lanterns to light the film.

Southwick came down the companion-way and into the cabin as the sentry announced him.

"She's still about a mile or more outside the gulf beyond Sant' Antioco. She's not making more than a couple of knots under topsails."

"The Captain's nervous of the gulf all right, but he may not have a decent chart."

Ramage quickly outlined his plans and his orders for Southwick, who protested at being given the gig. "That's the captain's boat," he said. "You should have her, sir."

"I prefer a cutter, and anyway the boat carrying your weight has to be light."

Southwick grinned and patted his stomach. "Have you chosen your men yet, sir?"

"No—I'd like to have Jackson and Stafford, but I suggest you muster the topmen and divide them up. Some Marines for the slowmatch, seamen for the grapnels. Oh yes, and boat-keepers: as we're towing our boats they might get painters tangled . . ." There was no need to elaborate on that risk.

"Can I go and tell the gunner now, sir?"

Ramage grinned and nodded. "Then we'd better get over to our ships. At least we won't have to bother to weigh or buoy the anchor cables!"

Southwick paused a moment. "Ten minutes for the slow-match—isn't that rather long, sir?"

"Ten minutes is not a very long time to get everyone down into the boats and row a hundred yards."

"I suppose not, sir, but I was thinking of the French boarding and putting 'em out."

"They won't know where to look; they'll be taken by surprise
and will assume the Merle and Muscade are fire-ships, so they'll
be expecting flames."

Ramage scrambled up the side of the Merle, a pistol-butt grinding into his ribs, and followed by Jackson and the rest of the
men in the red cutter, leaving behind only the boat-keeper. He
kept the painter clear of the chain-wales and port-lids as another
of the men let the boat drift aft and then made up the rope on
a convenient cleat with a cheery: "You'll be best off if we make
any mistake wiv the powder!"

Two seamen held lanterns while another two swung big mauls
to drive out the wooden wedges holding the battens in place
round the edge of the coamings to free the heavy canvas cover
protecting the thick hatch boards.

"Just get out three boards," Ramage said, and the canvas was
rolled back enough for them to be lifted up.

Even the weak light of the lantern showed that Ramage's
guess had been right, and the powder had been stowed in the
aftermost of the brig's two holds: the copper hoops of the powder barrels reflected a dull redness. They were well stowed with
shifting boards. "Bung up and bilge free," Ramage thought to
himself: the bung of each barrel was uppermost, and none of the
barrels rested against the side, or the bilge, of the ship. A wise
shipper always paid a premium and specified that his goods, if
in barrels, should be stowed "bung up and bilge free," but the
master of a ship carrying so much powder needed no urging: a
bung working itself loose as the ship pitched would mean, if the
barrel was not stowed bung uppermost, that a sixth of a ton of
powder would cascade into the bilges and, despite the copper
hoops, if one barrel rubbed against another, it could cause sufficient friction to ignite a few grains—fewer than a dandy would
bother to blow from his sleeve if he spilled some snuff—and that
would be enough to destroy the ship.

The top tier of barrels was only three feet below the level of the hatch coaming, and Ramage looked round for Stafford.

"You have those lengths of fuse?"

"Aye aye, sir." Stafford held up a canvas bag.

The sight of the bag made Ramage angry again. He had asked the gunner for lengths of slowmatch that would burn ten minutes, with a foot left over at one end. The damned man had backed and filled, saying he could not be certain of the burning time of a length of slowmatch between five minutes and thirty. Finally Ramage had decided to use the much less rugged fuse, and fortunately the *Calypso*'s magazine contained two types made from mealed powder, the finest available. But again the gunner had avoided specifying the speeds at which they burned, and an enraged and frustrated Ramage had made the man bring up his notebooks and found that they recorded that fuse made from good mealed powder burned at the rate of three inches in seven seconds and the other twelve inches in one minute. Ramage chose the slower and had then given the whole coil to Jackson and Stafford. After doing a quick sum, he told them to cut ten eleven-foot lengths. That would give each one ten minutes' burning time, plus a foot.

Five lengths had been handed over to Southwick for the *Muscade*, and now Stafford had five lengths for the *Merle*. Fuse burned fast, so for this sort of work long lengths were needed; on the other hand, with the longer fuse, as Jackson had pointed out, there was the advantage that when the fuse was first lit the flame was farther from the powder.

Already two seamen were calling from the outboard end of the starboard maintopsail yardarm to a third standing below. Ramage heard a thud as a rope dropped, then the rattle of chain. They were fitting the first of the grapnels which would hang from all the yards at varying heights, ready to catch in the French 74's rigging or any hull projection so that the *Merle* stuck to her like a burr on a woollen sock.

The topmen, without awaiting orders, were already aloft, checking over the gaskets holding the sails furled and slackening them, and making sure of the lead of halyards. As soon as they finished their work, the grapnel men would trace the leads of braces, sheets and tacks.

After glancing at his watch by the light of the lantern that Jackson was carrying (Ramage and Southwick had decided that apart from the 74 being too far away to see any lights, it would be quite natural for lanterns to be in use on board merchant ships at anchor) he found they were several minutes ahead of the rough schedule.

Ramage went back to the opened hatch and found Stafford and another seaman, Wells, inside and grunting as they gently tapped out the bung of a powder barrel using a small copper-headed maul.

Stafford glanced up and saw Ramage standing in the moon-light looking down at him. "Yer know, sir, gives yer a funny feelin' sittin' on top o' a hunerd an' fifty tons o' powder!"

"I'm sure it does. Try standing," Ramage said unsympatheti-cally. "And even though I'm up here, I doubt if the extra inch of deck planking gives me much of an advantage."

"S'pose not, sir, but this bluddy bung . . . ah! Here she comes."

The moonlight was bright enough for Ramage to spot the small hole in the top of the barrel and see how carefully Stafford wiped the bung clean of powder and put it down beside the maul. Then he pushed a finger into the hole, obviously testing how far it was to the powder, which always shook down like flour in a jar.

"Four inches," he said to himself. "That means the fuse goes in eight inches. So a foot to spare were just right."

He moved so that he was astride another barrel.

"Let's 'ave the maul, 'Arry."

Again he began tapping to lift the bung of the new barrel, at the same time blowing gently to disperse any grains that came out with the copper-sheathed bung. Quickly he pulled it out, wiped off any traces of powder, and passed it and the maul to Wells.

"Three inches," he announced after putting his finger into the bunghole. He saw Ramage still watching him. "The French contractors seem 'onest enough, sir: they don't sell short measure."

"There are no contractors," Ramage said. "Like our Board of Ordnance, they make their own."

"Supposed to be poor stuff though, ain't it, sir?"

"Yes—but don't get careless! It burns all right, but not as evenly as ours. That means if you fire five rounds from the same gun at the same elevation you'll get first grazes at five different places."

"Well, we won't have to bother here," Stafford grunted as he slid carefully across to the third barrel and called for the maul.

Ramage walked aft to find Jackson turning the wheel one way and then the other. "Just testing the wheel ropes, sir. Six turns from hard over to hard over."

"You might look at the rudder-head and tiller, in case of rot . . ."

"Done that already, sir," Jackson said. "By the way, the three axes are ready on the foredeck beside the cable."

Slight movements in the rigging caught Ramage's eye, and he saw four grapnels spinning slightly in the breeze like dead carrion crows suspended outside a gamekeeper's lodge. The three men were now working out on the end of the foreyard, rigging the remaining grapnels.

Ramage walked forward to where the second anchor was stowed in its chocks. It was well lashed in its place so that a heavy sea should not dislodge it. Yet if the brig and the 74 collided, one of the flukes might well embed itself in the planking of the Frenchman's hull, a stroke of luck one could not rely on but might encourage. He told a seaman to collect an axe from the foredeck and cut some of the anchor lashings. He waited until the man returned and described which to cut, not wanting to see the anchor suddenly drop over the side, because its cable was stowed below.

He walked aft to the lantern, looked at his watch again and saw they should soon get under way.

"Six minutes to go!" he bellowed so that all the men could hear.

At the hatchway he saw that Stafford and Wells had removed five bungs, and that one thin black line, a fuse, already led from the deck outside the coaming, over the top and down into the hold to the bung-hole of a barrel, where it disappeared like an escaping snake. Stafford would have pushed the fuse well down into the powder, using precisely the extra foot of length, and it was held in place by an encircling collar of cloth pushed down round it, holding it steady in the centre of the bung-hole.

A Marine was now standing by the coaming: his job was to make sure no one accidentally touched a fuse so that its other end was pulled out of a barrel.

Yet it was all too obvious!

As Ramage stood there looking at the hatch he put himself in the place of a French officer jumping down on to the *Merle's* deck from the 74 and seeing five sparkling and sizzling fuses leading down into a partly-open hold. In that moment he would know the *Merle* was not a fire-ship about to burst into flames and that he risked nothing if he snatched out those burning fuses and tossed them over the side.

He waited as Wells, under Stafford's direction, draped one more length of fuse over the edge of the coaming, then a third, fourth and finally the fifth. After a few moments, Stafford and Wells climbed out of the hold. Stafford, mopping his face, saw Ramage and said: "It's remarkable 'ot down there, sir."

"Come over here—now take a good look at it," Ramage said without comment.

"Yus, I see what you mean, sir: the first Frog on board is going ter see fuses and guess . . ."

"Throw one of those hatch boards over the side, put down two again—leaving the gap against the coaming—and then pull the canvas cover back in place across the hatch, putting a roll in the edge so that it doesn't touch the fuses. Then I doubt if anyone jumping on board would spot anything in the excitement—the fuses should have burnt enough that they'd have gone under the canvas and out of sight."

"Come on, 'Arry," Stafford said, "but be very, very careful wiv those two planks."

Ramage looked again at his watch.

"Four minutes to go," he shouted. "Topmen aloft, axemen to the foredeck, helmsman to the wheel, grapnel men to the sheets and braces!"

He wondered if anyone else had ever given such a bizarre series of orders. He watched the men moving about, sure-footed as cats and as shadowy in the moonlight.

"Two minutes to go. Topmen, are you ready?"

There were shouts aloft from both masts.

"Axemen, are you ready?"

Three yells came aft from the foredeck.

"Grapnel men, are sheets and braces sorted out?"

Laughs and shouts gave him the answer.

He went back to the hatch and was startled by the change: it would take a very careful examination to reveal that anything had been done to the hold since it was stowed in France or Spain; five thin lines hung down a few inches, but in the darkness no one would notice them; the hatch looked battened down, ready for sea.

"Excellent, Stafford and Wells. You'd both make good smugglers!"

"Excise men, sir," protested Stafford. "Always on the side of the law, we are."

Jackson was waiting by the wheel and Ramage looked yet again at his watch.

"One minute to go . . . Stand by, axemen. Right, cut the cable!"

A series of thuds as the blades bit through the rope, a hiss of the cable snaking out the hawse and a splash as it dropped into the sea told him the *Merle* was adrift.

"Foretopmen—lay out—let fall!"

The fore-topsail tumbled down, the moon now high and bright enough to give the sail some colour.

Slowly he went through the sequence of orders that set the brig's topsails and then the courses; orders that were adapted to the few men available. Jackson at the wheel needed no orders; he had already noted the approximate position of the French 74, although she was now too far away to see and had probably furled all her sails so that she did not show up against the hills and cliffs.

Ramage went aft to the taffrail and looked down at the cutter. The boat-keeper was asleep, lying curled up in the sternsheets. The painter was hanging clear, free of kinks, and Ramage decided to leave him, telling Jackson to give the man a hail once they neared the enemy.

Inshore, lit up by the moon, Ramage could see the *Muscade* under way on a parallel course and imagined Southwick looking across to make sure the *Merle* was all right.

Jackson said quietly: "It's made Mr Southwick ten years younger, sir."

"Has it really?" Ramage was startled at the remark because he had been so busy during the last hour on board the *Calypso* that, although he had been giving orders to Southwick—not many, because they were not necessary—he had not had time to notice his appearance.

"You know how it does, once he knows he's going to be able to get into a fight, sir," Jackson reminded him.

"But this isn't going to be a fight," Ramage said, finding himself puzzled again. "As I told you all before we left the *Calypso,* if the French capture us they'll treat the brigs as fire-ships and hang us all."

"Yes, sir," Jackson said in the stolid way that seamen had perfected over the centuries when they answered officers who clearly did not understand the situation.

The men at the sheets and braces had the sails properly trimmed, the topmen were down on deck and the axemen were hoisting the headsails. Soon they too were sheeted home, and the only man doing any work on board the *Merle* was Jackson, who turned the wheel occasionally a spoke one way and then another as he watched the luffs of the sails.

"Harvest moon," Jackson noted laconically, nodding his head to the east, where the full moon was now a golden disc well clear of the hills.

"Yes, the seasons race by. We're getting old, Jackson!"

"I was fighting the British afore you were born, sir," Jackson said dryly.

"If you live to a real ripe old age," Ramage said with affected seriousness, "you can come and work for me: I'll find you a simple job on the estate—like sawing up the big logs for winter."

"How many fireplaces would that be, sir?"

"Only a dozen or two, and the kitchens," Ramage said.

"So I can look forward to an interesting and restful old age."

"Yes," Ramage said, "we both can. You can vary the length of the logs and I'll measure them. We need to stay alive, that's all."

"I'll tell Stafford that if he turns up at the gates of Blazey Hall when he's seventy he might get a job, too."

"As long as he brings his own saw."

"Perhaps Rossi could start younger," Jackson said, his face expressionless. "The Marchesa might like to hear him singing and cursing in Italian from time to time."

Ramage ignored the implication of Jackson's remark, but it started him thinking. Stafford at the age of seventy—that would be in about forty years' time. By then young Lord Ramage would have inherited his father's title and be the ancient and eleventh Earl of Blazey, nearly seventy himself. Who would be the Countess of Blazey? Who would he have married? She might even be a widow by then. Or more likely Lord Ramage would, in the phrase so beloved by lawyers and biographers, have pre-deceased his father, his head long since knocked off by a round shot, and the earldom of Blazey, the second oldest in the country, would have become extinct, or been revived and given to some shoddy politician who caught the King's fancy.

He walked aft to throw off the gloomy thoughts, though he felt no embarrassment or irritation: standing on top of one hundred and fifty tons of gunpowder with fuses leading down into the hold, and steering for an enemy ship of the line, meant that anyone with the slightest imagination could be forgiven for a few passing reflections on mortality. Yet making a habit of reflecting on mortality was a quick way of driving a man to seek answers in the bottle. Anyway, he thought as he glanced down at the still sleeping boat-keeper, it is a glorious warm night with a steady breeze. Jackson's harvest moon, and an unsuspecting enemy just down the coast, with Southwick and the other brig abeam. Aitken and his convoy would by now be well on their way to Gibraltar safe from interference because they were sailing under the French flag . . . The *Calypso* seemed distant, another world. Paolo would have enjoyed being on this expedition, but he was learning more in Aitken's convoy.

Ramage sat down on the breech of one of the two 6-pounder stern-chase guns and looked at his watch. Two hours past midnight. The wind might have freshened a little, but the brigs were slow, and if the damned jibs did not stop slatting he would drop them. They had almost a soldier's wind so that for most of the time the headsails were blanketed by the forecourse. He knew he was now getting jumpy; when the slatting of sails irritated him, it was time to relax. He began walking forward to talk to the men.

Stafford and 'Arry—everyone, including Southwick and Aitken, always referred to him by that name—and the Marine guarding the ends of the fuses were sitting on the deck, their backs against the hatch coaming, and 'Arry was just finishing some lurid story concerning another man's wife in Scarborough: a woman, it seemed, possessed of inordinate desires and a weary and pliant husband.

"The three of you had better repeat to me what your orders are."

They looked at each other and Ramage pointed to the Marine, whose style of speaking derived much from the drill sergeants under whom he had served in the past.

"Hupon the horder 'Light fuses!' sir—that'll be from you—I 'old the lantern hopen in such a position that William Stafford, hable seaman, and 'Arry, hordinary seaman, can happly the end of each fuse to the candle flame. I make sure each fuse is burning steady an' when Stafford 'as hassured 'imself as well, we run like 'ell to the boat, which will be halongside the larboard quarter."

Stafford grunted. "An' we proceed to row like 'ell out of range an' back to the *Calypso*."

"You're sure you've used exactly a foot of fuse in fitting each one into a barrel?" Ramage asked him.

Stafford scrabbled about on the deck and then stood up, proffering a wooden stick with a fork cut in one end. "It's exactly eleven inches to the cleft, sir; I cut it meself. First I measured orf a foot o' fuse, nipped it with finger and thumb, then used this 'ere fork in the end to 'old a bight of fuse while I pushed it down into the barrel. It takes an inch to fit in the fork. Before I pulled the stick out I pressed the powder down 'ard wiv my fingers, and then once the stick was out I pressed down again, so the fuse is firm in the powder. Then we wound rags round like a bandage to 'old the fuse steady in the centre of the bung-hole."

The Cockney could have answered Ramage's question with a simple "Yes sir," but the fact that he had been sensible enough to get a stick of the right length and make a fork in the end showed that he was not blindly obeying orders.

"That was a good idea," Ramage said. "We need explode only

one barrel to send off the rest, but with fuses to five barrels we have five insurance policies."

The three grapnel men were sitting by the foremast on the starboard side, their grapnels swinging and spinning at various heights above them.

"One last check," Ramage said. "You've slung the grapnels at the right heights, so tell me what you do as we go alongside our French friends."

"I'm out on the foreyardarm, sir," one man said promptly, "an' I make sure the grapnels are swinging so they 'ook on."

"And then?" prompted Ramage.

"Well, that's all, sir."

"No, it's not, Smith, unless you want one hundred and fifty tons of powder to blow you over the moon."

"Oh yes," the seaman said sheepishly, "as soon as we hear you shout 'Abandon ship,' or we see the grapnels are securely hooked on, we bolt for the boat, sir."

"Which will be . . . ?"

"Larboard quarter, sir."

Ramage went on to find the three axemen, who were chatting with the topmen at the foot of the foremast. Having singled them out, he asked them about their remaining duties.

O'Rorke, who despite his name and the impression it gave of an Irish giant was a small, nimble man from Boston in Lincolnshire, who had first gone to sea as a young boy in the colliers bringing coal from the northern ports down to the Thames, took a pace forward.

"Grapnels, sir," he said at once. "As we go alongside we try and toss extra grapnels on board. Extra to the ones rigged from the yards."

"Are your grapnels ready?"

"Yes, sir, we've got two each; a fathom of chain and then rope on each one. The bitter end of the rope is made fast to something solid."

"And where have you got them?"

"Well, two on the fo'c's'le, sir. They're my two, on account of me being reckoned a good thrower. Longish ropes on my grapnels so we don't snub in the *Merle*'s bow too sharp. Two more by the forechains: Hurst here will be standing on the chains—"

"No," Ramage interrupted. "Hurst, you stay inside the ship: if we run alongside the Frenchman, you'd be crushed standing in the chains. And you, Gough," he said to the third man, "were you going to be standing in the main chains? Well, don't. I appreciate both of you are picking the best places, but you'll get killed. I can't lose two men—I want to be rowed back to the *Calypso* in time for a good breakfast!"

The three men laughed and two of them excused themselves, so that they could change the positions of their grapnels. Ramage, with a call to the topmen not to wait about once they heard "Abandon ship!" walked back to the wheel, pausing by the lantern to look at his watch. More than an hour had passed and he looked forward in alarm.

The cliffs of the headland north of Cala Piombo showed up well, and he could just make out the Torre di Cala Piombo like a thin tree stump on the top of a round hill. A dark blob this side of it showed where the French 74 was swinging to her anchor. Waiting for a convoy? Ramage speculated. Or perhaps expecting more 74s and attendant frigates to join her. Ramage wished he had not started wondering, in case any of them began to arrive.

The *Muscade* had slowly passed across the *Merle*'s stern so that as planned she was now on her seaward side. The French 74 would be windrode and heading westward, out of the gulf. Southwick would go alongside so that his larboard side would be against the Frenchman's larboard, his bow towards the 74's stern, while Ramage and the *Merle* would go starboard side on to her starboard. It was an elementary manoeuvre though, in battle, ships normally fought bow to bow and stern to stern.

Ramage could now see the 74, or rather her black blur, as a

more definite shape against the jagged cliffs anchored perhaps a mile from the shore and well placed in the bay so that the headlands protected her from winds and swells.

What sort of an anchor watch would the French be keeping? With the wind light from the west and the moon still rising in the east, the *Merle* and *Muscade* had two great advantages: first, coming from the dark half of the horizon they were approaching an enemy who loomed up stark against the moon, and second they had a following wind with no worry about how the brigs would beat out again.

The gap between the *Merle* and the *Muscade* was slowly narrowing: each ship was sailing up the side of a long, invisible triangle lying flat on the sea which had the 74 at its apex. Now they were a mile apart; soon they would be separated by only the width of the French ship.

Stafford had both lanterns hidden abaft the mainmast so their light could not be seen from ahead, and from the sound of it was lecturing 'Arry and the Marine about the finer points of picking locks. Having served an apprenticeship as a locksmith and been taken up by the press-gang while he was making a living at it—by working at night, Ramage understood, and without the owners of the locks knowing about it—Stafford was undoubtedly an expert.

The Marine, Albert Coke, was naturally berthed aft with the rest of the Marines in the *Calypso,* between the seamen and the officers, and his duties meant he did not mix so much with the seamen. This night's work with Stafford and 'Arry was, Ramage could tell, quite an experience. Hearing first-hand accounts of burgling expeditions against "some o' the best 'ouses in London"— a phrase Ramage had often heard Stafford use in the past when being teased by Jackson and Rossi—was obviously a new experience for Albert Coke.

Looking ahead, Ramage could see why they were now fast approaching the coast—or, rather, at night one always seemed to be going faster, although the speed remained the same. It was one of the tricks played by shadow, and with a moon this bright the shadow made the cliffs look like jagged pieces of coal held close to the face.

This time—indeed, for the first time ever that he could remember—he was approaching an enemy ship without sending the men to quarters. They were already as prepared for action as ever they could be, and their weapons were simply grapnels and lanterns, and some lengths of fuse . . . None of the *Merle*'s sixpounders would be fired; no muskets were even loaded. There was far too much danger, with all that powder about, for there to be any guns discharged in the *Merle*, although a few men had pistols in case of trouble later.

He thought for a moment what would happen if the French were suspicious and opened fire. A French round shot through the side of the *Merle* and into those barrels of powder would— well, they would know nothing about it although people would see the flash for fifty miles or more. The rumble might well wake up the mayor of Cagliari, who would assume there had been yet another earthquake.

C H A P T E R E I G H T E E N

ONCE again Ramage took out his watch—the hands were easy to see in the moonlight. He was not really interested in the time; he wanted to clear his mind of depressing thoughts, like approaching a French 74 in a brig laden with one hundred and fifty tons of powder. Time was of no consequence now; only distances mattered. The French ship—it was irritating not to know her name—was perhaps a mile away: the distance was difficult to judge because she was bow-on and against the black cliffs. A mile, say, and the *Merle* was making about four knots. In fifteen minutes it should be all over, one way or another.

He joined Jackson and bent over the compass, taking a rough

bearing of the *Muscade* and then of the French 74. He could imagine Southwick doing the same on board the *Muscade*.

The enemy a mile away to leeward: soon he would not be able to shout, except for the final orders in the last mad moments, in case the French heard the English words. So now was the time for his little speech; the one the men always seemed to expect, even though the words could only be banal.

"Calypsos," he called, "we have slightly less than a quarter of an hour to go." Surprising how being rather precise about the time gave the impression of carefully measured sextant angles of the Frenchman's mainmasthead and calculations using tables.

"I'm sure you can all see our target, and you can see the *Muscade* over on our starboard beam. The *Merle* and the *Muscade* are the two jaws of a pair of nutcrackers. You can see the nut dead ahead, almost in the shadow of the cliff. The only nut ever cracked with more than two hundred tons of powder!

"But our nutcrackers will probably only work if we get the nut squarely between us. We can rely on Mr Southwick and the *Muscade*. As far as the *Merle* is concerned, we have very little to do, but it has to be done correctly.

"First, I have to get this ship alongside that 74. If I go wrong, I expect Jackson will put me right." That drew a laugh from all the men, who knew that the pair of them had been in action together several dozen times.

"As I'm doing that, topmen will be clewing up the maintopsail and then the fore-topsail. Before that—in five minutes' time—you'll have furled the fore and main courses.

"You grapnel men will hook us on with at least six grapnels." He had to pause as the other men jeered and the grapnel men protested their skill. "As soon as the topsails are clewed up and the grapnels hooked on, Stafford and 'Arry will—when I give the order—light the fuses.

"By that time the boat-keeper, who at the moment is astern in the cutter, fast asleep, will with Jackson's help have the cutter ready alongside the larboard quarter. As soon as I hear from Stafford that the fuses are burning steadily, I shall order 'Abandon ship,' and we get down into the cutter and row seaward very quickly. Seaward because the French will find it harder to fire at us with muskets from over their bow, and because it is darker to seaward.

"If there is any problem with the fuses, we'll leave Stafford behind to deal with it because he has such nimble fingers."

Again that brought laughter and some teasing of Stafford, and when the men were quiet again Ramage said: "From now on, no more talking; sound carries on a night like this, and we want the sentries and lookouts in that 74 to remain merely curious why a couple of their brigs are coming up to them; we don't want 'em too suspicious. Not until we're alongside, anyway, when we'll allow them to begin to wonder!"

He looked across at the *Muscade* and then ahead at the Frenchmen. It was time to take in the courses.

"Man the main and fore clew garnets, buntlines and leechlines," he called, and within minutes the *Merle's* two biggest sails were furled on the yards. It was as if a great door had been opened forward: now he had an uninterrupted view of the sea and sky and the land: the orange disc of the moon, the hard black, wavy shadow of hills and cliffs, and the hint of a white line where waves were breaking and swirling among the rocks, like a hinge between the sea and the sky.

The French ship of the line was getting large now: first her royal masts, thin and spidery, rose above the dark hills behind; then Ramage could make out her topmasts and yards. And as he watched he could see out of the corner of his eye the *Muscade* exactly in position in relation to the *Merle;* both brigs were approaching the apex of the triangle.

Were ten minutes enough for them to get clear in the boats? He began to wonder, and the more he thought about it the more he wished he had added another five minutes. Southwick, for example, was not as nimble as the young seamen, and he would insist on being the last down into the gig.

What kind of explosion would one hundred and fifty tons of powder make, plus seventy-five tons on the other side? And—he realized his mistake in forgetting it—all the powder in the French ship's magazine: that would go up too, and she was unlikely to be carrying less than fifty tons. There would be something approaching a tidal wave; they would have to watch out for it as they fled. To be pooped by the tidal wave you caused yourself would be the crowning, or drowning, irony.

He could make out almost every detail of the Frenchman now: the rigging was black lace, like fishing nets drying on stakes, the yards the bare boughs of a tree in winter. The ship was swinging slightly from odd wind currents bouncing off the hills, or eddies as the sea rebounded from the base of the cliffs. Just enough of a swing that neither he nor Southwick would be able to approach on a course parallel with the Frenchman's centre-line; they would have to come in at a slight angle so that they could avoid her jib-boom and bowsprit if she swung, jinking by putting their helms over at the last moment so the brigs turned inwards, like two arms clasping a package.

The French ship was all black: she swung just enough for him to see that she had no strake of light colour or white to pick out the sheer. Her port-lids were closed so the guns were neither loaded nor run out. Her yards were not square—but then she was French, and if she stayed there at anchor for a week, they would still be almost a'cockbill. Southwick will already have noticed that!

She was lying to a single anchor; that was obvious from the slight swing, but Ramage thought he could make out the cable on the larboard bow. That too would make sense if she anticipated wind and swell from the south.

No shout and no challenge. Had the brigs been ships of war they would have had to be ready to answer the night challenge—lanterns arranged in a particular pattern—with an answer that differed only in the positions of the lanterns; but merchant ships were issued with neither challenge nor reply.

"Are you ready there at the fuses, Stafford?"

"Aye aye, sir; we have two lanterns."

He looked up at the main-yard and, making a trumpet with his hands, called softly: "Man the fore and maintopsail clew-lines and buntlines . . . Hands stand by the sheets . . ."

The ship of the line was now fine on the starboard bow.

"That's as far as she swings to starboard?" he asked Jackson.

"Yes, sir. I've been steering on that."

"You may have to come up a point at the last moment—"

"Sir—look at the *Muscade!*"

Stafford was calling urgently from the hatch and Ramage looked over to find Southwick's brig drawing aft and heeling over to larboard. No, not just drawing aft but being left astern!

She was listing, not heeling; the end of her main-yard must be almost in the water. Had she sprung a sudden leak? Was she capsizing? But even as he watched, almost rigid with apprehension, Ramage saw she was up by the bow and was not listing more: she seemed immovable. Obviously she had just sailed into a rock or on to a reef with enough force to lift up her bow; then she must have rolled over enough to heel the ship.

Suddenly the yards swung fore and aft and Ramage saw her topsails fluttering like shaken towels as sheets were cut and braces let fly to ease the pressure on the canvas and the masts.

Ahead the French 74 was anchored not more than five hundred yards from the *Merle,* and as he recovered from the shock of the *Muscade* and decided it was too late to worry whether there were reefs between the *Merle* and the enemy, Ramage realized that his nutcracker plan was ruined; the nutcrackers had lost one arm; there was now no way of squeezing from both sides.

Five hundred yards to go . . . Should he bear up and beat out of the gulf, picking up Southwick and his men as he went? If so he had to give the order to Jackson at this very moment— and he had to get both topsails and courses drawing again.

No, the fact that Southwick's brig had hit a rock was no reason why a French 74 should escape destruction, and the nutcracker plan was not the only way of doing it.

In fact, it was a dam' silly way: from her very shape and the thickness of futtocks and planking, the sides of a ship of the line were enormously strong; not only were all her guns arranged along her sides, firing out through the gun ports, but that was where she was designed to receive all the punishment in the usual battle of broadsides.

Any ship-of-war's weakest point was her bow: there the stays came down from the masts to the bowsprit and jib-boom; wrench away those two spars and there was a good chance of bringing down the foremast. And the ship, because of the batten-and-canvas bulkheads, was open from bow to stern. The bow itself was strong enough to withstand a heavy sea, but everyone feared being raked—having a broadside (or even a single gun) fired through the bow or into the stern so that the shot swept the unprotected length of the ship.

Very well, that 74's bow was like a bull's nose, the most tender spot.

"Calypsos!" Ramage yelled, "change of plan! We're not going alongside, we'll just—" But he broke off; there was no time to finish the sentence without creating confusion.

It was essential at times like this to remember that the ship's bow turned the opposite way to the wheel order.

"Hard a' port!" he snapped at Jackson, and as the American spun the wheel the brig's bow began to swing to starboard towards the French 74's jib-boom, which stuck out like a fishing rod from a river bank, moving gently across the horizon.

As soon as he was sure the brig was really swinging he said calmly: "Now up with the helm, Jackson, and jam us athwart his hawse!"

The American gave a bloodcurdling laugh as he spun the wheel the opposite way and the brig's bow started to swing back to larboard, so that the little ship began skidding sideways through the water, pivoting with rudder acting against sail, ensuring that she would smash at right angles across the Frenchman's bow, with that great jib-boom holding the *Merle* far more securely than a hundred grapnels.

"Hold tight, Calypsos!" Ramage yelled. "Secure those lanterns, Stafford!"

Then the crash came: like an enormous lance the 74's jib-boom rammed into the shrouds of the foremast and as the *Merle* slewed slightly, tore out the brig's whole mast with a crackling and rending that made Ramage think of a forest of dead trees toppling.

Then the *Merle* came to a stop. Towering above her starboard side was the French ship's bow, stark against the moonlight and now alive with shouts and hysterical challenges in French.

"Stafford—light the fuses!"

Then to Jackson: "Get the boat alongside!"

To the men forward: "Topmen, grapnel men, sheetmen—come aft!"

There was a light forward, then another. Stafford and 'Arry and the Marine Albert Coke were busy with the lanterns.

Jackson was cursing somewhere aft, cursing fluently at the boat-keeper. They had forgotten to waken him up, and now Jackson was having to waste precious seconds as the sleepy man kept the painter clear while Jackson hauled.

Now the French were screaming down at the *Merle*. They still did not realize they were being attacked; they thought that a clumsy French merchant ship had accidentally misjudged wind or current and become stuck athwart their hawse.

"I'm sorry, Captain!" Ramage shouted up in French. "I will come on board to make my apologies! What? Yes, Admiral, I will try to disengage myself this minute! Yes, sir—"

Stafford was nudging him. "Excuse me, sir, all the fuses are burnin' merrily . . ."

"Abandon ship!" Ramage bellowed. "Down into the cutter, m'lads, and then row like madmen!"

As he stood on the afterdeck of the little brig he was almost startled by the comparative silence that had suddenly come over the ship. The Frenchman's jib-boom creaked as it was pulled down by the weight of the *Merle*'s foremast and rigging, which still hung from it, and the *Merle*'s hull was grinding against the great ship's stem, but just round him, in the brig herself, there was only the thumping of bare feet running across the deck.

Ramage walked over to where Jackson had the cutter's painter hitched round a kevel.

"Two men missing, sir; I'm counting them."

How many minutes had elapsed since the fuses had been lit?

"Get down in the boat and wait three minutes, and then row away—"

"What are you—?"

"Do as you're told," Ramage snapped and ran forward, snatching up one of the lanterns as he passed the hatch, noting that the burning ends of the fuses were already halfway up the coaming.

He made for the wreckage of the foremast and as he approached he could hear the muffled voice of a man swearing.

"Where are you?"

"Here, sir, some bluddy ratlines have tangled me up."

Ramage put down the lantern and began feverishly hauling at the rope, suddenly conscious that Jackson was beside him. "Where's the other one, sir?"

By now Ramage had burrowed into the tangled rope and was within a few inches of the trapped man. "There's someone else missing—have you seen him?" Ramage shouted.

"Oh, that'll be Hobbs, sir," the man replied. "He was up on the yard. He got tossed overboard when the mast went, sir. I heard him shoutin' in the water."

With that, Jackson helped Ramage wrench the last of the ropes clear of the man and grabbed an arm to pull him to his feet. The man fell flat again with a grunt of pain.

"My leg, sir, I think it's busted. Leave me 'ere, sir, you'll all get blown up!"

"Lift him," Ramage told Jackson. "Now sling him over my shoulder."

Together Captain and coxswain staggered aft with the injured man. Jackson sniffed as they passed the hatch. "Those fuses are cooking well, sir."

Finally they had nearly reached the quarter when Stafford, 'Arry and several other seamen reached them.

"Come on, sir," Stafford said in an offended voice as he and 'Arry seized the injured man, "we wondered where you an' Jacko had gone."

Quickly they lowered the man into the cutter.

"Has anyone seen Hobbs swimming around?" Ramage shouted.

"I'm 'ere, sir," Hobbs said. "I swam round and was first in the boat!"

"Cast off," Ramage told Jackson. "Now, let's say goodbye to the *Merle!*"

With two men at each oar the cutter leapt through the water and as he looked astern Ramage was surprised how small the brig now seemed, jammed across the 74's bow.

"Didn't even break off the Frenchman's jib-boom," Jackson said, having a quick glance himself.

"But sent our foremast by the board without much effort," Ramage said. "Steer for the *Muscade:* I want to be sure Mr Southwick's gig hasn't been stove in."

Ramage looked round for the man with the broken leg. "We'll get a seizing on that as soon as possible."

"Don't you bother 'bout me," the seaman said cheerfully. "I just want to be far enough away to get a good view of the bang."

The words were hardly out of his mouth before a great flash like lightning lit every hill and mountain, showing an enormous column of eerily green water mushrooming from where the ships had been and followed a moment later by an echoing thunder-clap which made their ears sing and a blast that Ramage thought would burst their eardrums.

For a few moments there was stunned silence and then, as gulls began mewing, Stafford said: "Blimey, it's raining!"

The sky was clear. Ramage realized that they were being showered by spray from the explosion. And if there was spray—

"Duck!" he shouted. "Crouch down below the thwarts." At the same moment he launched himself across the body of the man with the broken leg.

Then pieces of wreckage from the *Merle* and the French ship of the line began falling from the sky as though an avalanche of trees was sweeping a mountain pass.

Finally it stopped and, with his night vision completely destroyed by the flash, Ramage was thankful for the moon to give him a sense of direction. The men resumed their places at the thwarts and Ramage found that only one couple had let go of their oar, which was quickly fished back on board.

"Right, let's find Mr Southwick and see what he thinks of our firework display."

"Beats anyfing I ever saw at Vauxhall Gardens," Stafford admitted, "but I fink I bin permentually deafened."

"'Permanently,'" Jackson corrected automatically. "No, it'll soon go, more's the pity."

Southwick and the gig saw the cutter first against the moon and hailed, and five minutes later both boats were lying along-side each other, the two crews exchanging stories.

Southwick scrambled into the cutter. "I'm sorry, sir, I let you down," he said sheepishly, "but I swear that reef isn't on the chart!"

"I know it isn't, and it's lucky we both didn't hit it. Anyway, we all overestimated the amount of powder needed!"

"I'm ashamed to say we had the best view, sir," the Master said. "And we knew you had escaped in time because we caught sight of the cutter in the flash. But the water it threw up—it even drifted down to us, and we're to windward. And the wreckage! We could see yards and great baulks of timber landing hundreds of yards away. The splashes showed up in the moonlight."

"The wreckage missed us," Ramage said thankfully, "but there were some enormous lumps crashing round. Well, by the time we get to the *Calypso* I'll be ready for breakfast."

CHAPTER NINETEEN

B Y NOON the *Calypso*'s Surgeon, Bowen, came to Ramage's cabin to report that Palmer, the seaman with a broken leg, was resting comfortably. "I gave him a drop of medicinal brandy, sir."

"Ah, so much better than the ordinary sort."

"Ah, yes indeed; it eases the pain like other spirits, but the seamen taste it so rarely that its effect seems magical," Bowen said with a straight face.

Ramage thought back. How long ago? It had been two or three years since Bowen had joined Ramage's ship and proved to be an alcoholic. A brilliant surgeon, he had had a flourishing practice in Wimpole Street until his patients were scared away by his drinking. Finally an impoverished wreck of a man went to the Navy, the only people who would pay him for practising his profession—and let him buy his liquor duty-free . . . But by chance Bowen had been sent to serve in a ship commanded by Lieutenant Ramage.

What followed had been desperate for Bowen and thoroughly unpleasant for Ramage and Southwick, but Ramage, having neither the time nor the authority to get rid of Bowen because the ship had to sail at once for the West Indies, was determined that his seamen's lives should not be in the hands of a permanently drunken surgeon. So once at sea he and Southwick had cured

Bowen by cutting off his liquor. It had been a dreadful night-
mare for them all; for days Bowen had been ravaged by delirium
tremens; during the worst hours when they sat with him both
Ramage and Southwick had themselves almost seen the imagi-
nary horrors that attacked the struggling, fevered man. And
finally it had been all over; Bowen was cured and now never
touched spirits; he could sit down to dinner and pass the wine
and prescribe medicinal brandy. He viewed the world with a clear
eye and, when needed, used a scalpel with a hand that did not
tremble.

"Palmer would like to see you, sir."

"Yes, I was going to call in the sick bay. I see you have no
other customers," he said, holding up Bowen's daily report. "It's
amazing how the prospect of action cures costive complaints and
rheumatic pains!"

"If we were in action once a week, I could retire and spend
my time working out chess problems," Bowen admitted. "When
you go into battle you have so few casualties that you won't get
rapid promotion, sir," he added dryly. "The Admiralty seem to
judge a captain's ability and bravery by the size of his butcher's
bill."

"I know," Ramage said evenly, "that's obvious from the des-
patches published in the *Gazette* and the subsequent promotions.
However, if the price of getting the command of a 74 is having
a thousand men killed and wounded round me over the years,
I'll happily stay with a frigate."

"Palmer wants to see Jackson as well. He won't tell me why."

"They're probably friends and Jackson knows where he's hidden his tobacco!"

"It's not that; it's as if he owes both of you money and can't
repay it."

Ramage shook his head, puzzled. "You're sure that the pain,
or the brandy, has not left him—well, a bit off his head?"

"No, he's sane enough. How did it happen—the broken leg?
He's not too sure."

"If he isn't sure then we'll never know. When we collided with the French 74, her jib-boom sent our foremast by the board and somehow Palmer was trapped in the rigging."

"How did he escape?"

"Some men pulled him out."

"After the fuses had been lit?"

"Yes, but they had plenty of time."

"Palmer didn't think so. You and Jackson, I suppose."

Ramage shrugged his shoulders. "The rest of the men were already in the boat."

"The Admiralty might say that when it comes to choosing between the life of one of its best young captains or an ordinary seaman with a broken leg, the captain comes first, sir."

"Probably," Ramage said dryly, "but the Admiralty are not responsible for taking the ship into action or the well-being of her men. Come along, we'll get Jackson and then see Palmer."

Ramage came up on deck to find the launch, pinnace and both cutters streaming astern, and forty or fifty men waiting in the waist of the ship after having been inspected by Southwick.

The Master came up to him. "I wonder how many masters have gone off to start destroying six ships at anchor, sir."

"Not many. In fact you may be the first, but the gunner and I will be following. What a waste of ships . . ."

"At least we know six of the largest are on their way to Gibraltar with Aitken, otherwise I'd be scuttling more," Southwick commented. "You're definitely keeping the *Passe Partout,* sir?"

"Yes, she may come in useful. She helps our disguise, too. A French frigate with a tartane in company is just what another French frigate would expect to see."

"By the way, sir, we know the name of that 74 now. She had it painted on a board at the entry port, and a couple of the men read it. *Scipion,* sir. Seems a funny sort of name, but they're sure of it."

"I know the name," Ramage said. "She's in the French List of Ships. Built at Toulon since the war, I believe. In fact she must be one of their newest ships of the line."

"Can I tell the men, sir?"

"Yes. I wonder if she was a flagship."

Southwick paused, took off his hat to run his fingers through his hair, and then gave a sniff to indicate his irritation. "We'll never know that now, unless the *Moniteur* reports it. That's the worst of blowing a ship to pieces; one doesn't get prisoners."

The boats left the *Calypso* and went to the anchored merchant ships. Ramage, thoroughly exasperated by the gunner, had given him those carrying powder but, weakening at the last moment, had told him he could scuttle them instead of blowing them up.

Ramage had noticed that at the north end of the gulf, to leeward of several of the merchant ships and near some huts, a group of fishermen were watching. At least, he assumed they were fishermen because they were near some fishing boats drawn up on the beach.

The fishermen must only just be scraping a living. The soil was barren; apart from olives, he had seen a few fig trees and vine terraces, so the harvest had to come from the sea. One of the French brigs to be scuttled carried a general cargo—everything from pots and pans to bales of hides, olive oil to sugar.

He had told Southwick to leave the brig to him, and not to be surprised if he saw it set a foresail. Taking Jackson, Stafford and a dozen seamen with him in the gig, he went over to the brig, saw that in fact she was lying to windward of the flat stretch of shore that the fishermen had taken as their village, and ordered the brig's cable to be cut.

With the gig towing astern, they watched as the brig drifted inshore under the windage on her hull and spars. They were a mile from the beach when a random current, flowing between the mainland and the island of Sant' Antioco, caught her and began to carry her northwards.

"Let fall the fore-topsail," Ramage said, "and get it drawing.

Jackson, take the wheel and steer for the fishermen's beach."

The seamen were going about their various tasks but obviously they were puzzled, and Ramage shouted to them: "Those fishermen over there: this ship represents a king's ransom to them, and we were going to scuttle her. We might just as well let her run up on the beach—no one will ever get her off again, and the fishermen can take their pickings as a reward for not bothering us. They're neutral, anyway."

Were they? Ramage suddenly found himself far from sure. About eighty years ago Savoy and Austria exchanged Sicily and Sardinia, so Sardinia now belonged to Savoy. But Savoy was at present under the French . . . Anyway, the only practical attitude to adopt was that anyone who did not shoot at you was friendly or neutral, and as a convoy anchorage it did not matter.

Jackson was far from impressed. "If we landed on their beach as survivors they'd have the shirts off our backs, sir; I can't see them giving us dinner."

"Think about all those Frenchmen we landed, then; they won't have been given a rotten fishhead or an empty wine fiasco to help them on the road to Cagliari."

"That's true, sir." The thought brought a grin to Jackson's face.

"And everyone speaking to them in Italian . . ."

Jackson nodded; he tended to forget the Captain spoke good Italian, and the effect that this could have.

"Can you put on a Sardinian accent, sir?"

"The *Sardi* . . . in this island alone there are probably two dozen different accents, quite apart from the fact it was owned by Austria until eighty years ago. Certainly I couldn't imitate the accent of this place, Sant' Antioco. Centuries ago they came from Genoa down to somewhere on the Barbary coast opposite here, then moved here when the Algerines oppressed them. They probably use as many Arabic words as Italian. Or archaic Italian words no longer used today."

Ramage felt slightly irritated by Jackson: until five minutes ago he was concerned only with being generous to some *Sardi* fishermen, and that in turn had led him to recall the Genovesi who, before the Spanish Armada sailed for England, went to North Africa; to Tabarka, Zembra and Djerba, and the Kerkenna Islands near by, in the constant hunt for new fishing grounds. Moslems, Normans, Christians, Catalans, Spaniards—all at some time or another had fought to get the tunny, the coral from the reefs, the slaves and the grain to be found in the triangle formed by Sicily, Sardinia and the Barbary coast. The language resulting over the centuries from such a mixing would be fascinating— and yet the nearest he could get to hear it now was letting this brig run ashore. There was so much of interest, so much to learn—and so little opportunity . . .

As soon as he was sure the wind would carry the brig down to the waiting fishermen—it seemed they had guessed what was about to happen—Ramage told Jackson to lash the wheel, left the topsail drawing, and ordered his men down into the gig.

Two hours later all the boats were back at the *Calypso* and being hoisted on board, and Southwick was already conjecturing whether the *Calypso* would catch up with Aitken's convoy.

"We'll be sailing less than 24 hours after them, sir," he commented.

Was it only 24 hours ago that Aitken sailed out past Isolotto la Vacca? The thought surprised Ramage, who, working backwards in time, found Southwick was right. It seemed more like a week.

"I can guess the course Aitken will take, sir, because I gave him some tips about the currents along the Barbary coast. There's a nasty inset into most of those big bays."

"The course from here to Europa Point is fairly direct," Ramage said sarcastically: "west by north, about seven hundred miles, and if we were bound for Gibraltar, I'm sure we'd sight them."

"Aren't we going to Gibraltar, sir?" Southwick was obviously startled.

"Yes, but we have some things to do first."

His satisfaction at surprising Southwick was short-lived; the Master's face took on the smile of some benevolent and overindulgent bishop; all he lacked, Ramage thought, was a cope, mitre and crozier. "Good," the Master said, "if there's some action I'll get a good look in now we've no lieutenants on board."

Ramage found himself strangely reluctant to leave the Golfo di Palmas; like so many other gulfs and bays in the Mediterranean, it held impressions of all the civilizations that had passed through it. Ramage was reminded of a piece of canvas with many portraits painted one on top of the other so that from different angles and in different lights one could see traces of the earlier works.

As the *Calypso* stretched past the Isolotto la Vacca with a brisk south wind and all plain sail set and drawing, Ramage looked astern at the *Passe Partout*, slicing along in the *Calypso*'s wake.

"Discipline in that ship for the next few days," Ramage commented to Southwick, "is going to be fierce!"

"Why, sir? Jackson's a mild enough fellow."

"Yes, but first Martin and then Orsini worked hard to clean her up: deck holystoned and a shine put on anything that would take a polish. Jackson doesn't know when Martin or Orsini will be on board again, but he's going to make sure she's sparkling."

"Just to show them how it should be done!" The idea appealed to Southwick. "Pity we can't put the gunner on board as Jackson's second-in-command."

"He'd beat Jackson," Ramage said, and knew exactly why. Jackson had enormous initiative, was not the slightest bit frightened of responsibility, and in action appeared never to have heard the word fear. But one word he did know was contempt; if he was contemptuous of a man, then that man ceased to exist; he became what in the West Indies was called a zombie, a dead man walking. Jackson would go about his business in the *Passe Partout* as though the gunner did not exist and the gunner, being the man he was, would be delighted, not insulted; he would probably start painting black lacquer on the guns, or passing all the round shot through a gauge to make sure they were completely spherical, with no bumps of rust.

"How are you heading, Quartermaster?" Ramage called, more to bring himself back to the immediate present than a wish to know if the men at the wheel were on course.

"Nor'-west a half west, sir," the helmsman said after glancing at the compass on the weather side of the binnacle.

And about 320 miles to go, Ramage thought to himself, if the wind does not head us so we have to start tacking.

Southwick supervised a cast of the log and came forward with the report that they were making six knots and the wind was freshening.

"We're not on the course the convoy took, sir," he said almost accusingly.

"Of course not. We're not going to the same place."

"I assumed that," Southwick said heavily as he noted the time, speed, course and position on the slate. Later, the details would be transferred to the master's log and to the captain's journal, and in due course, as laid down in the Regulations and Instructions, both volumes would be forwarded to the Admiralty, where Southwick assumed they would join an enormous and dusty pile of other logs and journals, unread and merely recorded in some index.

He was sure they were unread because he had served in ships where, for example, a captain had ordered that a man be given nine dozen lashes of the cat-o'-nine-tails and this was quite openly recorded, although two dozen lashes were the legal limit a captain could award; more than that could be ordered only by a court martial. Yet there had been no letter from the Board Secretary expressing their Lordships' displeasure, or even asking for more details.

No, a log or journal became important only if something went wrong, and something going wrong meant in effect losing the ship. Logs and journals were kept in case of trouble; a sort of coroner looking over your shoulder in the hope there would be an inquest.

Southwick's attitude towards life reflected in his cheerful face; he met tomorrow's problems tomorrow; he did not brood about them today. As he looked aft, to see if he had missed any details of the sketch he had made of the coast and which meant that not only had he carried out the instructions for masters but added to his own store of charts and views, he found himself startled that in the course of 24 hours, eight French merchant vessels and one 74-gun ship had been destroyed in the Golfo di Palmas, entirely due to the *Calypso*; six large prizes had been sent off to Gibraltar; and a small tartane had been kept as a tender to the *Calypso*.

He pencilled some more shading on to the sketch slightly to change the shape of the south sides of Monte Riciotto, one of the smaller mountains on San Pietro, and Monte Guardia dei Mori, the tallest.

Yes, Isolotto la Vacca also needed a little alteration. When he came to put on some watercolours later, he must remember the thin, distant line of the marsh and salt pans, and also the white sand beach near Porto Pino. The whole stretch of coast seemed peaceful enough now: just one brig heeled over on the beach near the fishermen's village and another ripped open on a reef at the other end of the gulf—they were the only signs of their visit. By now the brig at the village would have been looted by the local people, and as the months and years passed they would gradually strip the wood from the ship, using it to build or repair their own fishing boats. The towers of various shapes, sizes and heights—he wondered when they had last been manned by soldiers. Mr Ramage said Sardinia had been Austrian until about 1720, and Southwick could imagine them keeping a sharp lookout. Who were *they* fighting in 1720?

He asked Ramage, who had coincidentally just remembered another piece of history. "About a hundred years ago, around the turn of the century, Austria owned Sardinia, and Savoy had Sicily, and they exchanged them. I can't remember why—during the Spanish War, perhaps, because Spain occupied Sardinia for a while until she was defeated. Then in 1720 they exchanged *again*, Sardinia going back to Savoy, and Sicily back to Austria."

Ramage turned and looked astern. The changing fortunes of Sardinia, with Sicily beyond, were something that a Briton found hard to comprehend. Imagine having the ruler of your home, the island on which your whole being existed, exchange it all for another island. Until 1702 a Sardinian would have been a Savoyard; then until 1717 an Austrian, then Spanish when Spain occupied the island for three years; and then suddenly he would be a Savoyard again when there was a second exchange.

He laughed to himself at the thought that for the last two hundred years it was unlikely one Sardinian in a thousand knew or cared who owned him; any tax collector toured that wild countryside at the extreme risk of his life . . .

CHAPTER TWENTY

JUST after dawn three days later Ramage stood alone at the quarterdeck rail watching as the sun rising slowly began to light up the Pyrenees showing ahead, through the network of the rigging and each side of the great sails. This stretch of the Mediterranean, from the tiny French port of Collioure at the foot of the northern slopes to the Spanish town of Rosas about 25 miles to the south, always seemed one of the most beautiful parts of the western Mediterranean. Here the Pyrenees, having started over on the cold Atlantic side, and except for a few passes effectively sealing Spain from France, now tumbled down to the Mediterranean, as if thankful to find warmer water and bluer skies.

Here was the border between France and Spain, a border acknowledged in words by Paris and Madrid but of little consequence to the Basques and the Catalans living astride it, speaking their own languages and both contemptuous of the two nations they regarded as trespassers.

Somewhere over there, among the mountains and the coastal passes at which Ramage now looked, Hannibal had marched two thousand years ago with his fifty thousand men, nine thousand cavalry and 37 elephants, to stop the Romans invading Spain. Hannibal had originally come from Carthage, just south of Sardinia. Had he ever visited the Golfo di Palmas?

"That'll be Cap Béar on the larboard bow, with Port Vendres just to the north," Southwick said, having just come up from below. "With the glass you might pick out two towers, one low down and the other high up."

Ramage nodded: he knew this part of the coast well.

"Ah, the sun is just catching the snow on the top of Le Canigou, sir. Over nine thousand feet high, that mountain."

"And a blessing to navigators," Ramage commented. "An unmistakable shape with those double peaks, and snow for good measure."

"That's the trouble, the snow makes it difficult to get 'a good measure,'" Southwick grumbled. "Taking an altitude of Canigou to find the distance off is difficult because with any sun the snow makes it next to impossible to distinguish the peak. Still, no sun usually means the peak is in cloud . . ."

"You need a tape measure, not a sextant," Ramage teased.

Sitting at his desk, Ramage took out the French signal book and again turned to the list of semaphore stations. The entry he sought was brief:

"No. 28, Collioure (Pointe del Mich) . . . Albert St Laurent."

The reference to Pointe del Mich intrigued him. According to some notes in old sailing directions belonging to Southwick,

Pointe del Mich was the headland on the south side of the entrance to the narrow bay which, lying in the northern shadow of the Pyrenees, looked as if it had been made by a giant taking a bite out of the coast just where the mountains ended and the land rolled and then flattened into sand dunes and marshes, passing Perpignan and extending all the way round the Gulf of Lions to Marseilles. Then a glance at the chart made it clearer— Pointe del Mich stuck out to sea just far enough to be in sight of the next station to the north, number 27, and the one to the south, number 29, Port Vendres—the old "Port of Venus" of Roman times, well sheltered and, just now, well defended.

This was the difference between the islands of the West Indies and the Mediterranean, of course; from Grenada in the south of the Lesser Antilles to Jamaica in the north-west of the Greater Antilles, buildings and history were recent; little went back more than one hundred and fifty years. But here in the Mediterranean much of what one saw existed before Christ was born. As far as this stretch of coast was concerned, he recalled that the Moors, or Algerines, holding southern Spain were finally driven out only a few years before Columbus sailed to the New World, after creating most of the buildings of any beauty in Spain.

"Mr Southwick, sir!" the Marine sentry called from the door.

The Master reported: "We're two miles off the bay, sir: Jackson's already gone in with the *Passe Partout* and has anchored about a hundred yards beyond the cliff with the semaphore tower on it. They'll think he's gone close inshore to shelter from this south wind because anchoring on the north side, where the fishing boats are, would be a very rolly berth."

"Very well, I'll come on deck," Ramage said. He picked up the French Lieutenant's hat. "Damned man had too small a head for me," he complained. "I get a headache in five minutes."

"I've seen the mark on your forehead," Southwick said sympathetically. "Better be like me." He ran his fingers through his hair. "At my age no other Navy expects me to wear a hat. And if you don't mind me saying so, sir, that shirt of yours looks a little too fashionable. In these Revolutionary days I don't think captains in the French Navy have stewards with hot irons . . ."

"It's a hot afternoon; it'll soon crease. I refuse to wear that man's shirt; he has a chest as narrow as a boarding-pike!"

"I wonder what he's doing now?" Southwick said unsympathetically. "Can you imagine him trying to explain in French to a peasant speaking only Italian how the lieutenant commanding a semaphore station on the coast of Languedoc suddenly found himself and his men tramping across the goat tracks of Sardinia . . ."

"I can better imagine the look on the face of the person listening to him," Ramage said as he slipped a cutlass-belt over his shoulder and then tightened the belt holding up his trousers. He picked up his two pistols, after checking the priming. He slid the hook on the side of each pistol into his belt. "The shirt is not of Revolutionary cut or quality," he said ironically, "nor are these."

"The Marchesa will be glad you're using them, though," Southwick said. "I know she's going to ask."

Ramage led the way out of the cabin, climbed the companion-way and blinked in the sunlight as he came up on deck. The glare from the sails was almost blinding, but it was long enough past noon for shadows to be black and sharp among some of the peaks, crags and valleys of the Pyrenees.

"Ah, Le Canigou . . . it's a long time since I've been so close," he commented to Southwick. "An impressive brute . . ."

Now, looking ahead over the *Calypso*'s bow, he could see right into Collioure Bay. And memories, the chart and what he could now see met in nostalgic collision.

There was Pointe del Mich over on the larboard hand, a jutting headland with—he found the sight excited him—a semaphore tower at its top, a flagpole and Tricolour, and the same sort of huts for the garrison that he had seen at Foix. As the eye travelled inland and round to the head of the bay, there were two indentations in the cliffs with an old, round, lookout tower low down by a sandy beach; then came the immense fortress, which locally was called *Le château,* skilfully engineered and wedge-shaped so that guns on each side could cover the entire harbour entrance. But now, Ramage saw with his glass, no guns were mounted; shrubs grew along the battlements and clumps of some tenacious, dark green bushes stuck out of the grey stone walls. And then came the beach used by the fishermen and finally, on the north side of the bay, the citadel stood high on the hill, overlooking the tiny church whose circular tower was topped by a cupola. Perched on an outcrop of rock at the water's edge, the tower seemed to be built of wide bands of different-coloured stone, but many years ago it had been explained to Ramage that it had probably started life as a Roman watch tower—the lowest and darkest band of stone. Then the tower was repaired and heightened over the centuries so that the identity of the builders of successive bands was lost in time; not even recorded in legends. People like the Franks, the Normans (who may well have built on the church part) and the Moors, who were probably responsible for the cupola, turning the church into a mosque.

As one looked inland across the mountains above and west of Collioure there were many signs, if not of war, then of the fear of war. There was yet another round tower on a rugged hill overlooking the semaphore station; towering over that on the next higher hill was a small castle. On a more distant and higher mountain perched another signal tower, tall and remote as a hovering kestrel. Collioure's life for two thousand years must have been one of wars and threats; Hannibal's war elephants probably trumpeted their way through here because Collioure stood almost as a guardian at the northern end of the coastal pass through the mountains.

Ramage nodded towards the *Passe Partout* and told Southwick: "We'll sound our way in and anchor close under her stern. I don't know which of us will be weighing first but we don't want to get anywhere near the church or that reef beyond it."

"The island of St Vincent, they call it."

"The church, too. There's some legend that St Vincent arrived here in an open boat, landing on those rocks. Or perhaps he sailed from here. Anyway, it's all named after him. He'll be the patron saint of the village."

Half an hour later the *Calypso* was anchored in four fathoms, almost in the centre of a triangle joining the semaphore tower at the entrance to the bay, the *château* at its apex, and the church at the other side of the entrance, and Southwick and Ramage were busy supervising the hoisting out of the launch and both cutters. As soon as the three boats were lying astern on their painters, Ramage crouched beside the breech of one of the quarterdeck carronades, where prying eyes on shore would not wonder at his curiosity, and proceeded to inspect Collioure with his glass.

Already he could see the best way up to the semaphore station. There was a small, level, sandy beach in the first little bay inland of Pointe del Mich; the boats could land there, giving the men only a few feet to scramble up to where the track—devious and looking like a dead snake—led over the grey rocks and up to the tower.

No one at the semaphore station seemed to be interested in the *Calypso*. The tower was just like the one at Foix, complete to the canvas awning over the platform and the telescope on the tripod. There was one man up there, and most of the time he was sitting back in the chair, occasionally picking up a bottle of wine and leaning his head back. Only once in half an hour did Ramage see him swing the telescope south to look at the Port Vendres tower and then north to station number 27, and rising from the chair and grasping the telescope seemed to make heavy demands on his ability to balance.

There were four fishing boats drawn up on the beach facing the harbour entrance and although all the paint was peeling they had once been decorated in bright colours, red and blue predominating. But the other beach, between the *château* and the

church, was obviously the fishermen's favourite—it gave more
shelter when swells came through the entrance, and most of
their little houses were built just at the back of the beach, mid-
way between the *château* and the church, so they could choose
either sanctuary.

Nine boats were hauled out. One of them had been turned
upside-down and he could see that two planks had been taken
out of the hull. Three men were working on replacements, one
of them standing on a piece of wood and making chips fly with
his adze.

There were trees a few yards back along the beach providing
some shade, and he saw what at first glance seemed to be a row
of corpses sitting under them on the sand, their backs against a
low wall. When he looked more closely he saw they were women,
all dressed in black, some with black scarves round their heads
and others—they seemed to be younger—with white scarves.
But all of them had bundles of fishing net beside them, and all
had a leg extended and a bare foot sticking out from the hem of
their dress. The big toe, he saw, was used to poke through the
mesh of the net and keep a section taut as each woman methodically mended a tear, using a wooden net-making needle which
seemed to dart in and out like a pecking bird. Occasionally one
of the women would give a violent jerk with her body, as if
caught by a spasm of pain, but it was only to heave away the
repaired section of the net and draw over the next part, to be
extended by the big toe, inspected and if necessary repaired.

In the shade of the high wall of the *château*, which formed
one end of the beach and cut it off from the second, farther
round to the south, half a dozen men were making or repairing
fishpots, two of them trimming thin laths of wood, using a type
of spokeshave, while the others used the new laths to repair the
pots, bending them with a skill that came with the years.

The sails had been loosened from the lateen yards on two of
the fishing boats and men were sewing in patches. Each boat was
very beamy and shallow-draughted, unlike the boats one would

see on the beaches of southern England. The mast was stubby and the lateen yard was made up of two pieces of wood fished together in the middle, presumably to give a certain spring and also probably because straight wood was difficult to find. The forward end of the yard was bowsed down tight at the bow of the boat, lashed to a section of stem which stuck up an extra foot or so. The bow piece formed the pivot for the yard, so that when it was hoisted up the mast by the halyard, the forward end stayed low in the boat while the after end rose high, stretching the sail into its traditional triangular, leg-o'-mutton shape.

Ramage saw that the lower hills round the village were heavily terraced, and he could just make out the vines growing on them. Surely Collioure was renowned for its white wine, while farther south was Banyuls, which produced a sweet red to which the village gave its name? It was hard to remember; when he was last here, as a midshipman, such things did not interest him.

Captain Ramage, with a dozen important jobs to do, was dredging his memory for details of local wines . . . He swung his telescope round to the citadel, perched on its hill above the church as if to emphasize that in France today the State was above Church. He watched it for five minutes and saw no movement, noting the building was little more than a stone barracks. There were no guns, and more important, no flagpole. He suddenly realized that flagpoles were a great source of information because in Revolutionary France, where it was *de rigueur* to fly a Tricolour, every military establishment would have both flagpole and flag. The semaphore tower and its buildings had both; the *château* neither, nor the citadel. So the semaphore station was the only place where there would be soldiers or sailors; the absence of the Royal Navy from the Mediterranean made garrisons unnecessary for little ports like Collioure.

Jackson arrived on board with Stafford half an hour later, cheerful and obviously delighted at having brought the *Passe Partout* safely to Collioure.

"Only lost you once, sir," he told Ramage. "The first night out from Sant' Antioco, when we had that squall. The rain was so thick we missed your stern lantern and couldn't find it again when the squall passed."

"I'm not surprised," Ramage said, laughing. "The squall blew it out. The lamp trimmer thought he was going to get a flogging over that. We put up another lantern as quickly as we could."

Jackson sighed dramatically. "There I was thinking it was my clever navigation that found you again, sir; instead it was a new lantern! I must admit I thought you were pretty close when we saw the light again . . ."

Ramage assembled Southwick, the corporal of Marines, Jackson, Stafford and the three remaining bosun's mates, and said: "Stand round as though we are gossiping, just in case there are any prying eyes up at the semaphore tower. Now I want you all to listen carefully.

"We are here to destroy that tower, and I want it done so effectively that no signals can be passed until the tower is rebuilt—a week or so's work—unless they are taken by horseback from Port Vendres to the next station to the north of here, which has no name, only a number, 27. That's thirty miles' riding or more over rough and rocky tracks. Horses and horsemen are likely to be rare; donkeys are the usual transport here.

"You might wonder why I want to knock down this one particular tower when there are so many others. Well, it's so flat where number 27 is built that it would be easy to repair it. Number 29, at Port Vendres, will be too strong for us: the port is well defended, and even if we managed to destroy the tower, the French would build a new one very quickly because there's a shipyard there, which means wood, nails, shipwrights, carpenters and tools.

"But here in Collioure . . ." he gestured round him. "You can see it is a small fishing bay with a small anchorage. I imagine that boat being repaired over there exhausts the port's carpentry resources."

He paused a moment because Jackson obviously had a question. Ramage raised his eyebrows and waited.

"Excuse me asking, sir, and I don't want you to think we in the *Passe Partout* aren't enjoying it, but why knock down a tower at this end of the Mediterranean? Foix is much closer to Toulon, where the orders start from."

"Ah, that's a good question. Anyone know the answer—or wants to have a guess?"

They all shook their heads and Ramage said: "Jackson was near when he said Toulon is the source of orders. We want to cut the semaphore *now* to stop signals, or at least slow them down, somewhere between Toulon and the *action!*"

"What action?" Southwick exclaimed. "Action seems scarce round here—at least, until we knock down that tower."

"We're trying to stop the action," Ramage explained. "Within a day or so, the Spanish naval authorities at somewhere like Cartagena are going to get word from a fishing boat or a coastal vessel that a French convoy of six ships is sailing *westward*. They'll know that any convoy that far west can only be intended for Cartagena: there'd be no point in sending it to Almeria or Málaga because, militarily, Spain stops at Cartagena. Yet the reports will say the convoy is *well* to the westward of Cartagena and still steering west.

"So obviously the Spanish Admiral at Cartagena will make a signal to the French Admiral at Toulon, using the semaphore, asking him what it is all about, because almost certainly he would be the person to send off such a convoy and the only one who could explain why it is passing (has passed, I hope) Cartagena.

"The semaphores rattle and crash, and the Admiral in Toulon reads the signal, realizes he has not sent off any convoy to the westward, and sends back a signal to Cartagena ordering the convoy to be intercepted.

"The Admiral in Cartagena sends two or three frigates to sea and they chase poor old Aitken and the rest of them, and they end up dead or prisoners."

"Unless," Southwick said with one of his cheerful sniffs, "the Admiral in Cartagena can neither send nor receive a signal by semaphore for two or three days, by which time Aitken will be rounding Europa Point."

"Exactly," Ramage said. "I'm gambling that the Spanish Admiral is too lazy or too nervous of the French to send out frigates without orders. He may not have any—that's more than likely—and expects the Admiral at Toulon to order ships out from Alicante or Barcelona. It will take time for him to discover that Collioure's tower is out of action. Messengers on horseback will need a day to take a message from Port Vendres to station 27, and with luck semaphore replies will by then be held up by darkness between here and Toulon. With the French and Spanish benighted, Aitken has an excellent chance."

"Everyone in that convoy will owe us a lot," the Marine corporal said happily, sucking his teeth at the prospect.

"We'll see about that," Ramage said, "but in the meantime this is what we do, starting at sunset. First, we need half a dozen pairs of handcuffs . . ."

CHAPTER TWENTY-ONE

THE convoy was making good time and Aitken was pleased that his noon sight put them about twenty miles south of Cabo de Gata while dead reckoning had them forty miles short of it. Here, off the south-eastern tip of Spain, Europa Point was a clear run of a little under two hundred miles to the westward. In fact they would have to sail more than that "through the water" to overcome the eastgoing current constantly flowing into the Mediterranean from the Atlantic, but Aitken knew that it was more important that Cartagena, the last of the big naval ports, was now well behind them.

Almeria, just west of Cabo de Gata, was more of a commercial port, unlikely to hold any ships of war. From there to Europa Point and the safety of Gibraltar was only Málaga, again a commercial and not a naval port.

It was a miracle that the convoy had sailed so far without meeting a French ship-of-war that, as a matter of routine, would ask why the convoy was without an escort and, because it was so far west, whither it was bound. Until the last few hours, Aitken could always (using Orsini as his "voice") claim to be bound for Cartagena, and accept the scorn of a French frigate captain at being so bad a navigator to get so far south. Now he was too far into the channel between Spain and the Barbary coast to use that story.

He was well satisfied with the way his ships were being handled. He had divided the six of them into two columns of three and knowing the difficulty of sailing at night in the wake of a ship showing only a dim stern lantern, he led the larboard column with the bosun following him in the *Rosette* schooner and Rennick bringing up the rear in the *Matilda*. The starboard column was led by Kenton and the *Golondrina*, followed by Orsini in the *Caroline* brig, and then Martin with the *Bergère*. This left Orsini conveniently placed should his French or Spanish be needed—but also kept him safely between Kenton and Martin in case his station-keeping was erratic.

Aitken was surprised that the *Calypso* had not joined them. Not that Mr Ramage had said he would, but both he and Southwick would soon get exhausted standing watch and watch about, and they were deprived of most of their good petty officers. It was typical of the Captain's fairness that he had made sure the six ships of the convoy were well manned, although if they did not get through or anything happened to the *Calypso*, their Lordships would put Mr Ramage on the beach for the rest of his life. Still, there—Aitken's thoughts were interrupted by a hail from the foremasthead.

"Deck there! The *Bergère* has just hoisted a signal, sir."

Aitken picked up his glass and took his copy of the French signals from the binnacle box drawer.

Orsini had written a translation beside each of them and Aitken read the two hoists of flags without difficulty. The first said, *"Strange sail in sight"* and the second gave the direction, *"In the north-east quadrant."*

"Acknowledge that signal," Aitken told the bosun's mate and shouted to the lookout aloft: "Keep your eyes open; there'll be more signals soon."

Aitken's first reaction as a naval officer had been to detach one of his ships to investigate, and when he realized it he grinned to himself. Habits were hard to break. For the last two days he had been the master of a French merchant ship and, as senior of the other French masters, the commodore of the convoy. And an unescorted convoy, unless attacked by a squadron of Algerine pirates—the only danger along this coast—maintained its course, particularly with a good southerly wind and fine weather, minding its own business.

North-east quadrant. So the strange ship was on the convoy's starboard quarter and well down to leeward—too far away to be seen from the *Sarazine* but just close enough for her topsails to appear over the horizon and be sighted, tiny white specks, by the masthead lookout in the *Bergère,* the nearest ship. Merchant ships did not have lookouts at the masthead; ships of war, and prizes, did.

Martin would be pleased at being the first ship to spot the stranger, but they had sighted many strange sail in the last day or so, most of them small trading vessels, the larger ones preferring to sail in convoy.

What mattered now was whether or not the bearing of this strange sail remained the same. If it changed, then she was merely another ship on passage somewhere; if it stayed the same, then the ship must be beating her way up towards the convoy, and that could mean only trouble, because sailing on that course would otherwise take a ship to the Barbary coast, an unlikely destination.

He hoped Martin would have the sense to keep signals flying for as little time as possible. They had to use French signals and flags to keep up the pretence of a French convoy, but a French ship-of-war might get suspicious if too many signals were made across the convoy simply because all merchant ships, whatever their nationality, were as loath to make signals as small boys to wash behind their ears.

He picked up the slate and after a glance at his watch noted down the time of the signal. The "strange sail" could be an Algerine pirate. If she was, would she attack the convoy? Probably not as such but instead would try to cut out a single ship at the rear, Martin's *Bergère* or Rennick's *Matilda* most likely, because any of the other four going to help would then have to beat back to windward. The Algerine would know enough to guess that in the event of an attack the convoy would in fact most probably panic and scatter and leave the victim to her fate . . .

More than ten minutes elapsed before the *Bergère's* next signal, which the French system forced Martin to make in three parts:

"*Strange sail in sight . . . In the north-east quadrant . . . Is a frigate.*"

"Acknowledge," snapped Aitken. He was both annoyed and pleased. Martin was being sensible in repeating the signal "In the north-east quadrant" because that was obviously intended to tell Aitken that the vessel was deliberately steering for the convoy, not passing by. By identifying the ship as a frigate, Martin made it almost certain that the frigate was the *Calypso*. Yet . . . yet . . . Martin would himself have gone aloft with a telescope and had a good look. A ship identifiable as a frigate should also be recognizable as the *Calypso* because of the cut of her sails, even though her hull might still be below the horizon.

Aitken then cursed at his own slowness: Martin would have done all that and not have recognized the masts and sails as the

Calypso, so his signal meant just what it said—that the vessel was a "strange sail" and "a frigate," but not the *Calypso.*

Even then Aitken's Scottish caution made him think again. Supposing the frigate was the *Calypso?* How, using the French signal book, could Martin signal the fact? Aitken picked up his handwritten copy and looked at the last few pages, which gave in alphabetical order the names of all the ships of war in the French Navy, and the three-figure numbers of each of them so that by hoisting the three flags representing the numbers they could identify themselves. As he had guessed, the *Calypso* was still in the list under her original French name, although a neat ink line had crossed it out along with a dozen others—ships which had been sunk or captured. Yes, Martin was a bright lad; he would have thought of that and he would have given the three figures as the fourth part of his signal, knowing that it would be enough of a clue to set Aitken looking in the back of the signal book.

"Deck there! Fore-topmast lookout here!"

"Deck here," Aitken replied.

"I can make out a sail on the starboard quarter of the convoy, sir. Three masts, royals flying . . ."

"I'll send someone up with a glass!"

Aitken looked around, then decided to go himself, grabbing the telescope and making his way to the shrouds. Two minutes later, breathless, his shin muscles feeling as though they had been stretched three inches, he was standing beside the lookout. The *Sarazine* was surprisingly narrow below them; the mast seemed to be gyrating round the circumference of a fifty-yard circle.

The seaman pointed, and beyond the *Bergère* Aitken caught sight of a fleck of white.

"Royals set, eh?" he said doubtfully as he pulled out the eyepiece of the telescope. "You must have sharp eyes."

"Ah have that, sir," the man said firmly, thinking to himself that in Cumberland they poached just as skilfully as these

Scotsmen; aye and without all that funny talk and across hills just as high.

"You're right," Aitken conceded after three minutes' struggle with the telescope, trying to keep it focused. "Here," he said, "take the glass and see if you think she's the *Calypso*."

"Ah know that she isn't without needing the glass, sir," the man said, "but a bring-'em-near might tell me more."

Aitken thought back to his days as a midshipman, when the masthead seemed a second home, either because he had been mastheaded as a punishment or the captain wanted a ship identified. Those days, he thought ruefully, are long past. It was not the advance of old age; merely that he had lost the habit—and his nimbleness.

"French 36-gun frigate, sir; I forget the name of the class and I couldn't pronounce it even if I recalled it. Beating up for us, sir."

"Right," Aitken said, starting down the shrouds, "keep a sharp lookout with those poacher's eyes!"

As soon as he reached the deck, Aitken called: "Bosun's mate! Hands to quarters. The ship's company may have laughed yesterday afternoon at gunnery practice with six-pounders but it might make all the difference between spending next Sunday in Gibraltar or a French jail!"

On board the *Caroline* brig, the ship ahead of Martin's *Bergère* and the one astern of Kenton's *Golondrina*, Paolo Orsini had the slate and a copy of the signal book ready on the tiny binnacle box, and his telescope under his arm.

He could see the strange sail coming up fast now—the convoy was making less than six knots—and had finally decided she was French. Aitken had given very precise instructions about what the convoy was to do if attacked by French, Spanish or Algerines, and Paolo was thankful that an enemy frigate had not turned up earlier.

The reason was simple enough: the convoy was now in the narrowing channel leading to Gibraltar, so if he had to flee with the *Caroline* in a different direction from the rest, he would know once it was dark that by the following dawn land should be in sight to the north (Spain) or south (Africa), and as long as he steered westward he was bound to reach Gibraltar. It was not that he distrusted his celestial navigation, of course; simply that his quadrant must be damaged so that his altitudes of the sun were in error, because the latitude he calculated each noon was never quite the same as that hoisted by the *Sarazine* and the *Golondrina*. In fact his own answer that day, just over 49 degrees north, was (according to the French atlas he found in the former captain's cabin) obviously wrong because the *Caroline* could not be as far north as Paris.

Obviously Martin, by repeating the bearing, was telling Mr Aitken that the frigate was heading up to them, and Paolo knew from an inspection through his own glass that she was not the *Calypso*.

Baxter, his sharpest-eyed seaman, was up the mast now and shouted down that she was a French frigate; he thought one of the 36-gun class like the *Calliope*, a name which at first puzzled Paolo when he looked her up in the French list because Baxter pronounced it Cally-owe-pee.

Paolo looked round for a senior rating but apart from the man at the wheel the nearest was a Marine.

"General quarters!" he shouted. "Leave the port-lids down, and don't underestimate four 9-pounders. If we add up all the guns in the convoy—"

"They don't come to 36," a cheerful Baxter shouted down from the masthead, "but they'll make a lot o' smoke, sir, an' perhaps bring tears to the Frogs' eyes!"

Paolo looked astern to avoid laughing: he had dreamed hundreds of times of taking his own ship into action; he had imagined himself at the quarterdeck rail in full uniform, dress sword, telescope under his arm, snapping crisp orders to quartermaster, gunner, first lieutenant, master . . . But the ship in his dreams had been at least a frigate with a crew of two hundred and fifty,

not a bedraggled trading brig of three hundred tons with a bar-
nacled bottom, four guns and ten men. But at least the ten men
had exercised those four guns . . .

At that moment Rossi appeared from below.

"Better we fight that frigate with our tongues than our guns,
sir," he said in Italian.

"We may not have the choice, but you have the right idea,"
Paolo said, sarcastically. "We must think of the right thing to say
to the French. Like 'What a *bella figura* you make standing on
your quarterdeck, Captain!'"

Rossi chuckled at the thought as he went to Paolo's cabin to
get the key to the *Caroline*'s pitifully small magazine.

Rennick in the *Matilda* had long ago identified the distant ship
as French and at this moment had all his men, except for the
lookout and the man at the wheel, standing in a circle round
him.

"Mr Aitken's order, if the convoy is attacked by an enemy
ship, is to disperse," he told the men. "That means we all sail off
in different directions. But one of us is bound to be caught, and
if the Frogs put a prize crew on board her quickly enough they
can go after another ship. In fact if they're awake they can capture all six of us."

"Prison," muttered one of the Marines. "I've 'eard about them
French prisons."

"So have I," Rennick said grimly. "But you remember what
Captain Ramage always says . . . Come on, now!"

The men shuffled their feet and sucked their teeth, brows fur-
rowed with concentration, and increasingly embarrassed at
Rennick's impatience.

"Come on! Come on!"

"Surprise!" the Marine corporal yelled triumphantly. "Yer gotta
do somefing ter surprise the barstids!"

"Exactly," Rennick said, proud that it was a Marine and not
a seaman who had come up with the right answer. "Do the

unexpected. Now, what would that Frenchman not be expecting, eh?"

"Us to attack 'im," a seaman said firmly, as if disposing of that possibility once and for all.

"Exactly!" Rennick said once again, slapping his thigh and laughing with delight. "Mr Aitken can't give us any orders because of the signalling problems, so we must use our common sense."

He looked round at the eight men, the man at the wheel and the lookout aloft. Ten, led by himself as the eleventh. Well, it could not be helped. Surprise would have to provide the equivalent of the other two hundred and ninety men he would prefer to have.

"Our common sense tells us," Rennick said firmly, glaring round him for any sign of dissent, "that if we can save five ships of the convoy, we'll have won."

There were enough "Ahs" and "S'rights" showing agreement that Rennick promptly seized the moment to tell them his plan.

"So we ram the frigate with the *Matilda*."

Without knowing that he was repeating a tactic used by Ramage against a 74 only a few days ago, he explained: "We go for her jib-boom and bowsprit. If we can carry them away we'll send her foremast tumbling by the board."

"They won't arf be cross wiv us," a Marine muttered gloomily. "Still," he added, brightening up, "it'll be quite a sight!"

"Good, good," Rennick said briskly. "As soon as the Frogs recover they'll board us. We don't fight; we surrender. There'll be no dishonour. We'll be outnumbered about thirty to one, and if her foremast has gone, we've nothing more to do. So we'll be prisoners.

"Now listen carefully. Being taken prisoner means marching to prison, maybe across Spain and halfway across France. So make sure you've got shoes or boots, and put on two pairs of socks if there's room. And wear any thick coat you have. You'll look dam' silly now but later, trying to sleep alongside a mountain track in the snow, you'll be glad of every stitch you've got.

"Roll up blankets so you can put 'em round your neck like a horse collar. The French may steal them, but if they don't . . . And if you have any money, get below right now and sew the coins into a thick part of your clothing. You've ten minutes to do that, so dismiss!"

Orsini took one more look at the still distant enemy sail and knew she would never notice any unusual move by the *Caroline*. The idea had come to him just like that, "out of the blue," a very good expression the English used. But he needed Mr Aitken's approval before trying it—indeed, there might be a dozen reasons why the French would not fall for the trap, but it was worth suggesting, even if it made Mr Aitken angry.

Fifteen minutes later the *Caroline* was sailing with her larboard bow only a few yards from the *Sarazine's* starboard quarter, with Rossi at the wheel. Baxter was perched in the *Caroline's* foreshrouds carefully watching the *Sarazine's* quarter, which was close enough for him to lob a biscuit into the muzzle of one of her nine-pounders, and giving helm orders to Rossi, whose forward vision was limited by the fo'c's'le so that he could see only her masts and rigging. Orsini was standing on the *Caroline's* bulwarks right forward, gripping part of her anchor and waiting to get close enough to Aitken, who was sitting astride the *Sarazine's* taffrail, the mouthpiece of a speaking-trumpet to his ear.

"Can you hear me, sir?"

Aitken waved.

Paolo then explained his proposal, Aitken listening carefully. Finally, putting the speaking-trumpet to his lips, Aitken shouted: "It's a good idea and it might work. Try it. I'll leave the timing to you." He then shouted a word which Paolo could not understand, but Rossi called: "*Va bene*, sir, I know it."

Aitken gave another wave and shouted: "Good luck, lads; I'll see you all in Gibraltar!"

Paolo walked back to the wheel, his heart thumping with pride and excitement and his face flushed with pleasure, but he was met with a growl from Rossi. "For how long we stay in this position, sir? Any minute we lose our bowsprit through hitting the *Sarazine!*"

With a muttered curse Paolo returned from the dizzy realms of convoy tactics to the mundane problem of getting the *Caroline* back into her position as the second ship in the starboard column. The French frigate, he noted, was about a mile away and tacking once again in the long zigzag to get up to the convoy. On this tack he estimated she would stretch up to the head of the convoy and pass just across the *Golondrina's* bow, allowing for the convoy's forward speed remaining the same. Unfortunately there was no chance of any change in the wind's strength or direction; indeed, with the sky blue and dappled with small white clouds and the sun still hot, he was reminded of Trade wind conditions. The Mediterranean weather was being kind when the convoy needed it to be at its most treacherous.

Aitken watched the *Caroline* dropping back into position and had to admit that Orsini was ingenious, particularly considering his age. Was he sixteen yet? The idea might not save them, but certainly it was their only chance. The French frigate was obviously intent on getting ahead of the convoy, and that made sense because, as Aitken reminded himself, by now her captain would be sure the convoy was French, all the ships flying Tricolours, and would have no suspicions. The convoy knew he was their enemy, but the French captain was just following the usual routine. The only thing that would concern him was the whereabouts of the escort and why the convoy was so far south and steering west. And he would know that whoever was the senior captain of the convoy would probably be in one of the two leading ships. It was a pity, Aitken thought, that there had not been time to have the *Golondrina* and the *Caroline* exchange positions.

If only the *Calypso* would come in sight now! But even that would be too late; the French frigate was less than a mile away and fairly racing along, every piece of plain sail drawing. Ah, now she was clewing up her courses, because she needed only topsails for manoeuvring round the convoy—and, as if to show how right he was, Aitken saw the royals being furled as well. The way the frigate had tacked up to the convoy, never once overstanding a hundred yards, and the way she was being handled now, left no doubt that her captain was an experienced officer. Yet for Orsini's scheme that was an advantage; the more experienced the better.

CHAPTER TWENTY-TWO

THE SUN had just dropped behind the mountains in a blaze of red when the two cutters and launch left the *Calypso*, heading for the *Passe Partout*. Both peaks and valleys were darkening as shadows quickly lengthened, and Ramage steered the launch for the tartane, leaving the red and green cutters to circle as though keeping guard. The launch came alongside the tartane in full view of the semaphore tower, and the moment the boat was hooked on, several dozen seamen stood up, holding muskets. Ramage gave a loud hail.

Jackson appeared at the rail and, a few moments later, six seamen wearing handcuffs scrambled clumsily over the bulwarks one after the other and went down the ladder, covered by more men with muskets who had just appeared along the *Passe Partout*'s rail.

The six prisoners—it was obvious to any watchers on shore that they were prisoners of some sort or another—were pushed and cuffed in the launch and made to sit in the centre of the three middle thwarts, with the armed men already in the boat keeping them well covered.

The launch left the *Passe Partout* and when one of the cutters then went alongside her, the rest of the men on board climbed down into it and, with the other cutter, followed the launch, which was making for the first little beach inside the bay and just under the semaphore tower.

There was now neither wind nor swell waves, and the launch hissed as a few powerful strokes with the oars drove it up the sand. Seamen jumped out to hold the boat and first the guards with muskets scrambled up the sand to the foot of the cliff, turning to keep the boat covered.

Then the men in the boat drove out the handcuffed prisoners, who jumped down on to the sand, unbalanced with their wrists pinned together, and two of them sprawled flat on their faces.

Their cursing was so violent that Ramage, still in the launch, hissed: "Shut up, you fools!" Then sheepishly he remembered it was perfectly all right for them to speak and swear in English; it was the guards who were supposed to be French.

Leaving two boat-keepers, one of whom was busy securing the grapnel they had dropped as they came in, ready to haul the launch out again when required, Ramage went up to the armed men and the prisoners and waited while first one and then the other cutter ran up on the beach and landed its men.

Ten minutes later Ramage was at the head of a column of 48 men, most of whom carried muskets and four of whom had axes, keeping the blades concealed with rags. Near the head of the column stumbled six bedraggled men in handcuffs, all of them doing their best to look like prisoners. Wet hair, a few smears of sand and soil, and sodden clothes, made them seem pathetic figures, but a sharp-eyed onlooker would have noticed that each guard marching beside a prisoner, his musket at the ready, wore two pistols with belt clips, while all the other men with muskets had one pistol each. One would have to be very close to notice that none of the handcuffs was secured with padlocks; in fact the prisoners were having to hold them on.

The track up to the gateway to the semaphore tower was steep but smooth, the stony surface worn over the centuries by donkeys and peasants who had used it long before muskets and pistols existed.

Finally at the gate Ramage gave a sharp whistle and held up his arm to halt his men. A French soldier emerged from the guardhouse beyond the gate, weaving slightly and hastily pulling on a coat. He recognized Ramage as an officer and in a slurred voice politely asked his business.

"It is none of your affair," Ramage answered arrogantly. "Take me to your commanding officer!"

"But, sir"—the sentry gestured helplessly at the locked gate—"orders. 'Admit no one without him stating his business.' It's more—"

"—than your life's worth!" Ramage interrupted impatiently. "All right, go at once to your commanding officer and tell him that the Captain of the frigate anchored in the bay down there has urgent business with him and requires a room in which to lock some English prisoners."

The sentry nodded nervously, caught sight of the men in handcuffs and scurried along the track towards the buildings.

Ramage turned casually but hissed to the prisoners: "Make sure none of you drop those handcuffs until you hear me give the word 'Calypso!'"

The men muttered in reply and Jackson, now standing next to Ramage, said quietly: "Bit of luck they don't have a full guardhouse like Foix, sir. One man! Still, at least he keeps the gate locked!"

Ramage saw the sentry running back down the track, struggling to remove a large key from a trouser pocket.

"The commandant's compliments, sir. He asks that you come to his house at once!" He turned the key in the lock and swung the gate open. "I didn't have time to tell him you were not alone, sir, but—"

"Lead us to him; we have to sail before nightfall."

"Yes, sir, indeed, please follow me, I'm sure he will understand . . ."

He prattled on as he walked, but Ramage, realizing that the man was drunk rather than naturally stupid, looked carefully round the buildings. The only other soldiers in sight were two sprawled under a gnarled olive tree, their positions showing they had collapsed there drunk and would soon become the target for swarms of mosquitoes.

"How many of you garrison an important station like this?" Ramage asked amiably.

"Normally 35, sir, but we have two men in Port Vendres with venereal disease, and one awaiting court martial. So today there are 32. And the commandant, of course."

Four buildings just like the barracks at Foix; that larger house at the end of this track and towards which the sentry was leading them must be the commandant's. Beyond it, on the rising ground, the great semaphore tower stood like a section of a wooden wall, its lookout now off duty.

Where the devil were the rest of the garrison?

"Supper time, eh?"

"Ah—no, sir," the sentry said with an inane giggle, "the men are asleep. Today is the commandant's birthday, and everyone celebrated it. Some had a little too much Banyuls, and are . . . resting. The commandant . . ."

The commandant was very drunk. The door of his house flung open and a portly man, bald and bow-legged, lurched out holding a coat he was trying to pull over his shoulders, but in twisting his pear-shaped body to get an arm into the sleeve his belt came undone and he had to grab his trousers to prevent them falling.

The sentry stood paralysed, but Ramage moved quickly forward and, as if it was perfectly natural, said: "Permit me to hold your coat while . . ."

"Thank you . . . thank you," the commandant said as he did up the belt. Ramage held the tunic and the Frenchman slid one arm into a sleeve with an almost desperate thrust but, Ramage realized, that had been luck: with the second arm he obviously still saw three or four armholes but lunged at the wrong one. Ramage retrieved the waving wrist, slid it into the sleeve and with Jackson's help pulled the jacket into place.

"De Vaux, *lieutenant de vaisseau,* commanding the frigate anchored down there, sir!" Ramage said briskly.

The commandant looked blearily down into the bay, obviously startled. "*Sacré bleu,* all those ships! When did they come in? Should I fire a salute? I never know about these things. Anyway, my one gun is honeycombed, they tell me, and will explode if I fire it. You understand 'honeycomb?' Air bubbles trapped in the metal while casting? It is my birthday and the men gave me a party. But no honeycomb, which I like, but much Banyuls, which I also like. De Vaux, that was the name of a young man I met once, commanded a frigate, or a fleet. Navy, anyway; not a soldier."

He stopped talking and screwed up his eyes, trying to concentrate. "That makes two of you, because you are called De Vaux, too. All those ships down there!" He turned on the sentry. "Why was I not told? You are the lookout!"

"But, sir," the man protested, "I thought the tower would—"

"Thought, thought—you have never thought in your life! A fleet sails in and you keep the gate locked."

The commandant realized that there were several men behind Ramage and Jackson.

"You've brought some friends, eh? Here, sentry, get some more Banyuls. A cask. Collect mugs from the barracks. Toasts for the Navy. The Navy can toast me! Fifty-one years old and I can still chase the women."

The sentry hurried off, heading for the first barrack building. Ramage glanced at Jackson and raised his eyebrows for a moment. Then he waited for the sentry to emerge again.

The commandant, meanwhile, had been buttoning up his tunic with ferocious concentration but, starting at the bottom and putting the next to lowest button in the lowest buttonhole, the whole garment was now askew and too tight, giving him the lopsided appearance of a man tottering along a steep slope.

At that moment the sentry came out of the building clutching an armful of mugs. He was alone. No one in the building, Ramage guessed, was prepared to help him or, more significant, not interested, or capable, of drinking more wine with the newly arrived sailors.

All the pretence with the "prisoners" in handcuffs had been completely unnecessary—thanks to the fact that the commandant had been born 51 years ago today. Had his mother been a day earlier, or a day later . . .

Ramage looked round at his men, giving a wave which attracted their attention because they were all watching him.

"Calypso," he said conversationally, his voice pitched so that the men could hear him, and they split into four groups each heading for a hut.

The commandant, now obviously realizing that either the wine had warped his body or something was radically wrong with his coat, tried to look down the row of buttons, but the outward curve of his belly meant he could only see the top three. He craned his head forward to see the rest but the effort was too much and he toppled forward, sprawling flat on the ground as though crucified.

The groups of seamen passed the sentry who, concentrating on balancing the armful of mugs, took no notice of them—if indeed he saw them.

Ramage saw six pairs of handcuffs lying scattered on the ground, and their former wearers now had pistols.

"We'll leave him there," Ramage said to Jackson, gesturing towards the commandant. "He'll probably go to sleep."

He saw four of his seamen hurrying towards him, one coming from each of the huts. The first to arrive reported: "Nine men in the hut, sir, all blind drunk. We'll never get 'em on their feet!"

The other three seamen reported the same thing. Ramage remembered the two men he had seen sleeping under the olive tree and sent a seaman to see if they were insensibly drunk. Then the sentry arrived, the only man in the garrison, as far as he could see, capable of controlled movement.

Jackson caught his eye. "Knock him out and then put those handcuffs on his hands and legs," Ramage said. "And bring a pair of handcuffs for the commandant; we'd better secure him in his bed so that he doesn't fall out!"

He turned to the four seamen. "Very well, leave the drunks and meet me with your men at the tower; we'll do the job ourselves, since the wine has deprived us of French labour."

Half an hour later, while the commandant snored in his bed, his wrists secured beneath it by handcuffs so that he could neither sit up nor turn over, and the sentry lay in the barracks, unconscious and also secured by handcuffs, the Calypsos hacked at the heavy beams supporting the semaphore tower. It was just as substantial as the one at Foix, but the seamen who had been carrying axes sent it toppling without being relieved. After that, hands blistered and muscles aching, they handed over to other groups who took it in turns to destroy the whole structure, so that none of the wood could be used again.

While the men hacked, Ramage watched the bay below with his glass. Apparently no one down there had noticed the tower toppling. Nor was that surprising; the noise would not carry that far, and from the village they could only see the tower end-on, so that it seemed more like a tree trunk, and it was unlikely anyone would see it at the moment it toppled.

Finally Jackson came up to report: "There's not a piece of timber left that's more than two feet long, sir."

"Very well," Ramage said, closing the telescope. "We haven't disturbed anyone down there, so we'll march back in regular order to the boats. There's no need to spike that cannon over there," he added, remembering Jackson would not have understood the commandant. "It's honeycombed and they dare not fire it."

It was almost dark by the time the *Calypso*'s topsails filled aback and she did a long stern-board out of Collioure, followed by the *Passe Partout* which could easily wear round and pass the frigate on her way to the open sea.

Southwick had thoroughly enjoyed Ramage's recounting of the assault on the Collioure semaphore tower, which he had watched by telescope, and had promptly named it the Battle of Banyuls.

"With a bit of luck no one at the other two stations is going to know about it until tomorrow at the earliest," he commented.

"And those men up there aren't going to sober up tonight," Ramage said. "Even when the sentry recovers consciousness there's no one to hear his shouts. And by sunrise the commandant will have such a bad head that he'll be scared it'll fall off if he raises his voice. Anyway, a good job done with no casualties."

"Will it save Aitken, I wonder?" Southwick speculated soberly.

Ramage shrugged his shoulders. "It might. We've just done all we can; the rest is up to luck. Now, I want every bit of canvas set, and let's hope between here and Europa Point we sight the convoy."

CHAPTER
TWENTY-THREE

THE MEN in the six merchant ships watched the French frigate stretching along to cross ahead of them, spray slicing up from her cutwater like a rain shower. Few of them realized that to the frigate they were still friendly ships whose strange position warranted investigation; to them any ship flying a Tricolour, other than the *Calypso,* was an enemy, to be bluffed, evaded or, by some miracle, sunk.

Orsini studied her with his glass. She moved with the controlled power of a galloping stallion. Black hull unrelieved by a different-coloured sheer strake; sails patched but clearly serviceable. The lower part of the jibs dark from spray. Her port-lids were down, so obviously the French were not anticipating action, otherwise the lids would be triced up and the guns run out. The courses were neatly furled on the yards and so were the royals, and the topsails were drawing well. No gilt-work anywhere; not a glint of sun flickering on polished brasswork. The black hull had hints of purple in it, revealing aged paint exposed to too much hot sun and salt sea.

"Not such a nice sheer as the *Calypso*," Baxter commented to Rossi.

"Paint in a white or yellow strake and she'd look better," the Italian said.

"Yes . . . white would best bring up the curve, I think," Baxter said judiciously. "An' look at the rust marks down 'er side. And the rusty boom irons on them stunsail yards . . . Cor, Mr Southwick would go mad!"

On board the *Matilda*, Rennick had completed his preparations. Grapnels were ready to hoist from the yardarms, two men at the wheel had been reinforced by two more, in case any were wounded, and Rennick found that, faced with what seemed certain death within the next fifteen minutes, he was curiously resigned; there was none of the feeling of panic that he had always anticipated in the many occasions he had thought about such a situation. It was rather more an acceptance that he had made his plans, given his orders, and there was nothing left now but wait with as much patience as possible. He was sorry not to be seeing his parents again; he regretted no farewell handshake with Mr Ramage. But his men were cheerful, and it was up to him to make sure they continued cheerful until the very last moment when the *Matilda* rammed the Frenchman. He was puzzled that the *Caroline* had gone up to the *Sarazine* and hoped all was well with young Orsini. He liked the lad; it was a pity he was getting caught like this, at the beginning of such a promising career.

At first Aitken had been delighted with Orsini's plan but the more he thought about it the more it seemed a three o'clock in the morning idea that emerged after the brandy bottle had tilted too often and was embarrassing when looked at in the cold light of dawn. Still, beggars could not be choosers, and even if the attempt failed some ships might have a better chance of escaping as they dispersed in different directions. *Might*. If he commanded that frigate, no one would; still, the Frenchman might be content securing one prize instead of going on to the rest. He then dismissed that possibility, remembering Mr Ramage's warning that in war the most dangerous habit was to underestimate the enemy's strength, cunning or ability.

Kenton looked across at the French frigate as she came up fast on his starboard quarter, obviously intending to pass close abeam and then cut across his bow to get into position ahead of the *Golondrina* and *Sarazine*. He too found himself resigned to it; there was not a chance of these slow, tubby merchantmen doing anything except trying to bolt like hobbled cows when Aitken gave the order to disperse. The loss of this convoy, he suddenly realized, would wipe out all the *Calypso*'s officers except Wagstaffe, who was away in Gibraltar, and Southwick. The First, acting Second, and acting Third Lieutenants, Lieutenant of Marines, Midshipman and bosun. And he knew Mr Ramage would feel the loss even worse because he would not be there when it happened. Orsini was the Marchesa's nephew; he would have to tell the woman he loved that her nephew and heir . . .

Paolo Orsini found he now had a tendency to tremble. Well, not tremble, but there was a shaky sensation in his knees and his hands, and his stomach was knotted as though he had eaten a sour apple too quickly. Yet he knew it was not fear: he was just nervous about the timing, which had to be *preciso*.

He looked at Rossi, still acting as quartermaster and keeping a sharp eye on the two men at the wheel. Rossi looked just the same—a big, kindly Genoese with black curly hair and a little overweight, a friendly, round face and gleaming white teeth. Kindly to his friends, Paolo amended. He was full of good humour and had a collection of funny remarks which were just what a midshipman—just what the captain of a ship, Paolo corrected himself—needed at a time like this.

The French frigate was heeling to a puff, showing dark green weed on her bottom, despite the copper sheathing. As she heeled again he saw she had several sheets of copper missing round the bow. Not uncommon, of course; in most ships it became thin there, slowly dissolving away. There must be some scientific explanation.

"Getting close now, sir," Rossi said, with all the anticipation of a highwayman watching an approaching coach. The frigate was about eight hundred yards away on the *Caroline*'s starboard quarter, and still steering a slightly converging course that would take her close across the *Golondrina*'s bow.

But if he, Paolo Orsini, midshipman, acted too soon or too late they would all get sunk or killed or captured; it needed a little—well, a little finesse, to place the *Caroline* in the right place at the right time. Machiavelli, Borgia and—Orsini!

The right time to start, he decided with a calmness that astonished and delighted him, was now.

"Very well, Rossi! *Andiamo!*"

The Italian hissed an order to the men at the wheel and involuntarily walked closer to them, at the same time glancing frequently at the French frigate.

Slowly—too slowly? Paolo wondered—the *Caroline* swung to starboard out of the column as though intending to sail right across the bow of the French frigate. Baxter was calling orders to tend sheets and braces and Rossi, pausing a minute or two to compare the frigate's course and the *Caroline*'s, nodded contentedly.

Over in the *Matilda*, Rennick did not know whether to cheer or curse; Orsini had obviously had the same idea and, being nearer the Frenchman, the first opportunity.

Paolo was sure that the frigate bore away slightly the moment she saw the *Caroline* haul out of the line, to steer the same course as the convoy.

Mama mia, the two ships, merchantman and frigate, were closing quickly!

Rossi gave a sharp helm order, Baxter shouted more orders to the men at the sheets and braces, and in what seemed moments the *Caroline* and the French frigate were sailing side by side twenty or thirty yards apart, and Baxter was jabbing him in the side and hissing: "The bluddy trumpet, sir; yer need the speakin'-trumpet!"

Paolo grabbed it and ran to the side, waving at the group of French officers who were gathered on the quarterdeck and staring down at him.

"*Attention!*" he shouted in French. "For your own safety keep your distance—we are in the most terrible distress!"

"What has happened?" came back a startled hail.

"*La peste! La peste!* Every ship of the convoy has *la peste!*"

"The plague?" came back a horrified shout. "Where have you come from?"

Damn, he could not remember the place name Aitken had shouted, and he turned to Rossi. "Quickly, where was it Mr Aitken said?"

The seaman told him.

"Mostaganem—half the city seemed to be dying when we left!"

"But what were you all doing on the Barbary coast?"

"The Algerines! They captured the whole convoy, eleven ships. Six of us could pay the ransom and they let us leave. Then *la peste* struck. Every one of us has buried half a crew!"

"What are you doing now?"

"We do not have the strength to beat to windward—to Valencia or Cartagena. We are running for Málaga to quarantine there and get medicines!"

Paolo waited a few moments. He sensed it was working; that

his story was being believed because the frigate's officers could see how few men were handling the merchant ships. Right, now for the last throw of the dice.

"We cannot in all humanity ask you for men to handle our ships, but can you go on to Málaga and ensure the authorities have the hospitals prepared for six ships struck with *la peste?*"

"You will not be allowed to land the sick, but yes, I will go ahead and warn them. How many dead so far?"

"Thirty-three dead up to last night. I do not know how many more went today in the other ships. But for myself, I have lost seven. You can see—five of us left. We hope *la peste* left the *Caroline* with the last burial yesterday. But—who knows?"

Already orders were being shouted from the French ship's quarterdeck and first her forecourse and then the main course tumbled down as the gaskets were untied and the sails let fall. While both sails were being sheeted home and the yards braced up, the royals were being set.

The frigate bore away a point and began forging ahead. At the last moment the man Orsini took to be the Captain shouted a course to him. "You are steering a full point too much to the south!"

"Thank you," Orsini bawled back, "I will bring the convoy round. Thank you; meeting you was our lucky day!"

An hour later the French frigate's hull had disappeared over the horizon ahead of them. In the *Matilda*, Rennick felt curiously cheated but nevertheless relieved; he was unsure what Orsini had done, but it had worked.

In the *Caroline*, Rossi said: "You know, sir, if we *had* got the plague on board, it wouldn't matter whether we was French, Spanish, Dutch or anything: in Málaga or anywhere else they wouldn't allow anyone on shore or on board; we'd have to stay at anchor, or at a quarantine buoy, until everyone with the plague had died and then another three or four weeks had passed."

"I know," said Paolo. "Still, the two words, *la peste*, were the only things that could have saved us from that frigate. By the time she has Málaga prepared for our reception, we should be in Gibraltar."

"Deck there—foremast lookout here!"

"Deck here."

"Sir, there's another frigate coming up fast on the same course as that last bahstid."

Paolo felt almost sick. The last trick had been too easy and it was unlikely he could play the same ace twice in one game.

"Get aloft with the glass, Baxter," he said, not trusting his own knees to get him up the ratlines. "Make the signal to Mr Aitken for a strange sail, and the bearing," he told Rossi.

Two minutes later Baxter hailed.

"Deck there!"

"Hurry and report!"

"It's a French frigate, sir!"

"I guessed that!"

"She's steering for us, every stitch of canvas set, and another sail just astern of her!"

Two frigates. Paolo shrugged his shoulders; there was limit to what one's brain could accept. He turned to Rossi.

"As soon as Mr Aitken acknowledges, hoist 'Two strange sail.'"

"Mr Aitken has already acknowledged the first signal, sir."

"*Mama mia!* Then make the second," Paolo said impatiently, but Rossi did not move. Instead he was looking up at Baxter.

"Deck there!" the man hailed.

"Deck here," Orsini answered wearily.

"The first sail is a frigate, sir, and the second is a tartane."

"Very well," Orsini said and as he turned to Rossi he said: "Give me the signal book—I don't think the French have a signal for 'tartane.'" As Rossi handed him the handwritten sheets which had been sewn together to make a book, Orsini knew his hands were shaking, but he was surprised that Rossi should be grinning at the fact.

As he began to look through the signals Rossi murmured in Italian: "Sir—a frigate and a *tartane* . . . you remember!"

The *Calypso* and the *Passe Partout! Accidente!* Paolo glanced round at the other ships and then began giving helm orders: Captain Ramage would expect the convoy to be in regular order by the time the frigate and tartane caught up.

NEW! The Privateersman Mysteries

"Not content to outflank and out-gun C.S. Forester with his vivid and accurate shipboard action, storm havoc and battle scenes, **Donachie has made Ludlow the most compulsively readable amateur detective since Dick Francis' latest ex-jockey.**"

Cambridge Evening News

In this exciting new series—available now for the first time ever in the U.S. in hardcover and quality trade paperback—David Donachie re-invents the nautical fiction genre with his smart, authentic, action-filled shipboard whodunits set in the 1790s during Britain's struggle with Revolutionary France.

Donachie's hero, Harry Ludlow, is an admiral's son who was raised to serve. When he is forced out of the navy under a cloud, Harry becomes a privateersman in partnership with his younger brother James, a rising artist with his own reasons for leaving London. Together, murder and intrigue take more of their time than hunting fat trading vessels.

From the dark bowels of a troubled ship of the line to the rough-and-tumble docks of Genoa, Harry is stalked by the specter of murder. In the roiling waters of the West Indies and the Spanish colony of New Orleans, he is caught up in the intrigues of great nations and the power plays of men far from the control of their home governments.

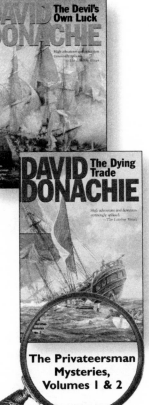

The Privateersman Mysteries, Volumes 1 & 2

THE DEVIL'S OWN LUCK
ISBN 1-59013-003-0 • 6" x 9"
320 pp., $23.95 hardcover

ISBN 1-59013-004-9 • 5.5" x 8.5", 304 pp., $15.95 quality trade paperback

THE DYING TRADE
ISBN 1-59013-005-7 • 6" x 9"
400 pp., $24.95 hardcover

ISBN 1-59013-006-5 • 5.5" x 8.5", 384 pp., $16.95 quality trade paperback

"High adventure and detection cunningly spliced. Battle scenes which reek of blood and brine; excitements on terra firma to match."
—*Literary Review*

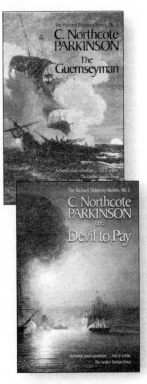